48 HOURS
TO
KILL

Also available by Andrew Bourelle

Heavy Metal

THE RORY YATES SERIES
(with James Patterson)
Texas Outlaw
Texas Ranger

48 HOURS TO KILL

A THRILLER

ANDREW BOURELLE

CROOKED
LANE

NEW YORK

Published in the United States by Crooked Lane Books, an imprint of The Quick Brown Fox & Company LLC.

Crooked Lane Books and its logo are trademarks of The Quick Brown Fox & Company LLC.

Library of Congress Catalog-in-Publication data available upon request.

ISBN (paperback): 978-1-63910-448-2
ISBN (hardcover): 978-1-64385-840-1
ISBN (ebook): 978-1-64385-841-8

Cover design by Patrick Sullivan

Printed in the United States.

www.crookedlanebooks.com

Crooked Lane Books
34 West 27th St., 10th Floor
New York, NY 10001

First Edition: December 2021
Trade Paperback Edition: August 2023

10 9 8 7 6 5 4 3 2 1

For Aubrey

Battle not with monsters, lest ye become a monster.
And if you gaze into the abyss, the abyss gazes also into you.

—Nietzsche

PROLOGUE

Abby
9 years ago

T HE TRUCK CAME around a bend, and the lake appeared in front of them, a giant shimmering sheet of blue glass. Speedboats and small yachts scored its surface like jets in the sky, leaving white contrails across the cobalt water.

Abby felt giddy. She sat in the middle of the truck's bench seat, with Ethan driving and Whitney to her right. The truck made its descent down the mountain highway. Pine trees blurred by. The windows were open, and the cool mountain air flowed in all around them in a whirlpool. Abby's hair danced around her.

They were going to the beach. On the drive, Ethan had said almost nothing. Whether he was hungover or just tired, Abby didn't care. Her brother was twenty-one and had his own apartment now and a new job, and she was just a kid getting ready to go to high school. She'd been afraid when he was moving out that he would forget about her, especially since his job was working as a bouncer in a strip club. What kind of guy who hangs around naked women all day and night still gives a shit about his kid sister?

But Abby had always been Ethan's number one. And vice versa.

When she was little, he'd been the one to watch her while their mom worked. He helped her with her homework and watched TV with her. Took her to movies. She didn't know what he was doing with his life—roughing up unruly customers when he was working? Partying with off-the-clock strippers when he wasn't? But it made her happy to know that she was still important to him.

"So," he said, turning the truck onto Highway 28, "you guys excited to be going to high school?"

"Sure," Abby said noncommittally.

Whitney shrugged.

The truth was that both of them were excited. Friday night football games. Homecoming. Boys. Dating. Parties. High school had been all they could talk about recently, but those things couldn't be particularly exciting to someone like Ethan, who could go to bars, gamble in casinos, stay out all night without a curfew.

Abby changed the subject. "How's the new job? Are the girls at the club really pretty?"

"Some of them."

He was slowing the truck, looking for an empty spot along the shoulder to park. Cars were jammed bumper to bumper. He began backing into a spot. It was a tight fit, especially since his new truck had a giant trailer hitch on the back, but he parallel parked with ease.

"Have you hooked up with any of them?" Whitney asked.

"Don't ask him that," Abby said.

Ethan grinned slyly. "All of them."

"Gross," Abby said, and she punched him in the arm.

*   *   *

A path wound its way down the slope through a wooded area. Clusters of beaches were hidden below along the boulder-strewn shoreline. Ethan carried a small cooler with a few beers for him and sodas for the girls, along with a towel and a paperback novel. Abby and Whitney carried their rafts and towels, navigating the trail carefully so their floats didn't get snagged on branches.

They finally came to the beach they were looking for and found it crowded.

"Where do you want to sit?" Ethan said.

Abby found her way through the blankets and towels on the sand, and they positioned themselves in a fairly secluded spot next to a boulder. They laid out their towels.

"Put on sunscreen," Ethan said. "Both of you."

"Okay, *Mom*," Abby said.

"Fine," he said. "Don't."

He flopped down on his chest, laying his arms above his head, and closed his eyes like he was going to sleep. His stubble shimmered in the sunlight like sand on his cheeks. Abby waited a few minutes and then put on sunscreen. She and Whitney rubbed it on each other's backs.

The beach was next to Coffin Rock, a sixty-foot cliff standing above the water, shaped like an upright pine casket from an old western. The backside sloped down to the shore. It was a steep climb among rocks and trees, but part of the draw of this beach was for people to come and cliff jump.

There were rumors about people dying when they jumped off the cliff. The water was so cold that it shocked them unconscious. Or they hit the surface wrong and broke their spines. Abby didn't know if any of it was true. She'd seen plenty of people do it without incident.

A group of guys, maybe high schoolers, maybe college, sat on towels nearby, drinking beer from bottles. They kept looking over at Abby and Whitney. After finishing their beers, they headed over toward Coffin Rock, scrambling up the backside and jumping off one by one, hooting with excitement as they came up out of the water. One of them made his way over to Abby and Whitney, smiling and shaking the water out of his hair.

"You girls want a drink?"

He gestured over toward the group, implying they had to come join the guys if they wanted one.

Ethan raised his head up off the towel.

"Oh. Hey, buddy," the guy said to him.

Ethan stood up, towering over the guy. The boy was younger than Ethan but already had a beer gut. He had shaved his facial hair into a thin beard, but the hair was patchy.

"What grade are you in?" Ethan asked the kid.

"I'm a freshman at UNR," he said.

"So, you're what? Nineteen?"

"Yeah. So?"

"You ever talk to these girls again," Ethan said, "I'll put you in the hospital."

The guy opened his mouth to argue, but Ethan wasn't finished.

"I'll hold you down," he said, "and rub sand in your eyes until you cry blood. You got it?"

"Jesus Christ," the guy said, starting to walk away. "I was just trying to be nice."

He retreated to his group, and the girls could hear low mumbles as he told his friends what had been said. Abby felt a little sick to her stomach—just the possibility of a fight had spiked her adrenaline.

"Geez, Ethan," she said, "we were just talking to them."

"We're not little kids," Whitney said.

"You two can do better than those idiots."

The boys started talking loudly, saying words like *douchebag* and *pussy*. Emboldened by their numbers, they talked about what they'd do to Ethan if he said anything else to them.

"I'll be back," Ethan said.

Abby thought he was going to fight the whole group of guys, and she opened her mouth to stop him. But he walked right past them without looking. He had a certain air about him—he wasn't pretending to ignore them; he simply was. The boys in the group eyed him as he walked past, but he had already forgotten about them. They were that insignificant.

"God, your brother's hot," Whitney said.

"Eww," Abby said.

She made a gagging gesture and acted like she was vomiting.

Ethan climbed slowly up the steep slope at the back of Coffin Rock. When he got to the top, he stood and looked down, as if contemplating something serious. The sun glinted off the blue water. She expected him to simply jump out, like the boys had, and drop feet first to the water below. Instead, he dove headfirst. He stabbed the water like a spear and disappeared in a small spout of white. Abby expected him to bob to the surface a moment later, but the water calmed without any sign of him.

Seconds passed.

He didn't surface.

"Oh, shit," Whitney said.

Abby rose to her feet. Finally, he broke the surface.

"Jesus," Whitney said. "He scared the shit out of me."

"Me too," Abby said.

They laughed together and watched as Ethan climbed back to the top.

He dove again and disappeared into the water, this time staying under for even longer.

"Jesus, Ethan," Abby said, "come on."

Ethan reappeared, throwing his head back, and she realized she'd been holding her breath. When he made his way back over, he collapsed onto his towel, breathing hard.

"You about gave us a heart attack," Whitney said.

"You stayed underwater for, like, five hours. I thought you were dead."

"I found a little cave down there," Ethan said. "At the bottom of Coffin Rock."

He explained that there was a gap in the cliff, about twenty feet underwater, a crack about eight inches wide.

"I could stick my whole arm in there," he said. "It seemed like a cool place to bury some treasure, you know, if I had any."

"If only you were a pirate," Whitney quipped.

"I want to see it," Abby said.

"The cave?"

"Yeah."

Ethan said he could climb up on top and make sure no one jumped. That way, Abby could swim over and look for the crevice without worrying if anyone would land on her.

"It's pretty deep," he said. "Probably hard to get to without jumping off the cliff. My ears hurt like hell down there."

"No," Abby said. "I want to jump."

"No way."

"You're not the boss of me," she said.

Ethan lowered his sunglasses to the bridge of his nose and considered her.

"I don't think it's a good idea, Abby."

"I'm going to do it. Either you can help me, or you can sit here and watch."

Ethan rose slowly to his feet. He was mostly dry now.

"Christ, you're obstinate," he said.

"Obstinate?"

"Willful," he clarified. "Stubborn."

She rolled her eyes.

"Pigheaded," Whitney said unhelpfully.

Abby gave them each the middle finger.

It was Ethan's turn to roll his eyes.

"You want to come, Whitney?" Abby asked.

"Sure," she said. "I'm game."

"You know people die doing this?" Ethan said.

"That's just an urban legend," Abby said.

They arrived at the slope, and Ethan started up. The trail was sandy at first, but soon they started to scale rocks. They were all barefoot. Ethan moved up the slope with ease, but Abby and Whitney both tread carefully.

"I'm not sure about this," Whitney said.

Abby wasn't sure either, but now she had to do it. At the top, Ethan stood a few feet from the edge. He held his arm up like it was a barrier he didn't want them crossing yet.

Abby looked down. The entire lake lay before her, the water shimmering in the sunlight. The people on the beach looked tiny.

"Holy hell," Whitney said. "It looks a hundred times higher from up here."

Abby's mouth was dry.

"I'm not doing it," Whitney said. "No way."

"I'm doing it," Abby said.

"You sure?" Ethan asked.

She stepped closer to the edge and felt a wave of vertigo. Her legs were trembling.

Ethan held her arm and balanced her.

"Okay," he said, "you want to jump out, away from the cliff. But you want to go straight down. Understand? Hit the water with your feet. Keep your arms flat against your body. Now, the cave—"

"I don't really give a shit about the cave," Abby said. "I just want to jump. I'll tackle the cave another day."

Ethan stepped back and made room for her. Abby looked over the edge. Wavelets lapped at the base of the cliff, and from here the sixty-foot drop seemed like two hundred. Abby's whole body was quivering.

She took a deep breath, let it out. Then another.

"You can do it," Whitney whispered. "You're awesome."

Ethan said nothing.

Abby put her foot on the edge and jumped out far from the cliff wall.

Right away, she knew the angle of her fall was wrong. She was leaning back, not going straight down. She flailed her arms, trying to right herself, but the blue surface was rising fast.

She hit the water with a smack, and all the breath burst from her lungs. The velocity shot her deep into the water. Her body instinctively took a deep inhalation, and suddenly her insides were filled with ice. She coughed and inhaled again, but there was no air. Only water. She tried to swim upward, but an invisible weight dragged her down.

Above, the sunlight came through the surface in heavenly rays. The water was impossibly clear—she could see up the cliff and even make out Ethan, as tiny as a toy action figure, looking down on her.

He wouldn't know anything was wrong. He would suspect she'd decided to look for the cave after all. From his perspective, she was just a blur under the water.

Ethan! Help!

But she could say nothing. The water around her grew darker, like she was swimming in a cloud of ink. She wasn't sure if she was sinking or if she was blacking out.

No! No please!

Something crashed through the surface above. Ethan was in front of her, grabbing her arms, looking into her eyes.

Then the water turned as black as oil, and Abby was gone.

* * *

She woke up coughing. She was lying on her side in the sand. Fluid drained from her nose. The water, so cold when it had gone into her body, felt warm coming up.

"Breathe," Ethan said. "Just breathe."

Abby started crying. She curled up in a ball. Ethan rubbed her arm. Whitney kneeled in front of her and told her she was going to be okay. Abby sat up and wrapped her arms around her brother and sobbed.

Someone began clapping, and then several people joined in the applause. Abby peeked through her watering eyes and saw that a small crowd had gathered around them.

"You saved me," Abby said, sniffling.

Ethan laughed. "It's no big deal."

"I'm serious," she said. "I could have died. You *saved* me."

He kissed her forehead. "Of course I did. I would dive into hell itself for you."

PART I

MONSTERS

CHAPTER

1

Ethan
2 hours until release

THE CELL WAS cold, as always this time of year, and Ethan kept the thin cotton blanket wrapped around him like a funeral shroud. Faint traces of his breath were visible in the gray-dark air, wisps of mist appearing with each exhalation. He could hear the sounds of the prison stirring, like some great creature coming to life. The scratch of cigarette lighters. The squeak of bedsprings. Coughs, wet and phlegmy. People rolling over, trying to get comfortable before morning roll call. A few muffled voices conversing in faraway cells, whispering at first but becoming less and less considerate as the minutes ticked by.

The window of Ethan's cell began to turn from black to blue. The glass was several inches thick and crosshatched with iron rods, and even in the best light it provided nothing more than a blurry view of colors and shapes. But the window was the only thing in the cell worth looking at, the only thing with any color in the ashen early light. As he lay awake in his bunk, he stared, watching the subtle changes as the four-by-sixteen-inch rectangle evolved from dark steel blue to indigo and finally to a light baby blue.

Below Ethan, in the bottom bunk, Jack was quiet too. Ethan couldn't hear Jack's breathing, which told him that his cellmate was awake.

"You up?" Jack said from below.

"Yeah," Ethan said.

"Figured you was," Jack said. "You get any sleep?"

"Some," Ethan said, although what little sleep he got was restless and lucid, where dreams and thoughts swirled around like paint in water.

"Today's the big day, huh?" Jack said.

"Uh-huh."

The springs squeaked below him as Jack rolled over.

"I don't want to sound faggy," Jack said, "but I'm gonna miss you."

Ethan laughed quietly. "I'll be back soon enough."

Ethan had been granted a forty-eight-hour furlough. For forty-eight hours, he would be free from the prison, able to walk outside instead of staring through a clouded block of glass. Able to walk among people besides cons and guards and caseworkers.

No house arrest. No ankle bracelets. No supervision whatsoever.

But the reason he hadn't been able to sleep wasn't excitement. Or anxiety. He'd spent the night, as he had every night of the past few weeks, thinking about his only sister.

Abby.

He was being released to attend her funeral.

2

Ethan
1 hour, 43 minutes until release

ETHAN HOPPED DOWN off the bunk and walked over to the toilet. The concrete floor was cold on his bare feet. He began to unload his bladder. Even though he had hardly slept, he felt only partly awake, and he stared at the wall. Jack lay behind him. There was no reason for embarrassment. They had to do everything in front of each other. Pissing. Shitting. Sometimes even crying when they got a letter from outside. When they masturbated in their bunks, they each did the other the courtesy of pretending they couldn't hear. There were no secrets from a cellmate.

He'd had a different cellmate for two years, a Black kid in for trying to knock off a convenience store in Las Vegas. He'd talked all the time, an incessant stream of stories and fantasies of what life would be like when he got out. Ethan was relieved when he was paroled. After that, he was alone for a while, but then they bussed Jack in from the Lovelock Correctional Center. He was pale, gaunt, and scarred. He'd been in prison for seven years at that point, but in the last two, there had been half a dozen attempts to kill him. Someone had finally gotten the idea to transfer him to a different prison to try to save his life.

It seemed to have worked. There had been only one attempt, and Ethan had been the one to save Jack, throwing his elbow into the assailant's jaw as he snuck up behind them in the yard. After that, Jack began to eat well, build up strength, and slowly form a friendship with Ethan. He joined Ethan in taking correspondence courses from Western Nevada College. He took a job within the prison, making teddy bears. He now had aspirations to be transferred to the

neighboring minimum-security facility—Carson City had three prisons—
where the cons could work with horses. He was from Montana and had grown
up with horses all his life. Jack was one of the few people in the prison who
actually felt guilt for what he'd done. But he'd settled into a life where he was,
if not happy, at least content to make the most of it.

While they never spoke of it, Ethan knew that Jack's serenity with his life
was at least in part because of their friendship. Jack was the rare person here
Ethan had any measure of respect for. The rest were sociopathic, emotionally
immature, or just plain stupid. Career criminals too dumb to break out of the
cycles they were in. Drug addicts who, despite years of sobriety in prison,
would get high within twenty-four hours of parole. Most thought only of
themselves, with no measure of empathy, let alone sympathy, for anyone or
anything.

Jack was nothing like them. He was a good guy. Ethan always thought Jack,
all in all, was a much better person than him. Ethan had been a professional
criminal and had more in common, if he was honest with himself, with the rest
of the cons than he had with Jack. He'd broken bones and bloodied noses. He'd
never killed anyone, but he'd pointed a gun in someone's face.

Jack had had no history of violence. Up until the day he shot four people.

* * *

They sat in the cafeteria, the two of them alone at a four-person table. Ethan
kept checking the time on his watch: a simple digital display on a rubber wrist-
band that he'd bought years ago at the prison commissary. He wasn't normally
a fidgety person, but he couldn't sit still. Not today.

The cafeteria was loud. There was nothing left of the quiet waking noises
from before. Now everything around them was raucous—grouchy and hungry
and anxious. Ethan and Jack ate in silence. The inmates were Black, White,
Latino. They had shaved heads and beards and tattoos. Some were boisterous,
posturing because of their insecurity. Others kept to themselves, trying to
escape notice. The longtimers and the lifers—the ones in for "all day and night,"
as the saying went—seemed at ease, tenured professors among the junior faculty
still figuring out how to survive. But beneath the pretense lived an atmosphere
of tension and fear. At any moment, a fight could break out. Prison was violent.
Brutality was second nature to most of the men.

Ethan had seen it before. During his first week, a man had been stabbed
one table over from him. As the man lay on his back, blood spread out over the
concrete floor into a wide red puddle that looked like spilled wine. One minute
life was discernible in his eyes. The next it was gone. It was unlike any death
scene he had ever watched in movies because there at least you could tell that the

actor was still alive, pretending, holding his breath and waiting for the director to call "cut." But death is visible. There's no faking it.

"Can I ask you something?" Ethan said.

"You just did."

"Can I ask you something else?"

Jack nodded.

"I don't figure you'd do it all over again if you had the chance, would you?"

Jack studied him seriously. He put down his plastic fork.

Ethan knew Jack's story. His twenty-year-old brother had become involved with some drug dealers, and they ended up killing him for reasons no one ever discovered. Jack and his other brother, who was only sixteen, took the law into their own hands. They started a gunfight on a neighborhood street in Carson City, two Montana cowboys with hunting rifles and shotguns against a house full of meth heads with machine guns. When the smoke cleared, there were five dead drug dealers and two dead bystanders, and Jack's kid brother had taken a bullet in the head. He was in a psych hospital somewhere, halfway to being a vegetable, and Jack hadn't seen him since his arrest.

"Would I do it all over again?" Jack said. "Not a chance."

Ethan had pressed on a bruise, so he didn't push the conversation further. But Jack seemed to sense there was more to his question, so he spoke up.

"Why? You thinking of going vigilante when you get out there?"

Ethan didn't answer. His sister's murder remained unsolved, and he'd been kicking around the idea of making inquiries, seeing what he could find out. He hadn't allowed himself to think far enough ahead to what he would do with the killer if he found him. Or her. Or them.

"Thing is," Jack said, "when we was asking around about our brother, trying to figure out who killed him, I kept thinking I'd do anything to make things right. I'd risk death, dismemberment, damnation—I'd risk my soul. I don't mean soul in any biblical sense. I know there ain't no god. I'm talking about my humanity. I'd put it on the line to fix things."

Jack's breathing went shallow. He opened his mouth, and his words came out choked.

"But my brother was already dead, so nothing we did made a damn bit of difference. There'd be people out there living right now if it wasn't for me. And my other brother wouldn't be in a hospital somewhere, collateral damage from my stupid need for revenge."

"Sorry to ask," Ethan said.

"Don't go doing nothing stupid while you're out there, Ethan," Jack said, staring at him to force the words home. "You're getting your shit together in here, and you could still have a pretty good life when you get out in a couple years. Don't go throwing it all away on revenge. Your sister's gone, and there ain't nothing you can do to bring her back."

*   *   *

Sometimes people joined Ethan and Jack for breakfast, but today they were alone until a Mexican kid named Miguel approached and said, "Hey, Lockhart, you a free bird today, huh?"

The kid smiled. His two top front teeth were missing, and he had a pathetic excuse for a mustache. Tattoos crept out of the collar of his shirt, like tentacles.

The kid had joined the prison a couple months ago, and within his first few days, he'd approached Ethan to tell him that he had worked for Shark, Ethan's previous employer. "We're keno buddies," the kid had said. Ethan didn't know what that meant, and he wanted nothing to do with any of Shark's associates. Prison was full of sycophants who tried to leech themselves onto bigger fish. A lot of prisoners liked the attention, but Ethan never greeted the kid with anything but cold indifference. To his credit, the kid got the picture and left Ethan alone.

Until today.

"Say what's up to Shark for me, will you?" Miguel said.

Ethan said nothing. He and Jack didn't want any company.

"Sorry about your sister, amigo," Miguel said, and walked away. "I seen her dance," he called over his shoulder. "She was as hot a piece of ass as I ever saw."

Ethan's blood raged inside him. His hands gripped the polystyrene breakfast tray, ready to snap it in two.

"Let it go," Jack said. "He's just trying to get under your skin."

Ethan forced a smile and let go of the tray.

He'd hardly eaten anything. The meal, if you could call it that, was made up of instant eggs, stale toast with a conservative spread of jelly, and a splotch of what was supposed to be oatmeal but looked and tasted more like old mashed potatoes. He had a small carton of milk, like he was in elementary school, but the expiration date had passed, and the liquid itself was room temperature.

They rose to dump their trays. Ethan spotted the kid, Miguel, watching him from across the cafeteria. He wasn't subtle about it. Ethan didn't know what to make of it, but he didn't give it much thought. He was going to be free within the hour.

Jack walked with Ethan, through the yard, toward the caseworker offices. They walked in silence. The air was cold, and their breath came out in white bursts. Other inmates were out already. The regular weightlifters were getting in their morning lift. Two guys were playing handball against the brick wall of C block. A group of kids was freestyle rapping in a circle. A guard with a shotgun in his hands sat on top of the metal walkway Ethan and Jack passed under.

They slowed when they approached their destination, both knowing there was more to be said.

"I'm sorry about your sister," Jack said, "but you got your head on straight in here. Don't do nothin' to jeopardize that."

"I always expected my sister to be a part of my life when I got out," Ethan said. "Part of the reason I wanted to change was to be a good brother to her. I don't know what's out there for me now."

Jack reached out and put a hand on Ethan's shoulder. It was an awkward gesture. They were friends, best friends, but here even the closest inmates didn't embrace or offer comfort. Even those who'd coupled up—the gay ones and the straight ones making do—rarely showed tenderness publicly.

Ethan told the guard he had an appointment with his caseworker. The guard called on the intercom, and while they waited for word to let him through the gate, Jack extended his hand, another rare gesture. Ethan took it. Jack's grip was strong, and he didn't let go.

"Don't do nothin' stupid," Jack said.

"Don't worry. I won't."

Ethan could tell Jack didn't believe him. When you spent all of your time with one person—most of it in a six-by-eight-foot concrete shoebox—you got good about reading the other person's thoughts.

3

Ethan
53 minutes until release

DARYL MAXWELL WAS waiting for him in his office, which was cluttered on every surface with file folders and paperwork. The walls in the office were painted the same dull color as the prison cells. Daryl had a window at the front of the prison. Outside were two rows of chain-link fence, with gleaming razor wire coiled on the tops and bottoms, in front of a gravel parking lot. Still, the view was much better than Ethan's thick ice block of a window.

Daryl looked at his watch and said, "You're running late. You're burning your free time, my friend."

Ethan sat in the wooden chair across from the desk. "My sister will still be dead when I get there," he said.

Daryl's cheeks flushed.

"Yes, well, I'm sorry about that." He picked up a file, opened it, and said, "Okay, let's go over this one more time."

"Do we have to?"

"Yes," Daryl said. "I need to make sure you understand your rights as a furloughed inmate."

Daryl Maxwell was forty-something with thinning hair and a paunch. He'd been Ethan's caseworker for four years.

"This almost never happens," Daryl went on. "Maybe at a minimum security facility you can get released without restriction. But at a max? Usually the family has to spring for a security detail to follow you around. Or at the very least you have to wear an ankle bracelet. But you, my friend, have the atypical blend of both a clean jacket"—he held up Ethan's file folder—"and a very good lawyer."

"Not to mention a caseworker willing to go to bat for me," Ethan added kindly.

"That might have helped," Daryl said. "And perhaps you have a powerful fairy godfather out there. Friends in high places?"

Ethan thought he knew what Daryl was implying but kept his mouth shut.

Daryl flipped to a court order inside the folder.

"So," he said, "what that means is you'll be released for forty-eight hours. The time starts at nine AM."

Daryl explained that prison guards would take him in a "three-piece suit"—a full set of restraints: handcuffs, leg irons, waist chain—to the bus station and release him there.

"When you return at nine AM Sunday morning," Daryl said, "you'll come to the prison. Not the bus station. Understand?"

"Yeah."

"The eastside entrance," Daryl said. "Where the gate is for cars to come in and out. I'll be there to welcome you home. Don't be late—not even a minute."

A few child's drawings were taped to the cinderblock walls of the office, and on a shelf sat a single framed photograph of a little girl with pigtails and a gap between her teeth. Daryl had told him once that his daughter was now a teenager living in Winnemucca with her mother. Ethan had asked why he didn't have any up-to-date pictures of her. *"Because she's a looker,"* Daryl had said, *"and this is a goddamn prison."* The message had been clear: Daryl didn't want every con in the joint to be lusting after his teenage daughter.

"If you're not there at nine AM on Sunday," Daryl said, "there will be an arrest warrant issued and an APB out on you at 9:01. Got it?"

"Got it."

"And even if you roll up at 9:05 or 9:10, that's a shitload of paperwork for me and a huge strike on the record for you. That's the kind of thing that could cost you years in front of the parole board."

That might be an idle threat to some prisoners, but to Ethan, such a potential consequence carried real weight. He was on track to be out in two years. He didn't want that number to balloon to five. Or ten.

Daryl handed Ethan a sheet of paper. On it was Ethan's information—age, height, weight, hair color—as well as legalese prose explaining that he was a convict on furlough.

"That's your ID," Daryl said. "If you have any interaction with law enforcement, that's what you give them."

"Can I use it to buy beer?" Ethan said.

"You can't drink, Ethan."

"It was a joke."

"Let's go over the rules again."

"It was a *joke*."

"I know, but let's go over them anyway." Daryl lifted his hand and started counting off with his fingers. "No alcohol. No drugs. No possession of weapons. No crime of any sort—don't even jaywalk."

Ethan nodded again.

"You can't drive. You have no license."

"I don't have a car."

"Well, don't borrow one from a friend. You get pulled over, you're coming right back here. Think of this as being on parole. Any violation of your release and you'll be arrested immediately, and it could—correction: it *will*—result in an extended sentence."

Daryl had all five fingers out, so he lifted his other hand and extended his index finger.

"No leaving the state," he said. "California ain't far away, but don't even think about crossing the border. If you get caught over there, they'll arrest you and there will be all kinds of extradition headaches."

He leaned forward and looked at Ethan earnestly. "Listen, my friend." He had a habit of calling all the inmates *my friend*, but Ethan thought he used it liberally with him. "You're going to get out of here at your first crack at parole. You've got two years left." He pointed at Ethan. "But don't forget your original sentence was twenty years. You could be in here that long if you screw this up."

Daryl explained that while Ethan was being released to attend his sister's funeral and memorial service, no one would be checking to make sure he was there.

"Technically, as long as you abide by the conditions, you've got forty-eight hours to kill however you want."

"I'm going to the funeral," Ethan said, irritated. "I'm not going to be snowboarding at Mt. Rose or playing slots at Circus Circus."

"And don't you even think about jackrabbit parole," Daryl added. "You try to make a run for it and you'll find yourself spending the rest of your life in prison."

Daryl sat back in his chair, as if he'd gotten something important off his chest. He pulled a business card off the little plastic holder on his desk and wrote something on the back in pen.

"Keep this with you. My cell is on the back. You run into any problems or questions about what you can and can't do, you call me, okay?"

Ethan tucked the card into his jeans pocket.

"Any questions?" Daryl asked.

"Do I get my stuff back, or do I have to wear this shit?" He looked down at his clothes. All the inmates wore jeans and denim shirts—that was the uniform. It wasn't as bad as in some prisons, but the outfit wasn't something Ethan would normally wear, that was for sure.

"You have to wear that," Daryl said. "You can wear other stuff while you're out there," he continued, "but you need to bring that crap back." He gestured to the clothes. "Otherwise they'll charge your account."

Daryl rose and extended his hand. Ethan took it. The grip was nowhere near what Jack's was.

"The entire time you're gone," Daryl said, "you'll still be a prisoner of the Nevada Department of Corrections. Don't forget that."

Ethan told him he wouldn't, and Daryl at least looked like he believed him.

Ethan felt like he was getting a different version of the speech Jack had given him. Perhaps they both sensed what was on his mind.

When Ethan found out Abby had been murdered, he'd been filled with such rage that he wanted to tear through the prison walls, wreak havoc on the world until he found his sister's killer. Until his furlough was granted, he didn't think he'd have a chance. But now, did he actually believe he could solve her murder in forty-eight hours when the police—with all they had at their disposal—hadn't been able to do it in three weeks? And if he could find Abby's killer, could he do it without—as Jack had put it—losing his soul?

Now that the day was here, all of that inner debate seemed moot. He realized the futility of that anger. He was helpless. He couldn't find Abby's killer. Not if he had a month, let alone forty-eight hours. Not by himself. Thoughts of investigating her murder were just the fantasies of a mourning man who hadn't come to grips with reality.

His sister was dead, and there was nothing he could do about it.

4

Ethan
7 minutes until release

T HE VAN LURCHED forward and jostled Ethan in his seat. He craned his neck to look out the window—another narrow slit like the one in his cell—but he was strapped in and couldn't get a good vantage. He saw telephone lines and the skeletal arms of trees. Other than that, he could only see blue sky—much clearer than the murky blue through the glass of his cell window—but still only a glimpse of freedom.

He smiled. He couldn't help himself. For the first time in five years, he was outside the prison.

His ankles were shackled together, and his wrists were in handcuffs that were chained to his waist. The cuffs were particularly uncomfortable on his left wrist where they pressed up against his cheap prison watch. He tried to wriggle his hands free, just to see if he could do it. The cuffs weren't tight, and he'd heard from people inside that you could get out of loose handcuffs if you had lubricant or were willing to do some damage to your wrist. It was a little-known fact. Still, Ethan couldn't do it.

The cuffs would be off soon enough, but he reminded himself that even though he'd be walking around like he was free, he would still be a ward of the Nevada Department of Corrections.

This furlough wasn't about freedom. It was about Abby.

He had been sad about her death—angry—but still it hadn't fully sunk in what was happening. He thought maybe the funeral would do that—make him understand that she was dead.

But even then he wasn't sure. They'd never found her body. Daryl had told him there'd been enough evidence to be sure it was homicide, not a missing persons case. But without seeing her stretched out in a casket, he wasn't sure his mind could fully grapple with the understanding.

Perhaps it was better this way. He wanted so badly to see her again that it might be best not to see her like that, pumped full of chemicals, as still as a plastic mannequin—only a shell of the living, breathing, beautiful girl she had been.

*   *   *

"How does it feel?" one of the guards asked him.

Ethan rubbed his wrists instinctively, as if the cuffs had been tighter and he'd been wearing them longer.

"Weird," he said.

He took a long, deep breath. The air was cold, as it had been in the prison yard an hour earlier, but it felt different somehow.

"You've got money for the bus, right?" the other guard asked.

Ethan nodded.

"Well, I think the next one leaves at nine thirty, so you better get in there and get you a ticket."

"Okay," Ethan said. "Thanks."

He felt an urge to be gracious to the two men, maybe even shake their hands. He also expected them to give him a small speech about not doing anything stupid, staying out of trouble, not being tempted by jackrabbit parole. But they simply stood watching him, unsure of what he was waiting for. They were only chauffeurs. No need to thank them or even say goodbye.

"Okay," he said again, and turned toward the station.

On the reflective glass of the entrance, he could see the guards climbing back into the van.

It was official: his furlough had begun.

5

Abby
5 years ago

ABBY CAME HOME from school and tossed her backpack on her bed. She had homework, but she didn't feel like doing it. This was her last year of high school, and she had major senioritis, but she had long since mastered the art of getting by on minimal effort.

She picked up the phone to call Ethan and see if he wanted to do something. Maybe see a movie. Go for a run at Rancho San Rafael Park. It didn't really matter.

There was no answer.

"Hey, it's me," she said to his voicemail. "Give me a call. Let's hang out."

He would call back. He always did, no matter how busy he was. Getting him to call back wasn't the issue, but getting him to hang out might be. Ethan had been MIA lately, and she didn't like it. Ever since he'd gone to work for the club and moved into his own apartment, things had been different. But he'd been particularly absent lately, working lots of hours. Or so he said.

It hadn't really bothered Abby at first. There'd been dates and parties and football games to occupy her time, not to mention *some* studying. But the school's guidance counselors were hounding her about turning in college applications, and it made her realize that the person she wanted to talk to about her future was her brother. She'd thought about just how long it had been since they'd spent any time together, and she realized she missed him.

She plopped down on the couch and turned the TV on. There was some kind of big manhunt going on in Sparks, and the local news had interrupted whatever daytime show was on for a live report. She flipped it over to Netflix to watch *Orange Is the New Black*.

She watched for about fifteen minutes, then her phone buzzed with an incoming call. She expected it to be Ethan, but it was Whitney. They texted each other a hundred times a day but rarely actually called one another. It must be something really interesting—some gossip from school—for Whitney to call instead of text.

She muted the TV and picked up the phone.

"Turn on the TV," Whitney said.

"It is on. I'm watching *Orange*."

"No, I mean the news. I think your brother's been arrested."

Abby's hand trembled as she reached for the remote. She turned over to the local channel—still talking about that manhunt in Sparks—and jammed her thumb against the volume button.

The screen showed a reporter standing outside a casino in Sparks. Police cars and ambulances sat in the background. Uniformed officers walked in and out of the frame. The reporter was saying something about an armed robbery. One suspect in custody, another still at large.

"Police have identified the suspect in custody," the reporter said, "as Ethan Lockhart of Reno."

Abby's heart was pounding—she'd never known it could beat this hard or this fast.

"Do you think it's him?" Whitney said.

"It can't be," Abby said.

She tried to sound confident, but the truth is she suspected it *could* be him. She'd long had her suspicions that he was doing more for Dark Secrets than checking IDs at the door and throwing out customers who tried to put their hands on the girls' tits. For one, he traveled around the city a lot. Not just the city—practically all of Northern Nevada. She'd call him and he'd be in Sun Valley one day, down in Mound House or Fallon the next. He'd say he was just running errands for Shark, the owner, but Abby couldn't think of why a strip club owner would have so many errands so far away.

With Whitney still on the phone, Abby sat down in front of her mom's computer and pulled up the site for the *Reno Gazette-Journal*. The top story was about the robbery, but there wasn't much to it. The newspaper didn't have any more information than the TV station.

"Hang on," Abby said. "I'm going to try to call Ethan."

She hung up and dialed. As she waited for him to pick up, she stared at pictures of Ethan on the bookshelf in the living room. Pictures of the two of them filled every shelf, from baby pictures to photos taken at a barbecue last summer. In all the pictures, Ethan had the same mischievous smile, like he was in on some joke that no one got but him.

"Call me as soon as you get this," she said to his voicemail, then hung up. She texted him as well.

CALL ME CALL ME CALL ME!!!

She paced around the room and thought about calling her mom.

No. No need to worry her until she knew something.

She called Whitney back.

"The *RGJ* just updated its story," Whitney said. "They've got a picture of him."

Abby refreshed the site, and there it was: Ethan's mugshot.

Her brother stared into the camera, trying to look tough, but the fear on his face was palpable. And something else. Sadness? Regret?

The smile that Abby loved so much was nowhere to be seen.

6

Ethan
47 hours, 59 minutes remaining

THE LOBBY OF the bus station was a plain room, with hospital-white floors and avocado-green paint on the walls. One person stood in line ahead of him and no one else. The other traveler, who looked and smelled homeless, was digging through his pockets, trying to find money to pay for a ticket.

Ethan heard the door open behind him and boots click against the tile.

"Prisoner!" the person behind him shouted. "Escaped prisoner!"

Ethan jerked, startled by the shouting, and spun around. A man was standing and pointing at him.

"Blake?" Ethan said, but there was no need to ask. Even if Ethan hadn't seen him in five years, his oldest friend was unmistakable.

Blake started laughing. Ethan stood, dumbfounded, and then he smiled and shook his head.

"You should have seen the look on your face," Blake said.

Blake was Ethan's figurative partner in crime when they were teenagers and his literal partner in crime when they were older. He couldn't stop howling, and in that sense he hadn't changed at all. He had the same mischievous cackle, the same misanthropic look in his eyes. Finally, he gained control of himself and walked over, his black cowboy boots clicking on the tile floor. He threw his arms around Ethan and gripped him in a tight hug. Ethan flinched instinctively. Then he put his arms—limp with surprise—around his friend.

He felt a pistol inside Blake's coat.

They broke apart. The homeless man and the employee behind the kiosk were staring at them. They turned back to their business.

"Goddamn," Blake said, looking Ethan up and down. "You look *big*. You been working out?"

"That's all there is to do inside. Lift weights. That and read books."

"You look good, man," Blake said. "I expected to see some hollowed-out piece of crap, like you just got back from Iraq. But you, man, you look like you've been training for the Super Bowl."

Ethan let out an uncomfortable laugh.

Five years of no drinking, no drugs, regular exercise, and regular meals had left him feeling healthy.

Blake, on the other hand, did not look so good. A couple inches shorter than Ethan, he had always been just as strong, just as fit. Now he looked thinner, nearly emaciated. He had dark crescent moons under his eyes, his skin looked pale, and gray was growing in at the temples of his slicked-back black hair. He looked like he either hadn't slept in days or had just woken up—it was hard to tell which.

"You look good too," Ethan said. His tone suggested he was only being polite, so he added, "It looks like you're dressing better these days."

Blake had black pants, black boots, and an expensive-looking leather jacket hanging open to reveal a blood-red dress shirt.

"Thanks," Blake said. He popped the collar of his coat. "New jacket," he said. "You, though—you look like you work at a Gap from the 1980s. How much denim can one person fit on their body?"

"They wouldn't give me my old clothes back. Can you believe it?"

"What I can't believe," Blake said, "is that you're standing here in front of me."

"More importantly," Ethan said, "what the hell are you doing standing here in front of me?"

"You didn't think we'd make you ride the bus, did you?"

*   *   *

The prison transport had left the parking lot, which Ethan was thankful for. He guessed there was nothing they would do or say about him leaving with Blake—nothing technically illegal about it—but he didn't want to draw any attention to himself.

The parking lot was nearly empty, just a shiny BMW parked in the front row and a few-years-old sedan at the back of the lot. Neither car seemed to fit Blake, but he pulled open the passenger door of the black BMW and held it for

Ethan, which seemed like an odd, showy gesture. The car was sleek and aerody-
namic, sparkling and freshly waxed.

"Nice car," Ethan said.

"You like?"

"Sure," Ethan said, although he was just being polite. A hundred-thousand-
dollar car was the kind of thing that might have impressed him five years ago.

The coupe was nearly spotless inside. It smelled of oiled leather.

"Listen to how quiet this thing is," Blake said.

Ethan could hardly tell the engine was running.

Blake pressed the gas—*now* he could hear the revving motor. Blake
punched the gas, and the tires chirped as the car sped out of the parking lot.

As they drove away, Ethan saw the shape of a person sitting in the sedan. It
could have been a government-issued car, and Ethan wondered for a moment if
someone was keeping an eye on him. He told himself he was being paranoid.

CHAPTER

7

Ethan
47 hours, 41 minutes remaining

"SHARK WANTS TO see you," Blake said. "I got strict orders to bring you in first thing."

They were sitting in traffic in Carson City. There was a highway bypass that went around the city's main congested thoroughfare, but it didn't make any sense to access it from where they were. So they just crept along with the traffic. Blake kept gunning the engine, stomping on the brakes, messing with the paddle shifters on the steering wheel as if he couldn't handle going this slow.

"What's new since I've been gone?"

Blake shook his head as if in disbelief. "A lot's changed, man. A lot."

"Give it to me."

Ethan felt antsy to get this conversation started. He wanted to get as much information from Blake as he could during the forty-five-minute drive from Carson City to Reno.

Even though he'd saved time getting a ride from Blake rather than taking a bus, he still felt the clock ticking on his furlough. If he wasn't careful, the time was going to flash by in a blink.

"Shark controls a majority of the action in the whole area these days. Reno. Carson. Tahoe. He's got fingers in all of it."

"So he's big time now?" Ethan asked.

"Like a real shark," Blake said. "He's the apex predator in these parts. The loan sharking and the fencing—that's all small potatoes for him now."

Shark had definitely paid the lawyer fees for Ethan to get his furlough. But if Shark was as powerful these days as Blake said, Ethan suspected he might also be the "fairy godfather" Daryl had been talking about. In order to get Ethan released without a security detail, Shark must have pulled some other kinds of strings.

Ethan wondered what Shark might want in return.

At the north end of town, out of the stop-and-go traffic, Blake stepped on the gas, zipped up over the hill that served as the gateway to Washoe Valley, then dropped down, slaloming around the other cars on the straight highway that took them toward Reno.

The wind coming off the mountains was blowing hard in the valley, and gusts buffeted the car. To the east, the Sierra Nevada rose up from foothills to mountain peaks, the tops thick with snow. To the west, Washoe Lake's surface was choppy. Everything seemed familiar and yet new, a strange contradiction created by five years of absence.

The posted limit was seventy miles per hour, but Blake passed the other cars like they were in a school zone. The speedometer was approaching 100. Still, the ride was smooth despite the wind. Ethan checked the rearview mirror. If the sedan had been tailing them, it was long gone now.

Ethan turned to say something and then noticed that Blake's pant leg had risen up as he accelerated. Tucked inside his boot was a small pistol. A tiny .38, he guessed, which probably held two shots.

"Do you know Stuart Kicking Bird?" Blake asked. "We played football against him in high school."

Kicking Bird had been a cornerback for Douglas County, and Ethan distinctly remembered the game they played. Ethan, a wide ride receiver, didn't catch a pass all game because Kicking Bird had been all over him. Ethan had been an all-district wide receiver because he was fast and strong, but mostly because he was tall—he could jump and pull down passes that other receivers couldn't reach. Stuart Kicking Bird had been a good three inches shorter than him, but he'd stayed glued to Ethan with the tenacity of a pit bull that had locked on and wouldn't let go. Ethan recalled the name because it was distinct and because he'd heard the announcer saying it—*"Pass knocked down by Kicking Bird"*—all night long.

"He was fast," Ethan said.

"Quick," Blake corrected, as if the distinction was important. "He's Shark's number two now. He's a cold-blooded killer."

Ethan was taken aback by the bluntness of the statement. When he'd worked for Shark, they'd roughed plenty of guys up, but they were never asked to kill anyone. If that kind of thing had gone on—and he didn't think it had, at least not often—Shark had had other people do it. With Blake speaking so forthrightly about murder, either it went on more frequently now or Blake occupied a higher position, where he was informed about such things. Or both.

"Remember about ten years ago," Blake said, "when there was that shootout in Carson City, a couple of ranchers from Montana going to war with a meth distributor?"

Ethan went cold. He knew about the shootout, of course—everyone in Northern Nevada could remember it. But Ethan knew the details more than others. His cellmate, Jack, was one of those "ranchers."

"Kicking Bird's sister was one of the people killed," Blake said. "He was a strung-out meth head back then. When she died, he kicked the drugs just like that"—Blake snapped his fingers—"like it was nothing. He went clean, but he didn't go straight. Started doing jobs. Not long after you went away, he started working for Shark. The two clicked like Butch Cassidy and the Sundance Kid. Now. He's one cold son of a bitch. I'm telling you, he's someone you don't want to mess with."

"I'm not afraid of Stuart Kicking Bird."

They were in Reno now, cruising up Highway 395. The city sat in a valley between two mountain ranges, the Sierra Nevada to the west, black and capped with snow, and the smaller brown hills of the Virginia Range to the east.

"And I'm not afraid of Shark either," Ethan said.

"Well, you should be," Blake said. "That's why I'm telling you all this. Things ain't like they used to be."

"What do I have to be afraid of?"

Blake gave him a look that said he should know. And he did.

Five years ago, Ethan's silence when he was arrested had bought him a lot. Shark had promised to "look after" his sister while he was away. He would provide for her financially; that was the understanding. With Abby gone, Ethan's loyalty would no longer be a certainty to Shark.

"As far as I'm concerned," Ethan said, "he broke his promise to me when he hired Abby to work at Dark Secrets. That's not what I meant when I said to look after her."

"Well, she's gone now either way. And Shark ain't got nothing left to make sure you keep quiet."

"So you think he'd take me out? Not take any chances?"

"No. You ought to be careful is all. Watch what you say. Show some respect."

Ethan shook his head, angry now. "Fuck that. I'm going to tell that son of a bitch exactly what I think of him hiring her to be a stripper, letting her get killed under his watchful eye. That asshole—" He stopped. He didn't know what more to say.

Blake took a long breath. "All I'm saying is that Shark and Kicking Bird, they ain't anyone to mess with. Things are different around here now."

Ethan wanted to tell Blake that he was around killers every day. That *he* had changed too. Instead, he bit his tongue and let Blake finish.

"I work for Shark," Blake said, "but you and I been friends since we were kids. Just trying to look out for you, bro."

* * *

Blake pulled off the highway and drove down Virginia Street under the famous "THE BIGGEST LITTLE CITY IN THE WORLD" sign. After dark, with neon lighting up the casinos, downtown Reno could disguise itself to look cheaply glamorous. Not nearly the spectacle of Las Vegas, but to inebriated tourists, it could pass as glitzy for a night. In the daytime, however, the pawn shops and homeless people took center stage, and you could see the cluster of downtown city blocks for what it was: a gambling hole that lured locals and addicts to spend their paychecks, pawn their family heirlooms, and waste their lives away looking for an easy fortune or a quick fix. In some ways, it was more of a sin city than Vegas. Vegas gave the pretense of glamour for retirees and frat boys and bachelorette parties. Reno's veneer wasn't nearly as shiny. It was easier to see through to the filthy underbelly. Downtown Reno was dirt and greed and addiction.

They drove over a bridge that spanned the Truckee River. A handful of restaurants and businesses lined this section of the waterway: a coffee shop, a bar, a bicycle rental. In the summer, the water would be churning with rapids and filled with kayakers. But right now the water was low, and it was way too cold for that.

They were getting close to Shark's club, and Ethan didn't think he could put off the question he really wanted to ask.

"Do you think Shark had anything to do with what happened to Abby?"

"No."

Ethan gave him a look that said, *Are you sure?*

"There's nothing to gain from it."

This was the truth. As much as he thought about it, Ethan couldn't figure out why Shark would want Abby dead. All it did was complicate the deal with Ethan.

"Would you know?" Ethan asked. "Is that something you'd be in on?"

"Probably," he said. "I'm usually in the loop about those things."

"And you'd tell me if you knew anything?"

Blake grinned, a smile that said, *Do you even have to ask?*

"Like I said, bro: I work for Shark, but you and I been friends a long time."

"I thought you might get out," Ethan said. "I thought what happened to me might be a wake-up call."

Blake laughed. "There's no getting out, man. Even when you do time, you're just taking a break." He reached over and slapped Ethan's knee. "Don't worry. When you get out, there'll still be a place for you. You'll be driving a car like this when the ink's still wet on your parole papers."

Ethan grunted noncommittally. He could tell Blake that he didn't want back in, that when he got out of prison he wanted a normal life, an honest job. But what was the point?

In prison, he'd had a lot of time to think about things he'd done, people he had hurt. Once, he'd been flirting with a girl at the El Cortez, a dive bar a few blocks from where they were now. When her boyfriend told Ethan to leave her alone, he twisted the man's arm behind his back, pinned him to the floor, and—even though the man was subdued, even though there was no need—twisted the arm in a direction it wasn't meant to bend. Something snapped in the socket. The guy screamed with all his breath, and Ethan and Blake laughed as they wandered out into the street, looking for more trouble.

Ethan didn't want to be that person anymore.

He assumed Blake still was. And always would be.

8

Ethan

46 hours, 50 minutes remaining

B LAKE PULLED THE BMW into Dark Secrets and stopped at the fenced gate
to the employee lot. An unspooled condom sat strewn on the cracked blacktop. Papers and fast-food wrappers and empty beer cans had collected against
the chain-link fence. The building's black paint was faded and chipped, giving
the facade a mangy look.

The place hadn't changed a bit.

Blake rolled down his window and punched in the code.

Ethan saw the numbers he pressed and noted that the code had changed
since he'd worked here. This was something Shark had taught him. Whenever someone was punching a code—at a locked door, at an ATM, at a
checkout line at the grocery—you should always look. You never knew when
the information might come in handy.

Dark Secrets was an enormous building. The club itself, with the main
stage, the bar, and several private rooms, only filled about half of the structure.
The rest was offices, dressing room, storeroom, kitchen, and a warehouse where
they kept the limousine used for private parties. The limo was parked outside
today, the roll-up door to the warehouse closed. A few vehicles were parked out
back: a Cadillac Escalade, which Ethan assumed was Shark's, and a few other
cars probably belonging to the skeleton crew working this time of day.

As they stepped out of the BMW, Blake said he wanted to smoke a cigarette
before they went inside. Ethan was anxious to get this over with, but he didn't say
anything. It felt strange to be standing here. When he was a twenty-one-year-old

kid, he thought he'd hit the jackpot when he was hired at Dark Secrets. The building—and the job—had seemed so glamorous. By the time he'd started to see past the glitzy facade to the ugliness underneath, he had already been lured by Shark's charisma. He'd drunk the Kool-Aid. Every step up the ladder felt more exciting than the first. Roughing up an unruly customer turned into breaking the fingers of people who owed Shark money. Which turned into walking into a casino wearing a mask and carrying an MP5.

"Look, man," Blake said, "there's something I've got to tell you."

The sky, clear earlier that morning, had begun to cloud up, and a grayness hung in the air.

"I probably can't come to the funeral," Blake said. "Definitely not the service tonight."

The earnestness of his apology was touching. Blake was his best friend, or had been once, but it had never occurred to him to expect Blake to come and stand by his side like a best friend might.

"Shark set up a high-stakes card game at the Neptune," Blake said. "High rollers only. Big money."

"You working the door?"

"No," Blake said proudly. "Got a bouncer from the club for that. I'm running the show. Making sure everything goes smoothly. Watch the money and divvy out loans if they need 'em. Make sure no one cheats. It's a hundred grand to buy in, and no limit after that. These guys are serious. The whole penthouse is reserved. They'll take naps here and there, but mostly they'll play straight through. Twenty-four hours at least. Maybe forty-eight."

Ethan thought about his own forty-eight-hour window of release. To think someone would spend that whole time at a table in a smoky room, looking at cards and making bets, seemed unfathomable to him.

"Here," Blake said, and he held out a playing card.

On the face side, it was an ace. On the backside was the design of a devil-looking creature with goat horns and claws, fangs overhanging its lips like a wolf. It had a serpentine tail that lay coiled around its feet, and it held a scepter topped with a human skull.

"That gets you in the door," Blake said. "I know you ain't gonna play, but if you get bored and want to keep me company . . ." He trailed off.

"If I show up with a hundred grand, you'll know I stole your car and sold it."

Blake laughed and pitched his cigarette, half-smoked, onto the pavement.

*   *   *

As soon as Blake opened the door to the service entrance, Ethan could hear the muffled sound of eighties hair metal blaring from the cabaret. They walked down the hall of plain sheetrock that no one had ever bothered to paint and past the dressing room door. Someone had written the letters *UN* with a black Magic Marker in front of the stenciled letters so the sign read "UNDRESSING ROOM."

Ethan thought they would walk directly back to Shark's office, but Blake went in the other direction, toward the club. Ethan hoped Shark was out there, but more likely he was in the back, and Ethan would have to wait until he was summoned.

He didn't want to wait—time was flying by on his furlough already.

They passed the kitchen and pushed through the curtain and into the club. What little light there was came from variously colored bulbs. Red was the dominant hue. It all had the effect of making the girls look better and somehow making the men look haggard and hoary, hiding the women's cellulite and acne while deepening the men's wrinkles and the circles under their eyes.

A girl danced on the stage. She had platinum-blond hair and balloons for breasts. "Stranglehold" by Ted Nugent was playing, and she swayed her hips seductively to the slow, building guitar. She had a couple tattoos here and there: a rose on her arm, a butterfly on one hip.

There were only a few men watching. Another girl was working the floor, an unrewarding endeavor when business was this slow. She was sitting with a customer, making small talk, but it didn't seem like he was going to shell out for a lap dance. He came to sip beers, watch the dancers, and get as much action with his eyes as he could for as little money as possible. The morning shift was the worst for the dancers—there was no money in it.

Ethan followed Blake to the bar, where a big bouncer was stationed, trying to look bored and tough at the same time. The manager, Cal, was tending bar, and his face lit up when he saw Ethan.

"Well, isn't this a blast from the past?"

As far as Ethan knew, Cal ran the club for Shark more or less legitimately. He had to be involved in the money laundering that went on, or at least aware of it, but otherwise his duties were entirely devoted to the club, not Shark's other dealings. He was a thin man with an elaborate comb-over to cover his balding head. He picked up a telephone, punched a few numbers, and said simply, "They're here." Then he took a swipe at the bar with a towel and tossed it over his shoulder, a practiced move that looked like something a bartender in a movie would do. "Can I get you boys something to drink?"

Blake ordered a bourbon on the rocks. Ethan asked for a glass of milk.

"Milk?"

"I haven't had a drink in five years," Ethan said. "I might get drunk off one sip."

On the stage, the music built toward its crescendo, and the girl jumped up on the pole, wrapped her bare legs around the metal, and flipped upside down. Ethan spotted brown incision scars at the bottom of each breast.

Cal said to the bouncer, "Bruce, this is Ethan Lockhart."

The bouncer appraised him dismissively. "I heard about you," he said.

The guy was a good two inches taller than Ethan and big. Strong, yes, but fat too. He had a neck like a Christmas ham, and his body was built like the trunk of an oak tree. One of his eyes was clouded over with a gray spider web covering the iris and pupil.

"Bruce played offensive line for Nevada," Blake said, like this should impress Ethan.

"You look like an O lineman," Ethan said.

"His brother played too," Blake said. Bruce and his brother Wayne were twins, he explained, and both had been working at the club for going on a year now.

"Remember when that was us?" Blake said, nudging Ethan's shoulder. "A couple of kids learning the ropes."

"You and your brother are named Bruce and Wayne?" Ethan asked. "Were your parents big Batman fans?"

"Like I never heard that before."

The song ended, and the blond-haired dancer left the stage.

"You able to see out of that eye?" Ethan said.

Ethan had meant the words as a jab, but Bruce didn't seem bothered.

"No," he said, closing his good eye, "everything's just a big blur." He opened the good one and looked at Ethan earnestly.

"Seems like a liability in this line of work," Ethan said.

Bruce shrugged. Ethan had wanted to get under his skin, but it wasn't working. Ethan opened his mouth to say that all the offensive linemen he ever knew were fat and slow—otherwise they'd play another position—but he stopped himself. This wasn't the prison yard—there was no need to show this kid who the alpha was.

The DJ said, "All right, everyone, we've got a special treat for you. Give it up for Sierra Rose."

With that, a spotlight hit the stage, and a beautiful woman strutted out to Michael Jackson's "Billie Jean." She moved in rhythm with the opening keyboard, stopping every few seconds and glancing seductively out over the empty room. She wore thigh-high white stockings, a short black skirt that barely covered anything, and a black leather jacket hanging open in front, revealing a white bikini top. Her hair was pulled up under a black fedora that she kept cocking on her head at certain points in the song.

Blake and Cal started talking about the poker game Blake was overseeing tonight and the possibility of bringing in a group of strippers to surprise the gamblers. Bruce pretended to be interested, but he kept his eyes on the dancer.

Ethan couldn't take his eyes off her either. He didn't remember any of the dancers being quite this dynamic. The girl on the stage was sexy, sure, but there was something about her, an electric charisma that not all the dancers had.

She pulled off her hat, tossed it behind her back, then swung her head in a wide arc that let her thick caramel-colored mane free. She caught Ethan's eye, and a smile came to her face, which he took at first to be flirtatious. But then her expression changed a little and she looked away, as if embarrassed. She moved around the stage with less flare now, going through the motions.

She had recognized him, but Ethan had no idea who she was.

They all watched her. Blake and Bruce would have seen this kind of thing every day—and Cal had been around it for two decades at least—but they all seemed to be caught in her spell.

A second song started—they always danced to two-song sets—and the girl continued to strut around the stage.

"What the hell is she doing?" Bruce grumbled. Ethan thought maybe he was complaining about the song, which Ethan didn't recognize, but then Bruce said, "Hey, Cal, she's not following the rules."

The girl spun on the pole and got down on her knees in front of the only two guys seated next to the stage. They craned their necks to look up her skirt, and she swaggered away, feigning coyness.

Ethan figured out what Bruce was talking about. Besides the hat, she hadn't taken anything off, not even the jacket. At this point in her set, she should have shed most of her clothes, if not everything except her thong.

Cal was irritated. "I don't care if we've got two guests or two hundred—you gotta give the customers what they want."

"Yeah," Bruce agreed. "And what they want is tits."

Ethan was trying to figure out if he had been away too long or if the girl really was as beautiful as he thought she was. He was halfway across the room, but he had excellent vision—twenty/ten at his last prison checkup—and he was fairly certain his female-starved mind wasn't playing tricks.

"Here comes Stu," Blake said, bumping Ethan on the shoulder.

Ethan pulled his eyes away from the dancer. Coming from a door at the back of the club was a thin Native American man with steady, sure steps. Ethan wouldn't have recognized him if he'd passed him on the street, but knowing who he was, he saw the resemblance to the teenager who had burned him on the football field twelve years ago. He was about six feet tall and trim—he hadn't bulked up like Ethan, but he was definitely in shape. He wore black dress pants and a black sweater, and his hair, also dark, was cut short. He wasn't flashy like Blake, but something about his outfit—the dark, no-nonsense of it—gave him an air of seriousness that Blake lacked. Blake's carefully constructed appearance made him look like a wanna-be gangster. Stuart Kicking Bird, without trying, looked like he was one.

"Stu," Blake said. "This is Ethan Lockhart."

Kicking Bird nodded slightly, barely acknowledging the introduction. He did not extend his hand.

"We played football against each other once upon a time," Ethan said.

Kicking Bird looked at him with an expression that suggested he was not only trying to remember Ethan but was trying to remember a time when he did something as pedestrian as play football. As if it had happened in another life.

"I'm sorry to hear about your sister," Kicking Bird said, a statement that seemed thoughtful enough, but it was as if a computer delivered the words. His eyes were cold, his tone flat.

"Yeah," Cal said from behind him, trying to compensate for not saying anything earlier, "we were all really sad to hear about it."

"Thanks," Ethan said.

"Yeah," Bruce added, as slow to participate in the conversation as he probably was on the football field. "She was a real pretty girl."

Ethan felt a spark of irritation. A pretty girl? That was the only thing the guy could think to say?

"Come on, Ethan," Blake said, clapping him on the back. "Let's go see Shark."

"Not you," Kicking Bird said, and Blake stopped. "Shark says you're excused. Go over to the hotel and start getting things ready."

Blake had a wounded expression. He didn't want to be left out of the reunion. But he wasn't going to defy Kicking Bird.

"Sounds like a plan," he said.

He gave Ethan another hug. "Come visit me, brother," he whispered in Ethan's ear. "Top floor. The Neptune."

"Sure," Ethan said, knowing he wouldn't come.

Bruce led the way, with Ethan following and Kicking Bird bringing up the rear. They walked past the stage, and Ethan looked up at the girl. She locked eyes with him, and now her expression was different.

She was worried. For him.

9

Ethan
46 hours, 22 minutes remaining

B RUCE PUSHED THROUGH the door to the dressing room—or "undressing" room—and Ethan followed. One wall held lockers and the other three were lined with mirror stalls where the girls sat to change their outfits and put on makeup. The room was empty now except for the fake-breasted blond who had been on the stage earlier and a Black girl with leopard-print tights and no top. Both women eyed them in the mirror as Ethan walked in with Kicking Bird and Bruce. They made no effort to cover themselves.

The room stank of perfume that covered an underlying reek of pungent sweat.

"Take your clothes off, Ethan," Kicking Bird said.

"What?"

"We need you to strip."

"Why?"

"You can figure that out."

"You think I'm wearing a wire?"

"They actually don't use wires anymore," Bruce said matter-of-factly. "More like a sticker with a little wireless transmitter. That's what I seen on TV."

Ethan could picture him sitting in his apartment, alone, eating a bowl of ice cream and watching *Law & Order*.

"It's a precaution," Kicking Bird said. "You can't see Shark unless you do it."

"I've got better things to do than sit around with you assholes," he said. "I agreed to come here as a courtesy to Shark."

"And because Shark paid for the lawyer who filed the paperwork for your furlough, it seems reasonable that your courtesy would extend to this request."

Ethan looked back and forth between Kicking Bird and Bruce. He caught the Black girl's eye. She had turned around and wasn't even pretending to watch them from the mirror anymore.

"Go ahead and take it off, honey," she said. "No need for modesty around here."

Her comment cut the tension, and Ethan snickered. Bruce chuckled too. Kicking Bird was silent.

Ethan pulled off his jacket, dropped it on the floor, and unbuttoned his shirt. He pulled his T-shirt over his head, kicked one shoe off and then the other, unbuckled his belt, dropped his jeans.

He stood in his socks and prison-issue boxer shorts.

"All of it," Kicking Bird said.

Ethan pulled the socks off and then dropped his boxers. He stood for all of them to see.

He heard a pair of heels clicking in the hallway, and someone pushed through the door. It was the girl from the stage. She froze in place, looked at Ethan, let her eyes fall to his chest, then his stomach, then lower.

"Oops," she said. "Sorry." She looked at Kicking Bird. "I mean, sorry for interrupting."

Her cheeks were turning red.

"Sit down," the Black girl said. "Enjoy the show."

Ethan kept standing. Bruce came over and picked through Ethan's clothes, looking for anything resembling a bug. When he was finished, he dropped them on the floor, and Kicking Bird gave a single nod to say Ethan could get dressed.

Ethan pulled his jeans back on and started to put a hand through the arm-hole of his T-shirt when the girl from the stage walked up.

"Hi," she said, smiling.

"Hello?" He said it like a question.

She'd thrown on a sweatshirt and pulled her hair back in a ponytail. Up close, she was even more beautiful than she'd been from the stage. She had luminescent skin and the kind of eyes that could hold you prisoner. She was stunning, there was no doubt about it, but with her sweatshirt on and her hair pulled back, she looked more like the pretty girl next door than someone you'd see in a strip club. Which was probably what the men loved about her so much. She wouldn't appeal to all of the customers, but to some, she could be the best of both worlds, sweet *and* sexy.

"You don't recognize me, do you?"

Ethan shook his head apologetically. He was trying to place her stage name—"Sierra Rose"—but couldn't remember any of the girls going by that. Besides, she was too young to have worked at the club five years ago.

"Whitney," she said. "Abby's friend."

"Oh my god," he said. "Whitney?"

Suddenly she became recognizable. The little girl his sister used to run around with was buried in the features of the stunning woman standing in front of him. The eyes, the nose, the way her teeth lined up when she smiled—they were all clues to a mystery he hadn't been able to figure out. And now that the mystery was solved, he felt silly for not seeing it before.

He became quickly aware that he was still shirtless, so he tried to pull the fabric over his head as he blundered through their reunion. He put the shirt on backward and had to pull it off and start over. She had been embarrassed on stage, and now it was his turn.

"I didn't know you worked here," he said, trying to find the right armhole. "The last time I saw you, you were . . ." He trailed off, trying to remember.

Whitney had always been a cute kid, but he'd been seven years older than her. Once she and Abby had hit their teenage years, he hadn't been around much. He'd been busy working for Shark.

She was smiling big and bright, and he realized he was doing the same. He finally got his arms and head through all the right holes. He didn't quite know what to say to her. He felt like saying "You look great" or "You're all grown up now," but neither of those seemed appropriate.

Bruce broke the silence for them.

"Any day now," he said.

Bruce pointed to his wrist even though he wasn't wearing a watch. Kicking Bird seemed indifferent to the conversation. The other girls had turned back to their mirrors.

"Well," Whitney said, "it was good seeing you."

"Yeah, you too."

"I guess I'll see you tonight at the memorial," she added.

"Yes," Ethan said, "see you then."

Two more girls came into the dressing room, new girls Ethan didn't recognize. They eyed him curiously. One of them made an exaggerated sound like she'd tasted something good.

The Black girl who had been there all along said, "I know. You should have been here two minutes ago."

Whitney pulled on a pair of sweatpants with the word "PINK" stenciled on the butt. She pushed her feet into a pair of unlaced tennis shoes and, without so much as a hello or goodbye to the other girls, left the room, a gym bag slung over her shoulder. Ethan, finishing tying his shoes, watched her go. He thought she might look back at him, but she didn't.

It was surreal to see her, this girl from his childhood, in this place from his adulthood. The two—the club and the girl—didn't seem to fit, and it reminded him all over again about how his sister had worked here. She didn't fit either. Not in the way he thought of the two. Abby was all that was good in the world—his kid sister who could do no wrong, not in his eyes anyway. She had a sarcastic sense of humor, she could be crass, and she was as stubborn as a person could be, but she was, at heart, a wonderful person. The club, on the other hand, was full of filth—the customers and the employees alike. It represented all that was bad from his past.

Abby never belonged here.

"I'm ready," he said, rising to his feet.

Kicking Bird told Bruce to go to the garage to check on something.

Bruce went through one door, and Ethan followed Kicking Bird through the other. The hallway was narrower than he remembered, the ceilings lower. Being here reminded him of a time when he was in high school and he'd had to go to his old elementary school to pick Abby up. It had been a few years since he'd been in the building, and he was shocked at how small the lockers looked, how tiny all the desks were. Of course, everything was the same; he'd been the one to change. The bowels of the club felt that way now—familiar, recognizable, but somehow different and smaller than he remembered them.

Kicking Bird knocked once and opened Shark's office door without waiting for an answer.

Shark stood in the center of the room, wearing, as he always did, loud clothes and bright jewelry. He could have been standing there for minutes, for all Ethan knew, as if it was perfectly ordinary to stand as still as a statue, waiting for his office door to open.

"There he is," Shark said, his smile wide. He had stubby, uneven teeth, like someone had filed them down. "I can't believe it."

"Hello, Shark," Ethan said.

Shark appraised him up and down. "Goddamn," he said, "you got big."

Besides being older, Shark hadn't changed much. With a flat smashed-in nose, skin as pale as paint and as rough as sand, and a mouth full of tiny teeth, Shark did look somewhat like the ocean predator he was named for. He wore a lime-green dress shirt, a salmon-colored tie, a lavender blazer, gold bracelets on both wrists, rings on several fingers.

"Isn't it a little early in the morning for clothes that bright?" Ethan said.

Shark laughed—a thick, husky sound, like a bear coughing—and threw his arms around Ethan. Ethan flinched. Then hugged him back. He couldn't quite help it. Shark was as evil a person as there was, but he might be the closest thing to a father Ethan ever had.

10

Ethan
46 hours, 7 minutes remaining

SHARK'S OFFICE WAS messier than Ethan remembered, less impressive. Before, the wood-paneled walls had seemed to give it a rustic appearance, like a cabin, but now the décor looked cheap and out of place. On each side of Shark's desk were clusters of aquariums. The ones to his left contained snakes and various reptiles, tarantulas, scorpions. To the right, they were full of fish, orange and red and yellow. Most of the aquariums seemed empty now, but Ethan figured whatever creatures were inside were probably hiding under rocks or blending in with the sand. The collection had impressed him when he was younger, but now the glass seemed unclean, the fish not all that exotic.

The wall behind the desk was still lined with glamour shots of many of the girls, some so old their hairdos had gone out of style. Shark only hung photos of the girls he'd slept with—a growing trophy display from when he first opened the club. Ethan was thankful he didn't see a picture of Abby. Or Whitney.

Shark sat behind his desk, and Ethan took a seat across from him. Another chair sat next to him, but Kicking Bird leaned on Shark's desk, facing Ethan instead, closer to him than would be socially acceptable in a normal office meeting. Shark's shorn hair, always buzzed close but not off, had more gray in it than it'd had five years ago. His face was looser, his jowls beginning to look like those of a bulldog. He was heavier, but not much. He had always been squat and solid, but not really fat. He was someone who could wear a business suit and rub elbows with high society, or he could put on a T-shirt and walk into a drug den, and no one—not even men bigger and stronger—would mess with him.

Ethan noticed a photo sitting on the desk, facing outward for visitors to see, of Shark standing on the deck of a small yacht, a bikini-clad girl under each arm.

"I bought a boat after you went inside," Shark said, noticing where Ethan's eyes had gone. "If it wasn't cold as hell right now, I'd take you out in it."

Ethan was ready to skip the pleasantries—he didn't care about Shark's boat—but he figured it was probably necessary to participate in some measure of small talk.

"*You* bought a boat?"

Shark had once shared with Ethan that he couldn't actually swim, and given his name and his affinity for fish, Ethan had always thought that was funny.

"You don't have to be Michael fucking Phelps to appreciate getting a blow-job in the middle of Lake Tahoe," Shark said.

They chatted like this for a few minutes. They talked about business in the club and life in prison, both of them being deliberately vague. Kicking Bird didn't speak. The music from the club—a pop song Ethan didn't recognize—came through the walls in muffled distortion.

Finally, Shark's tone changed to indicate he was getting down to business. He asked, "So you're out for two days, huh?"

"For the memorial tonight and the funeral tomorrow. And an extra night, so—I don't know—I can be with my family, I guess."

"You go back Sunday morning?"

"Sunday morning."

"No guards? No tracker on your ankle?"

"Nope," Ethan said. "I guess I have you to thank for that."

Shark sat back in his chair and shook his head. "The lawyer? That was nothing."

"Well, thank you." He tried to say it earnestly, to show Shark that he meant it—despite what he was going to say in a few minutes—and to express his thanks for more than the lawyer.

"I never heard of someone getting a furlough without some kind of security detail or at least an ankle bracelet," Shark said. "That's why I thought you must be working for the feds."

Ethan wondered if Shark was playing with him, but Shark had never been one for modesty. Daryl had alluded to Ethan having a friend in high places—a fairy godfather—who helped arrange the terms of his release. He must have been mistaken.

Shark leaned forward, his expression changing. "You know I can smell a lie like it's dog shit stuck to your shoe. I'm a human lie detector."

Ethan knew this to be true. Shark had made his reputation long ago as a card player who could always tell when people were bluffing. It was a skill that came in handy later as a fence and a loan shark. One day, sitting around the club, Blake and Ethan had tested him on it. They told lies and truths about the most trivial things—their favorite colors, their favorite movies, what they ate for breakfast—and Shark knew every single time.

"Are you working for the feds?" Shark said, all trace of joviality gone. "Don't you lie to me, 'cause I will know."

Ethan glanced at Kicking Bird, hovering so close to him, and then back to Shark. He worried for a moment that the movement of his eyes might give Shark the wrong impression.

"I'm not working for the cops, Shark. Not the feds. Not anyone. I didn't dime you out five years ago. Why would I screw you over now?"

Ethan felt his pulse quicken. What would happen if Shark thought he was lying?

Shark sat back in his chair, satisfied.

"I just wanted to get that cleared up."

Ethan leaned forward. "I don't have the same lie-detecting superpowers as you, but I've got a question too. Did you have anything to do with Abby's death?"

Ethan's limbs felt shaky. His heart was pounding harder than he wanted it to.

"No," Shark said softly, and the answer seemed heartfelt. "Of course not. I liked your sister, son. She was a sweet girl. I told you I'd look after her, and that's—"

"When I asked you to look after her," Ethan said, "I didn't mean hire her to take her goddamn clothes off."

"Now, listen," Shark said, putting his hand down on the desk. "That was her idea."

Ethan was beginning to boil. "I don't give a shit whose idea it was," he said, standing up and leaning over the desk. "You shouldn't have done it."

Kicking Bird stood up, ready to intervene, but Shark waved him off.

"Ethan," Shark said, "take a deep breath."

Ethan stared at him and then he turned away. He walked a few paces out into the room. He looked at one of the snakes, lying curled under a heat lamp. It looked back at him with cold reptilian eyes.

"You know anything about paying people under the table?" Shark said. "Laundering money. Making illegal money look legitimate. Know anything about that?"

Ethan thought this was a rhetorical question, but Shark seemed to be waiting for an answer.

"No," Ethan said.

"It was hard to *give* your sister money, pay for her school and bills and things. She's out there paying cash for everything, and she ain't got any income to show for it. She got audited by the IRS. Twice."

Ethan listened. He studied Shark's face but couldn't tell if he was lying.

"Coming to work here was her idea. It was easy to make everything look legal that way. About once a month, at the end of her Friday night shift, there was a fat envelope waiting for her under the bar. A nice tip from an anonymous customer."

He pointed to himself as if it wasn't obvious who the anonymous customer was.

"All of that was for you." He pointed to Ethan. "For your loyalty."

"And my silence."

"Yes. Both. But for you all the same."

Ethan figured the truth was probably somewhere in the hidden details of Shark's story. Abby might have suggested she come to work for the club, but Ethan wasn't naive enough to believe Shark hadn't planted the idea. He would have told her it was hard to give her money, explained how laundering worked, probably said something like, "If only you had a legitimate job where I could pay you extra."

Ethan opened his mouth to ask Shark why he didn't have her serving drinks instead of dancing—those girls wore black from head to toe, jeans and turtlenecks, to make sure customers saw them only as waitresses. Abby could have done that job just as easily. But he said nothing. Shark's speech about loyalty had done its work on him. He didn't want to seem ungrateful. The man had provided for his sister—whether Ethan liked the manner in which he did it or not—and he'd paid for Ethan's lawyer, both when he was arrested and for his furlough application.

"It's so messed up," Ethan said. "She was murdered, Shark. I can't even wrap my head around it."

"I know, son," Shark said, sitting back in his chair again. "That's one reason why I wanted to talk to you today. I'm prepared to help you do something about it."

Ethan looked back and forth between the two men. Kicking Bird was unreadable. Shark looked pleased with himself, as if he'd made Ethan the offer of a lifetime.

"You're aware, Ethan, that I'm a man with some connections," Shark said. "Stu and I will look into your sister's murder. Find out what happened. We've got certain talents and methods the cops don't."

"What's the catch?" Ethan said.

"Who says there's a catch?"

"Come on," Ethan said. "I'm not new to this."

Shark frowned in mock confusion.

"Well, if you're offering," he said, "there is one little thing you could do. But really it's more for your own good than mine."

Ethan listened. His heart rate had finally slowed, and now it was speeding up again.

"All I'd ask is that you try not to be upset when you go back to prison on Sunday."

Now it was Ethan's turn to frown. His confusion was real.

"You know," Shark said, shrugging, "if things have changed a little bit while you were gone."

Ethan understood.

Jack.

He wouldn't have known except for what Blake had said about Stuart Kicking Bird losing his sister. Jack—or his brother—had killed Kicking Bird's sister. Before switching prisons, Jack had been the victim of several murder attempts. But once he started hanging out with Ethan, those attempts had stopped. Things were starting to make sense.

Ethan glared at Kicking Bird, trying to intimidate him, but his old football rival just looked back as insouciant as always.

"You've got to be kidding me," Ethan said to Shark. "You got me out of prison for this?"

"I didn't get you out," Shark said again. "I just paid for the lawyer. But when I heard you wanted out, I thought it was a nice chance for us to tie up some loose ends."

Ethan wanted to storm out. Now that he knew what they were planning, he wanted no part of this conversation. His mind was racing with what he could do to stop it, but he knew the first step was keeping cool in this moment.

"Now I'm going to do you this favor," Shark said. "Find out what happened to Abby. And all you have to do is just live and let live."

"Favor?" Ethan snapped. "You owe *me*, Shark. I just did five years in prison and I've got at least two more. I could have dimed you out and walked."

"I appreciate that," Shark said. "But if you'd dimed me out, you wouldn't have walked far."

Ethan digested the threat.

"You promised me you'd look after her," Ethan said. "If you think you can find out what happened to her, just do it. For me. Don't bargain with me to look the other way while you murder someone."

"Okay, I will do you that favor," Shark said. "But I'm not bargaining. You *will* look the other way. Understand, Ethan, that I could have had this done at any time, but I held off out of respect for you. Now that you're out and don't have to be there, it's time."

"You mean now that I'm not there to stop it?"

"I know you're friends with this guy," Shark said, "but your loyalty is to me."

"I don't work for you anymore."

Shark grinned wide, showing his sawed-off teeth.

"You know," he said, "things have changed around here since you left."

"So I hear."

"Stu's become my right-hand man," he said, nodding to Kicking Bird. "If you weren't in prison, you might be my left. I always liked you, Ethan."

"Well, at least you have Blake."

Shark shook his head. "He's a good kid. Loyal. But he isn't you, Ethan. I always wished he'd been pinched instead." He put his finger to his lips and made a *shh* sound. "Don't tell him I said that."

"Things have changed with me too, Shark. When I'm done with my bid, I'm going clean. I don't want anything to do with this place anymore."

"We'll talk about it again before you go back," Shark said, as if Ethan's words were inconsequential.

Ethan didn't respond. He had no intention of seeing Shark again before he went back.

As if he could read Ethan's mind, Shark said, "A few of the girls and I will be at the funeral. I want to pay my respects."

Ethan felt his anger surging again. He didn't want Shark at Abby's funeral. He rose to leave, and made it to the door before Shark told him to stop.

"There's something I want to show you before you go," he said. "In the warehouse."

Kicking Bird's eyes darted to Shark's: a look of surprise—the first real emotion Ethan had seen on his face since he'd walked into the club.

"It's all right," Shark said to Kicking Bird. "I want him to see."

"See what?" Ethan said.

Shark grinned again. His black eyes narrowed, and his face, in that moment, reminded Ethan why people feared him.

11

Abby
5 years ago

A BBY STEPPED OFF the bus and headed toward the county courthouse. She was ditching school. Her mom had forbidden her to go, but Abby thought someone should be there for Ethan. It was a warm spring day. The grass on the courthouse lawn was losing its winter brown, with green stalks coming up in patches. Trees were blooming. It felt like a day for new beginnings, which was unfair—this was the day Ethan was going to prison.

She walked through the metal detector and looked around for where to go. The halls were filled with police officers in uniform and lawyers dressed in plain black suits. The other people looked like the dregs of society: men with missing teeth and sunburned faces, women in thrift-store clothes with babies in their arms.

From the lawyers to the criminals, everyone looked like they inhabited this world comfortably. They knew where to go, how to speak the requisite language.

Abby felt lost.

A man—obviously a lawyer, with shiny black shoes and slicked hair to match—noticed her as he passed.

"You don't look like you belong here," he said. "Can I help you, young lady?"

She told him what courtroom she was looking for.

"The Lockhart sentencing," the man said. He pointed down the hall. "I can walk you there."

"That's okay," she said.

The courtroom wasn't quite what she'd expected. There weren't vaulted ceilings and big windows, no mahogany benches like church pews. The seats were more like movie-theater chairs, and the judge's bench was a simple raised desk with a wood-paneled counter. The seal of the state of Nevada was mounted on the wall like a portrait.

Abby sat in the back and waited.

There were lawyers, police, a couple reporters she recognized from the local TV stations. They brought in Ethan in a blue jumpsuit with "WCSO," for Washoe County Sheriff's Office, stenciled on the back and front. He wore handcuffs and ankle shackles that were connected to a chain around his waist. He walked with a hunched-over shuffle, like an old man with back and knee problems. The room was only about half full, but he didn't see her sitting in the back.

They uncuffed him before he sat down.

When the bailiff said, "All rise," she did so dutifully, as did Ethan. She watched his back as the judge came in from a back doorway and told everyone to be seated.

The judge, a barrel-chested man in a black robe like a big paper sack, explained the purpose of the hearing.

"A jury has found you guilty of armed robbery," he said. "Today is your sentencing hearing."

The district attorney went first, calling witnesses—an employee of the casino, the floor manager, the guard who'd been shot—who discussed how they were traumatized by what happened. The casino manager talked about how business had been hurt. The guard said he couldn't work again and was collecting disability.

Then it was Ethan's lawyer's turn. He was a tall, bony man—a praying mantis in a suit—and he seemed to unfold as he rose out of his chair. He said he had no witnesses.

He'd asked Abby and her mom to testify about Ethan's character, but Abby was eight days shy of her eighteenth birthday, and the lawyer wouldn't let her do it without her mom's consent.

The judge asked for Ethan to speak.

"I'm sorry for what I did," Ethan said. "It was a stupid mistake. I don't ask for leniency, your honor."

They moved on to the recommendations from the district attorney and Ethan's lawyer. The DA called for the maximum sentence: ten years for the crime, plus another ten for use of an automatic weapon.

Ethan's lawyer explained that Ethan was repentant and had no history of criminal behavior. He reminded the judge that forensic evidence showed the gun Ethan had carried was not the gun used to injure the security guard.

"The real criminal is still at large," he said. "Don't punish Mr. Lockhart for what his accomplice did."

The judge asked Ethan to rise again, and he did. He stood straight. He didn't seem to be trembling, as Abby was.

"Mr. Lockhart," he said, "while we know that you did not shoot your gun during the perpetration of this robbery, the crime you are accused of is egregious. It is brazen, reckless, selfish. It's malicious and immoral. This is not the crime of a petty criminal."

Abby's heart was pounding.

Please, God. Please.

"Moreover," the judge continued, "your unwillingness to aid in the arrest of your accomplice is even more troubling. If you truly felt sorry for what you had done, you would have helped law enforcement find—as your attorney put it—the real criminal at large. Your expression of remorse is therefore unconvincing."

Abby stared at Ethan's back. Tears blurred her vision.

"Ethan Lockhart, you are sentenced to twenty years in prison."

Abby put her face in her hands. Her body convulsed with sobs, which she tried to keep as quiet as possible.

"Bailiff," the judge said, "if there are any members of Mr. Lockhart's family here, he may have a few minutes with them before you take him into custody. Are there any members of the Lockhart family here?"

Ethan said, "No, your honor."

Abby jumped to her feet. "I'm here," she yelped.

She hurried down the aisle. Ethan turned, an expression of pure surprise on his face.

Abby pushed past a uniformed deputy and threw her arms around Ethan's neck. She sobbed. His strong arms wrapped around her. She'd always felt safe in those arms.

"It's okay," he whispered to her. "It sounds worse than it is. I'll be eligible for parole in seven or eight years. I'll be out in ten at the most."

"Ten?" she bawled.

"Shh," he said. He rubbed her back, and she loosened her grip on him.

He put his mouth right next to her ear and whispered quietly.

"My boss is going to bring you some money from time to time," he said. "To help you out. Don't tell Mom where you got it, okay?"

He looked into her eyes, and the mask of strength he was wearing started to break apart. His eyes became glossy with tears. His mouth struggled to speak without crying.

"I love you, Abby. You're the only thing that matters to me in the whole world. You have to live a good life. Be good. Be happy."

"It's not fair," Abby said.

"It is fair," he said. "I'm getting what I deserve. But I'll be out someday, and I'll make you proud of me. I'll be the big brother you deserve."

The bailiff stepped forward and told them to finish their goodbyes.

Two deputies positioned themselves between them. Two more put all the chains back on Ethan.

"Goodbye, Sis."

She pushed the cops out of the way and hugged him again. He couldn't hug her back because of the chains. The cops pulled her away, gently but forcefully, and walked him through a door in the back of the courtroom. He turned his head and held her eyes until they pushed him through the doorway.

She hurried outside, ran to the side of the building, and collapsed against the wall, crying.

A few minutes later, one of the TV reporters approached her. "Excuse me, would you mind if we interviewed you for channel—"

"Eat shit," Abby said.

She stopped crying, but she didn't get up. She hugged her legs to her body and stared out at the world. The sunlight was unusually bright, the glare extreme, as if she'd just gone to the eye doctor to get the drops that dilate your pupils.

Ethan's lawyer came up the sidewalk, walking in a long, slow gait.

"You okay?"

"What do you think?" she said.

He set his briefcase down and sat next to her. His pant legs rose up past his dress socks, and a few inches of his thin legs were visible, his skin white and scaly.

"Is there anything you can do?" she said. "An appeal? A retrial?"

"Sorry," he said. "The evidence is about as strong as it gets."

Cars drove by like it was a normal day, oblivious to the girl, sitting by the courthouse, whose world as she knew it had just come to an end.

"Our only hope was a light sentence," he said. "I thought we might get some leniency too. But the DA's pissed because they couldn't get him to roll over."

"Give up his accomplice?" Abby said.

"Well, yeah, that's what they said in there, but they want everybody—the whole operation, Shark included. Your brother's too smart for that."

Abby continued staring out at the road like nothing had changed, but her mind was racing. Ethan had given her practically no details about what had happened. She had always assumed the so-called accomplice had been his best friend, Blake. But Shark? The owner of the strip club? How was he involved?

The lawyer was talking to her as if she knew more than she did.

"I've got to run," he said, putting his hand on her shoulder like they were old pals. "You take care of yourself."

He rose to his feet. Abby craned her neck to look at him.

"Your brother loves you very much," he said. "Shark's going to take good care of you."

She nodded, only beginning to understand the subtext of his words.

As he walked away, a seed of an idea planted itself in her mind.

12

Ethan
45 hours, 33 minutes remaining

SHARK AND ETHAN stood waiting while Kicking Bird unlocked the door to the warehouse. The door had never been locked back when Ethan worked here. Once they stepped through, he could see why it was.

A man was sitting on a metal folding chair in the center of the warehouse. His hands were cuffed together, and the chair sat atop a large sheet of clear plastic spread over the concrete floor. Bruce leaned against a nearby workbench, doing something with his phone.

The handcuffed man was Black, probably in his late twenties, although it was hard to tell because his face was bruised and swollen. His head hung down so his chin was almost touching his chest. A few strings of pink saliva dangled from his mouth. A chill ran through Ethan as he thought the man might be dead. But his chest rose slightly, then fell.

There were no ankle shackles, and the man wasn't tied to the chair, but he was in no condition to run off.

The music from the club was reduced to the thump-thump of bass.

"Wake him up," Shark said.

Kicking Bird pulled something out of his jacket pocket and waved it under the guy's nose. He jerked awake, almost tipping the chair over.

Shark, Kicking Bird, and the kid—Bruce—stood in a half circle in front of the guy. Ethan stood off to the side so he wouldn't be confused for anything more than a witness. The guy looked back and forth between Shark and Kicking Bird—he seemed to ignore Bruce—and opened his mouth to speak. Shark raised his hand to silence him.

"I want to know what you told them."

"Told who?"

The guy was a bad liar. Ethan didn't need Shark's special lie-detection powers to see that.

Shark looked up at the ceiling and took a deep breath, like a parent trying to be patient with a petulant child.

"Don't start by lying to me," he said. "You talked to the feds, Anton. Fact."

The guy, Anton, shook his head. He tried to raise his arms in some kind of gesture but then dropped them again when he remembered they were cuffed together. "No, Shark. I swear."

Shark flicked his arm against Bruce's shoulder—a gesture that told him to do something. The big lineman started toward the bench, almost lost his footing on the plastic on the floor, and then kept going.

"Turn the radio on while you're over there."

An old boom box sat on the bench, and Bruce flipped it on. An eighties metal song was playing, and he turned the volume up. Ethan knew why: to drown out the screams.

Bruce came back with a pair of what looked like tree trimmers, except they were stainless steel. The handles were at least six inches long, with one thick, sharp blade and a curved edge to press the blade against.

"Bone shears," Shark said to Ethan. "Coroners use them for ribs mostly, but they work for fingers too. A hundred bucks on the internet but worth every penny."

He told Bruce to give the cutters to Stu.

"I want to do the thumb," Bruce said.

Shark shook his head. "The bone's too thick. Last time Blake tried, he made a mess of things."

Ethan felt a wave of nausea hearing what Blake was willing to do for Shark. He wasn't sure if they were having this conversation to scare Anton or if there really was this running debate about which finger to sever.

"I can do it," Bruce said. "If you cut at the joint, I bet the thumb will come right off."

"Give the cutters to Stu," Shark said.

Anton tried to rise, but Bruce shoved him back down on the seat.

"I'll tell you," Anton said. "I'll tell you whatever you want to know."

"Yes," Shark said, "you will."

Bruce wrapped Anton in a headlock and held one of his arms with his free hand. Kicking Bird grabbed the guy's fingers. Anton moved his hand as much as he could, but Kicking Bird worked patiently. There was no need to hurry; the outcome was inevitable.

"Get in there and help them," Shark said to Ethan.

Ethan didn't move.

Finally, Kicking Bird got a good grip on Anton's smallest finger and twisted it back, almost to the point of breaking it. Anton gasped in pain, and Ethan had the sick thought that the poor bastard hadn't felt anything yet.

Kicking Bird slid the blade around Anton's finger, and there was a pause that seemed to last longer than it really did. Like the entire room held its breath. Anton stared, wide eyed, as if thinking—just for a moment—that maybe they wouldn't go through with it. This was just a threat. A scare. A bluff.

Kicking Bird squeezed the handles together. The blades cut only through skin at first. Anton couldn't scream or beg—he was too busy gasping for air. Hyperventilating. Then the bone gave way and there was a snapping sound like a dry branch breaking. The finger dropped onto the plastic sheet like a discarded scrap of food. Blood ran into Anton's lap.

Ethan felt the room spinning. He tried to take a deep breath, but he smelled blood and thought he might throw up or pass out, or both. He willed himself not to.

Bruce let go of Anton and stood back to watch. His chest rose convulsively, a wheezing sound was all that escaped from his open mouth, like his airway had been reduced to a pinprick. Shark stepped forward and slapped him in the face.

"Shut up."

Anton quieted. His chest still rose and fell in rapid succession, but he was silent now, staring at his hand in disbelief. His lap was soaked with blood.

"Who did you talk to with the feds?" Shark shouted.

"Hughes," Anton said, his voice raspy, like he hadn't taken a drink in a week. His eyes were wet with tears. "Brian Hughes."

Shark turned to Kicking Bird. "That same bastard," he said, exasperated. "He doesn't give up."

Kicking Bird gave Shark a slight nod but didn't respond.

"What did you tell him?" Shark asked Anton.

"I don't know. Some of the jobs we did."

He started naming them. A jewelry store robbery. Stolen cars. A prostitute they buried in the desert.

"What kind of evidence do they have?"

"Nothing." Anton shook his head. "Nothing, man, I'm telling you—"

"Did you wear a wire?"

"No," Anton said, and this answer seemed honest—clearly different from the way he had answered before his finger was cut off. "He wanted me to, but we hadn't gotten there yet."

"What else?" Shark said.

"Nothing, man. I swear."

"Did you mention keno?"

"No way."

Ethan frowned. There it was again—a reference to keno that he didn't understand. Shark nodded, satisfied.

Then the begging began.

Anton told Shark that if he let him go, he would leave town, Shark would never see him again. "Or I can tell that fed some fake shit," he said. "Send him in the wrong direction. I can play him if that's what you want me to do."

Shark turned his back to Anton and sauntered, in no hurry, over to the bench. Anton kept talking while Shark looked around at the tools. He picked up a flathead screwdriver, considered it, then put it back down. He settled on a framing hammer. It was big, probably eighteen inches long, and made of steel. Shark hefted it by the rubber grip, weighing it and weighing his choices.

Ethan knew there was really no choice. Only one way out of this for Anton. Shark walked back over the plastic.

"Shark, I swear I was going to tell you."

Anton started to rise, but Bruce pushed him down by the shoulders.

Shark raised the hammer. "You stupid"—he brought it down—"son of a"—again—"bitch!"

Each time the metal hammerhead struck Anton's skull, there was a pinging sound, like a muffled bell. Anton slumped back in the chair but didn't fall. Blood crawled down from his hairline in a trickle. Shark dropped the hammer, and the metal rang out against the concrete.

"Finish him, Stu."

Without a word, Kicking Bird circled around to the back. Bruce stepped off to the side to watch. Kicking Bird had a knife in his hand—Ethan hadn't seen where it came from. Kicking Bird took a fistful of hair, pulled Anton's head back, and put the knife to his throat. No hesitation. He sunk the blade in and sawed through the cartilage of Anton's windpipe. Anton made a thick gurgling noise, like a drowning person coughing up water. Blood came out in a pulsing waterfall. Anton's body slid off the chair and fell onto its side on the plastic.

Ethan felt dizzy and concentrated on not falling over. He wouldn't look away though. He didn't want Shark to smell any weakness. And he needed to see—to witness—what these people were capable of. Even now, as it was happening, he knew that any time in the future—two years from now, five years from now, ten—if he was ever tempted to go back to work for Shark, he needed to remember this moment.

Bruce was smiling like he'd done something exciting, gotten off a roller-coaster or spotted a celebrity.

"That was awesome," he said.

Kicking Bird was already down to business. He moved Anton's body around so it was lying flat. He took the metal chair and set it aside. Then he went to the corner and pulled the plastic toward the body. Bruce joined him. Within seconds, the body was wrapped up like a present, blood smeared on the inside of the clear plastic. Kicking Bird sealed the bundle closed with duct tape. Bruce grabbed a bottle of bleach and a rag off the workbench and knelt to clean the chair Anton had sat in. Kicking Bird came over and began cleaning the bone shears and framing hammer.

"Desert or lake?" Bruce asked Shark, squatting on one knee to wipe up a splotch of blood on the concrete.

Shark took out a leather-bound ledger from his jacket pocket and looked inside.

"Desert." He handed the ledger to Bruce. "Stu will help you. Blake's gonna be busy with the card game, and your brother is helping him."

Shark leaned against the bench and watched the other two work. It seemed as if they'd all forgotten Ethan.

He opened his mouth to speak. It was dry. "Am I done here?" he said, his voice unrecognizable to himself.

Shark walked over to him. "You see why I was asking about the feds?"

Ethan didn't answer. He didn't think it was that kind of question.

"I got to be careful. They're after me."

He put a hand on Ethan's shoulder, and Ethan willed himself not to pull away.

"I like you, Ethan. I always have." He patted Ethan's cheek like he was a child. "Of course," he said, "I liked Anton too."

13

Whitney
45 hours, 25 minutes remaining

W HITNEY SAT IN her car with the engine running. The heater pumped cold air into the cab before it started to turn warm. She turned on the radio, flipped through the stations, turned it off. She noticed she had clamped her hands into fists, and she forced herself to loosen them.

She'd pulled through the gate into the customer lot and positioned herself so she could see the front door as well as the back lot. She wasn't sure how long Ethan would be or which exit he would come out of. Only a few other cars were in the lot, so she had a good vantage on all the exits.

When Ethan had disappeared into the back with Stu and Bruce, she had looked up at Cal behind the bar. He was glaring at her. The song was almost over, so she knew she better give the men in the club a good finale. She hadn't been able to take her top off with Ethan in the room. He hadn't even recognized her, but she still couldn't let him see her like that.

With Ethan gone and thirty seconds left in the song, she pulled off her jacket, unzipped her skirt and dropped it on the floor, and with the final crescendo of the song, untied her bikini top and gave the audience what they wanted.

She'd felt sick to her stomach.

Afterward, she'd gone to the bar and asked Cal if she could have the rest of the day off.

"What the hell was that?" he said. "The first song is to tease them. The second is to show them what they came to see."

"Sorry," Whitney said, faking sincerity. "I'm not feeling well. Can I go home?"

"You just got here."

"I know, but you've got enough girls."

A few men had been trickling in, but the club was still practically empty.

"With Abby's memorial tonight," she said, "I'm not feeling it."

Whitney hated to use this as an excuse, but the comment seemed to work. Cal's expression changed from irritated to sympathetic.

"Okay," Cal said, "get out of here."

She hadn't expected to see Ethan when she'd gone into the dressing room, much less naked. She'd made sure not to strip in front of him on stage, and it turned out he had to strip in front of her backstage.

He looked good too.

When she'd come into the dressing room and seen him standing there, it had taken her breath away for a moment. He'd always been svelte, athletic, but he'd put on a lot of muscle in five years. His shoulders were broad and defined, his chest and stomach muscles carved out of stone. Fat veins ran up his biceps like serpents slithering under the skin.

Seeing him, she got a taste of what she did to men on a nightly basis.

That wasn't why she was waiting, though. He might need a ride. He might need a place to stay. He might need a friend.

With Abby gone, Whitney could sure use one.

14

Ethan
45 hours, 22 minutes remaining

ETHAN DID HIS best to act normal as he walked through the club. As he passed the bar, Cal asked if he wanted a lap dance—on the house, for old time's sake—and he was even able to act nonchalant about passing on the offer. But it was an act—as soon as he pushed through the front door and into the cold air, he stepped to the side and allowed himself to vomit. The bile came up white and hot, splattering against the pavement. He retched several times. He stood up straight and took a deep breath. The cold air felt good on his clammy face. A chimney of steam rose from the vomit.

He heard the whine of an engine and stood, wiping his mouth with his jacket sleeve. A blue Prius pulled up beside him. The window buzzed down, and inside sat Whitney.

"You okay?"

"Better now," he said. "I ate too much breakfast."

He could tell she didn't believe him.

She reached into her gym bag on the backseat and pulled out a bottle of water. She held it out to him. He took a drink, swished it around in his mouth, and spit.

"You want a ride somewhere?" she said.

"I don't want to put you out."

She rolled her eyes. "Get in the car, Magic Mike."

He filled his mouth with water and then spit again before climbing in.

"Where to?"

Ethan leaned back in the seat, took a deep breath, and closed his eyes. "Can you take me to my mom's house?"

"Sure thing." She put the car into gear. "She'll be glad to see you."

Ethan shook his head. "No she won't."

*   *   *

Whitney zipped the car down a side street, bypassing downtown, and circled around the university toward their old neighborhood.

"So how've you been?" Whitney said, her tone indicating she knew the absurdity of the question. She was making a joke because neither of them knew what else to say.

"I don't mean to be rude," Ethan said, "but I need to think for a minute."

She was quiet.

Ethan couldn't stop thinking about what he'd just witnessed. He tried to shove the images aside and focus on what Shark had said to him.

All Shark had wanted was to get Ethan out of the prison for a couple days— to get rid of Jack's protection. Or maybe what he'd said was true: He hadn't pulled any strings to get Ethan out, but was simply taking advantage of the situation that had presented itself.

There was something about the way the kid Miguel, who used to work for Shark, was staring at them this morning that told Ethan he was the one Shark had tapped for the job.

"Do you have a phone on you?" Ethan asked.

"Yes."

"May I make a phone call with it?"

Whitney pulled a phone out of her sweatshirt pocket, pressed a button to unlock it, and handed it to Ethan. The interface was different from the last phone he'd owned, but he recognized the green icon with the telephone receiver on it. Ethan pulled his case worker's card out of his pocket and punched the digits on the screen.

"Daryl Maxwell."

"It's Ethan."

"Hey," Daryl said, sounding excited, like he was hearing from an old friend he hadn't talked to in a while. "Miss me already?"

CHAPTER

15

Daryl
45 hours, 3 minutes remaining

D ARYL TUCKED HIS cellphone to his ear as he walked back through the prison grounds. He'd been out by the eastern wall, talking to a kid who'd been studying for his GED but had skipped his last two tutoring sessions. It was cold outside, but still a lot of the inmates were out and about. The prison was more than a hundred and fifty years old, and the buildings and infrastructure around him had a Frankensteinian appearance, an odd combination of old sandstone walls and rusted iron catwalks along with modern structures made of plastic and gleaming steel.

"How's freedom treating you?" Daryl asked Ethan.

Lockhart was one of his favorite inmates. He wasn't sure why. Ethan was a big guy, tough. He could handle himself in prison. But underneath that was an ordinary young man who'd taken a wrong turn in life. Daryl knew the details of his arrest and had always felt the hefty sentence was unfair. Ethan was doing more time than a lot of guys who were worse offenders.

Ethan ignored the question. "Could you do me a favor?" he said.

"Depends."

"My cellmate," Ethan said. "Jack. Can you get him out of the general population? Put him in solitary until I get back?"

"What the hell for?" Daryl stopped walking. "Tell me what's going on, Ethan."

"Nothing," Ethan said. "I have a bad feeling."

Daryl didn't say anything. He lifted his head and took a deep breath. If Ethan was out there getting into trouble, it was exactly what Daryl had told him not to do.

"Before he was transferred," Ethan explained, "there were a bunch of attempts on his life. And even one or two after. If I'm not there . . ."

"To protect him?" Daryl finished for him. "You've got a pretty high opinion of yourself, don't you, Ethan?"

"Could you ask him?" Ethan said. "Give him the option."

It was a strange request, but Daryl was pragmatic about his decision-making. He doubted there was much of a threat to Jack—at least not more than there was for any given inmate on a particular day—but his mantra was *"better safe than sorry."* He didn't want to clock in for work tomorrow to find that this guy Jack had been knifed in the shower.

Still, Daryl was only a caseworker, and moving someone from general to solitary wasn't the type of thing he could just do with a phone call. He'd have to provide paperwork, some justification, and still the higher-ups might not go for it.

Daryl took a deep breath. "Okay. I'll try. But you owe me."

"Thanks, Daryl," Ethan said.

Daryl wanted to give Ethan his spiel about staying out of trouble, but the phone beeped to indicate the call had ended.

"Son of a bitch," Daryl said, staring at the blank screen on his phone. "He hung up on me."

16

Ethan
44 hours, 56 minutes remaining

"What was that all about?" Whitney asked after Ethan hung up the phone.

"Long story," Ethan said.

There wasn't time for him to tell it. They had arrived at his mom's house.

Ethan sat in the car and stared at the house where he'd grown up with Abby. The siding was the same, only faded and flaking paint. The concrete walkway was a lighter gray than he recalled, as if the sun had bleached it over the past five years. The front door—had it always been that beige color? Ethan couldn't remember.

Ethan and Abby had different fathers, but there had never been a regular father figure around. Their mom had had boyfriends off and on, but no one Ethan had ever looked up to or liked. Since she usually worked more than one job to keep up on the mortgage payments, she'd often left Ethan to keep an eye on Abby. He and his mom had butted heads a lot—he wasn't a particularly good kid—but that was the one area where she trusted him completely. And he'd never betrayed that trust. When he'd been running around town with Blake or partying with the football team, that's when he got into trouble, but his mom put up with it because he took care of his sister.

It wasn't until she was old enough to take care of herself that things really started to go wrong. He wasn't around much after high school. He worked odd jobs here and there—washing dishes, roofing houses, moving furniture—making enough to get his own apartment. He'd never been cut out for college, not that he wasn't smart enough. He had a good memory, particularly with numbers and puzzles and patterns, but he just couldn't see himself sitting in a lecture hall, taking notes, studying for exams. And he didn't have any interest in racking up a bunch of student loan debt. When he turned twenty-one, he went to work for Shark and thought he'd hit the jackpot. Here was a job—both in the club and the extras Shark asked for on the side—that he could stick with. But it never occurred to him what kind of example he might be setting for Abby. His mom knew, though, and when he was arrested—something she thought was inevitable—she said she never wanted to see him again.

Whitney opened her door and started to get out, but Ethan didn't budge. "Come on." She tugged on his arm. "It's going to be fine."

He stepped out into the cold but hesitated on the sidewalk when he saw, several houses down, a sedan sitting parked in the street. He couldn't be sure, but it looked like the one from the bus station parking lot earlier that morning.

"Hang on a sec," he said to Whitney, and he started down the sidewalk.

The car's engine started. It was pointed toward him, so if it was going to drive forward, it would go right past him. Instead, the car backed into a driveway and turned around the other way. It moved quickly and was gone before Ethan got to it. Again, the driver was only a shape behind the wheel.

He hadn't thought to look at the license plate number and wished he had. He didn't know what he could do with the information, but it wouldn't have hurt to have it.

"Anyone you know?" Whitney asked.

"Not sure," Ethan said.

Whitney led the way, as if this was her childhood home, not his. She knocked on the door, and when there was no answer, she tried the knob. It turned, so she opened the door and announced herself.

"Mrs. L?" she said. "Anybody home?" She stepped inside. "It's Whitney Potter. I've got a surprise for you."

Ethan cringed at her tone. This wasn't going to be a good surprise.

They found his mother in the living room. She was curled up on the couch, a blanket wrapped around her. The overhead light was dimmed, but not off. The TV screen was black. His mother was doing nothing. Simply lying awake in the gray light.

The house smelled of cigarette smoke. The ashtray on the coffee table was overflowing with butts.

Whitney came over and knelt next to the couch.

"I brought someone to see you," she whispered.

Ethan's mom's eyes shifted to him. "So they let you out for your sister's funeral."

"Hi, Mom."

She looked away, back to the black screen of the TV. Ethan wondered what kind of pills she was on, and how many.

It was only afternoon, but the gray sky and dim lighting made the day seem later. His mother looked fifteen or twenty years older than he remembered. She'd always been attractive—he'd been in many fights in school when boys would joke about how much they wanted to screw his mom—but it seemed like time had caught up to her. She wasn't yet fifty, but she looked well past it. A half-inch of pure white hair sprouted from her roots before the color was covered by a cheap dye job. Wrinkles spread out from her pale lips, mapping a lifetime of sucking on cigarettes. The bags under her eyes, always there from being a single mother, were now charcoal black. She looked like she hadn't slept a minute in the past three weeks.

Ethan came over and knelt down next to Whitney.

"I'm sorry, Mom."

"You're sorry?" she said, her voice raspy. "For what?" She said it like a question, but her tone was sarcastic.

"I'm sorry I wasn't here."

She stared, the black holes of her eyes burning into him.

"That isn't what you should be sorry about."

She sat up slowly, reached for a pack of Camels on the coffee table, and fumbled with the lighter. Finally, she got it lit, took a long drag, and exhaled. She pointed at Ethan with the two fingers that held the cigarette.

"You being gone was the best thing that ever happened to your sister."

Whitney rose and stepped back, knowing not to get involved.

"The problem was when you were here. Working at that strip club. Doing God knows what for that criminal son of a bitch."

Ethan lowered his head. There was no point in arguing. Everything she said was true.

"When you went away," she said, "I was *relieved*. I thought, maybe now Abby will stop looking up to him and have a chance to do something good with her life."

She pulled on her cigarette, exhaled through her nose.

"But you'd done all the damage you needed to already. She followed right in your footsteps. Going to that disgusting club." She gestured to Whitney with her cigarette. "With this one."

Whitney looked like she'd been slapped but didn't say anything to defend herself.

"Leave Whitney out of this," Ethan said. "It's me you're mad at."

He rose and walked a few feet away, looking to a bookshelf covered in knick-knacks and picture frames. A dozen pictures of Abby at various ages stared back at him. One of her as a little girl, her hair in pigtails, a gap in her smile where a baby tooth had fallen out. A senior picture of her sitting cross-legged, her elbows on her knees and her chin on her fist, her smile big and proud. There was a picture of Abby with Whitney, probably from middle school, where the two wore their cheerleading uniforms and stood back to back, arms crossed, smiling brightly. Whitney was recognizable but different—a cute kid hiding the beautiful woman she would become. An explosion of grief struck his heart as he thought of Abby and how she would not continue to grow, to change.

There were no pictures of Ethan.

They were silent for a long time. His mom finished her cigarette and stubbed it out. Whitney came over to Ethan and touched him gently on the arm. "We should go," she said softly.

She was right. He wanted to be able to comfort his mother, but it was clear she would prefer to be alone than be around her son.

"I've got to get something first," he said.

He walked down the hall toward his old bedroom. After he had moved out when he was twenty-one, his mom had always kept his room more or less as it was. She'd taken down his posters from the walls, but the bed had remained, as well as his old football trophies and some of his clothes. Before his trial, when he was out on bail that Shark had paid, he'd cleared out his apartment and brought over some boxes of stuff, clothes mostly, but also his TV, his stereo, a mountain bike.

But she'd converted the room into something else entirely. There was a small table with a sewing machine on it, a papasan in the corner, a quilt hanging on the wall. Whitney stood in the doorway, watching him. He stepped past her and walked back down the hall.

"Mom," he said softly. "I know you're pissed at me, but I need to know where my suit is. I can't go to the funeral dressed like this."

"I don't want you there at all," she said.

"I'm going," he said, firm this time.

She took a deep breath. "Abby took all your stuff. I told her I was going to throw it all away, and she came and got it."

"Do you have a key to her place?"

"It's a crime scene," she said. "You can't go there. The cops told me they'd let me know when I could go and clean it out."

Whitney put her hand on Ethan's shoulder again and mouthed something to him. He squinted, unsure what she'd said. She leaned in to whisper. In five years, he hadn't smelled anything like her.

"I have a key."

Ethan nodded.

"We're going to go now, Mom."

Ethan started toward the front door.

"If I had known they would let you out," she called to him, "I never would have let the FBI talk me into declaring her dead."

He stopped. "What?"

She was looking toward the window, even though the blinds were drawn. "I would have let her stay a missing person forever if it meant I didn't have to see you."

"What are you talking about?"

Daryl had said there was enough evidence to know for sure she was dead.

"*You* declared her dead?" he asked.

"The FBI told me to."

"The FBI? Why is the FBI involved?"

"I don't know, Ethan," she snapped. "I talked to the Reno PD, the FBI. Hell, I don't know who all was here, asking questions."

Ethan stared at her. "But the FBI talked you into declaring her dead?"

"He said it would help with the investigation," she said, her tone defensive and angry. "Something about making it easier to call it a murder investigation."

Ethan didn't know much about murder investigations, but none of this made any sense.

"Who told you that?"

"Some young guy," she said. "I don't know his name. His card's around here somewhere."

"Where?"

"In the kitchen."

He headed that way, and she called after him, near tears, "I didn't know what to do. It's not like I had anyone here to help me."

Hope ballooned inside him. *Could Abby still be alive?*

He rummaged through the clutter on the kitchen counter: piles of papers, unopened mail, bills with past-due notices. There was a bundle of bananas that had gone brown, a box of Cheez-Its lying on its size, spilling out some of the orange squares.

He pushed the mess around, frustrated. He turned to call back to her, but Whitney was there, and she placed a gentle hand on his back.

"I'll help you," she said.

Her touch had a calming effect. She searched the counter, and he moved to one of the drawers where his mother had always kept paperwork and other junk: batteries, scissors, pens, tape.

Finally, Whitney spotted a business card wedged under a magnet on the refrigerator. She handed it to Ethan. The card was for a Reno cop named Calvin

Taylor, not an FBI agent. There was an office address, phone number, and email address. There was a number on the back, presumably a cell phone.

"I think this is the cop I talked to," Whitney said.

"You talked to the cops?"

"Of course I did," she said. "I'm her best friend. They wouldn't be doing their job if they didn't ask me any questions."

He put the card in his pocket.

He went to say goodbye to his mom again. She'd lain back down on the couch, how he'd found her.

She didn't look at him, and for a moment he thought she wouldn't say anything. Then she said, "You know what I told God when I found out she was gone?"

Ethan waited.

"I told Him if I had to lose a child, why couldn't it be you?"

Ethan said nothing. If there was a god, he would have said the same thing.

CHAPTER

17

Jack
44 hours, 32 minutes remaining

JACK STOOD ALONE in the yard. The air was cold, and he was tempted to go back to his cell, but fresh air was a precious privilege in prison. Inmates braved worse weather than this—snow, rain, one-hundred-degree heat—to be outside when they had the chance.

The few picnic tables were usually barred territory. You had to be in a gang or protected or sucking someone's dick to get a place there. Otherwise, the only place to sit was the ground.

A few men played a pickup game of basketball, taking turns complaining about how rock-hard the ball was and how it wouldn't bounce for shit. Other men were jogging. He and Ethan usually spent their yard time at the weight benches, which were always crowded. But today, without Ethan, Jack didn't feel like navigating his way through the other inmates to do any lifting. Ethan was like the popular kid at school who let Jack tag along with him. Jack didn't quite know what to do or how to be without him. So he figured he would spend the time standing by himself, breathing in the cold, fresh air.

He noticed someone looking his way. In the fifteen minutes he'd been out here after lunch, he'd seen this same person looking at him twice now. It was the kid who had talked to them that morning, Miguel.

His nerves were on high alert. Something was up.

Jack started walking, as if he was just taking a stroll, and repositioned himself against the stone wall on the far edge of the yard. This way, if the guy made a move, Jack would see him coming. There was no way to sneak up behind him. And being at the center of the wall, he couldn't get backed into a corner.

He looked back at the kid. Miguel locked eyes with him and made no effort to look away. The kid smiled, showing both of his missing front teeth. He stuck his tongue through the hole, a gesture Jack wasn't sure how to interpret.

But it couldn't be good.

Jack looked around for guards. There would usually be at least three monitoring the yard, but he could only find one on the far side. If they cleared out like this, that usually meant they'd been paid off. There was still a guard tower within view, but from this angle Jack couldn't make out if anyone was up there.

He figured he should walk in the direction of the one guard who'd remained on duty, but then he spotted Ethan's caseworker, Daryl Maxwell, accompanied by another guard, entering the yard from the administrative office wing. Maxwell and his guard—a guy as big as Ethan and known for excessive force—were closer. So he headed that direction.

Suddenly, there was a burst of shouting. Miguel was in a fight with another guy about his size. They were throwing wild, inaccurate swings at each other, and a crowd was starting to form. The guard who'd remained in the yard headed over to break them up. But something was off. These guys weren't really trying to hurt each other. Which told Jack the fight was a distraction. Someone else was about to be attacked.

He knew who it was going to be.

Jack whirled around just as a big man with a ponytail—like Thor from the comic books he used to read—came at him with a shiv. Jack backpedaled. Thor thrust the blade forward, but the guard who'd been with Maxwell rushed in from his periphery. Thor didn't see him coming, and a club came down on his head with a loud crack—a sound like two pool balls colliding. The guy's legs went wobbly. The guard brought the club down again, harder, and the god of thunder collapsed into a gelatin heap.

Jack's heart was racing like a horse at a full gallop. Daryl Maxwell, who looked just as shaken as he was, stepped up next to him.

"Holy shit," Maxwell said. "I think Ethan Lockhart just saved your life."

"Come again?" Jack said.

Ethan, Maxwell explained, had called and asked him to put Jack in protective custody.

"I'm guessing that's okay with you considering what nearly just happened."

"Sure," Jack said, stunned—wondering what the hell Ethan was up to if he got wind of this.

More guards were running in, pushing the rubbernecking cons out of the way. Jack's attacker lay unmoving in the dirt. A snake of blood slithered out from under his blond hair.

Miguel and the guy with the shiv hadn't counted on Maxwell showing up with an escort. If he hadn't, Jack would be the one on the ground, only instead of being knocked unconscious, he'd be bleeding out.

Daryl gestured with his arm, and the two of them walked side by side toward the yard's exit.

Jack looked around for Miguel and saw that his fight had ended without fanfare. From a crowd of inmates, the kid glanced over at Jack. He had an expression like he'd put a big chunk of money on his favorite sports team and they'd lost in a blowout.

CHAPTER

18

Ethan
44 hours, 22 minutes remaining

THEY SAT IN the Prius, the engine idling and the heater pumping warm air into the cab. Throughout the neighborhood, the grass in the lawns was brown. The trees were skeletal.

They'd talked for a few minutes about the encounter with Ethan's mom, but there was only so much to say. Whitney thought his mom would come around—she just needed time—and Ethan assumed his mom would hate him forever. Now they sat in a comfortable silence, Ethan unsure what to do next, and Whitney, he assumed, willing to take him wherever he asked.

He held the card they'd taken from his mom's refrigerator and stared at it.

"Do you have a place to stay tonight?" Whitney asked. "I mean, it doesn't look like you'll be staying with your mom."

"I don't know where I'm staying," he said. "I could probably—"

He was going to say that he could probably go to Blake's poker game and sleep in an empty bed in the suite they'd reserved, but Whitney interrupted him.

"You're welcome to crash at my place," she said. He said nothing, and she quickly added, "The couch is pretty comfy."

"I might take you up on that."

"Did you want to go to Abby's?" she said. "To get your suit."

He glanced around to see if the sedan might be back, but it wasn't. He looked back at the detective's business card.

"Will you take me somewhere first?"

Whitney put the gearshift into drive.

"You want to go see that cop?"

"Yeah," he said. "None of this makes any sense to me."

* * *

"I'll wait here," Whitney said, putting the car in park in front of the police station.

"You can come if you want," Ethan said.

"Maybe he'll be more open with you if I'm not there," Whitney said. "But I want to hear what he has to say, so take good notes." She tapped her finger against her skull. "Mental notes, I mean."

She pulled out her phone and started swiping through screens.

Ethan walked into the front reception area. The tile floors of the lobby looked almost yellow in the fluorescent light. A man in uniform—younger than Ethan but probably older than Whitney—sat at a welcome kiosk, typing into a computer. The room was silent otherwise.

Ethan pulled the card out of his pocket and said he wanted to see Detective Taylor. He showed the card to the man at the desk.

"Who may I say is here?"

"Ethan Lockhart."

The man made a phone call. Ethan checked his watch. He wanted to shout, *Hurry up! Time is running out!*

A few seconds later, the officer hung up and told Ethan, "I'm sorry, but he's in a meeting."

Ethan leaned over the counter, locked eyes with the guy, and said, "Tell him I have important information about the murder of Abby Lockhart."

"Oh," he said.

"And I'll only talk to him," Ethan added.

CHAPTER

19

Taylor
44 hours, 5 minutes remaining

CALVIN TAYLOR SAT at his desk, snacking from a Ziploc bag of baby carrots and looking over the files from a shooting a few months back: a jilted ex killing the new beau of his estranged wife. A court hearing was coming up, and Taylor was reviewing the files, to be prepared to testify.

He knew the case inside and out and was mostly stalling until his shift was over. Still, he'd told the desk officer to tell Ethan Lockhart to get lost. He'd heard the guy was getting out of prison on furlough to attend the funeral, but Taylor hadn't had anything to do with that case since the very beginning. The FBI had snatched it away because of its possible connection with the gangster who ran Dark Secrets. Giving the case up hadn't sat well with him at the time, but he'd since moved on—there were plenty of murders and missing persons cases to keep him busy.

Abby Lockhart and her brother were not his problem anymore.

His phone rang again.

When he picked up, the clerk passed along Ethan's message.

"He says he'll only talk to you."

"All right," Taylor said, taking an exasperated breath. "I'll be out in a minute." After he hung up, he said to himself, "Always on a goddamn Friday."

He took a moment to stash the bag of carrots in his desk and put the domestic shooting file away. He didn't know what this guy was after, but he could see he wasn't going to get rid of him without talking to him. He headed down the hall, pushed the button to electronically unlock the door, and stepped out into the lobby.

Lockhart stood by a row of chairs, anxious enough that he couldn't even sit down to wait. He was White, probably about thirty, a couple of inches taller than Taylor, and as solid as a brick wall. Like a lot of cons, he clearly lifted weights. He was wearing denim from head to toe—apparently the prison hadn't even let him change clothes. In his facial features, Lockhart resembled his sister. When she'd first been dubbed a missing person, Taylor had borrowed a handful of pictures from the mom. She'd been quite beautiful, and Ethan was a handsome young guy as well. They looked like a couple of All-American kids who should have had bright futures, yet somehow one of them had ended up in prison and the other one had been murdered.

"Ethan Lockhart?" he said. "Calvin Taylor."

Taylor extended his hand, and the young man took it.

He had a firm handshake but wasn't trying to posture. Sometimes cons tried to break his damn fingers they squeezed so hard. But Taylor had spent his life around tough men and wasn't intimidated. To his credit, Ethan Lockhart looked like he had no interest in trying to be intimidating. He looked like a big brother trying to make sense of a world where a loved one could be violently taken away. Taylor had seen the look a thousand times on the faces of people reeling from senseless murder like this. He felt a pang of pity for this young man.

Taylor punched a code into the door, hiding the keypad with his body. Once they were out of the lobby, Taylor said, "Do you really have vital information, or did you say that to get my attention?"

Lockhart cracked the hint of a smile.

"Thought so," Taylor said.

"Just like you weren't actually in a meeting."

Taylor chuckled. "Got me. Is it okay if we sit in my office instead of the interview room?"

"We can sit wherever you want," Lockhart said. "You're going to be doing most of the talking."

CHAPTER

20

Ethan
43 hours, 57 minutes remaining

D ETECTIVE TAYLOR'S OFFICE was a cramped little room with a small wooden desk, some filing cabinets, a rolling cushioned chair behind the desk, and a small wooden one in front. A metal bookshelf full of binders instead of books sat against the wall. There was no clutter on the shelves. The desktop was empty except for an inbox and an outbox, and a fat Rolodex full of faded manila address cards.

Taylor gestured for Ethan to take the chair opposite the desk. As the detective lowered himself into his own chair, he unbuttoned the bottom of his sports jacket, and Ethan glimpsed a pistol hanging close to his body in a shoulder holster. It was a blocky thing, probably a Glock. As he settled into the seat, his jacket shifted and covered the gun back up.

"So you're out of prison," Taylor said, "and you want the scoop on your sister's case. Am I right?"

"I'm just trying to understand what happened," Ethan said.

"You're not going to try to solve this thing on your own, are you?"

Taylor seemed to have a no-nonsense, cut-through-the-bullshit way about him, which Ethan appreciated.

Taylor was a fifty-something Black man with close-cropped gray hair and some bulk around the middle of a once-athletic frame. He wore a weariness on his face that suggested he'd been at this a long time. He'd clearly seen a lot, but it hadn't necessarily hardened him. He still had a friendly composure.

"No one tells me shit in prison," Ethan said. "I'm just trying to get a little clarity before I go back on Sunday."

"You might be in the wrong office," Taylor said. "The feds took the case from us."

"Why?"

"Why do you think?"

"Shark."

"You said it. Not me."

"Can you tell me what you do know?" Ethan said.

"I can't say a lot. It's an ongoing investigation, even if it isn't ours."

Ethan leaned forward. "Well, maybe you can answer this. How do you know Abby is dead? There's no body."

He felt a chill saying those words about his sister.

Taylor stared at him, hesitant.

"I'm not going to go public with this," Ethan said. "I'll be back in prison in"—he looked at his watch—"in, like, forty-three hours. I just want to know what happened to my sister."

Taylor seemed satisfied.

"First of all, we classified her as a missing person, but we treated the case as a homicide based on the evidence at the scene."

Ethan swallowed. "Are you saying there's a chance she's just missing?"

"Not likely." Taylor held his hands up like he was weighing something in each. "When I had the case, I determined that your sister was almost certainly dead. I hate to say it, but that's the truth. Still, I'm scrupulous when I investigate a crime. I cross all my *T*s and dot all my *I*s. I don't like to declare a victim deceased till I have a body. I don't like making assumptions."

"So if you were still investigating," Ethan said, "you wouldn't have had her declared dead?"

"No. I think that's weird, to be honest with you."

Ethan's breath caught in his throat. "I thought so too."

They were quiet for a few seconds. Ethan hadn't noticed it before, but now he could hear Taylor's clock ticking on the wall.

"There was a lot of blood at the scene," Taylor said. "Forensics estimates at least a liter, probably two. Your sister was a petite girl. She probably only had three and a half liters in her whole body. She lost a third to a half of her blood. We're talking a class III or class IV hemorrhage. Fatal without medical help."

Ethan felt a wave of dizziness. He thought of the blood coming out of Anton that morning and pictured that amount gushing from Abby. The balloon of hope that had been inflating inside him popped. Taylor's phrasing—*"fatal without medical help"*—had been the needle.

"And you're sure it was Abby's blood?"

Taylor nodded. "The DNA matched with hair taken from her hairbrush and some of her baby hair, which we got from your mom."

"Any leads?"

"Obviously the FBI thinks it knows something." He shrugged. "But we had no major leads. No clear evidence at the scene. No fingerprints or DNA that couldn't easily be explained. No murder weapon. No sign of a break-in."

"So the killer could have been someone she knew? A friend?"

"Or someone she worked with. Or she just didn't lock her door."

The clock ticked.

"I don't really know how you decide jurisdiction," Ethan said. "Why is Shark their case and not yours?"

"Some bureaucrat requested their help making a case against Shark a while back. Technically, we're working in conjunction with the feds' organized crime unit. But that's PR. Shark's case is theirs. We don't have much to do with the investigation anymore."

Taylor took a deep breath, as if pondering how much more to share.

"My gut tells me it wasn't Shark," he added.

Ethan waited for clarification.

"For one," Taylor said, "we made some discreet inquiries into Shark's whereabouts that night. He's got a solid alibi, and so do all of his people."

"Stuart Kicking Bird?" Ethan asked, unsure if he should let on he knew the names of Shark's associates. But, of course, Taylor would know that he used to be a part of Shark's crew.

"Yes. He was at a casino practically all night. Security video confirms it."

"Blake Freeman?"

Taylor nodded his head. "Yes. And the two football players. And Anton Trujillo. Even the new guy from the Midwest. Every single soldier of Shark's was doing something else that night."

Ethan didn't know who the new guy from the Midwest was, but he assumed the football players were Bruce and his brother Wayne. Anton, of course, was the man he'd just seen murdered.

"Another thing," Taylor said. "What happened to your sister isn't really Shark's style."

"What do you mean?"

"Shark's enemies tend to disappear without a trace."

Ethan thought of Anton. Of the efficient way Shark's crew had killed and disposed of him this morning. If they'd wanted to kill Abby, they could have just done it in the warehouse. No need to come to her home and leave behind a liter or two of blood.

"Can you tell me who I should talk to at the FBI?"

"Name's Brian Hughes."

Ethan tried not to show any reaction. It was the same name Anton had given up to Shark before Kicking Bird cut his throat.

Taylor reached for his Rolodex.

"My peers keep telling me I need to put all this stuff online," Taylor said, flipping through the Rolodex. "Go digital. But I'm old-fashioned. Here it is."

He pulled out a manila card and wrote down the name and number for Ethan on a sticky note. Ethan could see the card contained a handwritten address in addition to the phone number. He was seeing it upside down, but he memorized the information.

"He's a young guy," Taylor said. "Has a reputation for being aggressive, getting busts, making things happen. He's risen within the ranks pretty fast, I think."

Taylor seemed to realize he'd implied something negative about Hughes and tried to correct himself. "Don't get me wrong," he said. "He's an all-right guy. Been to a barbecue at his house. It's just, you know, whenever someone rises that fast, it means they know how to play the politics game. Which is something I've never really done or even known how to do. I solve cases. Or try to."

Ethan found himself wishing Taylor was still on Abby's case. He seemed like a good cop.

"I appreciate you being so forthcoming," Ethan said. "I'm an ex-con, after all. I mean, I'm *currently* a con."

"Doesn't mean that what happened to your sister wasn't a tragedy."

Taylor handed him the sticky note with the phone number on it. "I'm not sure he'd be thrilled I gave out his number, so if he asks . . ."

Ethan nodded. "I'll tell him my mom gave it to me."

As they rose to their feet, Ethan felt overwhelmed. How naive had he been to think he could walk out of prison and solve his sister's murder in forty-eight hours? He was more confused than ever.

Taylor walked Ethan down the hall and pushed through the door into the lobby. Whitney had come in—she'd probably gotten cold in the car—and was talking to the cop behind the counter. He was obviously into her. One look was all it took to see that.

When Ethan locked eyes with him, the cop had an expression like he'd been caught doing something he wasn't supposed to.

"Ma'am," Taylor said when he saw Whitney. "Nice to see you again."

"Detective," she said politely, and gave him a head nod.

As Taylor closed the door behind him, Whitney smiled at Ethan, and he felt warm inside from it. Then he thought of Abby and felt guilty for being happy, even for a moment.

21

Ethan
43 hours, 6 minutes remaining

WALKING THROUGH THE parking lot, Ethan looked around for the sedan, but there weren't any cars that resembled it. Maybe he was just being paranoid and the car he'd seen at his mother's wasn't the same one he'd spotted at the bus station.

Before they got to her car, Whitney's phone started ringing.

"I don't recognize this number," she said, holding out the screen to him.

"My caseworker," Ethan said.

She swiped and handed the phone to Ethan.

"Well, you were right," Daryl said.

Ethan's stomach twisted. "Is Jack okay?"

"If we had gotten there two minutes later," Daryl said, "your cellmate might be in the infirmary right now. Or the morgue. Probably the morgue."

"But he's not hurt?"

"He's fine. The guy who came after him, though, he's in an ambulance headed to Carson-Tahoe Hospital. He might never wake up after the hit the guard put on him."

Whitney started the car and Ethan sat down in the passenger seat next to her. Ethan let out a relieved breath.

"Thank you, Daryl," Ethan said earnestly.

"There's someone here who wants to talk to you."

After a pause, Ethan heard a new voice on the phone.

"Hey, partner. I guess I owe you a thank-you."

Ethan had never heard Jack's voice coming through any kind of mechanical device before. Somehow his accent sounded thicker, like a country music star talking on the radio.

"If you were gone," Ethan said, "there's no telling what kind of cellmate they'd stick me with. I was looking out for my own interests."

"How'd you know?"

"A hunch," Ethan said.

"Shit." Jack said the word like it had two syllables—*shee-uht*.

Ethan looked out the window at the brown foothills rising up and away from the city. He wasn't sure how much he could tell Jack. He wouldn't trust a landline in the prison not to be bugged, but this was Daryl's cellphone. It was unlikely anyone would be listening in. Still, Daryl was sitting right there and might be able to hear what Ethan was saying. Even if he couldn't, he could see Jack's face and hear everything he said back.

"There were two of them," Jack said. "A big guy. Looks like Thor. You might have seen him in the yard. He was going to do the hit while another guy created a distraction. Mexican kid. Missing teeth. You know who I'm talking about?"

Ethan did. Shark's guy, Miguel.

"Can Daryl hear me?" Ethan said as softly as possible.

"I don't think so."

Ethan tried to choose his words carefully in case anyone was listening in.

"There's a relative of someone who died when you and your brother . . . you know."

"Mm-hmm."

"He works for somebody I used to know."

"I know what you mean," Jack said matter-of-factly, not giving anything away to Daryl by his reaction.

"I think maybe they wanted me out of prison," Ethan said. "Saw an opening to get to you. I can't figure out if they had something to do with my sister."

"Mr. Maxwell's wanting me to give the phone back now," Jack said, his tone neutral, as if Ethan had told him about a plate of scrambled eggs. "You just remember what I told you this morning."

A second later, Daryl was back on the phone.

"What did he tell you this morning?" Daryl asked.

"Same thing you did," Ethan said honestly. "Don't do anything stupid."

"Well, are you?" Daryl asked. "Doing anything stupid?"

"I've been drinking beer and snorting coke all day," Ethan quipped. "Oh, and I'm driving without a license. And I'm about to cross the state line into California."

"Very funny."

Ethan thanked him again for saving Jack and assured him that he was staying out of trouble.

As Whitney drove him to his sister's place so he could look for his suit, he borrowed her phone again and dialed the FBI agent's number. The call went to voicemail. He didn't leave a message. He didn't feel confident the agent would call back if he did.

He set the phone back in the console between their seats.

"Ever since you picked me up, I've been running you all over town, borrowing your phone. We haven't had a minute to catch up. I'm sorry."

Whitney flashed him a smile.

"That's okay," she said. "It's just nice to see you, Ethan."

22

Ethan
42 hours, 35 minutes remaining

WHITNEY PULLED THE car into a tract of townhomes. A narrow strip of black-top ran between two rows of three-story apartments, each painted a pastel blue or pink or green, colors that might have looked vibrant on a sunny day but were sickly underneath the ghost gray sky.

"These are nice," Ethan said, surprised that his sister could afford something like this. "Did she live alone?"

"Yep," Whitney said. "Abby and I were roommates a couple years ago, but not for long." She put the car in park and smiled at Ethan. "Sometimes best friends don't make good roommates."

Ethan thought of Jack. If anything, their forced proximity had made them friends. They learned to overlook the qualities that irritated them about one another. And, perhaps more importantly, when they looked out at the other options available to them—drug addicts, murderers, pedophiles—they were thankful for each other.

Whitney parked in a visitors' lot at the end of the row of townhomes, and they started walking down the drive they'd come up. The townhomes faced each other in mirror images, identical except for the colors. Each had an entry door on the bottom level next to a garage, and there were balconies on the second and third floors, presumably the living rooms and master bedrooms.

Ethan could smell cooking meat—someone was grilling on their deck.

"This is it," Whitney said, stopping at a green door.

Ethan had expected to see some kind of yellow police tape, but there was nothing like that. Instead, there were blackish blots around the doorknob and doorjamb.

Stains from where the police had dusted for fingerprints.

Whitney stuck her key into the lock and turned, trying not to touch the powder-stained handle itself. She held the door open with her forearm and gestured for Ethan to go inside.

There was nowhere to go except into the garage or up the stairs to the second floor. As he stepped on the carpeted stairs, he kept his feet to the outside, thinking he might somehow be destroying evidence walking in the middle, where Abby's killer must have walked. He knew he was being irrational. The police had collected everything they were going to. They'd taken pictures and scraped for hair samples and dusted for prints. He saw no bloodstains on the carpet. Abby must have been wrapped in something when her killer removed her body.

At the top, Ethan reached around the corner and found the light switch. The panel was covered with the same powder, and suddenly Ethan's hand felt dirty.

The second level consisted of a living room and a dining area next to a kitchen. It was spacious. No walls separated the three rooms, only counter space. A large area rug lay in the crook of an L-shaped couch, but otherwise the whole floor was covered with white tile. In the space where the kitchen, living room, and dining room converged, the floor was stained with a purplish soapy scum.

It was where they'd found Abby's blood.

A liter.

Probably two.

Ethan's knees went weak. He knelt and put his hand on the floor—far from the bloodstain—to steady himself.

Whitney knelt down next to him and put an arm around him.

"Let's get some fresh air," she said.

He didn't respond, but she rose up and walked over to the balcony. He found the strength to follow her. Outside, he put his hands on the railing and leaned over, head down, taking in long, slow breaths.

The air was cold and felt good inside his lungs.

Whitney rubbed his back.

Ethan was beginning to feel better when, from the mirror-image townhome across from them, a man stepped out on his balcony with a plate and a set of tongs, and opened up his grill where a chicken breast was cooking. He did a double-take when he saw Ethan and Whitney, no doubt wondering what someone was doing in the home of the girl who'd been killed across the street from him.

"Whitney?" he said.

"Hi," she said back.

Ethan got the impression Whitney might not remember his name, and the guy must have sensed the same thing because he reminded her. "Robert," he said. "Robert Winther."

"Of course," she said politely. "How are you?"

He was a stocky man with pudgy features. A man Ethan was sure had been thrilled to have a stripper live across the way, who had probably monitored his windows closely for any movement from Abby—any excuse to step out on the balcony to talk to her, or a reason to go check the mailbox at the same time she did.

"What are you guys doing?" he asked. "Are you okay?"

"We're okay," she said. "We came to get a few things. This is Abby's brother."

The man's eyes went wide, and his mouth hung open. "Oh man," he said. "I'm so sorry about Abby. She was a wonderful person."

"Thanks," Ethan said. "Do you mind if I talk to you about Abby, anything you might have seen living so close to her."

Robert frowned. "I already told the police everything I know."

"Can you tell me what you told them?"

"Uh, I guess so." He looked down at the roadway below, measuring the space that separated them. "I could come over after I eat."

"No," Ethan said. "The police might still consider this a crime scene."

"We have permission to be here," Whitney added quickly, "but I don't think they want anyone else here."

Robert invited them over to his place to talk.

"We'll be over in a few minutes," Whitney said. "We'll give you time to eat your dinner."

The man went inside. Because of the proximity of the townhomes, Ethan could see directly inside the man's apartment. He could see the TV, the couch, the kitchen counter. He figured the guy could see into Abby's apartment just as well.

CHAPTER

23

Ethan
42 hours, 1 minute remaining

ETHAN AND WHITNEY went upstairs and browsed through Abby's closets. There were no boxes like the ones he was looking for. Whitney suggested they search the garage, but Ethan wanted to look around first. When he had gone away, Abby had still lived with their mom. He'd never seen her in a place of her own. He recognized some of her stuff. A lamp. A bookshelf. Decorative candles. A stuffed animal she'd had since she was a little girl. Other things were new. The furniture. Paintings on the wall. A large flat-screen computer sitting on a desk.

The apartment looked like the home of a grownup. When Ethan had lived alone, he'd lived in an obvious bachelor pad, with thrift-store furniture, a fold-out card table where he ate his meals, and a dartboard with a hundred dart holes in the drywall around it. His sister had been younger, but she'd lived like a real adult. She had style, taste, money enough to decorate her house the way she liked. Ethan didn't know what his style and taste were. If he was out, he wouldn't know what to do with a place like this. He would have asked Abby to help him choose furniture, pick paint colors for the walls.

On the way downstairs, passing through the living room, he spotted two picture frames. One was a picture of him. He'd been in his early twenties. She must have been in high school when she took it. He had a smile that he didn't even recognize, an ornery smirk. He looked happy, but there was also something in his eyes that he didn't like. A dark confidence. The background was his mom's backyard. Abby had probably taken it when he'd swung by the house to visit. But who knew what he'd done before or after he'd gotten there. For all

Ethan could remember, he might have broken someone's fingers that morning and come by for a snack.

The other picture was of the two of them together. Abby was probably only one year old in the pic; he was about eight. They were posing in front of a faded green backdrop. She was giggling—the pure happiness of a toddler enjoying herself. And Ethan looked happy too. The look in the eyes—the misanthropic I-don't-care-about-anything gaze he had in the other photo—was not yet there. Here, there was no sign of the man he would become.

* * *

Ethan opened the door to the garage and fumbled for the light. When it came on, he said, "Holy shit."

His Dodge pickup truck sat in the garage, a huge behemoth in a tight space.

"She still had my truck?" he said.

"Oh yeah," Whitney said. "She planned to give it back to you when you got out."

He'd bought the truck used when he first went to work for Shark. He always planned to upgrade to something nicer, but seeing it now, he felt that it suited him more than something fancier like Blake's BMW.

"I figured she would have traded it and got something a little more practical."

"No way. She had to do all kinds of work to it to keep it running. New brakes. New fuel pump. Alternator. I can't remember what else. Transmission, I think."

"Transmission? It would have been cheaper to get a new car."

She shrugged with a grin. "She wanted to surprise you."

The truck barely fit inside the width of the garage, but the space was deep, so there was room at the back wall for a bicycle, a cooler, some storage bins. They squeezed around the truck and found Ethan's boxes there, pushed into the far corner away from the other things. Whitney helped him go through them. She found his suit folded up inside a plastic bag from a dry cleaner.

Ethan kept digging around. He found an old pair of jeans, a hooded sweatshirt, some work boots. He looked longer and found some boxer shorts. He told Whitney he was going to change his clothes. He wanted out of the prison-issue denim.

"I'll wait in the hall," she said, then added, "Of course, I've already seen you naked, so you've got nothing to hide."

He laughed and pulled off his shirt.

"Stay if you want," he said. "What do I care?"

She smiled at him and left.

She came back a minute later with a plastic garbage bag for his other clothes. "You look better," she said.

He felt better. He'd worn jeans every day for the past five years, yet somehow these felt more comfortable. His old sweatshirt, the steel-toed boots, they all felt like home to him.

"Here," Whitney said, leaning down and pulling something out of one of the boxes. "You should wear this too."

It was a leather jacket he used to wear when he worked for Shark.

Ethan hesitated. He'd bought the jacket when he'd started making some money. He'd wanted to look a certain way. Cool. Tough. Now it seemed like part of an outfit. A uniform. Like Blake, showing up today looking like he wanted to be a gangster, Ethan had bought the jacket wanting to look the part.

"Let's take it with us," Ethan said.

At the door, Whitney stopped. "Oh yeah, you wanted to talk to Abby's weird neighbor."

"He may have seen something helpful. People coming or going. Who is he?"

He was a sales rep for a pharmaceutical company, she explained.

"He comes into Dark Secrets sometimes. I think he used to sell prescription drugs to Shark before those companies really started cracking down on that stuff. He's not a regular exactly, but he is a big tipper, which the girls always remember."

Once, on a slow day, Abby had told him she was looking for a new place to live. He'd said the townhome across from his was vacant.

"I wouldn't say we were friends with him," Whitney said, "but we put up with him because he gave us pharmaceutical samples every now and then." When Ethan raised his eyebrows, she said, "What? You're no saint, my friend."

"Fair enough."

24

Ethan

41 hours, 25 minutes remaining

T HE GUY INTRODUCED himself to Ethan again. He beckoned them to come upstairs. The layout of his apartment was identical to Abby's, although he hadn't decorated it nearly as nicely. He was probably in his thirties, a little older than Ethan, but he had a carefully manicured haircut that gave Ethan the impression of someone trying hard to look younger than he was.

He offered to make coffee or tea and looked hurt when they declined, as if he was expecting this to be a social visit.

"Do you want to sit down?"

"No," Ethan said.

"We can't stay long," Whitney said. "We were really just hoping you could fill us in on anything you might have seen at Abby's place."

"Well, the night, uh, it happened," he said, stumbling over his phrasing, "I did hear her arguing with her boyfriend."

"Her boyfriend?" Whitney said. "She had a boyfriend?"

She gave Ethan a look that said, *If she had a boyfriend, I would have known.*

Robert went on. "Well, I'd seen him over there a bunch. For a couple months at least."

Ethan wandered over to the window as he listened. They'd left a light on in Abby's apartment, and he could see directly into her living room. He guessed that from the floor above, the guy could see into her bedroom just as easily.

"Whoever it was," Robert said, "they had a fight. I know these units are close together, but you usually can't hear what's going on next door. I could totally hear them yelling."

"Did you tell the cops?"

"Yeah," Robert said. "The detective. A Black guy. I can't remember his name."

"Taylor?"

"Sounds right."

"I was so worried about it that I took a picture of the guy as he was leaving."

Ethan stared at him. Did he have a picture of the murderer?

"Did it occur to you to check on her?" Ethan asked. "Or call the police?"

"Like I said, the guy wasn't exactly a stranger. And Abby was still alive when he left. The blinds were open, and I saw her moving around inside. But I felt weird enough about the whole thing to take the picture. I wish now I would have called the cops."

Robert explained that Abby's lights were still on when he went to sleep.

"When I woke up the next day, I went to my cabin in California. I didn't know anything happened until a day later, when the cops called to ask me some questions. I rushed back to show them the picture and tell them what I knew."

Robert said he'd been traveling the last three weeks for work. He'd only come back to go to the funeral.

"I'm a little freaked out staying here," he said, "knowing what happened across the street. I'm thinking about selling this place."

Ethan's heart was beating fast, and he felt a sick sort of anxiety in his stomach.

"Do you have a copy of that picture?" Ethan asked.

Robert went up the stairs to the third floor. Ethan and Whitney looked at each other. Whitney had a hopeless, confused expression on her face, and Ethan could only assume he looked just as pained.

He followed Robert up the stairs.

"Oh," Robert said, surprised to see him. "I was going to bring it back down."

He handed Ethan a photo printed on glossy paper. A glance out of the corner of Ethan's eye showed him that Robert had a desktop computer with a laser printer.

The angle of the photo was from a high vantage point, probably the third floor of the apartment. The image showed a man, early to mid-thirties, leaving Abby's place. It was a good photograph considering it was taken at night and without the man knowing. The camera had been zoomed in. Abby's front light was on, so the guy was fully lit. Dark hair. Handsome. Square jawed. Fit.

He might simply have been caught in an unfavorable moment, but he had the appearance—both on his face and in his stance—of looking to see if anyone was watching him leave.

He looked like the kind of charismatic douchebag who would go to a strip club and pick up one of the dancers.

Ethan felt queasy thinking about his sister with this guy.

Whitney came up the stairs to join them.

"You seen this guy before?" he asked.

"I don't think so."

"In the club?" Ethan prompted.

"Maybe," she said. "Lots of guys come in there. You know how it is."

Ethan sat down at the desk where Robert's computer was.

"Let's go back downstairs where it's more comfortable," Robert said.

Ethan ignored him. He held the picture with both hands, staring at it. His hands were shaking.

"What time was this?"

"Midnight," Robert said. "A little after. The time doesn't show on the print-outs, but my camera time-stamps the pictures."

Ethan looked around the room. The camera sat on the guy's bedside table. Ethan knew nothing about cameras, but this one looked expensive.

Ethan walked over to the window and opened the venetian blinds. He looked at Abby's apartment. On the top floor, the blinds were open, and he could see directly into her bedroom. From here, he could see part way into her second floor, but the angle was bad. The front door was clearly visible, the angle to it nearly identical to the one in the photo.

He tried to determine where Robert had taken it. Because of the zoom, he couldn't quite figure it out.

Robert came over next to Ethan and gestured to the picture. "Like I said, I already told the cops about this. I don't know what they've done with it."

Ethan didn't look up from the photo. But when Robert came and stood next to him, his eyes shifted to Robert's feet. There were indentations in the carpet, as if a lamp or something similar had stood there. He counted three impressions—each about the size of a quarter—before Robert shifted his feet and covered two.

Ethan stared at Robert. They were uncomfortably close.

"You've got a nice camera," Ethan said. "You take lots of pictures?"

"Sometimes. It's a hobby. I travel all over the state. California too. I like to take it with me and see what I can find to shoot."

"You got any hanging up?" He glanced around, taking in the room: a closet door, a bathroom, the desk and computer. No pictures on the walls.

"I hang them in my cabin," Robert said.

"Sure."

Ethan walked to the closet and opened it.

"Don't. Hey. What the hell are you doing?"

Standing in the closet, upright, was the tripod, its three legs still spread the same distance as the three indentations in the carpet.

Robert hurried toward him. "This is my house. You can't—"

Ethan spun around, his hand clenched into a fist. He hit Robert in the face with a quick, hard jab, and the man went over backward like he'd slipped on ice.

Whitney let out a clipped scream of surprise.

Robert lay on the floor. A red mark in the shape of a fist was tattooed to his cheekbone. Ethan had pulled the punch, hitting him hard, but not as hard as he could have. Punching with his full strength was a good way to hospitalize a guy. Or break his own hand.

Ethan watched Robert for a second to make sure he was breathing.

"What did you do that for?" Whitney said.

Ethan didn't answer. He sat at the desk and started opening the drawers. He found a series of hanging files, each labeled and organized alphabetically. He pulled a few of them out, and each one looked like a different client for his pharmaceutical sales. Then Ethan opened the lap drawer and found what he was looking for. There, among a scattering of pens and paperclips and business cards, was a large white envelope with the word *ABBY* written in block letters.

Inside were more pictures. A handful were of her talking to the guy Robert had photographed leaving her place. The two of them sat at Abby's kitchen table and on the couch, discussing something. They could have been a couple, or he could have been a door-to-door salesman peddling a water softener. There was nothing romantic in the pictures.

But as Ethan flipped through the photos, the images became pornographic. Abby in her underwear. Abby naked. Abby having sex with the guy from the other shots, straddling him with her back to the camera, the angle just right to show the profile of one breast. The man's face was visible, even clearer in these pictures than the one Winther had shown Ethan.

"Oh my God," Whitney said. "That sick *asshole*."

Nauseated, Ethan sat back in the chair and looked up at Whitney. There were tears in her eyes. She put a hand on Ethan's shoulder.

"What do we do?" she said.

Ethan shook his head. "Nothing."

"He should be arrested," Whitney said. "Do you think he—"

She didn't finish, but Ethan knew what she was asking. He looked at Robert, unconscious on the floor. He had a hard time seeing the guy get the better of Abby.

"No," Ethan said. "It's not him."

Just some lonely, pathetic voyeur.

He'd probably wanted to help the police but couldn't tell them what he'd been up to. So he made up some bullshit story about taking the guy's picture out of concern for Abby.

Ethan wondered if they really had been fighting. And if the guy got any pictures of it. He asked Whitney to help him search the computer and camera for more. The camera's memory was empty—no photos. And the computer was password protected. Neither of them knew enough about computers to even try to get around it.

Ethan stuffed the pictures back into the envelope and folded it in half. He shoved it in his pocket, which was getting crowded—Daryl's and Taylor's business cards, the sticky note with the FBI agent's phone number, the prison inmate identification form Daryl had given him, and the playing card Blake had handed him for admittance to the poker game. He riffled through the desk drawers for something to put it all in and found an empty business envelope with a preprinted return address in the corner. He shoved all the cards and papers into it, placing it in the pocket opposite the one with the pictures of Abby.

As Ethan did this, Whitney went through the drawer of the bedside table. She came out with a handful of pill bottles. There was a white paper sack from a pharmacy, and she shoved the bottles in there, then put the bag into her purse.

"To hell with that guy," she said, and they left him unconscious on the floor.

25

Ethan
40 hours, 41 minutes remaining

T HEY PICKED UP some Thai food and went to Whitney's apartment to get ready for the memorial service. Neither of them ate much. Both were quiet, unnerved by all that had happened and nervous about the memorial.

When Whitney asked him what he was going to do, he didn't want to let on that he'd left prison that morning considering trying to find Abby's killer. Now that he was out and actually digging around, the prospect of accomplishing that goal seemed impossible. He felt hopelessly out of his depth, swimming in deep water with the shore nowhere in sight.

Whitney set up her ironing board for Ethan to iron his suit. She took a shower while he tried to get the wrinkles out. The effort seemed almost futile. He hadn't worked an iron in five years. It seemed strange that he could be out of practice in such an everyday activity, but he was.

When Whitney had finished showering, he took one too. He stood under the hot spray, trying to enjoy the warmth. It was his first private shower in five years, and in prison, the temperature and water pressure were always inconsistent. The water was either cold or scalding hot, either came out in a trickle or like a sandblaster. The shower didn't help as much as he'd hoped. He didn't feel any more relaxed.

When he stepped out of the bathroom in a towel, he found Whitney ironing his suit, doing a much better job than he had. It was wrinkle free. She was in a towel as well, one wrapped over her chest with another around her hair. He thanked her and she smiled at him. Her legs, barely covered, were tan and muscular. Her neck, exposed with her hair up in the towel, was long and lean and spotted with moisture.

"I used some of your shampoo," he said. "And bodywash."

She leaned over and moved her face close to the crook of his neck. "Smells good on you," she said, and laughed.

"I probably shouldn't go back to prison smelling like this," he said.

She giggled and unplugged the iron and left it standing on the ironing board to cool. She went into her bedroom, and Ethan put the suit on. The white dress shirt was snug, and his muscles—bigger than they used to be—bulged under the material. The collar was tight as well, and wrapping a tie around his neck felt uncomfortable. Like putting his head in a noose. The pants were snug, and the jacket gripped him around the shoulders. He felt like if he flexed he could tear the back out of it. The shoes had always given him blisters if he wore them too long.

Whitney was still getting ready, so he stepped out onto her balcony. She had a fine one-bedroom apartment, not as big as Abby's, but just as nice. It was in a tall condominium, and the view was spectacular. The balcony overlooked the Truckee River and downtown Reno. The sun was setting and the casinos were lit in the graying light. The sky was full of clouds, soft pink in the dusk. The color changed every second as the sun set, transforming to a bright red, then a dark crimson—almost like blood—before turning purple, leaving the clouds a lumpy bruised color.

Ethan was in a surreal world. This morning, he'd woken up in a cell like he had every day for five years, and now he was leaning over a balcony, looking out over the city. He'd seen a man killed today. He'd punched someone out. He'd stood over the stains where his sister had lost two liters of blood.

Even more strange than all that, none of what he'd found out about his sister made any sense. Why had the FBI taken over the case? Why had they needed to declare her dead? Who was the man in the photographs? Why didn't Taylor say something about him? Who—if anyone—had helped him get out of prison? Who the hell was following him in the sedan?

And the biggest question of all: Was there a chance Abby was actually alive?

Whitney stepped out onto the balcony. She was wearing a simple black dress and black heels. Her hair was down and straight, styled conservatively for the occasion. She wore light makeup. She looked quite different from the flashy dancer he'd seen on stage that morning, but, if it was possible, she was even more stunning.

"You clean up nice," she said.

They had a few minutes before they needed to leave, and Whitney asked him if he wanted a drink.

"Nah," he said, "I might as well stick to the rules."

"You're not allowed to have a drink?"

"No drinking. No drugs. No driving." He ticked them off his fingers just as Daryl had that morning. "No leaving the state. No possession of weapons. No crime of any sort."

She laughed. "I'm guessing punching a pervert qualifies as a crime."

"Well," Ethan said. "Five out of six ain't bad."

The air on the balcony was growing colder each second, so they went inside. She didn't get a drink for herself either. She sat on the sofa with her legs crossed, and he sat perpendicular to her on the love seat, trying not to look at them.

"Don't take offense to this," he said, "but how did you and Abby end up working at Dark Secrets? I wouldn't have expected that. For either of you."

Whitney pursed her lips and shook her head. She explained that they'd gone to work at the club together. Neither of them had been doing well at the community college. Whitney had been taking nursing classes but felt the career wasn't for her, and Abby was bored by classes that repeated what she'd already learned in high school. They applied to the club on a whim at first, and then, once they saw how much they could make, they came up with plans to do it for a few years, make some money, and get out. It had always seemed a bit like a game to her—some fun adventure she and Abby were on together.

"Without Abby," she said, "I don't really know what I'm doing there."

Ethan listened without commenting. He didn't want to sound judgmental. He'd worked there himself.

"To be honest, it's a bit of a rush," Whitney said. "You've got these men in the palm of your hand. It makes you feel kind of—I don't know—powerful. It's flattering in a way.

"Before a shift, a night shift when things are really crazy, you do a couple shots, maybe take a pill, and the whole night's this big blurry party. You're dancing and smiling and, you know, just sort of *on*, and the whole time men are giving you money hand over fist."

Ethan thought about his own employment with Shark. Most of the job did feel like a party. And it was only the mornings after that he'd question the actions of the night before.

"Sometimes," Whitney went on, "it's pretty gross, though. When you stop to think about what you're doing. Or on a slow dayshift. When you've got some perv coming in wearing a thin pair of basketball shorts with no underwear and he wants lap dance after lap dance." She shuddered. "Days like that, I don't feel much better than a prostitute."

"Did you two ever date the guys who came in?" Ethan asked. "Like this guy in the photographs. You think he was from the club?"

"Abby *never* dated the guys who came in," Whitney said. "At least not that she ever told me. I dated a guy from the club once," she added. "Big mistake. Never again. Long time ago. Christ, I couldn't tell you the last time I got laid."

Ethan paused and then said, "I bet I've got you beat there."

CHAPTER

26

Ethan
38 hours, 21 minutes remaining

T HE FUNERAL HOME was more crowded than he'd expected. His mother was dutifully there to greet people, but she hardly looked up to the task. She'd brushed her hair and put on some makeup, but she looked as if she wanted nothing more than to crawl back onto her couch and stare blankly across the room. Someone was talking to her by the door, and he and Whitney slipped past her. She didn't make eye contact, but Ethan knew she'd seen him.

The air in the funeral parlor was thick with the smell of synthetic potpourri. In the low lighting of the room, he hardly recognized anyone. Some of the women were clearly from the club, with too much makeup for the occasion and skirts that were too short. They didn't have Whitney's talent for adapting to different environments.

Other people might have been classmates, but Ethan didn't recognize them. He was in a room full of strangers, yet he felt like people were watching him and talking about him. "That's her brother," he heard one woman whisper, "the one from prison."

There was a casket, which Ethan didn't understand. It was made of dark-stained wood with faux-gold trim, and it was positioned next to what appeared to be the central focus of the service: a display of photographs and a table of important artifacts, like a teddy bear from when she was a child, pom-poms from when she was a cheerleader, and some jewelry. There were a couple of her favorite books from childhood: *The Monster at the End of the Book*, which Ethan had read to her over and over again when she was a toddler, and *The Hunger Games*, which she'd been obsessed with in high school.

A few dozen photos were displayed on a bulletin board: pictures of Abby from every age of her life, from a little girl with freckles to a grown, beautiful woman flashing an amazing smile. In one picture, she wore a blue graduation gown with her cap askew on her forehead, the yellow tassel almost hanging in her eyes. In another, she and Whitney posed together in green and pink dresses, presumably for prom, which Ethan had been gone for. The photos showed no evidence that Abby had worked as a stripper. And here, as at his mom's house, there were no pictures of Ethan.

The top half of the casket was open, and there was a note taped to the side of it inviting people at the service to drop in keepsakes, whatever reminded them of Abby. The casket, the instructions explained, would be sealed before tomorrow's funeral. Inside it were a variety of items: photos, a lipstick case, cards, CDs.

Ethan found himself in the corner, watching the people. He looked for the guy from the photographs but didn't see him. The TV shows always said killers liked to attend memorials—it was a thrill to see the aftermath of what they'd done—but everyone looked normal as far as Ethan could tell.

It occurred to him that maybe the sedan he'd spotted earlier might be here, so he headed toward the parking lot to check. He didn't expect to find the car, but looking for it at least gave him an excuse to step outside for a few minutes. He inhaled the cold air and strolled through the parked cars. He didn't see any that looked like the sedan he'd seen, but he wasn't ready to go back inside. He walked around the back of the building and found a loading ramp and a funeral home employee smoking a cigarette. When he saw Ethan, he pitched it and turned to go inside. There was a punch pad at the back door, and he entered a code to open it. Ethan couldn't quite see the digits, but he was close enough to track the pattern of the guy's fingers.

He could hear traffic from the highway and see the neon glow of the casinos. The sky was still overcast, and it seemed to catch the light of the city, making a soapy gray ceiling from horizon to horizon.

Whitney found him outside.

"You okay?" she said.

"No," he said. "You?"

"No."

They were quiet, then Whitney took his arm and said, "Come on, let's get out of here."

On the way to the car, Ethan stopped.

"I'm going to say goodbye to my mom," he said, and turned back.

Whitney accompanied him, and they found her inside, staring into the casket.

"Mom," he said softly.

She met his eyes. She'd made an effort to cover her haggard appearance with makeup, but she still looked like a woman living through the worst few weeks of her life.

"Whitney and I are going to go, Mom. We'll be back tomorrow."

As he started to step away, she said his name.

"She loved you so much," she said. "Ever since she was a baby, she looked up to you like you hung the moon. She never looked at me that way."

She began to cry. Whitney stepped away to give them a moment.

"I loved her too," Ethan said, his voice breaking. "I felt the same way—"

"No you didn't," she said. "I don't know if there's any stronger admiration than a little sister looking up to her big brother. You never saw it."

Ethan wiped his eyes.

"I know you loved her, Ethan," she said. "Maybe a brother's love for his little sister is something special too. But the way she looked at you, the way she lit up whenever you came by, you took it for granted. You took her for granted."

He stared at her, wishing he was the kind of son who could comfort his mother, who could say the right thing to ease her pain.

Instead, he said nothing, and she turned and walked away.

CHAPTER

27

Ethan
36 hours, 37 minutes remaining

Back at Whitney's place, Ethan took his tie off and draped it over the iron-ing board, which was still set up in the living room. He laid his jacket there as well and undid the top buttons of his shirt. He sat back on the couch and rubbed his head.

Whitney changed into sweatpants and an AC/DC T-shirt. She went to the fridge and brought back two beers. This time, Ethan didn't object.

Two out of six rules broken.

Whitney stretched out on the couch, crossing one leg over the other. Her feet were bare. Her nails were painted red. Ethan felt drained, as if all his energy had leaked out through some invisible wound. He hadn't had a drink in five years, and every sip made his stomach warmer. A tingling feeling was spreading out to his limbs. He eyed the bottle. Not even half empty.

"I'm getting a buzz from this," he said, and let out a forced laugh.

Whitney's bottle was tucked between her legs.

"That felt really weird, didn't it?" she said. "The memorial."

Ethan nodded and took another drink.

"I can't believe she's gone," Whitney said. "You hear that all the time when people die, I guess. But it really doesn't feel like she is."

Ethan agreed with her. Open investigation or not, without a body on dis-play, it was hard to accept that she was dead. Hell, even an urn with ashes would have done it. But a corkboard with photographs and a casket full of junk? That wasn't enough.

He wondered if, given everything he'd heard from his mom and from Detective Taylor, he couldn't emotionally accept Abby's death because he simply wanted it to be untrue. He kept finding himself hoping that somehow she would turn up alive and well. He was almost certainly deluding himself, but he couldn't let it go.

"I'm confused about the whole thing," Ethan said. "No body. The FBI telling Mom to declare her dead. This guy in the picture. Even you didn't know about him, right?"

"It's a little weird Abby didn't tell me she had a boyfriend."

"If that's what he was."

"What else would he be?"

Ethan shook his head. He'd seen the pictures. If the guy wasn't her boyfriend, he hated to even think about other possibilities. A paying customer? He couldn't believe Abby would do that, but he had been shocked when she became a stripper.

"You know," Ethan said, "even me getting let out of prison for the weekend feels like there's something going on I don't know about. Everyone seems surprised as hell that I'm not on house arrest or that I don't have a guard with me at all times."

He stood up and walked toward the sliding-glass door on the balcony. The city lights glowed in the darkness beyond the glass. In the reflection, he could see Whitney sitting on the couch.

He thought about what Jack and Daryl had both told him that morning. *"Don't do anything stupid. Revenge won't solve anything. You've got a future ahead of you."*

"Tomorrow," he muttered, "I'm getting some goddamn answers."

"What?"

"I'm going to figure this thing out. I'm going to find out what happened to Abby. I owe her that."

Whitney swung her feet onto the floor and sat up. This was the first time he'd vocalized this to Whitney, and her face seemed to light up. "How are you going to do that?"

"I'm going to start with the FBI agent Taylor mentioned. If that doesn't tell me what I want to know, I'll start from the beginning. Talk to Mom again. Talk to the cops." He paused. "Talk to Shark."

"You're not a detective," Whitney said.

"I'm sure as hell not," he said. "But I can get answers. That's something I used to be pretty damn good at."

He had the flash of memory of bending a guy's pinky finger back. *"Okay, okay,"* the guy had gasped before Ethan went ahead and broke it. As the guy was screaming, Ethan threatened to break the thumb—even though snapping the first hadn't even been necessary.

"Do you really think you can figure it out?" Whitney said. "In one day? The police and FBI have had three weeks."

"I can do things they can't. I got the pictures from that shithead neighbor, didn't I? They'd need a warrant and would have to wade through a bunch of lawyer bullshit."

"What are you going to do, strong-arm the cops? The FBI? Shark?"

She was questioning the viability of his plan, but he could tell she was excited—she wanted to find Abby's murderer too.

Ethan thought about it seriously. Ever since he'd learned of his furlough, he'd been kicking around the question. How far was he willing to go?

He looked her in the eyes and said, "I'm going to do whatever it takes."

CHAPTER

28

Abby
2 years ago

ABBY WALKED DOWN the corridor of Plexiglas stations. On her side were the visitors, talking to the inmates through telephones. On the other side were the men, tattooed and bearded and hard. Even the small ones looked scary. Several inmates called to her from the other side. Their voices were muffled, but she could see their faces, hear the stifled shouts of "Damn!" and "Hey, sexy thing." One woman, visiting a boyfriend or a husband, slammed her phone into the receiver and stormed off, pissed that whoever she was visiting was catcalling the young girl walking by.

Abby was always careful what she wore when she came to visit. Loose jeans, baggy sweatshirts, no makeup. It didn't matter—seeing a pretty girl drove them nuts.

She found her assigned seat and waited. Ethan walked up a minute later. It made her sick to see that he fit right in with the others: he looked tough, hard, mean. The meanness softened when he saw her, but it didn't go away entirely.

"Hey, Sis," he said into the phone.

"Hey, Brother."

She put her hand to the glass, and he did the same. It was a futile gesture—their hands were still a foot apart.

She asked him how things were going inside, and as usual, he was vague in his response. Everything was fine. Nothing was new.

He asked her about school, and she answered with the same elusiveness. She didn't want to tell him she had failed all her courses last semester because she never went to class. She didn't want to tell him she wasn't cut out for college.

But she did need to tell him something.

"So I got a new job," she said coyly.

"Yeah?"

She bit her lip. "Please don't be pissed."

He waited. The glass between them was scuffed and smeared from other people putting their hands against it.

"I'm going to start working at Dark Secrets," she said. "As a dancer."

His eyes burned into her, and for once she was thankful for the glass barrier.

"Not funny, Abby."

"I'm not joking."

"You are *not* going to work at Dark Secrets," he said.

"Yes I am."

He set the phone down on the desk surface. He looked like he was bottling up enough anger to go on a killing rampage. He looked away and took deep breaths through his nose, then picked the phone back up.

"Abby," he said, "I know that if I tell you not to do this, your stubbornness will come out and you'll do it to spite me."

She opened her mouth to object, but there was some truth to what Ethan was saying. Whenever he tried to play the big-brother card and tell her what to do, she always dug her heels in and stood her ground, determined to show him that she wasn't a little girl he could boss around.

"But I don't want you around those people," he added. "I'm serious. You can be stubborn the next ten times I tell you to do something, but this is one time when you should listen to me."

"*You* worked there," she said.

He held up his arms. "And look where it got me."

"I'm not going to be knocking over casinos, Ethan."

He stared at her. "Please," he said. "Do this for me."

She thought, *I am.*

"I'm sorry," she said. "It's something I need to do. You'll understand someday."

He smacked his fist down on the table. A guard pacing the stalls behind the inmates raised his eyes and moved his hand to the baton on his belt.

"Calm down," Abby said.

"Goddamn it, Abby. I swear to god, if you don't quit that job, don't bother coming to visit me again."

He slammed the phone into its cradle and walked away.

She kept a strong face as she walked back down the gauntlet of catcalling prisoners and through the security checkpoints. In the parking lot, she climbed into the truck and breathed deeply. She willed herself not to cry. He would get over it. He would calm down.

But in her heart, she knew he wouldn't. She would return next week, and the first thing he would ask was whether she had taken the job. If she said yes, he would hang up the phone and walk away.

As long as she worked at the club, she shouldn't bother coming back.

CHAPTER

29

Ethan
34 hours, 23 minutes remaining

ETHAN LAY ON Whitney's couch, staring at the ceiling in the blue light. He was warm, wrapped in a blanket. The couch was more comfortable than his cell bunk, the room's temperature much better than he was used to. His prison cell was cold in the winter, hot in the summer—rarely a happy medium.

But despite all the comforts he wasn't accustomed to, Ethan couldn't sleep. He kept checking his watch. More than an hour had passed since he lay down, but instead of relaxing, his body had only grown more tense. His heart wouldn't slow down. He'd told Whitney he was going to get up early, but lying on the couch felt like a waste of time. He'd chewed up more than a quarter of his window of freedom already. Why kill another six or so hours waiting until tomorrow?

He rose, pulled on his jeans and boots and sweatshirt. Whitney had a laptop on the kitchen table, and fortunately there was no password required. It was different from what he was used to—the computers in the prison classrooms were old, with no internet access—but he figured out how to open a web browser and search for a map database. He typed in the address of the FBI agent that he'd memorized when he was in Taylor's office, and studied the route. It was a three-mile walk. He didn't have any money for a cab. He thought about taking Whitney's car, but he wasn't sure what Whitney would think of him borrowing her car without asking, and didn't want to wake her up. He'd already inconvenienced her enough.

He put his arms through the sleeves of his leather coat. It felt like he was putting on a uniform, stepping into a character he used to play. It didn't feel right on him. He wasn't that person anymore. But he didn't have a choice. It was cold out and he needed more of a coat than his prison-issue jean jacket. Besides, if he was going to find out what happened to Abby, maybe he needed to be a little more like his old self.

He considered leaving Whitney a note but decided against it. He would probably be back before she woke up. He opened her door and closed it quietly. It locked behind him.

30

Ethan
33 hours, 53 minutes remaining

E THAN WALKED THROUGH the dark streets. On each side of him, residential houses stood quietly, their front lights lit, their interior lights dark. Inside each one, families slept. He thought about what it must be like to have a normal life like those people. He felt sorry for himself for a moment but then pushed the self-pity aside. His life was his own doing.

It was only a few miles, but by the time he reached the street he was looking for, his hands were frozen claws. He was reading addresses stenciled on the curb when it caught his eye: a sedan like the one he'd seen earlier sitting in a driveway. The engine was off. No one was inside. Ethan checked the address.

This was Brian Hughes's house.

One mystery solved.

The FBI agent in charge of investigating Abby's murder was the one who'd been following him. But why?

It was an ordinary home. Two-car garage. Pine tree in the front yard. Bushes along the walkway to the front door. He went up the front walk, trying to be as quiet as possible. The porch was dark. On each side of the door was a thick blurred pane of glass, similar to the window in his prison cell, and he could make out the faint glow of light coming from somewhere inside. A TV perhaps.

Was he really going to do this? Knock on an FBI agent's door in the middle of the night?

"You've been trying to keep tabs on me, you son of a bitch," Ethan muttered. "I'll let you know exactly where I am."

He raised his fist and pounded on the door. He rang the bell several times and then pounded again. Through the flickering light inside, Ethan could see movement. He'd been right: someone was up late watching TV.

The front light came on, and Ethan squinted.

The door opened.

"What the hell is going on?" the man who opened the door said. "It's the middle of the—" He stopped as the recognition came over his face. He knew who Ethan was. Ethan recognized him too.

It was the man in the photographs with Abby.

The man—Brian Hughes—cracked a partial smile. It wasn't friendly. It was a sly smile, as if he couldn't help himself. It could have meant a lot of things, but Ethan only registered one: *"I fucked your sister."*

Ethan pushed open the door with one arm and shoved Brian Hughes backward with the other. Hughes's smirk morphed to shock.

"Wait," he said.

His tone was calming, as if he were trying to soothe an angry dog, but this was a distraction—as he spoke, he brought one arm around from behind his back, a pistol in his hand. Ethan lunged. He caught Hughes's wrist before he could aim the gun and held the arm away from them so the barrel pointed over his shoulder. Ethan didn't think the guy wanted to shoot him—he was just trying to take control of the situation before things escalated. But now that Ethan had his arm, there was no way out of this for either of them without escalation.

Hughes used his free arm to try to punch Ethan in the throat, but Ethan threw his other arm up in time to clumsily block the blow. He grabbed the deflected arm with his own free hand and held tight to Hughes's other wrist. Their bodies were close, their faces only inches apart. Ethan was definitely stronger, but as an FBI agent, Hughes would have some training in hand-to-hand combat. Ethan didn't want to underestimate him. He had the advantage right now, but it might not last long.

"Ethan," Hughes said, his voice no longer calm. "I want to t—"

Ethan head-butted Hughes—hard—and as the agent rocketed backward, Ethan yanked the gun out of his grip.

Hughes lost his balance and fell onto his butt. Ethan swung the door shut behind him and stomped toward the man, holding the gun by the barrel like a hammer. He had just assaulted an FBI agent in his own home, and he would be in serious trouble for it, but right now, he was so angry he didn't care.

Hughes crawled backward, one arm up in protest or self-defense or both. Ethan threw the gun across the living area where it landed next to the TV. If he held onto it he might use it.

"Wait," Hughes said again. "I can explain."

Ethan pulled the envelope out of his jacket pocket and held one of the pictures in front of Hughes's face.

"Explain this," Ethan said.

He dropped the pictures and grabbed Hughes by the collar of his sweatshirt. He brought his fist up. He'd been bottling up his rage ever since he'd gotten the call about his sister, ever since he'd gone to prison, perhaps ever since he'd been born. He was a landmine and Brian Hughes had stepped on him. He couldn't stop himself—he was going to explode.

"I got you out of prison!" Hughes shouted.

Ethan hesitated. "What?"

"I called in some favors," Hughes said. "You're out of prison because of me."

Ethan tried to process this.

He let go of Hughes's shirt and stood. His rage was dissipating—for now, Hughes had disarmed the bomb.

"You're my fairy godfather?" Ethan said.

"Your fairy *what*?" Hughes said.

31

Ethan
32 hours, 25 minutes remaining

ETHAN SAT ON a recliner in the living room, which had a big-screen TV, a few items of furniture, and nothing else. The walls were a boring yellow, and the carpet was thick and unworn. Everything looked fairly new, like a model home, only decorated without much taste.

Hughes walked from the kitchen with two beers in one hand, the other hand holding a frozen bag of vegetables to his forehead. He set one beer on the coffee table in front of Ethan and sat on the opposite end of the couch with his own.

"No thanks," Ethan said, staring at the beer. "It's a condition of my release that I don't drink."

"I bet you're not supposed to attack FBI agents either."

"I bet FBI agents aren't supposed to sleep with strippers working for gangsters."

"Touché."

Hughes was wearing track pants and a University of Nevada sweatshirt. Both looked brand new, like he'd stopped at the UNR bookstore on his way home from work. Everything about him was slick and polished—a carefully constructed facade. The kind of asshole he could see Abby falling for.

Hughes had gathered up the pictures and put them back in the envelope, which now sat on the coffee table.

"That creepy neighbor," he said. "What a sicko."

"You know about him?"

"The detective from RPD showed me a photo of me outside the apartment. I never talked to the guy. Which was good, considering what he knew about me."

Ethan took a deep breath. "You want to tell me what the hell is going on?"

"I'm impressed that you found me. And quickly. You've been out, what, fifteen hours?"

"You had me under surveillance," Ethan said. "Did you think I wouldn't spot you?"

Hughes looked embarrassed. "Tailing somebody is a lot harder than people think. You need two or three cars to do it right."

"And you couldn't get that?"

"No, it was never anything official. No one in the bureau knows I helped you get a furlough. But I was curious where you'd go."

Ethan waited, quiet. Hughes grinned. It was that sly, pleased-with-himself expression he'd had earlier.

"I wanted you out," Hughes said, "so you'd look into your sister's death. I didn't know you'd come looking for me. How did you find me anyway? You spotted my car? Got someone to track the plates?"

Ethan didn't want to tell him that he'd spotted the address on Taylor's Rolodex. Hughes thought he was here because of some real investigative work, when really it was just that Taylor had come to a cookout here once. Ethan hadn't even realized Hughes was the guy in the pictures until he'd opened the door.

"I've got my sources," Ethan said.

Hughes seemed to accept this and move on. His investigation, he said, was at a standstill. When he'd heard that Ethan was applying for furlough, he made some calls to make sure he got out—without any kind of security detail. He knew Ethan had worked for Shark and had taken a twenty-year sentence instead of ratting him out. If anyone could get close enough to Shark to find out what happened, it would be Ethan.

"I didn't expect you to solve the case," Hughes said. "Honestly, I wanted you to stir some shit up so something might break loose and we'd get some new leads."

Ethan was confused. He couldn't put all the pieces together.

"You think it was Shark?" Ethan said.

Hughes rolled his eyes and flopped back against the couch, exaggerating his disbelief. "Yes. Jesus Christ. You were smart enough to find me, but not smart enough to figure that out?"

Ethan felt a twinge of anger toward the cocky asshole.

"I know Shark's capable of it," Ethan said. "But there's no reason for him to have done it. Without Abby, he risks losing my silence."

Hughes exhaled, frustrated.

"Your sister was going to rat Shark out," Hughes said. "She'd been working with me for months, getting closer and closer to him. She was about to start wearing a wire to try to get us what we needed to take him down. The only reason she hadn't already was because, well, it's kind of hard to wear a transmitter under your clothes when your job requires you to take them off."

Ethan's insides twisted, like his intestines were a nest of snakes, flopping and rolling and coiling around each other. He thought of Kicking Bird cutting Anton's throat that morning. He imagined it was Abby in the chair instead of Anton.

"What the hell was she thinking?" Ethan said. "Why would she do that?"

"To get you out of prison," Hughes said.

Abby had been negotiating terms for Ethan's release, he explained. If she brought them enough evidence for a conviction, Ethan would be granted immunity.

Ethan stood up, paced in front of the TV.

"I'll be out in two years anyway," Ethan said. "Christ, even if you arrested Shark tomorrow, it might take that long to get through a trial. She'd go through all that trouble to get me out, what, a month early? Six months tops. I bet you didn't tell her that, did you?"

"She knew how much time you had. She wanted to do whatever she could to help. She said it didn't matter if you had ten more years or one more day. She did it because she loved you."

Ethan whirled on Hughes, fists clenched this time. "You son of a bitch. You fed her to that monster."

Ethan leaned over and picked up the envelope.

"How much shit would you be in if your bosses found out about this?"

"A lot. And I would appreciate it if you didn't say anything. I cared about Abby. I really did."

Ethan pictured Hughes going into the club, pretending to be a regular customer, looking for a dancer he could pick up and try to turn. If he couldn't get her to work for him, at least he'd get laid.

Ethan wanted to grab Hughes and punch him until he went limp. And maybe even then he wouldn't stop.

Or he could take the photos and get the guy fired.

"Abby was amazing," Hughes said. "She was so full of *life*." He regretted his choice of words immediately. "I mean—"

Ethan held up the pictures. "You're going down."

"Wait." Hughes said, following Ethan to the foyer. "Ethan."

"You got her killed," Ethan said. "You turned her against Shark."

"You got her involved with Shark in the first place," Hughes snapped. "He wouldn't have been in her life if it wasn't for you."

The words hurt Ethan like a physical blow.

There was a mirror hanging in the foyer. He looked at his reflection: a big thug in the same leather coat he used to wear when he was working as muscle for his old boss. He punched the reflection. Glass shards rained down onto the tile. Hughes flinched at the outburst, but he didn't say anything.

Ethan leaned against the wall. He let his shaky legs slide out from under him, and he sat on the floor.

"You can be mad at me," Hughes said. "But the killer is still out there. That's where you need to direct this anger."

"You're right," Ethan said, his voice soft now, almost a whisper.

His hand was bleeding. The cut was small, but a surprising amount of blood was curling around his fingers, filling the creases in his palm. He closed his fist and rubbed the blood around with his fingers. It was slippery.

Hughes went into the kitchen and came back with a towel. Ethan pressed it against the cut, and Hughes sat on the floor, leaning against the opposite wall.

"She said she didn't have anything incriminating yet," Hughes told him, "but she offered to find evidence for us if we'd cut you a deal."

Ethan felt nauseated. Most of the girls in the club knew little about Shark's criminal enterprises. Sure, they knew he was engaged in illegal activity, but they weren't privy to any details. The only way a girl could get close enough to learn the kind of information Hughes would be looking for was by becoming a trophy with her picture on Shark's wall of conquests.

"If you really liked her," Ethan said, "you would have told her how pointless all this was."

Hughes lowered his head. "Look, I'm trying to make this right."

"How?" Ethan said. "By getting me out of prison?"

"The investigation into Abby's murder is cold. We've got nothing. I'll be able to bring Shark down eventually—I've got a guy on the inside, way deep in Shark's organization. But my guy doesn't know about Abby. Says he wasn't in the loop about this one."

He knew who Hughes was talking about, but kept that to himself at the moment.

"So what did you expect from me?"

"I don't know. Like I said, the investigation was cold. I wanted to stir things up. Insert a new element into the equation."

"You play awfully loose with other people's lives," Ethan said.

He checked the cut. The bleeding had mostly stopped, leaving a web of maroon stains on his hand.

"Listen," Hughes said, "I didn't expect you to find out about me, but now that you have, it could work out even better. Just get me any information you can on Shark. Anything that will help me make a case. That's your revenge—seeing that bastard behind bars."

Ethan stood, and Hughes followed.

"In fact," Hughes said, unable to soften the excitement in his voice, "you know so much about Shark's organization from the old days, you don't really need to find out anything. With my guy on the inside and your testimony about the old stuff, that would be—"

"Is your guy on the inside Anton?"

Hughes looked stunned.

Ethan put his hand on the doorknob. "I wouldn't count on him being much help anymore."

He opened the door. The cold came in like a flood of icy water.

"He was supposed to make contact today," Hughes said. "Where is he?"

Ethan stepped outside, taking the bloody towel with him.

"Probably the same place as Abby," he said. "Thanks to you."

CHAPTER

32

Ethan
31 hours, 42 minutes remaining

E THAN STOOD OVERLOOKING the city. He was on the west side, off McCarran, where the elevation rose and the neighborhoods encroached on the foothills. To the north, he could see downtown. The casinos were lit up in green and purple neon. He could make out Whitney's building near the river. He wished he'd taken her car. The cold was vicious. He had no gloves, no hat. Only a sweatshirt and the leather jacket. He pulled the hood up and buried his hands back in the coat.

The clouds in the sky had finally broken open, and the stars were out. An airplane took off from the airport, rising fast over the eastern foothills.

To the south, away from the other casinos, stood the Galaxia, tall and silver like something out of a science fiction movie, and further away the Neptune and the Sandstorm stood side by side, the first glowing an aqua blue, the second emanating a soft orange light. They were miles away. Somewhere in the Neptune, in one of the suites, Blake would be overseeing a card game of high rollers. Ethan needed answers, and he didn't know where else to get them.

He set off in that direction.

* * *

The casino felt like a sauna. He found a slot machine in a corner and sat down to get warm. He was exhausted. He asked a cocktail waitress in a gaudy outfit what time it was, and she said it was just after three. He felt shaky, hungry. He thought about finding a restaurant in the casino and getting something to eat—some protein for energy—but decided he couldn't wait. He went in search of the hotel elevators. All around him, slot machines rang and clattered and called to the patrons.

The whole place was decorated in a cartoonish ocean theme. The carpet was aqua-colored with designs of fish, seahorses, and octopi. Cheap-looking statues of mermaids with seashell bikini tops and mermen with tridents stood stationed among the slots. Glass jellyfish hung from the ceiling on wires. There was a massive aquarium that put the ones in Shark's office to shame. It was full of multicolored fish, ranging from a few inches to several feet long. The stale air smelled of cigarette smoke.

He found the elevators and pressed the button for the penthouse. A trashcan stood between the elevator doors, and Ethan tossed in the bloody towel Hughes had given to him.

When he came out on the top floor, he knew which door it was because Bruce from the club was sitting on a stool outside. As Ethan got closer, he saw that it wasn't Bruce. It was his brother. Practically identical in every way—even the clothes he was wearing—except for the eyes.

"Hey, Wayne," Ethan said, trying to be as friendly as possible. "I met your brother today."

Ethan reached into his pocket and pulled out the playing card Blake had given him. He held it up for Wayne to see the demonic creature illustrated on the backside.

"You the guy just out of prison?" Wayne said. "Abby's brother?"

Wayne extended his hand, and Ethan took it.

"I'm real sorry about your sister," he said.

"Thanks," Ethan said.

He liked Wayne more than his brother already.

Wayne pulled out a keycard from his pocket and slipped it into the door lock. The light indicator flashed red, and he had to try again. This time, green flashed, and Wayne pushed the door open.

"Good luck," he said, which didn't make any sense to Ethan until he realized Wayne thought he was here to gamble.

CHAPTER

33

Ethan
30 hours, 17 minutes remaining

WHOEVER HAD DESIGNED the Neptune had wisely abandoned the kitschy ocean theme in the hotel itself. The suite was high class. There was a large, spacious room with high ceilings and a number of offshoot bedrooms. In the middle of the room was an octagonal poker table with a felt green top and a wooden-inlaid border, complete with drink holders and chip racks. Six men were seated: five players and a dealer. Judging by the cards laid out, Ethan thought they were probably playing Texas Hold 'Em. The players turned toward him momentarily and then turned back, apparently assessing with a glance that he was not a player.

Blake stood at the back wall, which was made up of floor-to-ceiling windows. The lights of the city lay sprawled behind him, a nebula of glowing streetlights and car beams and casino neon.

Blake smiled big as he walked toward Ethan. He shook his hand vigorously and gestured for him to come over to the bar. Liquor bottles lined the counter. Blake asked what Ethan was drinking.

"Nothing," Ethan said, and then noticed how dry his mouth was. "Water, I guess."

Blake pulled a bottle out of the refrigerator and handed it to Ethan. "We've got milk," he said with a smirk.

"Sure," Ethan said, knowing he could use the protein.

Blake poured whole milk into a tumbler and handed it to Ethan. Then he took a handful of ice cubes out of a silver dish and put them into a glass. He poured himself about three fingers of bourbon and took a drink.

Ethan downed the milk and took a long drink of water.

"Glad you could make it," Blake said. He kept his voice low, not whispering, but trying not to be a distraction to the players. "You need a place to sleep? We've got the whole suite. Plenty of beds."

Ethan shook his head.

"Where you staying?" Blake asked. "Your mom's?"

Ethan didn't answer. He was watching the poker players. They looked to all be in their forties or fifties. Most were smoking. One had a cigar. There were drinks all around. Ethan wondered if the men got the drinks themselves or if Blake did it—a glorified bartender.

"These guys are just getting started," Blake said. "Some of them will go for twenty-four hours straight. Then they'll take a nap and go at it another twelve. It's unbelievable."

Ethan came around the bar and helped himself to another glass of milk.

"That stuff's for white Russians," Blake said, "so make sure to leave a little."

Ethan raised the new glass to his mouth, and Blake said, "Jesus Christ, what happened to your hand?"

"I punched a mirror," Ethan said, "like an idiot."

Blake laughed.

"I want you to tell me what you know about Abby," Ethan said.

Blake stopped laughing. He slurped the last of his bourbon.

"I think Shark killed her," Ethan said, "and I want to find out for sure."

Blake set the drink down. He had an expression that said, *Oh man, this again?* He gestured for Ethan to follow him.

They walked into one of the bedrooms. The room held a small night bag—Blake's things, Ethan assumed—and a black briefcase lying over the taut, still-made bed.

The money.

With five gamblers and a hundred grand buy-in from each, that meant there was at least half a million in there. And Blake would need extra to dole out loans as needed. That's where Shark would make his real money from the night. High-interest loans to people with the means to pay a steep vig.

How much was in there? A million?

"Man," Blake said, "I told you I don't think Shark had anything to do with it."

"Who else could it be?"

Blake threw his arms up. "Who couldn't it be? It could be anyone in the world."

Ethan stepped closer. "When people close to Shark go missing, is it usually because of Shark or because of someone else?"

"That doesn't even make sense, man. We've been over this."

Ethan let his anger subside. He stepped away and sat on the edge of the bed. "I saw him kill someone today," Ethan said. "That guy Anton. You know him?" Blake nodded.

"They cut his finger off and then slashed his throat. Oh, and Shark beat him with a claw hammer. I saw it. Shark wanted me to watch it."

"I'm sorry you had to see that," Blake said.

"I've seen people killed before," Ethan said, "but never someone tied up and tortured like that."

"We tortured people before," Blake said. "You and me."

"Breaking a finger isn't the same as cutting it off."

He locked eyes with Blake. He let the stare ask the question: *Have you killed people?* Blake squirmed away and walked toward the door and leaned against the wall. He pulled out a cigarette.

"I told you things have changed," Blake said. "Shit like that ain't all that uncommon anymore. I get rid of bodies. Dump 'em in Lake Tahoe or bury them in the Black Rock." He took a drag off his cigarette and blew a smoke ring. "I prefer the lake. I get blisters on these pretty hands every time I have to dig a hole out in the desert."

Ethan pictured Abby wrapped in a tarp, dumped over the side of a boat. Or dropped into a hole as faceless men shoveled dirt over the plastic. Ethan recalled Shark telling Bruce to take Anton's body into the desert right after he'd looked in a leather-bound ledger.

"What's with Shark's ledger?" Ethan said. "He handed it to Bruce after they killed Anton. What does he keep track of in there?"

Blake ignored the questions. He put his hand on Ethan's shoulder and leaned closer. "Listen to me, man." His voice was low and sharp. "I don't want to have to bury you too. You need to stop this line of thinking. It ain't good for you."

Ethan glared back. He hadn't known what to expect from Blake. That he might come clean when confronted a second time?

"You look tired, man. Why don't you go into one of these rooms and catch some *Z*s. You'll feel better after that."

"No," Ethan said. "I'm okay."

He thanked Blake for the invite and headed toward the door. Blake urged him to stay a while, hang out. Blake was bored babysitting these guys. He'd traded their cash for chips; now all he had to do was stick around to see if any of them wanted to buy more—and to make sure there was no trouble.

"I offered to bring some girls in from the club and give these guys a little show," he said. "Give them a break. But they don't want any distractions. Can you believe that? They'd rather sit around a table looking at each other than have some tits shaking in their faces."

"It sure sucks that you're bored," Ethan said. "I'm sorry you don't get to torture and kill people every night."

"Hey, man, don't be like that."

Ethan ignored him and walked out.

* * *

He rode the elevator down to the casino level. He headed for the door, stopped, turned, couldn't make up his mind what to do. The casino noises rang around him. He went to the giant aquarium and looked in at the fish.

A cocktail waitress stopped to ask if he needed anything. She held her serving tray at her side, like a Frisbee, and put an arm on Ethan's shoulder.

"You okay, hon? You look like you've had a rough night."

She was pretty, blond, with heavy makeup and a voice that was both high and raspy, a sexy combination that fit her. She was older than him by at least a few years, but she was attractive. She could have worked at Dark Secrets as easily as the casino.

"What can I get for you, handsome?" she said, and she rubbed her hand up and down his arm, from shoulder to elbow, making no effort to conceal how much she enjoyed feeling his muscles. "I get off in an hour, if you're sticking around."

He pictured himself lying on top of her, her nails digging into his back. That seemed like just what he needed: a good lay—his first in five years—to distract him from how his entire world had fallen apart. But what would happen when he rolled off her? Abby would still be dead, and he'd still be no closer to knowing who killed her.

"Sorry," he told the waitress. "There's something I've got to do."

He went back to the elevator and rode it up. He thought about the line he was crossing. There would be no going back after this.

In the hallway, he told Wayne he'd forgotten something, and the big bouncer opened the door for him again.

This time, Ethan *was* here to gamble.

He was gambling with his life.

34

Ethan
29 hours, 26 minutes remaining

INSIDE, ETHAN REACHED up and, as quietly as possible, swung the bar of the door guard to the locked position. Wayne wouldn't be able to get in. At least until someone inside unlocked the door for him.

There was no sign of Blake, but one of the gamblers said, "He's in the head," and pointed. Ethan crossed the room and opened the bathroom door.

"Occupied," Blake said over his shoulder. He had his legs apart and was shooting a stream of urine into the toilet.

Ethan grabbed him by the shoulder with his left hand. With his right, he punched Blake hard in the back where his kidney should be. Blake gasped and twisted. Urine splattered across the toilet tank and the wall. Ethan snatched a fistful of Blake's hair and shoved his face downward. Blake grabbed the side of the bowl, but Ethan seized his arm and twisted it behind his back.

"What the hell are you doing, man?" Blake said, but then his face was in the yellow water.

He struggled, but Ethan was stronger. Finally, Ethan pulled Blake up into a standing position and shoved him into the shower. His body caught on the curtain and pulled the rod down on top of him in the tub.

"I went to prison for you!" Ethan roared. "Now you're going to tell me something useful."

"Are you crazy?"

Blake's hair was wet and askew, glued across his forehead and sticking up.

"Remember when we used to break guys' fingers to get them to talk?" Ethan said. "We'd start with the pinky then make our way to the thumb. Let's see how you fucking like it."

Blake's jacket hung open and the pistol inside was visible. Blake moved his hand slightly, and Ethan shook his head.

"You grab that gun," Ethan said, "I'm going to take it away from you and beat you with it."

Outside the door, he heard commotion. Wayne's stomping feet. Someone had opened the door for him.

"Where?" he heard Wayne ask.

"In the bathroom," one of the gamblers said.

"Shit," Ethan mumbled.

The door banged open and the big lineman stood filling the doorway.

"Stay out of this, Wayne," Ethan said.

"Break his goddamn legs!" Blake yelled.

The big guy came at him, faster than Ethan would have expected. He grabbed Ethan's jacket and tried to pull him toward the door. That was a mistake: treating him like a drunk at the club he could just drag away.

Ethan swung his right fist into Wayne's ribs. It felt like punching plywood, but the big guy flinched and grunted. Ethan brought his left up, but Wayne threw his own arm up to block. That left him exposed, and Ethan came in with a right, thrown hard and fast. He aimed for Wayne's temple but his fist landed on the guy's cheekbone instead. Wayne's head rocked to the side, and he stumbled back two steps. He threw both arms out to catch himself on the doorway. He was spread eagle and dazed, and Ethan took advantage. He brought his leg up and kicked Wayne directly in the solar plexus with the sole of his boot. The lineman somersaulted backward out the door and came to rest lying facedown.

Ethan came out of the bathroom. Wayne was getting up. Slowly.

Ethan knew he should be on him, taking him out of the picture before he had a chance to recuperate. But he didn't have anything against the stupid kid. And this wasn't prison. In prison, a fight meant hospitalization or death for someone. He didn't want to do that to this guy if he didn't have to.

"This is between Blake and me," Ethan said, circling Wayne. "From the old days. Go back out in the hall."

Wayne said nothing.

The gamblers were all standing and watching.

"A thousand on the big guy," one of them said.

"They're both big," another said.

"The *bigger* guy."

Wayne seemed emboldened by this vote of confidence. He swung his log of an arm at Ethan, who leaned back in time for the swing to go wild. Ethan drove his own right into Wayne's exposed ribcage. Wayne grunted again, but it didn't stop him. He swung back with his left, and this time he connected. It was a glancing blow—hitting Ethan's cheek, grazing his nose—but it was enough to disorient him for a split second. Wayne's right fist hit Ethan in the gut, and he felt the air leave his lungs.

He tried to stagger away to catch his breath, but Wayne didn't let him. He grabbed Ethan, wrapped his big arms around him like he was tackling a quarterback, and lifted him off the ground. He rammed Ethan's body into the wall. The drywall cracked behind him.

Wayne was leaning into him, like a boxer holding his opponent against the ropes, dealing Ethan one body blow after another.

Ethan grabbed Wayne's head—big, like a melon—and tried to jam his thumbs into his eye sockets. Wayne squirmed, and Ethan got the leverage he needed to slip away. He backpedaled into the room. He hit the poker table and rolled on top of it and landed on his feet on the other side. Cards and chips and beer bottles dropped onto the carpet.

Wayne rubbed his eyes. Blake was standing in the doorway of the bathroom. He'd pushed his wet hair back from his forehead, and he wore a look of detached amusement. The gamblers were arguing about odds.

Wayne approached.

No more dicking around, Ethan thought. *Pretend this is prison and take the guy out.*

"Wayne," Ethan said, "did you know I played wide receiver in high school?"

"So."

Wayne was close now, the two of them squaring off.

"I was also a pretty good punter," Ethan said, and he stepped forward and drove the steel toe of his boot up into Wayne's groin. He put his body into it, like he was kicking a forty-yard field goal.

Wayne squealed and bent over holding his crotch. His face was parallel to the floor, and Ethan swung his fist in a hard uppercut. The crunch of Wayne's nose was audible, and his head jerked back. An arc of blood swung up from his nose like a whip. Droplets splattered the ceiling ten feet above them.

Wayne collapsed onto the floor in a fetal ball.

He was either unconscious or in too much pain to move, Ethan couldn't tell which.

Ethan heard the unmistakable click of a gun being cocked.

"Enough of this MMA bullshit," Blake said.

He was pointing his pistol at Ethan's face.

CHAPTER

35

Ethan
29 hours, 20 minutes remaining

ABOUT TEN FEET separated Ethan from the barrel of the gun. Ethan stepped toward Blake.

"I'm not messing around, Ethan."

"Are you really going to shoot me?"

"Yes, I'm really going to shoot you."

Ethan kept walking. Blake backed up.

"We're not in the warehouse with a big sheet of plastic underneath us. I don't think you want to fire a gun in a hotel."

"You still don't understand who you're dealing with, do you?"

Blake continued backpedaling, and Ethan pursued. Then Blake's back hit the glass wall. "Don't move, Ethan."

"You're really going to kill your best friend?" Ethan said.

"You stuck my head in a toilet. I'd say *best friend* is probably pushing it."

"Then do it," Ethan said.

"I'm not—"

Ethan twisted left and grabbed Blake's wrist and forced the gun to the side. Blake didn't pull the trigger. Ethan drove his fist into Blake's body. Again and again and again—four big body blows. The glass window shook behind him.

Blake doubled over and Ethan yanked the gun out of his hand. He ejected the magazine and tossed it across the room. Then he ejected the shell in the chamber and it bounced on the carpet. He tossed the empty pistol over his back.

"Ethan," Blake said, wincing as he spoke, "you're dead, you know that? Shark is going—"

Ethan grabbed Blake by the jacket, spun him away from the window and shoved him across the room. He crashed into the poker table and sent more chips bouncing to the floor.

The gamblers stood watching.

"What?" Ethan said. "You're not going to bet on this one?"

They all headed for the door, like they smelled smoke and realized they were in a burning building.

Blake was trying to stand, and Ethan came from behind and hit him again in the kidney. He crumpled, and Ethan kneeled over him, driving his fist over and over again into Blake's ribcage. Blake squirmed and thrashed, and finally Ethan stood over him, breathing heavy.

His old friend was gasping in short, shallow bursts. Tears were leaking from his eyes. Ethan figured he had a broken a rib or two.

"I asked you nicely two times," Ethan growled at him. "I want some goddamn answers, Blake."

"I don't," Blake said, his voice coming out in bursts, "know . . . anything."

"Tell me something that will help me," Ethan said. "You've been on the other side of this before. You know what would be useful to me."

"I don't."

Blake looked on the verge of sobbing, like a child trying hard to be tough, to be grown-up, but failing. "You're my friend," Blake said, his voice cracking. "Why are you doing this?"

Ethan thought about not taking this any further, but he'd come this far. If prison had taught him anything, it was that if you start something, you'd better be prepared to take it all the way.

He grabbed a fistful of Blake's hair and began dragging him to the bathroom. Blake tried to stand and ended up sliding and staggering the whole way. Ethan shoved him into the bathtub, his head near the faucet. Blake writhed inside the tub, tangled up in the plastic curtain.

Ethan started the water and reached down to plug the drain. Cold water blasted Blake in the face, and he squirmed to get away from it. Ethan put his foot on Blake's chest and pressed down.

"You better tell me something before the water gets too deep."

Blake grabbed the rim of the tub and tried to pull himself out. He pushed against Ethan's leg. He tried to reach behind his head to pull the stopper on the drain, but Ethan grabbed his arm and twisted his little finger nearly to the point of breaking.

"Help!" Blake screamed. "Help! Somebody help me!"

"Help yourself!" Ethan yelled.

The water was almost to Blake's lips. He craned his neck to bring his mouth another inch above the surface. It kept rising. Another few seconds and the water would be over his mouth.

"Okay," Blake said. "Okay."

"What?"

Blake spit water out of his mouth and said, "The ledger! Shark's ledger!"

Ethan reached down and shut off the water. He eased the pressure off Blake's chest enough for him to bring his head farther out, but he left his boot perched there in case he wanted to press down again.

"Tell me."

"He writes down where all the bodies are," Blake said. "You can look in there and see if any of the entries match Abby's disappearance."

Ethan waited, considering what Blake said.

"If they dumped her in Tahoe, you'd never find her," Blake gasped. "But if they put her in the desert, you could dig her up."

Ethan felt numb. "So they killed her?"

Blake shook his head, splashing water. "No, man. I don't know. I'm just saying this is one way you *might* be able to find out."

Ethan almost asked why Shark would take the chance of recording the locations in the first place—especially in Lake Tahoe where the bodies wouldn't stay in one place anyway—but he realized he didn't need to. The answer was easy: ego. Shark wanted to keep track of his trophies. Just like the photos on his office wall.

Ethan reached into the tub and pulled the stopper.

*   *   *

Ethan gave Blake his hand and hauled him out. Blake was nearly useless, and Ethan did most of the work. It took all of Blake's strength to sit upright and lean against the tub. His soaked clothes leached water into the grout of the tile floor.

"So this ledger," Ethan said. "Is there some kind of code?"

"Code?"

"Yeah, code," Ethan said. "So if the cops get their hands on it they don't know what it says."

"This isn't James Bond," Blake said.

Actually, Ethan was thinking of *The Untouchables* and the ledger that brought down Al Capone. Maybe that kind of thing was just in movies.

Ethan left the bathroom and went into the bedroom he and Blake had sat in before. He took the briefcase and headed back. He paused for a moment to look over Wayne, who remained limp on the floor, his face in a muddy blood puddle.

"When I leave," he called to Blake, "you better get Wayne to a hospital. Maybe yourself too."

Ethan walked back to the bathroom, where Blake was curled up, holding himself. He looked half the size he had earlier that day, the little boy Ethan used to run around with, not the man he'd grown into.

Ethan held up the briefcase for Blake to see.

"Don't do it," Blake said. "Shark's already going to be pissed, but this . . ." He hesitated. "This is like signing your own death warrant with a big black Magic Marker."

"I want you to do three things for me," Ethan said. "I know you're going to go crawling to Shark as soon as I leave, but I want these three favors."

Blake was holding his ribcage, breathing carefully and deliberately. The ankle pistol was visible, but it might as well have been a hundred miles away. He was in no shape to make a move for it.

"First," Ethan said, "don't tell him that you told me about the ledger."

"I'm not suicidal."

"Second, tell him he can have his money back when he tells me what happened to my sister."

Blake shook his head in disbelief. "You're the suicidal one."

"Third," Ethan said, "tell Shark you're hurt too bad to do anything this weekend. Lie on the couch and stay away until nine o'clock Sunday morning." With this, Ethan leaned over so his face was close to Blake's. "Do not side with Shark against me."

Blake hesitated, then nodded, a sad expression on his face. Ethan didn't think he was sad that their friendship had come to this. He was sad because he didn't expect to see Ethan again. Or when he did, Ethan would be wrapped in plastic, and Blake would be shoveling dirt over his face or pushing him over the side of a boat.

* * *

Ethan left the hotel room and waited for the elevator. His pant leg was soaked. His right hand was bleeding again.

Inside the elevator, mirrors surrounded him on every wall. His reflection looked crazed, eyes wide and angry. His pupils, dilated from the adrenaline, were large black saucers consuming his irises. His skin was pale, the skin around his eyes dark and purple. He looked haggard and hungry and animalistic.

He had spent five years trying not to be the person he saw in the mirror. But there he was: the monster he never wanted to be again.

PART II

ABYSS

CHAPTER

36

Abby
2 years ago

ABBY SAT NEXT to Whitney in the dressing room at the club. Before they'd gone into the room, Whitney had looked around, made sure no one was watching, and pulled a Sharpie out of her bag. She'd written the letters *UN* in front of *DRESSING*. They'd giggled together and walked inside for their first shift at Dark Secrets.

The stalls were mostly full, but Abby and Whitney found places next to each other. They started with their makeup. Lots of blush. Heavy eyeliner. Shiny lip gloss.

The girls around them worked in various states of undress. They gabbed. They argued. Everyone spoke loudly over the thumping bass coming from the club.

Cal came in and went over the order of dancers like it was a batting lineup for a baseball game.

"We're going to have a packed house tonight," he said. "No dicking around back here. When you're not dancing, I want you out on the floor getting those lap dances. If cheapskates want to talk, move on to the next sucker."

The other girls hardly paid attention, but Abby and Whitney listened to every word. They didn't want to screw up on their first night.

"Hey, Cal," Abby said when he was finished.

He came over and stood next to them. Abby was in her bra and underwear. She was determined not to show how uncomfortable she was. If she couldn't handle being this close to the club manager, what was she going to do in fifteen minutes when she had to strut out on that stage?

"You ladies nervous?" he asked. "First day and all."

"A little," Whitney admitted.

"Could you do us a teensy favor?" Abby asked, holding her thumb and index finger a quarter inch apart.

She flashed him her most unscrupulous smile—one that said, *I'm trying to manipulate you, and you know it, and it's going to work anyway.*

"What's that?" he said, crossing his arms.

"Could you bring us a couple shots?" she asked. "To calm our nerves."

"Go get 'em yourself." He pointed to the door.

"You see, the thing is," Abby said, "the first time I go out there I want it to be on stage. I want to dive right in. Full immersion. If I walk out to the bar, it would be sort of like I dipped my toe in the water first."

He looked back and forth between Whitney and Abby, bemused.

"Okay," he said. "Sure."

He headed for the door.

"Oh, I want tequila," Whitney said.

"And Jameson for me," Abby called.

"You'll take what you get," he said, and pushed through the door. A moment later, they heard him swearing from the hallway. "Who the hell wrote this?" he said.

They both burst into laughter.

Abby eyed the clock in the dressing room. They had about ten minutes before she had to go on. Whitney would go after her.

Abby took off her bra and pulled on a tight white camisole. She stretched white stockings over her legs and hooked them on her garter belt. She fastened her tall, cherry-red heels, the only thing in her outfit that wasn't white. Whitney was wearing a baby-doll negligee, which was puffy and purple.

Cal came in with two shots.

"Tequila Sauza," he said, "and Jameson Irish Whiskey."

"You're the best, Cal."

"Yeah, yeah," he said. "Don't make a habit outta this."

Abby took the shots and set them on the desks in front of their mirrors. She rolled her chair over next to Whitney so that the two of them could look in the same mirror.

"Damn," Abby said, "we look good."

"Yeah, we do."

Abby looked behind them in the reflection at the other girls. A curvy blonde in a bodystocking was heading out the door. A Latina woman with a pink corset pushing her breasts up practically to her chin was wrapping a feather boa around her neck and getting ready to leave. Another woman who'd just been dancing came walking in, naked except for her thong, carrying her teddy and her shoes.

In the intense lights of the dressing room, Abby could spot pimples on the girls and cellulite on their thighs and dark circles under their eyes. One woman was tweezing errant hairs at her bikini line. Another was putting makeup on the veins on her arms to cover up her tracks. The women were pretty, but most of them were worn out, sexy but in a trashy, used sort of way. And the ones who weren't, the young ones—if they gave it a few years, they'd look like the rest.

Abby felt suddenly nervous about this. She'd convinced Whitney to do this with her, sold it as a fun game—something to do for a couple years to make some money. Would Whitney end up like the thirty-five-year-old in the corner, covering her age spots with powder and pulling in half the money she used to, trying to squeeze one more year out of her body while she figured out what to do next? Abby would never forgive herself if that happened.

She was more worried about Whitney than she was about herself. She was here for one reason only—to help Ethan. She'd wanted Whitney to join her simply because she didn't want to do it alone. Maybe that made her a bad friend. She hoped Whitney would understand one day.

Everything she'd said to Whitney about having an adventure together was a lie. She was doing this so she could find something that would help her brother. She knew Shark was responsible, the smarmy gangster who dropped by the house every six months or so, saying he was checking in, leaving her with an envelope of money.

"This is from Ethan," he'd tell her. "They get paid well inside making license plates. Did you know every license plate in the state is made by prison inmates?"

Such bullshit. She hadn't bought it, even when she was eighteen. When she turned twenty-one, he told her the IRS was watching his money closely, and he needed a new way to pass along her payments.

"Why don't you come work at the club?" he said. "You've got the looks for it."

Abby had laughed in his face. But then she'd thought about it all through the night. Here was her chance to do something for Ethan. She figured she could get inside the club, get close to Shark, find something on him that the cops or the feds would be interested in.

Ethan had already served three years. She didn't care if she could cut ten years off his sentence or only one. She didn't want him to stay in there a minute longer than he had to. But first she had to be convincing as a stripper. Make everyone, including Whitney, believe she was here for a good time and money and the thrill of making men do anything she wanted.

"Hey, new girl," said one of the veteran women whose tits had started to sag. "You're up."

"All right!" Whitney said, trying to encourage her.

Abby lifted her shot glass and clinked it against Whitney's. They downed the drinks, and each let out a loud whoop. The other girls looked at them like they were silly kids, but they didn't care.

Abby's breath burned.

"Go get 'em," Whitney said. "Show these bitches how it's done."

Abby strutted out of the room and down the hall. She entered the backstage waiting area.

"Okay, gentlemen," called the DJ. "We've got a real special treat for you tonight. Give it up for the newest addition to the Dark Secrets family, making her main-stage debut—Miss Scarlet Grace."

Abby marched out on stage to the opening vocals of Def Leppard's "Pour Some Sugar on Me." She popped her hips to the words. Then, when the music started, the drums and guitar, she swaggered around the stage, looking at all the men staring at her. She grabbed the pole and swung herself around, whipping her hair back.

The club was packed, every table full of men, the women making the rounds getting guys to pay twenty bucks for a one-song lap dance. One girl pressed a man's face between her fake cantaloupes. Another waved her ass in front of a guy in a suit, hiking her skirt up so he could get a good look at the red panties underneath.

The air was hot and moist and smelled like a locker room after a football game.

I can do this, Abby thought. *For Ethan.*

The men in the front row waved ones and fives that they wanted to tuck into her underwear. She flashed her biggest smile and strutted over to give them what they wanted.

CHAPTER

37

Whitney
28 hours, 52 minutes remaining

WHITNEY LAY AWAKE in the darkness. She'd been able to sleep for a few hours, but now she was staring at the stationary ceiling fan above her bed. She was thinking about Ethan. She'd had a crush on him years ago, when he was just out of high school and she was still a little girl. She'd thought she was long past it, but seeing him today and then spending the afternoon with him, all those old feelings had tiptoed back into her mind.

She knew she shouldn't be thinking about this on the eve of Abby's funeral, but she was lonely. And horny. She hadn't had sex in a year. She'd dated a guy she'd met at the club, an advertising rep at the *Gazette-Journal*, and he'd turned out to be a giant douchebag. After that, she'd vowed never to date someone from the club again. And when you're a stripper, you don't often meet guys any other way.

She knew a one-night stand with a guy on weekend furlough from prison wasn't a good idea, but this was Ethan. She'd known him most of her life. He was a good person despite what his criminal record might say.

She got up to use the restroom. The room was chilly out of bed, the tile cold on her bare feet. She made up her mind to check on Ethan. What happened afterward would depend on whether he was sleeping. She didn't envision that she'd throw her arms around him, but she could invite him to sleep in the bed. That would be nice; they wouldn't have to have sex.

She threw on a T-shirt and a pair of Victoria's Secret sweats, and opened her bedroom door to check on him.

The couch was empty.

She looked around the apartment. There was no sign of him. The pillow she'd given him lay without an indentation from his head, the blanket was unfolded but piled on the couch cushion. The room was bluish gray, the only light coming from the city outside through the sliding glass doors.

She stepped out on the balcony. The cold was stimulating. Her breath came out in thick frosty clouds. The concrete was like ice on her bare feet.

Below, the city was as quiet as it could be. She had an idea that she might see him, walking away from the building or walking to it, or sitting on a park bench, but he was nowhere. The park was empty, its lamps lighting the pathways for no one to use. Traffic lights on the streets flashed red and green for no cars.

The world looked absent of people, and the absence turned her thoughts to Abby.

They'd spent many summer evenings sitting on this balcony, looking out over the city, sharing a bottle of wine, talking about girl drama at the club, reminiscing about high school. Talking about any and everything—all of their problems had seemed so big before but obviously weren't, not now in the shadow of Abby's death.

It didn't feel real. Here it was the eve of Abby's funeral and still, somehow, Whitney found herself thinking it would be nice to invite Abby over to share a bottle of wine and watch a rom-com.

She'd never felt such loss before. That's why she'd waited for Ethan outside the club. She needed someone to share it with, someone who was hurting as bad as or worse than she was.

She wished she hadn't made him sleep on the couch to begin with. She should have invited him into bed. Not for sex. Just someone to hold. If they'd made love, that would have been okay too. Anything to take her mind away.

She went back inside and slammed the door on the cold. She dropped onto the couch and wrapped herself in Ethan's blanket.

CHAPTER

38

Shark
28 hours, 31 minutes remaining

S HARK WAS ASLEEP under satin sheets and a plush comforter, but a ringing cellphone was pulling him out of his dreams. He looked up from his pillow. Anzhelika, his latest sex doll, was sitting upright in bed with her smartphone in hand, texting or looking at Facebook or who knew what. She was a twenty-one-year-old Russian hooker who'd jumped at the chance to simply take her clothes off for customers instead of have sex with them. Shark had brought her over for cheap, put her to work, then lured her into his own bed with cut-rate meth. The light from her phone lit up her fake tits, which he'd paid for. He'd known she wouldn't be able to sleep. The idiot had taken a snort before they had sex even though he had warned against it.

Kids these days. No foresight.

"Knock that off," he said, nudging her thigh. He dropped his head back into the pillow. "I'm sleeping."

"It not me," she said. "It your phone that keep ringing."

The phone had stopped so he decided to dismiss it. It started ringing again a few seconds later.

"What the hell?" he said.

He sat up and looked around. The phone was on the nightstand next to the baggie of crystal. The bag looked a little lighter than when he'd drifted off to sleep.

Caller ID showed the call was coming from Blake.

"What do you want?" he snapped. "You know the rules: unless I'm at the club at this hour, call Stu."

"I guess he's still in the Black Rock with Bruce," Blake said apologetically. "It's going straight to voicemail."

There was something in Blake's voice: apology, yes, but something else too. Fear maybe. Or pain. He sounded like he had the flu and had been puking all night.

"I'm waiting," Shark said.

Blake took a deep, audible breath. "Lockhart showed up at the game. He beat the shit out of me. He really messed Wayne up. And . . ." He hesitated, afraid to deliver the bad news.

"Don't tell me," Shark said.

"He took the money."

Shark threw the covers back and jumped out of bed. He started pacing around the room.

He was naked, and Anzhelika made an attempt to whistle like the men in the club whistled at her. She was no good at it.

"You better be joking," Shark said into the phone.

Anzhelika went back to looking at her screen.

Blake assured him that he wasn't, and his voice sold it more than his words did. It was pain in his voice. Definitely pain.

Shark grunted in frustration, then started asking questions. How bad was Wayne? Could they get out of there without calling an ambulance? What happened to the gamblers? Where did he think Ethan had gone?

And finally: "How the hell did he know about the game to begin with?"

"I told him," Blake admitted. "I thought he might come and hang out. Maybe he'd need a place to crash for the night. I never thought in a million years he would come in throwing punches like Liam fucking Neeson."

Shark sat on the edge of the bed and ran a hand through his hair. Anzhelika set her phone down and kneeled behind him. She fixed his gold chains, which were hanging down his back instead of his chest, and then she started massaging his shoulders.

"Get Wayne out of there," Shark said. "I'll come over and clean up the mess."

He needed to contact all the players and assure them they'd get their money back. And depending on the condition of the suite, he might need to straighten things out with the hotel manager.

"I'm sorry, Shark," Blake said.

Shark hung up on him.

Anzhelika wrapped her arms around his shoulders. "Because you are awake," she said, running her fingers through his chest hair and down to his stomach, "you want we should have round two?"

"Don't you have your own apartment?" he said, throwing her arms off him and standing up.

She flashed him a flirtatious smile. "You sure you don't want—"

He belted her in the face, and she rolled off the side of the bed onto the floor.

She sat up, her eyes floating in tears. She dabbed at her lip with her finger and came away with a splotch of blood.

"You going to Abby Lockhart's funeral?" Shark said.

"Yes," Anzhelika said.

"Maybe you'll get to meet her brother," Shark said. "Right before *his* funeral."

CHAPTER

39

Ethan
28 hours, 4 minutes remaining

ETHAN APPROACHED THE funeral home. His body had cooled after the fight, and his sweaty shirt was now like a cold, wet towel against his skin. He was shivering. The briefcase shook in his hand. He gritted his teeth together so they wouldn't chatter. He'd passed a bank that displayed the time on a digital sign. It was almost five AM. The world would be waking up soon.

He curved around to the back of the building. He stared at the punch pad, trying to remember the pattern the employee had made with his finger. He punched the four numbers he thought the man must have used, and the display flashed red. *Shit.* He wondered if there was any danger of entering the wrong code too many times. Would it set off some sort of alert? He closed his eyes and pictured the pattern again. He decided on another option, only one number different. He steadied his fingers, trembling from the cold, and punched in the code. A green light flashed on the display, and he yanked the door open. Inside, he leaned against the wall and let himself get warm.

There was a single caged bulb—like the ones in prison—that gave the cinderblock hallway an eerie yellow glow. He walked inside and peeked into the room where they apparently did the body preparation. He reached for the light switch and found a large hand-sanitizer dispenser mounted on the wall. The switch was on the other side. The room lit up to reveal a combination of offwhite furniture and pieces of stainless-steel equipment. There was a strange-looking machine with a tall, cylindrical glass tank, which he assumed was the embalming machine.

He found the viewing room. The lights were on a dimmer, and he turned them up. He stared at the photos of Abby, taking the time he hadn't been comfortable taking earlier when the parlor was full of people. He looked at each picture, picking out his favorites and coming back to them again and again.

Finally, he approached the casket. He set the briefcase down and looked for the latch to release the lids. He opened both the upper and lower sections so the entire inside was in view.

There were more artifacts now: cards and notes, pictures of her with friends. Everything lay on a flat white cushion that covered the casket floor. He tried to remember how the items were lying inside, then he reached in and gathered them all up and set them on the floor. He felt around the edges of the cushion and pried it up.

He walked back to the room where they worked on the bodies. The air smelled antiseptic. A big box of plastic gloves sat on the counter next to the stainless steel table. He took two and stretched them over his hands. A variety of tools lay on a metal stand nearby, and Ethan took a couple of those too: a long pair of surgical scissors and a dissection knife at least a foot long.

He saw a pair of steel shears that looked similar to what Kicking Bird had used to cut off Anton's finger. Bone shears. He left those where they lay.

Back in the viewing room, he went to work on the latch of Shark's briefcase with the tools. It took some work, but he finally pried it open.

Inside the briefcase were rows and rows of cash, bundled together. The bundles were different sizes with different kinds of bills, which made sense because it all came from different sources—Shark's money and the five gamblers' deposits. Ethan made a quick effort to count but then gave up. He didn't care enough to take the time.

He took the bundles and arranged them in the bottom of the casket, spreading them out as evenly as possible. He put the cushion back in its place, then picked the items up off the floor and placed them back in as well. He arranged them more or less the way they'd been before.

He closed the casket lids. The clicks were loud in the silent room.

On his way out, he returned the knives to their original positions next to the stainless steel table.

The funeral home's dumpster was enclosed behind a locked fence, so Ethan carried the briefcase with him down the street. He followed the river path toward Whitney's apartment. The water looked black and gray.

He threw in the rubber gloves, then tossed the empty briefcase out over the river. It landed on the surface with a smack, and the lid flopped open. It floated along the current, then was pulled under.

CHAPTER

40

Ethan
26 hours, 25 minutes remaining

ETHAN WAITED OUTSIDE Whitney's building for a few minutes, unable to open the locked door. Yesterday when she'd pulled her car into the garage, he hadn't caught the access code.

He stood in the light of the sunrise, which wasn't warm but was better than what he'd endured most of the night. He figured someone would come along sooner or later, heading into or out of the building, and he was right. A woman in pajama pants under a long trench coat came out with a corgi on a leash. She held the door so he could enter the building, not thinking for a moment that he might not belong.

Inside the elevator, he felt the weight of his exhaustion. He'd been holding it off, but now, so close to Whitney's apartment, it was as if his body sensed it could relax. He'd been awake for twenty-four hours—and he hadn't slept well before that.

He took the chance that Whitney was awake and knocked gently on her door. She came to the door wrapped in the blanket he'd used on the couch.

"You okay?" she said, her voice slurred from sleep.

"Sorry," he said. "I didn't mean to wake you up."

"It's all right."

Back on the couch, she drew her knees to her chest, pulling the blanket around her, and made room for him to sit. He collapsed onto the cushions. On the glass coffee table, there was a cup of water she'd put there for him before he went to bed. He drank it all.

"I was worried about you," Whitney said. She seemed awake now.

"Sorry," Ethan said again. He rolled his head around his shoulders and cracked his neck.

The curtains were open to the balcony, and the sky was growing bluer and bluer by the second.

"Did you get any sleep?" she said.

Ethan shook his head.

"Holy crap! What happened to your hand?"

"I got in a fight," Ethan said. He didn't bother to explain that the cut had actually been from punching a mirror.

"With who?"

"Wayne. That guy from the club."

"Oh," Whitney said glumly. "I like him."

"I did too."

"Are you hurt? I mean, besides your hand."

"Nah," he said, but it wasn't entirely true. Ethan's ribs felt tender, and when he made a fist, his hand throbbed.

"Did you hurt him?"

Ethan took a deep breath. "Hopefully not too bad."

"Hopefully?"

"He wasn't conscious when I left."

Whitney tucked her legs under her. "Holy shit, Ethan, what did you do?"

His instinct told him not to involve Whitney more than she already was. But he'd been up all night trying to figure things out, unaided, and he hadn't gotten very far. Maybe he couldn't do this alone after all.

"I found out some things," he said, and he told her what he'd done and what he knew.

He told her everything except where he'd hidden Shark's money. She asked, but he wouldn't say.

"Better you don't know," he said.

When he was finished, Whitney took him by the hand and guided him off the couch. Her touch was electricity, and for a moment, he thought she was going to take him into the bedroom. But she stopped at the bathroom and pulled out a first-aid kit and a bottle of peroxide from a drawer next to the sink. He thought it was unnecessary, but he let her tend to the cut on his hand anyway. She washed the dried blood with a wet, warm cloth, then poured peroxide over the gash. The liquid foamed up around the cut, but it didn't hurt. She dabbed his hand dry and placed a knuckle Band-Aid over the skin.

"Before I dropped out of college," she said, "I was studying to be a nurse."

She lifted his hand and kissed the injury.

"All better," he said.

Their eyes lingered on each other for a moment. He wanted to pull her in and kiss her, and he was sure she wanted the same thing.

When he did nothing, she smiled and said, "Are you hungry?"

"Starving."

* * *

Together, they made breakfast. He tended to the bacon while she made pancakes. When he was finished, he used the bacon grease to fry eggs. While the two of them cooked, they said little. They danced around each other in the small kitchen, smiling, touching each other unnecessarily, her hand on his shoulder, him touching—briefly—her waist.

She was barefoot and wearing a pair of sweatpants and a Reno Aces T-shirt. She wore no bra underneath, and her breasts pressed against the fabric, her nipples hard in the chilly air. Ethan tried not to look.

The blinds were pulled back from the windows, and outside the dark had been replaced by the bright light of sunrise.

When they sat down to eat, Whitney asked Ethan what his next step was.

"I've got to get that ledger," he said. "Somehow."

"How about I get it for you?"

"No. Thank you, but no." Ethan already felt like he was putting her in danger by being in her apartment. He didn't want to involve her any further.

"It's the only way," she said.

"I'll find another."

He opened his mouth to protest, but she launched into her plan. Shark would likely be looking for Ethan at the funeral, which would leave his office at the club unattended. Even after what Ethan had pulled last night, the funeral should be safe. Shark might attempt to talk to Ethan, but he wouldn't try to hurt him—he would have to know the police and the FBI might be watching. They could be undercover or at least spying on the proceedings. Meanwhile, Whitney would go to the club and sneak into Shark's office. It made more sense for her to do it. No one would think twice about her being there.

"As long as the ledger's there," she said, "I'll get it. Let's just hope he doesn't keep it with him all the time."

It seemed like a decent plan, but Ethan didn't like the idea of putting Whitney at risk.

"I'm not going to the funeral now," Ethan said. "I don't have time for that."

What he didn't say was that he wouldn't miss his sister's funeral for anything *if* it actually felt like her funeral. But he didn't see the point of standing next to an empty casket. Finding out what happened to her was the only way to get any closure.

"You have to go to the funeral," Whitney said. "That's the whole reason they let you out. It will raise all sorts of red flags if you miss it."

"It will look suspicious if you're not there," Ethan said.

"Not as suspicious as you not being there," she said. "And you can't just walk into the club and ask for the ledger. Even if Shark's not there, Stu will be. Or Bruce. Or both."

Ethan sat back. Much of his food sat uneaten on his plate. They'd made enough for four people, but he'd lost his appetite and had to force himself to eat what little he did.

"We'll get you a cell phone," Whitney said. "A prepaid one. So we can communicate. If anything seems suspicious, I'll split."

"I don't think it's a good idea, Whitney."

She reached out and put her hand on his arm. "Abby was my best friend," she said.

"Fine." Ethan exhaled, hoping he wasn't making a mistake. "We'll do it your way."

CHAPTER

41

Taylor
26 hours, 9 minutes remaining

TAYLOR PULLED HIS unmarked car into the valet turnaround at the Neptune Hotel and Casino.

"Sir," an enthusiastic valet said, "may I have your keys?"

Taylor showed him his badge.

"Leave it here," he said.

"I understand, sir," the kid said. "If you won't be long, you can just—"

"I might be all goddamn day," Taylor said, "but you're not moving my car."

Perks of being a police officer.

The concierge greeted him as soon as he came through the door into the hotel lobby.

"Checking in, sir?" the concierge asked him.

Taylor showed him his badge.

"Hotel manager, please."

"Of course."

Taylor waited. The inside of the casino was filled with silly fish-themed decorations, but the lobby of the hotel was meant to look glamorous. Gleaming marble floors. High ceilings with absurdly large chandeliers.

The first time you set foot in the casino, you might be impressed. But the hundredth? Everything looked fake. An opulent pretense.

A man in a suit approached and introduced himself as Armando Garcia, the night manager. Taylor explained that they'd received a report that a couple banged-up guys were spotted limping through the casino.

"No," Garcia said. "Nothing like that happened. My employees would have reported it to me."

"Can we check the footage on your security cameras just to be sure?"

"Sorry," Garcia said. "That would be against our policy. Unless you have a warrant, I can't show you any security footage."

Taylor nodded, still trying to act polite. The Galaxia had pulled the same crap when they'd tried to get footage of Kicking Bird at the bar the night Abby went missing.

"Okay, I'll work on getting that warrant," Taylor said. "In the meantime, because we've been getting so many reports about the Neptune lately, I'm going to ask some undercover officers to take a close look at what's going on here. We're going to crack down on drug dealers making sales on Neptune property, prostitutes working illegally in the casino—"

Garcia looked mortified.

"—and I'll put a call into the Nevada Gaming Commission," Taylor added, "and let them know there have been reports of the Neptune stacking the deck at its blackjack tables, rigging its roulette wheels, and not paying full amounts on slot machines."

"Let me call my boss," Garcia said. "Maybe we can allow you to look at the video footage."

"Go ahead," Taylor said. "I'll make some calls while I wait."

"Um," Garcia said. "Let's go ahead and take a look. We have nothing to hide."

"Thanks for your cooperation."

* * *

Taylor and the night manager stood in the security room of the casino, looking at a bank of computer screens with different camera views of the hotel and casino. There were a lot of cameras, and Taylor wasn't sure where to look.

Garcia began rewinding the footage on a handful of recordings. People walked backward through the casino. Cards flipped up into their hands on blackjack tables. Slot machines sucked coins up like vacuum cleaners.

Taylor wouldn't normally be investigating something like this, a couple beat-up guys limping through a casino. That probably happened every night. But whoever called it in said he recognized one of the guys—a big bouncer from Dark Secrets.

Because it was Dark Secrets, the lieutenant in charge had called Taylor at home and asked if he wanted to look into it. Normally, he would have passed—Shark was the FBI's problem, after all—but his gut told him to check it out.

"Stop," Taylor said, pointing to one of the monitors. "That one."

Garcia pressed a button and the image froze.

Two men were coming out of a hotel elevator, the smaller one holding up the bigger one, whose face and shirt were covered in blood.

The picture wasn't that good, but Taylor thought he recognized them both. Blake Freeman and one of the twins who worked for Shark, Bruce or Wayne Capullo.

"I guess you were right," Garcia said. "None of my employees reported this to me. The men are being pretty discreet."

Taylor fought the urge to laugh—there was nothing discreet about a six-five, three-hundred-pound man hobbling through a casino with his nose gushing blood.

Taylor asked to see footage from inside the elevator they'd exited. The frozen image on the screen was time-stamped, and Garcia quickly rewound the video to a few seconds before that.

The image was much better. Taylor had been right about both of their identities. And Blake Freeman didn't look much better than his companion. He didn't appear to be bleeding, but his face was grimacing, and it looked as if his hair was all wet and in disarray.

"Do me a favor," Taylor said. "Rewind the tape a little further. Let's see if anyone else comes down before them."

Sure enough, a few minutes earlier, another recognizable person stood in the elevator, his eyes wide with adrenaline, his face full of rage.

"Ah, there you are," Taylor said aloud.

"You know that guy?" Garcia said.

"I wouldn't have," Taylor said, with a chuckle, "except he was sitting in my office yesterday."

CHAPTER

42

Ethan
25 hours, 35 minutes remaining

T HE FUNERAL WASN'T until eleven o'clock, and Ethan asked if he could take
another shower. He'd sweated badly during the fight, but more than that,
he simply felt dirty.

He stripped off his shirt and inspected himself in the mirror. There were no
visible bruises where Wayne had hit him, but his ribs were sore. He squirted
some of Whitney's toothpaste onto his finger and did his best to rub his teeth
clean and get the rotten taste of violence out of his mouth.

In the shower, he stood under the hot water, thinking, letting the spray
massage his neck. Steam rose around him, and he inhaled the warm air.

He heard the door open and, through the curtain, saw Whitney enter the
bathroom. She was blurry through the curtain, but he could see her pull her
shirt off over her head and then step out of her sweatpants. She drew open the
curtain.

"Let's stop fighting this," she said, and stepped into the shower.

She let the water soak her hair. The light chocolate locks turned to dark coffee. Rivulets of water chuted down her body. He was a foot taller than her, and
she reached up and guided his head down so they could kiss. He kissed her hard
and clumsily and then wrapped his arms around her and pressed his body against
hers. His cock, already hard, pushed against her stomach. She stroked it gently
with her fingertips, and it responded in throbs. He leaned down and kissed her
neck, then her collarbone, then lower. Warm water cascaded down her breasts,
and he put his mouth over a nipple, which grew hard against his tongue.

She let out a moan. She held onto his shoulders for balance and stepped up on the sides of the bathtub. He steadied her with his hands on her hips in case the footing was slippery. Now she was as tall as he was, and she took his erection and guided it inside her. He pressed her against the porcelain wall behind her. She gasped as he went deeper until he was all the way, his body contoured tightly against her. They fit together as if they were molded as one piece. He kissed her, she kissed him, and they started to push against one another, out of sync and then finding a rhythm. He held onto her tightly, feeling a raw, hungry need for her.

"I haven't had sex in five years," Ethan whispered. "I might not last long."

"It's okay," Whitney said. "I'm ready."

He pressed into her, his hands on her butt, guiding her movement. She gripped him tighter, her body growing tense, every muscle rock hard. She threw her legs up and wrapped them around his waist. She made a loud noise—a gasp and a moan with a little bit of a scream. He felt himself building and building toward a climax, ascending inside a mountain, expecting the peak to be any moment but rising higher and higher until, finally, the volcanic explosion rocked through his entire body.

He held onto her, his mouth on the crook of her neck, her wet hair clinging to his skin. His cock continued to spasm inside of her. She lowered her legs. He kissed her and leaned back enough to take in her eyes, blue prisms he wished he could stare into forever.

She was smiling, big and expressive—a happiness that couldn't be faked. Ethan felt it too, and for a moment there was no such thing as sadness and self-hatred.

"Wow," she said, and they started laughing together.

Ethan hugged her. He didn't want to let go.

43

Ethan
24 hours, 41 minutes remaining

ETHAN WAS WORRIED that someone would spot them together, and somehow word would get back to Shark that Whitney was helping him. He wanted her to go shopping for supplies by herself. She only finally convinced him to go with her if they went to the Walmart north of town, on the way to Cold Springs, where no one would know them.

"None of your coworkers have trailers up there?" he asked.

Whitney gestured to her condo. "Does it look like we live in trailers?"

"You and I both know that the strippers don't all live like this."

"We're dancers, thank you very much."

"Sorry," he said. "You and I both know the other *dancers* don't all live like this."

Ethan knew from experience that some of the girls blew their money on drugs or supporting unemployed dirtbags. Or they had kids or parents to look after. Few were like Whitney—single, responsible, levelheaded. And they probably didn't make as much as her either. He guessed she was one of the club's top earners.

The morning was cold, and traffic seemed light. They sat in silence on the ride. Ethan caught Whitney smiling.

"What?" he said.

"I was just thinking."

"Thinking what?"

"I was wondering if we'll have time to do that again after we get back."

"I don't know," Ethan said. "It feels weird to try to squeeze in sex before the funeral."

This silenced her. She stared at the road ahead, the happiness that had been on her face all morning now gone.

"I'm sorry," he said.

"No," she said. "I'm sorry. It was a stupid idea."

He almost said nothing, but he didn't want things to be weird between them. He reached out and rested his hand on her jeans.

"This morning was wonderful," he said. "Best five minutes of my life. It's just, well, everything is so messed up right now. I'm out on weekend leave from prison for God's sake."

Whitney was silent for a second, then her pursed lips broke into a grin that she couldn't stop. "Five minutes? More like sixty seconds."

He laughed. "I didn't hear you complaining."

*   *   *

At Walmart, they walked through the brightly lit aisles, unsure how to find what they were looking for. They finally located the prepaid cell phones and debated for a few minutes about which one to buy before Whitney grabbed the most expensive one.

"I'm buying," she said. "You can pay me back. I know you're good for it."

Ethan didn't argue. He wished he'd saved a bundle of Shark's money. At least a few bills. That would have been a smart thing to do.

Whitney suggested they go ahead and buy a shovel.

"Worst-case scenario," she said, "we don't need it."

The lawn and garden area was closed for the winter, but they found a rack of shovels in the hardware section. Ethan grabbed one with a long handle and rounded steel blade. Whitney insisted they buy two.

"I'm with you on this," she said. "All the way."

It was difficult for them to wedge the two shovels into the car, but they finally figured out a way, with the handles sticking between them in the front seats.

On the drive back, Whitney said, "You mind if I ask you a question?"

"Shoot."

"Abby never really knew the details of what happened when you got arrested. We read the court transcripts, but it seemed like there was a lot, you know, hidden between the lines."

"I didn't want her to know. I was trying to shield her from who I really was."

"But you told Shark to look after her."

"I never thought he'd hire her to dance," Ethan said. "I thought he'd send her an anonymous envelope of cash every now and then. I really wasn't thinking."

"So what did happen?" Whitney asked. "When you got arrested?"

Shark had been interested in putting together jobs, Ethan explained. Instead of being a fence for stolen goods or the guy who could launder money, he wanted to steal and make the money himself. So he had the idea that two guys could knock off the Silver Coin Casino. It was a small casino, no hotel, a simple layout with the cage in the center of the floor. Most casinos were like mazes, but this one had easy access from four corner doors. And in the daytime, there was only ever one guard on duty. Two guys could go in and take them before they knew what hit them: one to climb up over the cage, the other to keep watch and keep his gun on any security guards or patrons who wanted to be heroes.

"Shark gave us two MP5s. Told us, 'You gotta put the fear of God in them. Shock and awe—like George Bush.' I didn't even load my gun. The magazine was empty."

"But Blake's was loaded?" Whitney said.

He exhaled. "Blake's was loaded."

When they went in, their first goal was to take out the security guard. But neither of them could find him—he was probably in the restroom—and the scattering of people in the casino were freaking out because two armed men in ski masks were running around. So they went to the cage, and Blake climbed over, shouting at the employees inside. He held his gun up with one arm, like he was Rambo, and shoved them and told them to fill garbage bags with all their cash. Ethan circled the cage, pointing the empty gun at patrons and telling them to get down on the floor. He kept a look out for the guard but didn't see him.

Blake tossed two bags of money up over the cage and climbed out. He jumped down and handed Ethan one of the bags. There really wasn't that much in it. They'd only taken what was in the drawers. They hadn't hit a safe or anything like that. Ethan had his back turned, and Blake was picking up the other bag, and that's when the security guard popped out from behind a bank of slot machines.

He had a little pistol and told them to freeze. Blake raised his gun and opened fire on the guy.

Ethan and Blake ran in opposite directions, but Ethan's escape route was in the front of the building, and a police car was rolling into the lot just as he made it outside. He took off running, tossing the gun in a flowerbed and stuffing the money bag in a garbage can.

He ran into Victorian Square in Sparks and dropped his ski mask, trying to seem like another pedestrian browsing the storefronts. But he was wearing all black, and at this point there were lots of cops out looking for him.

"The cops spent all their energy going after me," Ethan said. "Blake drove away unnoticed."

Whitney's car was approaching downtown. The streets were nearly empty except for a few homeless people wandering around, bundled up and pushing overloaded shopping carts, and some kids on skateboards trying to ride a hand-rail in front of Walgreens.

"Back then, Shark wasn't quite what he is now," Ethan said. "He'd launder drug money at the club and sometimes fence stolen stuff. But mostly he was just a loan shark. That's what Blake and I did—we were the muscle making collections. But I guess Shark fancied himself something more. I thought what happened to me might sober him up a bit. Maybe he'd quit while he was ahead. Looks like the opposite happened."

Whitney stopped the car at the gate to her condo. She punched the code for the gate to lift. This time, Ethan memorized the numbers.

Whitney pulled into a parking spot and said, "I know you robbed a place, but what you did doesn't sound *that* bad. You didn't shoot the guy."

"I got an extra ten years because of the MP5," Ethan said. "The legislature had just passed the law the previous year. Shark and his brilliant idea to scare the crap out of everyone with automatic weapons . . ."

"They could do that even though your gun wasn't loaded?" Whitney asked.

"The DA argued that I dumped the ammunition and they just never found it. They knew I wasn't the one who shot the guard. The gun didn't match the bullets. But they threatened me with twenty years if I didn't cooperate. And—"

"You didn't," Whitney finished.

"I didn't."

"The guard didn't die, did he?"

"No," Ethan said. "His vest saved him. But he had some permanent nerve damage. One of his arms doesn't work right. His hand is stuck in a sort of claw shape. He testified at the trial and held up his hand for the jury to see."

They left the shovels in the car but carried the Walmart bag containing the burner phone with them to the elevator.

"God. Those assholes. They didn't deserve your loyalty."

"I deserved to be locked up. Just because Shark and Blake deserved it too didn't make a difference. If I had been the judge in the case, I would have given me the max too."

"You are nothing like Shark and Blake," Whitney said.

The elevator lifted off the ground and started upward. There were no mirrors in this one, which Ethan was thankful for.

"I'm a little bit like them," Ethan said. "Enough that I don't deserve to be walking around the street."

Whitney put her hand on his shoulder to comfort him, but he wasn't in the mood now. "You're a good person," she said. "You didn't even load your gun."

"The reason I used an empty magazine isn't because I'm not capable of killing somebody. Just the opposite. I didn't load the gun because I figured if I had, I would have used it."

Whitney was quiet, then said, "I don't think I could ever kill anybody."

"Everybody probably could if they had to," Ethan said. "The things I did back in those days, it was almost like I wanted to."

The elevator door opened, and Whitney reached for her keys.

"But that's not you anymore," Whitney said.

Ethan didn't say anything, but he thought, *I'm not so sure.*

* * *

Whitney ironed a dress that she would wear, a different one from what she'd worn the night before. She said she'd hurry over to the funeral if she was done at the club in time. Ethan asked if he could iron his suit again, but Whitney offered to do it for him.

There was a digital clock on the stereo system, and Ethan kept watching it. Part of him wanted it to speed up so they could get through this. Another part of him wanted it to slow down. He had less than twenty-four hours before he had to report back.

"Let's go over the plan again," he said.

Whitney sprayed a mist of water onto Ethan's dress pants and ran the iron over them, back and forth, the water hissing as it boiled away.

"Don't worry about me," Whitney said.

"And if Kicking Bird is at the club . . ."

"Stu?" Whitney said. "He's harmless."

Ethan put a hand on her arm. "No. He's not."

"I know him," Whitney said.

"Whitney," Ethan said firmly, "I watched him cut a guy's throat with no more feeling than if he was slicing a Thanksgiving turkey. Stuart Kicking Bird is not harmless."

She unplugged the iron and looked up at him. Her expression told him she'd gotten the message.

Once they left—him for the funeral, her for the club—the whole situation would change. They were in a strange moment before the standoff would escalate. A brief space where they could slow down the racing clock and pretend that their lives weren't out of control. Ethan knew this was his last moment resembling anything like normalcy with Whitney.

He reached down, wrapped her in a hug, and lifted her into the air. She bumped the ironing board, and the iron teetered but stayed upright.

"Oh," she said, surprised, and wrapped her legs around his waist.

Their faces were inches apart.

"It looks like we have some time after all," he said, and he carried her to the bedroom.

Abby
4 months ago

ABBY ORDERED A beer. It seemed like a beer kind of night.
"What's with the rose?" the bartender asked. He was a young guy, her age, with muscular arms and a tattoo of a snake wrapping itself around his forearm. "Got a blind date?"

"Something like that."

She took her beer and her rose and went to find a table. She wore jeans, boots, and a red sweater. She wanted to look good—not dressed up, just impressive.

The bar was in Carson City. She and Whitney had stopped here once on the way back from snowboarding. It was popular, with kitschy signs and memorabilia on the wall. A jukebox played classic rock songs. She'd wanted a place where it was unlikely anyone who knew her from Reno might spot her.

She didn't wait long.

"I'm supposed to meet someone here with a white rose," said a handsome man in a suit.

She picked the rose up, examining it like it was the first time she'd seen it. "Well, what do you know," she said. "I've got one."

"I'm Brian Hughes," he said, extending his hand.

She took it. "Nice to meet you."

"And you are?"

"Sit down," she said.

"It's nice to meet you too, Sit Down."

He was young for an FBI agent, maybe a little older than her brother, but not much, and handsome in a polished way that would have driven Ethan nuts. He emanated student-body government, fraternities, country clubs. She saw guys like him all the time when she was dancing, but usually she could see through the genteel facade to find that they weren't that cute, weren't that charming, probably weren't as rich as they let on.

She thought there might be something more to him.

"What can I do for you?" he asked.

"You're leading the investigation into Stanley 'Shark' D'Antonio?"

"Yes."

"How close are you to bringing him in?"

"I can't tell you that."

"So not close?"

He looked perturbed—an expression that told her she'd hit the bull's-eye. He took a drink of what looked like a soda without alcohol. The straw made a slurping sound when the glass was empty.

"What are you drinking?" Abby said.

"Nothing." He set the glass down. "I'm on duty. This is business."

Abby took a long pull from her beer. "I want to get information for you," she said, "so you can build a case."

"And who are you?" Hughes said. "A jilted ex?"

"I work at Dark Secrets," she said.

He sat back in his seat and made no effort to hide his smirk.

"So you're a stripper?"

"A dancer," she said. "Yes."

"And what do you know that could help me?"

"Not much," she said. "Not yet."

He looked around, bored, irritated that he'd driven all the way down here for a lead that didn't look like it was going to pan out.

"I can find out whatever you need to know," she said. "I'm close to everyone at the club. Blake Freeman. Anton Trujillo. The new guys, Bruce and Wayne. Cal Burnside. I'm sure you're keeping an eye on those people. And I can get closer to Shark."

"You didn't mention Stuart Kicking Bird," Hughes said.

"He's hard to get to know," she said.

"Look, miss," Hughes said, "I'm sure you've got the best of intentions, but it doesn't sound like you've got much to give me. You haven't even told me your name."

"I'm Abby Lockhart," she said.

His expression told her that the name meant nothing.

"Ethan Lockhart's sister."

His eyes woke up. "As in Ethan Lockhart in prison for armed robbery?"

She nodded.

"As in Ethan Lockhart who probably committed the crime working for Shark?"

She hooked her thumb toward herself. "As in Abby Lockhart who gets a regular cash payment to buy her brother's silence."

Hughes's eyes went from awake to alert.

"Holy shit," he said.

A server was passing by, and he waved her down. "Sam Adams please," he said. "And another for her."

He leaned forward in his chair, elbows on the table.

"Can you get your brother to testify?"

"That's not what I'm offering," she said. "I'm offering to get you what you need. *I'm* offering to testify."

"So what do you want?" he said.

"I want my brother out of prison," she said. "Can you do that?"

"I don't know."

Abby set her beer down and stood up. "Then goodbye."

"Wait," he said, reaching out and grabbing her wrist.

She felt the urge to jerk her hand away, but there was something in his touch—or the expression on his face—that stopped her.

"I can figure something out," Hughes said.

She sat back down. He was excited and began bombarding her with questions. She could tell him almost nothing he wanted to hear, but he didn't seem to care. He was drunk on possibility.

Abby felt caught up in it too. Since that day in the courtroom, when Ethan had hugged her goodbye, she'd longed to help him. She'd finally mustered the courage to call the local FBI office and demand to speak to the person in charge of investigating Shark.

There was a lot that still needed to be done, but she finally felt like she might actually be able to accomplish this.

"You know this is going to be dangerous?" Hughes said. "You seem like a nice girl. Do you know what you're getting yourself into?"

Abby thought of the day she'd jumped off the cliff at Lake Tahoe. She'd wanted to be fearless, like Ethan.

This time, she thought, *I'm jumping in to save you, big brother.*

CHAPTER

45

Ethan
22 hours, 20 minutes remaining

THE TAXI DROPPED Ethan off at the funeral home. The wind was blowing hard, and icy tentacles crawled into the cracks of his suit. He hurried up the walkway, his shoes clicking on the gray concrete. A flagpole stood in the brown grass, and the lanyard whipped noisily against the pole.

His mother was waiting inside the door. She looked pallid. A few people—the first to arrive—stood behind her in the viewing area.

"Stand with me," she said, scowling at him with palpable distaste.

Without a word, Ethan turned and stood alongside her to wait for the rest of the mourners to arrive. She wasn't ready to forgive him, obviously, but she needed his help in handling the expected formalities of the occasion. He would do it without complaint. His mother even asking him to stand with her was a step.

As people arrived, Ethan and his mom greeted them with hugs and handshakes. They said "Thanks for coming" over and over. Ethan hardly knew any of them, but they looked at him with knowing expressions: he was Abby's brother from prison.

Ethan kept his eye out for the FBI agent, Hughes, but he didn't show. Neither did the pervert voyeur who lived across from Abby, not that Ethan expected him after he'd knocked the asshole out cold.

When it was almost time for the service, Ethan spotted a big Cadillac Escalade pulling into the lot. Shark stepped out of it in a lavender suit that was almost restrained for him, along with three girls from the club. Two looked unfamiliar and very young, and the third Ethan recognized from the old days. The wind pushed against Shark's suit, pulling his tie out and flipping it like a rag. The girls held down their skirts and pulled their jackets tight around them. One of them had a bruise at the corner of her mouth that she'd tried to hide with makeup.

Inside the door, the dancers tried to straighten their hair, which had been blown into disarray. Shark fixed his tie.

"Ms. Lockhart," Shark said, "my deepest condolences."

Ethan's mom did not respond. She fixed Shark with a stare that would have made most men squirm, but Shark seemed unperturbed.

The dancer Ethan knew gave him a hug and said it was good to see him. Then Shark extended his hand to Ethan and said, "Good to see you, son."

Ethan took it. Shark held his grip tightly. Ethan's mom turned away and walked into the parlor.

"Might we have a moment to talk?" Shark said.

"Not now," Ethan said, still squeezing Shark's hand. "Wait until the casket is in the ground."

Shark didn't let go. He was stronger than he looked.

"Show some respect for the dead," Ethan said.

"Of course," Shark said. "Your sister was a lovely person, Ethan." He flashed a malevolent grin. "Shame what happened. Did they ever find her body?"

Ethan wanted to grab him around the throat and throw him to the ground, squeeze until he crushed Shark's windpipe. But he couldn't do anything. He pulled his hand loose from Shark's and stepped aside. With a smile, Shark went into the parlor, and Ethan followed.

His mother had saved him a seat.

CHAPTER

46

Whitney
22 hours, 5 minutes remaining

WHITNEY PULLED UP to the gate for employee parking, rolled her window down to punch in the code, and waited while the motorized fence rolled to the side. The wind pushed a tumbleweed across the blacktop. In the back lot, Shark's Escalade was missing, but Stuart's pickup was there, as well as Bruce's Chevy Tahoe. She wished Ethan had beaten him up last night instead of his brother. Bruce always leered at her, and it gave her the creeps.

She took a deep breath and slung her gym bag over her shoulder and headed toward the door. Music played from the cabaret, a country song. She passed one of the girls in the hallway, who asked why she was so dressed up.

"Abby's funeral," she said. "I'm heading there now."

The woman's face changed. "Oh, I'm so sorry. I wish I could go."

Whitney peeked through the curtain into the club. Bruce was leaning against the bar like he usually did. Cal was behind it. Two girls were working the room, but the place was dead. There was no sign of Stu.

She walked toward Shark's office and poked her head in, knocking as she did. She was thankful for her charade—Stu was sitting behind Shark's desk, scanning through some kind of paperwork. He looked up at her.

"Where's Shark?" she said.

"At the funeral," he said. "I thought you would be there."

She stepped into the doorway to show him her outfit. "I'm heading there now," she said. "I just had something to tell him first."

He said nothing. A leather-bound journal lay on the corner of the desk.

She went to the dressing room and sat down at the station she usually used.

She pretended to rummage through her things. No one else was in there, but she felt like she was being watched.

CHAPTER

47

Ethan
22 hours remaining

THE MINISTER TOOK the dais next to the table of Abby's things. He began quoting from the Bible, and it was clear he had never met Abby nor taken the time to learn anything about her.

"Are you going to say anything?" Ethan whispered to his mom.

"I wouldn't be able to get through it," she said.

She looked at Ethan with pleading eyes.

"Will you say something about her?"

The minister asked everyone to bow their heads, and Ethan rose. Murmurs rolled through the audience like waves.

"I'd like to say something," Ethan said.

He towered over the minister.

"Oh," he said, stepping backward. "Okay."

Ethan turned to face the people in attendance. There were about thirty. No doubt that if Abby had died when she was in high school the audience would have been five times as big. But since she made her living as a stripper—or maybe because her brother was in prison—many of her older, more respected friends had stayed away.

"I'm Abby's brother," Ethan said. "Most of you probably know that."

The audience was silent, their eyes cemented on Ethan.

Ethan hesitated, not sure what else to say. What positive spin he could possibly put on this. He became suddenly aware of how tired he was. It was hard to believe that his talk with Jack in prison was only yesterday—and he hadn't slept one second since.

"Let me tell you about Abby," he said. "You all knew her, but none of you knew her as well as I did. Except," he added, "maybe our mom.

"I remember when I was seven or eight, I would ask Mom if I could hold her, and I would just stare down into the face of my baby sister. Her skin was so soft and she had this new-baby smell. She would stare at me. Even before she learned to walk, she had her own amazing personality. It was incredible for me to see, as a child, how much she was her own person even when she was a baby. She had this amazing laugh when I tickled her feet. Long before she could talk, she loved to jabber nonsense words, like she knew exactly what she was saying.

"I know it's supposed to be a little while before babies start to smile, but that's not how I remember it. I remember her smiling all the time. Even when she was a newborn. And that's how I remember her throughout her life—smiling. She had this extraordinary, magical expression that brought joy to my heart like nothing else ever has. Even when I was mad at her, she could flash that smile and my heart would melt. She made everyone around her want to smile too."

Ethan paused. He thought about going on and telling a story or two about Abby. But most of the people in the audience were crying already. Maybe he had said enough.

"That's how I hope you'll remember Abby," he said. "Smiling."

48

Whitney
21 hours, 45 minutes remaining

WHITNEY CHECKED HER phone to see how much time had passed.
"Shit," she said.

One of the girls, a newbie named Janelle, came into the room, naked except for a thong, boots, and a cowboy hat. She'd been on stage dancing to Garth Brooks's "Friends in Low Places." The rest of her clothes were in her arms.

"Hey," she said, overly friendly.

Whitney rose and left the room.

She glanced out into the club, looking for Stu. He wasn't there. She peeked into the kitchen. One of the cooks was leaning against a table, texting. There was no food on the grill. She walked out into the club. Another new girl was taking the stage, prancing out to a Britney Spears song.

Bruce eyed Whitney as she approached. His eyes were squinted, his face puckered. His bad eye seemed especially cloudy, if that was possible.

"Hey, guys," she said to him and Cal. "You okay, Bruce? You look like you're in a bad mood."

"Nothing a blowjob wouldn't fix," he said.

"Gross," she said, rolling her eyes. She turned to Cal. "Hey, I need Wednesday night off."

She didn't. She was killing time. In fact, she didn't think she'd ever step foot in the club again. Even if the ledger didn't confirm Ethan's suspicions, it was time to do something with her life besides shake her ass in front of sex-starved strangers.

She'd started to make small talk with Cal, but then Stuart came out of the back.

"I better get going," she said.

She passed Stuart, who didn't make eye contact. She went back into the dressing room, grabbed her bag, and headed for Shark's office.

Her heart was thumping—fast, full beats that seemed to shake her whole body. She pushed the door of the office open, looking around as if someone might be there, even though everyone was accounted for.

She flipped the ledger open. Most of the pages were empty. The ones that weren't had strings of numbers. Stuffed in a pocket in the back were a bunch of keno notes. Whitney had lived her whole life in Nevada and had always thought keno—a lottery-style game offered in nearly every casino—was one of the more boring ways to gamble, barely a step up from bingo. Keno didn't seem like the kind of game Shark would be interested in, but here was a pile of receipts showing this appeared to be his game of choice.

Was this even the right ledger?

She looked around but didn't see anything else that fit the description. She shoved the book into her bag and hurried out of the office. She made it to the back exit when Stu called her name. She stopped. The door was cracked. She thought about running.

He walked toward her, taking his time. Cold air seeped in.

He locked eyes with her, and she wanted to wilt under the stare. His irises looked black in the fluorescent light.

"Do you want me to pass that message along to Shark?" he said.

"No," she said. "That's fine. I'll probably see him at the funeral."

"My condolences," he said. The words were devoid of feeling.

"Thanks," she said, and she pushed out the door.

Halfway through the lot, she turned her head and looked back.

Stuart Kicking Bird was watching her.

CHAPTER

49

Ethan
21 hours, 15 minutes remaining

T HEY WERE STANDING in the cemetery, a half circle around the casket, the wind whipping against them, when the police cars pulled up the gravel drive. The first car was unmarked, a black sedan similar to the one Brian Hughes had used to follow him. The two behind it were black and whites.

Ethan watched as Calvin Taylor stepped out of the first and was joined by four uniformed officers. They didn't approach. They had enough respect for that.

Shark stood across the hole from Ethan, his harem clustered around him. Shark was glaring at him with an expression that said, *They're here because of you, you asshole.*

"There is a picture of you in there," Ethan's mom said, gesturing to the casket. "I put it in this morning. I may be angry, Ethan, but I know how much Abby loved you."

"Thank you," he said, then added, "How did everything look in there?"

"Very nice," she said.

The cemetery was a bleak sight. The grass was brown with winter. The other grave markers were gray and gothic. A leafless tree stretched over the congregation, its skeletal limbs twisting and whining in the wind. The minister made a few perfunctory remarks. He seemed to recognize that everyone was miserable in the cold.

The casket began to lower.

Ethan kept his eyes on Shark. The corners of Shark's mouth curved upward, as if he couldn't help himself.

You probably wouldn't be smiling like that, Ethan thought, *if you knew where your money was.*

Ethan's mom squeezed his arm. "Would you like to come back to the house?"

"Sure," he said.

He knew he couldn't spend any time with her, but yesterday his mom wouldn't even speak to him. It was important that he make an effort. He could at least ride back to her house and have Whitney pick him up there.

If Taylor didn't arrest him, that was.

People started to leave. Ethan spotted Shark waiting for him next to a tree.

"Give me a minute, Mom," Ethan said. "I'll meet you in the car."

"Nice speech," Shark said when he approached.

"Somehow the words 'fuck you' don't seem strong enough."

Both of them glanced over at the police. Taylor and his entourage were hanging back for now. They knew Ethan wasn't going anywhere.

Shark's grin disappeared and he stared at Ethan, deadly serious.

"I want my money."

"I want to know what happened to my sister."

"I don't know how many times I have to tell you this, Ethan. I didn't kill your goddamn sister."

"Bullshit."

Shark stepped forward and got into Ethan's face. Ethan was taller, but everything Shark had done stood there with him and Ethan felt outmatched.

"You are in no position to negotiate," Shark said, his words almost a snarl. "The only deal is this: you give me the money and you go back to prison alive. You might not go back with all your fingers, but I'll let you go back alive."

"If you kill me," Ethan said, "you'll never get it. No one knows where it is but me. And it's a lot of money, Shark. I looked. I don't think you want to lose that."

"I don't have to kill you, Ethan. There are other people I can hurt." Shark tilted his head toward the cemetery, and Ethan followed his gaze to his mother opening her car door.

Ethan grabbed Shark and shoved him against the tree.

"You hurt her, you son of a bitch, and your whole goddamn world will burn."

"Won't you be in prison?"

"I'll get out eventually," Ethan snarled. "I will find you. I will tear down everything you built. And then I'll kill you. What you did to Anton will look like a fucking massage compared to what I do to you."

Shark laughed—Ethan's rage seemed to have no effect on him. Shark pushed Ethan's hands off him and straightened his suit.

"If that money isn't in my hands by the time you go back in, you won't be able to stop me from anything. Feels pretty helpless, doesn't it? To be locked up and unable to stop certain things from happening?"

Abby. Was that an admission?

Shark took a couple steps away and then turned back to Ethan. "You're playing a game you don't even know how to play, Ethan."

"I've got your money," Ethan said. "I think I'm doing okay so far."

"Five years ago," Shark said, "you walked into that casino with an empty gun. You're no threat to me."

"You waited until I was out of prison to try to kill Jack," Ethan said. "I'd say you have some respect for what I can do. You know your hit failed, right?"

"Doesn't matter. Your buddy is dead. You think cons are the only ones I got in my pocket?"

Ethan felt his insides clench.

"It costs more money to get a guard to do it. But now?" He winked at Ethan. "Definitely worth it."

Shark turned away but saw Taylor approaching and waited. Taylor was alone, but the other officers seemed to be ready to run forward if something happened.

"Looks like you might be going back to prison early, Ethan," Shark said, making no effort to hide the smugness in his voice.

"If he arrests me," Ethan said, "I won't be able to tell you where your money is."

Taylor was close now.

"Just the two people I want to talk to," Taylor said.

"You two know each other?" Shark asked, looking back and forth between Ethan and Taylor. "Very interesting."

"Ethan came by my office yesterday." The wind whipped Taylor's overcoat. "He wanted me to fill him in on his sister's case."

"You find my sister's killer yet?" Ethan said.

"No, did you?"

Taylor stared at him for a few seconds. He'd been friendly yesterday, but today he was all business.

Ethan still liked him.

"I'm not here about your sister," Taylor said. "I'm here to find out what happened at the Neptune last night."

Neither Ethan nor Shark responded.

"You were there," Taylor said, gesturing to Ethan, and then to Shark. "And so were two of your employees."

"What a coincidence," Shark said. "Which employees?"

"I think you know."

"I don't know what my employees do on their days off."

"In that case," Taylor said, fixing his eyes on Shark, "you may be excused." Ethan could tell Shark didn't want to leave. He wanted to hear what was said. Shark turned to Ethan. "Come see me before you go back, old friend. We still have some catching up to do." Then he faced Taylor. "And you, Calvin, you know the number for my lawyer. Next time you want to talk to me—use it."

When Shark was gone, Taylor said to Ethan, "I'd like you to come down to the station with me and answer a few questions."

"Are you arresting me?"

"If I have to."

Ethan looked over toward the place where his sister's casket had been lowered. Men were shoveling in dirt. He looked past it to the rows of grave markers and the fenced neighborhood that lay beyond. He could run, but he didn't see how he could get away. Not against Taylor's quartet of officers.

"Listen," Ethan said, trying to bring back the friendliness he and Taylor had used with each other the previous day, "my sister was just put in the ground. I'm about to go spend some time with my mom. This time tomorrow, I'll be back in prison. Why don't you drive down to Carson City and we'll have a long chat? I'll tell you everything you want to know."

"Let me guess," Taylor said. "If I bring you in right now, you'll lawyer up and you won't say a goddamn thing."

"You guessed it."

"And what if you don't return to prison?" Taylor said. "What if you go AWOL?"

"If I'm not back at prison by nine AM tomorrow," Ethan said, and then nodded toward Abby's grave, "they'll be lowering me down into the ground next to my sister."

"We're on the same side here, Ethan."

"You said you're not even looking into Abby's murder anymore."

"Maybe it's time to take another look."

"Won't that get you in trouble with the feds?" Ethan said, the friendliness gone.

"Technically, we're working together," Taylor said diplomatically.

"Well, technically Brian Hughes was screwing my sister before she died," Ethan said. "Did you know that?"

"Had a hunch."

"Are we done here?"

"Ethan," Taylor said, taking a let's-be-honest-with-each-other tone, "you're playing a dangerous game here."

"No one else seems to be willing to play it."

"I want to find your sister's killer," Taylor said. "But I have to do it by the book."

"Maybe that's the problem," Ethan said, and he walked away.

He waited for Taylor to call out to his men to arrest him, but Taylor said nothing.

As Ethan walked toward his mom's car, he called Daryl Maxwell.

"Hey," he said into the phone, "I think Jack is still in danger."

50

Ethan
20 hours, 59 minutes remaining

"WHAT DO YOU mean?" Daryl said.

"Someone's still going to try to kill him," Ethan said. "A guard maybe. Someone who can still get to him."

"That's ridiculous," Daryl said, but Ethan could hear the hesitation in his voice. Maybe it wasn't so ridiculous after all. Maybe this kind of thing did happen in prison.

Ethan walked toward his mother's car as he spoke. The wind whistled around him.

"I need you to do something—anything that will protect Jack," Ethan said. "Move some people around. Change the guard rotation. Whoever is supposed to be delivering his meals. It's got to be in his food, right? How else could they get to him and get away with it?"

"I'm a caseworker, Ethan. I don't have any say over what guard works where. Hell, I don't even know most of their names."

"Pull some strings," Ethan said, his voice getting louder and more agitated. "Call in some favors. Do something."

"Wait," Daryl said. "Slow down."

Ethan gave him time to think. He had reached the car and stood next to it. His mom looked at him through the window, and Ethan held up a finger to ask her to wait.

"What makes you think someone is going to try to kill him in solitary?"

"I was right last time, wasn't I? Trust me."

"You said it was a hunch."

"It is a hunch."

"No," Daryl said. "This is not a hunch. You *know* something. You're getting into some kind of trouble. Jesus, Ethan, we talked about this."

Ethan was quiet.

"You know I can revoke your furlough privileges with one phone call."

"Don't you do that," Ethan snapped.

The line was silent for a moment. Ethan had never talked to Daryl that way before. The two usually joked around. Ethan could practically hear Daryl coming to a realization—Ethan wasn't the likable, reformed guy he always seemed to be. For the first time, Daryl was probably understanding why Ethan was in prison.

Ethan had to change tack.

"Daryl," he said calmly, "I appreciate everything you've done for me. You know me. You know that I'm not out here doing anything bad. I was right the first time. If I'm right again and you don't do anything, you'll have to live with that guilt. I know most of the employees in that prison don't give a shit if we live or die, but you've got a conscience, Daryl. You wouldn't want anyone to die if you could have done something about it."

"Okay," Daryl said after a long pause. "I'll see what I can do."

"Thank you, Daryl."

"Don't hang up," Daryl said, and Ethan caught himself with his finger over the "End call" button. He had hoped to get off the phone before his caseworker could ask him any more questions about what he was up to.

"Listen to me for a second, Ethan. I was walking through the prison earlier, and I was thinking about you. You know what makes you different from all the guys in here?"

"I have a conscience too."

"Most of the people in here do," Daryl said. "There are some psychopaths, but most of them are like you. Regular people who've done bad things. And now they're stuck in a hard world to be good in. But the difference between them and you is that they're too stupid and self-destructive to change."

Even in the cold, Ethan felt a chill crawl up his back. Daryl was right. The inmates were good at blaming everyone else, but the truth was most of them were their own worst problems.

"The guys in here," Daryl said, "if you give them a chance—any chance—they're going to screw it up. You're different, Ethan. At least I thought you were. I don't know what you're doing out there—and I don't want to know—but before you get yourself deeper into whatever mess you're in, you need to think about what kind of person you are. Are you the Ethan I see, with some kind of normal future ahead of you? Or are you going to screw it up?"

Ethan knew Daryl was right, that he was jeopardizing his future—not to mention his life. But what Daryl didn't understand was that there are some things worth risking everything for.

For Ethan, finding Abby's killer was one of those things.

Maybe a regular person could let it go. Maybe your average law-abiding citizen would recognize that it wouldn't do any good.

But Ethan wasn't one of those people. He had to know, and he would do whatever it took. In that way, maybe he was more like the other cons than he had ever wanted to admit.

"Message received," Ethan said.

Daryl hung up.

Ethan reached for the passenger door and then stopped himself. He held up his finger for his mom to wait another minute. He called Whitney—she had programmed in her number—and paced in the cold while the phone rang.

"Hey," she said, her voice full of excitement.

"Where are you?"

"My place," she said. "I got it. I hope it's the right one."

"Any trouble?"

"No. Stu was there. He gave me this weird look, but I think we're safe."

Ethan didn't like the sound of that.

"I'm coming over there now," he said. "Get your stuff together so we can leave as soon as I make it."

He walked around to the driver's side of the car and opened the door.

"Sorry, Mom, I need to drive. And I'm not going to be able to come over to the house."

He had to get to Whitney as quickly as possible. Both of them needed to be gone from her apartment in case Kicking Bird came looking for them.

"Are you allowed to drive?" his mom said.

"No," he said, sliding into the seat, "but that's the least of my worries right now."

C H A P T E R

51

Whitney
20 hours, 48 minutes remaining

WHITNEY HAD CHANGED into jeans and a sweatshirt. She grabbed gloves and a coat out of her closet. She wished she had something that would fit Ethan: coat, gloves, hat—anything. They hadn't even thought to buy work gloves at Walmart. He'd be stuck with his jeans, sweatshirt, and leather jacket, which were folded in a pile on the couch next to the ironing board.

A knock rattled her door. She froze. It was too soon for Ethan to be back. She was on the tenth floor of the complex; solicitors never came and the neighbors all kept to themselves.

She lifted a couch cushion and tucked the ledger underneath, then stepped quietly to the door. She peeked through the spyhole. Bruce from the club stood in the hall.

She tiptoed away from the door and called Ethan.

Another knock.

"Bruce is here," she whispered into the phone. "He's at my door. Stu must have figured out I took the ledger."

"Does Bruce know you're there?"

"I don't think so."

"Be quiet and hide. Do not answer the door. I'll be there soon."

CHAPTER

52

Ethan
20 hours, 46 minutes remaining

ETHAN SPED THROUGH the streets toward the river and Whitney's apartment. The engine whined as he pressed on the gas and accelerated around a slow pickup truck.

"Ethan, what the hell is going on?" his mom said.

"We're going to Whitney's," he said. "She's in trouble."

"What have you done now?" she said, her voice full of anger. "What kind of trouble are—"

"Listen, Mom. I think Shark killed Abby. I'm going to find out for sure. Whitney's helping me."

"You need to leave this to the police," she said. "The FBI."

"They're all useless," Ethan said, swerving into oncoming traffic to get around another car, then yanking the wheel back as an oncoming van honked its horn. "You might think I'm crazy, but I need you to do me a favor."

She was quiet. One of her hands was gripping the armrest on the door, the other was pinned to the dashboard.

"I need you to go somewhere safe. Check into a hotel. Don't stay in your house tonight."

"I'm not staying in a hotel."

"Mom, goddamn it! Just until tomorrow."

CHAPTER

53

Whitney
20 hours, 44 minutes remaining

WHITNEY STOOD IN her bedroom, trying to control her breathing. She listened. She could hear her refrigerator's motor and the familiar clatter of her hot water heater. But she heard nothing from the hallway.

When she'd hung up with Ethan, Bruce had called through the door: "Whitney," he said, trying not to sound like the douchebag she'd always known him to be. "This will go a lot easier on you if you just give the book back. You know I always liked you. I won't let anything happen to you."

But since then, there'd been no other sound. Had Bruce left? He must have.

She snuck back over toward the door, moving slowly, making sure her bare feet didn't bump into anything. She looked through the spyhole.

He was still there. She expected him to raise his hand and knock again, but instead he was backing up. She realized what he was doing a moment too late.

He charged the door like a battering ram.

CHAPTER

54

Ethan
20 hours, 42 minutes remaining

H E PULLED ONTO Whitney's street and skidded to a halt in front of the building.

"One more thing," he said.

"What?"

"Don't call the police. Give me until tomorrow morning. I'll be back in prison, and if you want to report all this, you can do it then."

She stared at him, her lips pursed, her face pale with fear.

He didn't wait for her to answer. He leaned over and kissed her cheek, then jumped out of the car and ran to the building's outer door.

It was locked.

Ethan ran around the side of the building to the parking garage gate. He typed in the code he'd seen Whitney use, and the metal door started to lift. He ran, rolled under the gap, and sprinted to the elevator. He punched the "Up" arrow and waited. He thought about taking the stairs, but it was ten flights. The elevator would be quicker.

Even if he had to wait.

"Come on," he said, and balled his fist, pounding it against the metal door.

CHAPTER

55

Whitney
20 hours, 40 minutes remaining

WHITNEY LAY ON her carpet, blinking her eyes, trying to orient herself. The door had crashed into her, colliding with her forehead and knocking her back against the wall. She felt like she'd lost a few seconds, maybe longer. Bruce was wrestling with the door, trying to get it out of the way. He turned it sideways and threw it out into the hallway.

Whitney put her hand to her forehead and pulled it away. Her palm was wet with blood.

"Oh my God," she said, trying to crawl away.

Bruce grabbed her by the hair and dragged her into the apartment. She let out a scream, and he smacked her in the face.

She crumpled to the floor. Her forehead throbbed. Her lip—now broken and bleeding—screamed at her. She couldn't think straight. She was moving in slow motion while Bruce walked around her at regular speed. He leaned over her, shouted questions, but she couldn't understand what he was saying. All of her attention was taken by the pain.

Bruce surveyed the apartment as if he was looking for a place to rent. Something caught his attention, and he walked over to the ironing board. He leaned down, grabbed the cord of the iron, and plugged it into the outlet.

Whitney tried to crawl backward into the kitchen, but Bruce grabbed her by the hair again. She clawed at his hands, pounded on his legs, but the blows had no effect. He flung her like she weighed nothing, and she rolled onto the floor next to the ironing board.

He pinned her down with one arm and reached up to grab the iron with the other.

"Tell me where your boyfriend is," he said, "or I'm going to burn your pretty face off."

56

Ethan
20 hours, 39 minutes remaining

ETHAN HEARD HER screaming before the elevator door opened. He ran down the hall, saw the door agape, and threw himself inside.

Whitney was lying on the floor, and Bruce was crouched over her. He held her iron inches from her face. She was clawing at him and pushing him, but she might as well have been fighting a bear.

Ethan vaulted himself over the couch. Bruce looked up in time for Ethan to drive his right fist into the big man's face. A shockwave of pain ran up Ethan's arm from his fist to his elbow. Bruce's nose crunched with a noise much like his brother's had the night before—and he tumbled backward off Whitney and crashed against the ironing board. The iron fell onto the carpet.

The pain in Ethan's hand was ferocious. He unfurled his fist, and fresh bolts tore through his arm all the way to his shoulder.

Whitney rolled over. She was sobbing. Ethan helped her to her feet with his non-demolished hand.

"Are you okay?"

She didn't respond. There was a gash in her forehead and her lip was bleeding, but she didn't look burned.

Bruce rose onto one knee. Blood gushed from both nostrils. Water streamed from his eye sockets.

"Get back," Ethan said to Whitney, and this time she seemed to hear him.

He shouldn't have been surprised by the lineman's speed—Wayne had been fast too—but he was. Bruce wrapped his arms around Ethan, lifted him, and drove him down into Whitney's coffee table. The glass shattered, and the frame gave way. Bruce came down on top of Ethan. The air was forced from his lungs.

Bruce straddled him like a schoolyard bully and began throwing punches at his face. Ethan flailed his arms and was able to divert most of the blows, but a few came through, each sending a thunderclap of pain through Ethan's skull.

"My brother's in the fucking hospital!"

Ethan lurched upward, grabbing for Bruce's throat with his good hand like he was trying to choke him. The big guy leaned back, as Ethan intended. He threw his leg up and got his calf around Bruce's neck. He flexed and straightened his powerful leg, yanking the big man backward. Bruce rolled away.

Ethan jumped to his feet. The iron was facedown on the carpet. Smoke rose from its metal edges. The cord was still plugged in. Ethan snatched it up with his left hand. Bruce was up on his knees, and Ethan hit him with the hot face of the iron. The metal hissed against his skin. He recoiled from the burn and fell onto his back. Ethan pounced, the iron above his head.

"No!" Bruce yelled.

Ethan brought the iron down like a knife, jamming the pointed side into the socket of Bruce's one good eye. The socket sizzled.

Bruce began to shriek, his body shuddering and convulsing, but Ethan pushed down harder. It wasn't until he smelled burnt flesh that he realized what he was doing. He pulled the iron away. Bruce's skin stuck to it like pizza cheese.

The man rolled and shrieked, holding both hands to his face. The screams were earsplitting, and Ethan knew he had to shut him up. He slammed the metal iron into Bruce's skull as hard as he could.

Bruce collapsed, limp, on the carpet. He lay unmoving, like a bear in hibernation.

Ethan oriented himself. Whitney was standing at the threshold between the living room and the kitchen, her hands up to her face in horror.

"Is he dead?" she said.

Ethan looked closely. Bruce had a goatee of blood coming from his nose. His right eye—the one that was already blind—was open, and the clouded iris stared out. The other socket was red and swelling, the lids melted open like they were made of wax, the eye behind them soupy like undercooked egg white.

Bruce's chest rose with an inhalation.

"He's alive," Ethan said, "but he'll never see again."

The air stunk—burnt flesh and burnt eyeball—and Whitney seemed to notice it at the same time Ethan did. She began making a retching sound.

CHAPTER

57

Ethan
20 hours, 36 minutes remaining

E THAN DROPPED THE iron. It fell on its side next to the burnt triangle in the carpet where he had retrieved it. He yanked the cord out of the socket with a spark.

"Is everything okay in here?"

A man stood at the door, a twenty-something guy in a plaid shirt and black-rimmed glasses. His skin went pale as he took in what he saw.

"Call nine-one-one," Ethan said.

The guy didn't move.

"Hey!" Ethan shouted, and this shook the guy from his trance. "Call nine-one-one!" The guy reached into his pocket for his phone, and Ethan added, "Go back to your apartment until they get here."

Ethan went to Whitney. He held her face in his hands and examined her eyes. Her pupils weren't dilated. She grabbed him around the neck and held onto him tightly. Her whole body shook.

"Whitney," he said, as calmly as he could manage, "I have to go. You stay here. Get medical attention. Go ahead and tell the police what happened. I'm sorry. I'm sorry about everything."

She pulled away and looked him in the eyes.

"I'm coming with you," she said.

He thought about arguing, but they didn't have time for that.

"We're leaving in one minute," he said. "Grab anything you need. Clothes. Phone. Coat."

Ethan rolled Bruce onto his side so the blood wouldn't run down his throat and choke him. He felt a lump in Bruce's jacket pocket and pulled out the big guy's cell phone. He pocketed it.

Whitney—who seemed to be thinking straight now—grabbed the ledger from under the couch cushion. She shoved it and Ethan's clothes into her gym bag. She ran into the bathroom, and when she returned she had her first-aid kit and the bag of pills they'd taken from Abby's neighbor. Then they were out the door.

The neighbor who was calling 911 peeked out from a crack in his door. As they waited for the elevator, Ethan said to Whitney, "Do everything I tell you and I'll let you live, you bitch."

When the elevator doors closed, he said, "Sorry. Now there's a witness who heard me threaten you. You'll be able to tell the cops I kidnapped you."

"I would never do that," she said.

"You might have to."

*   *   *

Ethan drove without knowing where to go. His suit jacket had ripped down the center of his back, and his pants seam had split at his buttocks. His face throbbed from where Bruce had hit him, and his right hand was already starting to swell. He was more worried about Whitney than he was about himself, though. They needed a place to go to collect themselves. A gas station bathroom. A rest stop. Something.

He did a U-turn.

"Where are you going?"

"We need a place to regroup," he said.

"Yeah, but where's that?"

"Somewhere no one will think to look for us."

He drove to Abby's apartment.

58

Jack
20 hours, 3 minutes remaining

JACK LAY ON his bunk, flipping through an old copy of *Range* magazine. Down the hall, he heard a guard rolling in the lunch cart through the cell block. It took a while, Jack knew, for the cart to make its way down the hall. He was hungry. He'd hardly touched his breakfast. He'd grown accustomed to prison food over the years, but breakfast was the grossest meal of the day. Lunch usually wasn't too bad, although still a far cry from the venison steaks, beef raised on his parents' ranch, and home-cooked vegetables he'd grown up with.

The cells in solitary weren't much different from those in general population. Here there was no bunk bed, but otherwise everything was the same: metal toilet, metal mirror, metal sink. The same taupe paint on the cinderblock walls.

There were two major differences, though. One was that solitary was quieter. He was in a corridor lined with other cells, but the hall was separated from the rest of the facility. Besides the occasional sound of someone coughing or blowing his nose or shooting a jet of urine into the toilet, the corridor was relatively quiet.

The other difference was that you didn't get to leave but for about forty-five minutes a day, stretching your legs in a secluded little courtyard.

It could be tedious and claustrophobic, but Jack didn't mind. In his previous prison, he'd spent a lot of time in solitary. Every time someone tried to kill him, the prison officials would place him away from the other inmates for a few weeks for his own protection. If it wasn't for the limited time outside, he would prefer it to being back with the rest of the inmates. At least while Ethan was gone. The only real problem was that being alone, without a cellmate to talk to or the noise and distraction of the general population, meant there was nothing to keep his thoughts from drifting to why he was in here. What had happened to his brother. What he'd done.

He'd been young and stupid. He thought shooting a person wouldn't be much different from shooting a deer or an elk. But that hadn't been the case. Shooting a person was its own thing—far worse than he'd ever imagined.

The guard pushing the cart arrived at Jack's cell, accompanied by another with one hand on a submachine gun strapped to his chest. Jack swung his feet down off the bunk to receive his lunch.

"How you doing today?" the guard pushing the cart said.

"Can't complain," Jack said.

Jack didn't recognize the guard. He was a young guy with a high-and-tight buzzed haircut. Ex-military, Jack figured. He'd been in the army himself. He could spot the type. The other guy, the one watching to make sure inmates didn't make any moves during the food transfer, was a longtime regular in the solitary hallway.

The guard opened the hinged slot, which was big enough to slide in the tray.

"Wait!"

Jack and the two guards both looked down the hallway. Daryl Maxwell was shuffling down the corridor, holding a paper bag in one hand and his arm up with the other.

"Hang on," he said, approaching. "I need to talk to this one. He's going to have lunch in my office."

Daryl held up the bag, and Jack saw the Cracker Barrel name and logo on the paper. He couldn't help but grin—what the hell was Ethan up to now?

The guard delivering the food had a perturbed look on his face. Prison guards liked to do things by the book, and this wasn't by the book.

"Don't worry," Daryl said, clapping the guy on the back. "You get a paycheck whether this guy eats your food or not."

Daryl fixed him with his eyes, and the guard seemed to flush. There was a subtext in Daryl's words, and Jack could read it as clearly as the guard could.

Jack's smile faded.

He removed his hands from the lunch tray and said to the guard, "I'll take the Cracker Barrel, thank you very much."

CHAPTER

59

Ethan
19 hours, 47 minutes remaining

E THAN PARKED THE car in the visitors' lot of his sister's townhome complex.
It didn't look like the spying neighbor was home, but Ethan made sure all
the blinds in Abby's apartment were closed anyway. He took Whitney by the
hand and led her to the bathroom, taking a wide arc around the stain.

He found a washcloth under the sink and held it under warm water. He
dabbed the blood off her forehead. He had her lean her head back over the sink
so he could pour peroxide on the cut. A large lump was growing on her forehead, as if someone had taken a golf ball, split it in two, and slid one half under
her skin. Her bottom lip was swollen as well.

He kissed her forehead.

"All better," she said, but her eyes were overflowing with tears.

What had happened was a lot for Ethan to handle, let alone for someone
like Whitney, who had never seen violence like that.

She helped him redress the cut on his hand, reopened in the fight, but the
cut was the least of his worries. His right hand was swollen badly. The veins and
tendons had disappeared underneath a mound of puffy flesh.

"Is it broken?" Whitney asked.

Ethan tried to make a fist and winced.

"Something in there must be," he said. "It's got to be more than a sprain."

* * *

Whitney sat at Abby's kitchen table. Ethan filled up glasses of water for both of them, then had to carry them one by one to the table, to avoid trying to use his broken hand. He opened Abby's freezer and, just as Brian Hughes had done last night, found a bag of vegetables and carried it over to the table. He laid his hand on the surface, palm down, and balanced the frozen vegetables on top. Whitney rummaged around in the sack of medication she'd taken from the neighbor, and she popped a pill into her mouth and offered one to Ethan.

"No thanks," he said, and added, grinning, "that would violate the conditions of my release."

She let out a clipped laugh. "*That* would violate the conditions?"

He started counting with his fingers. "As long as I don't take drugs or leave the state, they might still take it easy on me."

Whitney laughed, and he laughed too. They weren't laughing at his joke so much as the ridiculousness of their situation. It was gallows humor—in the face of what they were up against, what else could they do but laugh?

Whitney's laugh went away.

"What?" he asked.

"I've got bad news," she said. "I don't think I got the right ledger."

Ethan put Shark's ledger and Bruce's cell phone on the table. Stuffed in the back of the ledger were a bunch of old keno receipts, which Whitney pulled out and spread on the table. There were a few folded envelopes, but inside them were only more keno receipts. One of the envelopes had the word *SHARK* written on the outside, but otherwise none of the receipts or envelopes contained any writing. The only writing was the numbers in the ledger. Whitney turned to the front pages and showed Ethan how each entry in the journal was just a string of numerals, spaced out in one- or two-digit increments, from 1 to 80, just like the number range of a keno card.

"These are just keno numbers," Whitney explained. "For some reason, he keeps track of the numbers he plays."

Ethan clenched his jaw.

"Blake," Ethan said. "That son of a bitch told me there was no code."

"You think that's what this is?"

"Who keeps track of the keno numbers they play?" Ethan said. "There's no way Shark would do that unless it was hiding something else."

The entries were written in at least four different styles of handwriting, each distinct. Ethan assumed the handwriting depended on who disposed of the body that day.

They were quiet for a few seconds. Ethan was thinking.

"Do you know where Blake lives?"

He would have to find Blake and beat it out of him.

"An apartment in Sparks, I think," she said. "But I've never been there."

That left Shark and Kicking Bird who probably knew the code. Cal might know, but he doubted it. And if Ethan walked into Dark Secrets, he'd probably leave wrapped in plastic.

Something nagged at Ethan's brain.

He snatched up his cell phone to dial Daryl Maxwell. He hesitated. There was no way—given how their last conversation had gone—that Daryl would help him anymore. He thought for a moment, then pulled out the number for Brian Hughes.

Hughes picked up right away.

"I need a favor," Ethan said.

60

Daryl
19 hours, 14 minutes remaining

DARYL SAT IN his office, with Jack Fisher sitting across from him, devouring his Cracker Barrel meal. Daryl's nerves were shaken. If he was right about what had just been about to happen, one of the guards in the prison had been about to poison an inmate. Daryl had somehow gotten caught up in something with Ethan Lockhart, and he didn't like it. He needed to make some phone calls, starting with the warden. He had to get Ethan's furlough revoked and get the police involved in whatever was going on.

A second after having this thought, his intercom buzzed, and Valerie, the prison switchboard operator, said, "Daryl, there's a Brian Hughes from the FBI on line two for you."

"FBI?" Daryl said.

"Yes, sir. He says it's urgent."

"Hello?" Daryl said, picking up.

"Daryl," said the voice on the other end of the line. "I just sent you an email. Would you mind opening it?"

"What the hell is going on?" Daryl asked.

"This will go a lot quicker if you just take a look."

The voice sounded young, confident. Daryl had no idea if the man was who he said he was, but his computer was right in front of him, so he opened his inbox. Sure enough, there was a message from someone named Brian Hughes with a dot-gov account. He clicked on it. The message was empty except for a photo attachment.

"Go ahead and open the picture," Hughes said. "Don't worry. It's not a virus."

Daryl glanced up at Jack, who was ignoring him completely. He looked like a guy who hadn't had a decent meal in years—probably because he hadn't.

Daryl clicked on the attachment, and a picture appeared on his screen of four men on a golf course.

"I'm assuming you recognize three of those men," Hughes said.

Daryl did. One was his boss, the warden. Another was the Nevada attorney general. The third was the governor.

The only one he didn't recognize was a young, handsome man, smiling broadly. On his head, instead of a typical golf visor, was a black ball cap with an American flag on the crown.

"I know people in high places," the voice on the other end said. "I need a favor. Help me out, and I'll pay you back someday. Refuse, and I'll make your life a living hell. Understand?"

Daryl's mouth was dry.

"What do you need?" he croaked.

"I'm going to patch Ethan Lockhart in on our call."

61

Ethan
19 hours, 7 minutes remaining

"I GOT YOUR BUDDY sitting in my office again," Daryl said when Ethan came on the line. "This is beginning to be a regular thing."

"Is he okay?"

"I think you were right," Daryl said. "Again."

"What makes you say that?"

"The look on the guard's face when I showed up with takeout," Daryl said. "There might have been a little something extra in your buddy's lunch. I could be wrong, but I've got a hunch."

"It's good to trust your hunches," Ethan said.

He was surprised how nonchalant Daryl was about this—he'd just learned, or at least suspected, that one of the guards at the prison had tried to assassinate a prisoner for money. But maybe he was putting on a show for Hughes's benefit, who was listening on the line without interfering.

Ethan asked if he could talk to Jack.

"How you doing, man?"

"Stuffed," Jack said. "Your boy Daryl hooked me up."

Ethan laughed. It felt good. Like he and Jack were sitting in their cell, joking back and forth during a simpler time.

The moment was short-lived.

"There's an FBI agent on the line," Ethan said. "But this is off the record. You can say what you need to say."

"All right," Jack said, although he sounded skeptical.

"So the guy causing the distraction yesterday, Miguel. You know who I'm talking about?"

"Yeah, worked for your old boss," Jack said.

"Remember he said something like we were in the keno club together?"

"Rings a bell," Jack said. "Neither of us could figure out what the hell he meant by that."

Ethan hesitated. Should he really be saying this when Hughes could hear? He didn't have a choice.

"We stole a ledger from Shark, but we can't read it. It's coded to look like keno numbers."

"Okay."

"Shark didn't use it back when I worked for him, but I think Miguel didn't realize that. He thought I'd know what he meant. I need someone to tell me how to read the code."

"I'm reading you," Jack said.

Ethan felt relieved. He didn't have to say anything—Jack knew what he was asking for.

"I'm sorry," Ethan said.

"I'll give it my best shot," Jack said. "But you're going to have to convince your caseworker buddy here to send me back out into general."

Ethan pictured them in Daryl's office: Jack gesturing to Daryl as he said this, Daryl's face screwed up in confusion.

Daryl came back on the line.

"What's this?" he said. "First you want me to take him out of general population. Now you want me to put him back in. He's safer in solitary, Ethan. All he has to do is not eat the food. I can bring him his meals."

"It's not that," Ethan said. "I need some information, and the only way I can get it is for Jack to go back in."

Daryl was quiet. He was putting everything together in his head. Despite Daryl's chumminess, he was still a prison official and Ethan was an inmate. Ethan shouldn't be asking this type of favor from him.

"What information do you need?"

"Daryl, the less you know, the better, don't you think?"

Daryl snapped. "Hell yes, the less I know the better. I already know too much. I know you're in direct violation of your furlough, out there getting involved in who knows what. I ought to revoke your release right now. One phone call and I bring you back in. Give me one reason why I shouldn't."

Ethan didn't answer. Hughes did.

"I already gave you the reason," he said.

"Jesus Christ," Daryl said. 'I'm going to be sick."

"I'm going to find my sister's killer, Daryl," Ethan said. "No one else is going to figure this out. I have to do it."

"And you're okay with this?" Daryl said, and they all knew he was directing his comments to Hughes.

"I am. And so are you."

"Daryl," Ethan said, "you've always been good to me, and I appreciate it. But I need to do this. I have to. You've got to let Jack out into the general population."

"Jesus Christ."

The problem with Daryl was that he was a good guy. Prison wasn't a place for good guys, not even the employees. Most guards and caseworkers were bribable. Some took money regularly, others just once in a while.

But there were anomalies, and Daryl was one.

"All right," Daryl said. "Jack's got one hour. Then I'm going to let him call you one last time. After that, I'm going home. I'm turning my goddamn phone off for the rest of the day. I don't want any more to do with whatever the hell is going on."

"Thank you," Ethan said, genuinely grateful. He knew he had placed a difficult choice in front of a man who would rather the world be black and white.

"I'll be here tomorrow morning when you come back to prison—and you better be here," Daryl said.

"I'll be there."

"I'll help get you processed," Daryl said. "Then I'm transferring you to another caseworker. I don't want to work with you anymore."

This stung. There weren't many people in the world who believed in Ethan, and Daryl had been one of them. Had.

"I'm sorry I put you in this position," Ethan said.

"Save it," Daryl said, his voice heavy with disgust.

Before he could hang up, Hughes said, "Oh, and Daryl?"

"Yeah?"

"I was never on this phone call," he said. "Got it?"

"The sooner I forget you, the better," Daryl said, and hung up.

When he was gone, Hughes said to Ethan, "That worked out well. We make a good team, don't we?"

"Go to hell," Ethan said, and he hung up too.

Hughes was using him—he would use Hughes. But they sure as hell weren't friends.

Ethan looked at Whitney, who was watching him with an anxious expression.

"Now what?" she said.

"We wait."

CHAPTER

62

Jack
18 hours, 40 minutes remaining

JACK APPROACHED THE entryway to the plate factory. He recognized the guard, a thirty-something guy with red hair and a spattering of freckles. Despite his age, he looked like he hadn't started shaving yet. He was known for bringing in drugs for prisoners. For a steep price.

Jack and Ethan had no use for a guy like him, and he had no use for them. So they were never on his good side or bad side. But he had always been friendly to Ethan. He recognized an alpha when he saw one.

The guard—Snyder was his name—nodded to Jack as he approached.

"Heard you had a close call this morning," he said.

"Not that close," Jack said, trying to sound tough.

He didn't normally subscribe to the bullshit macho code prisoners went by, but there were times when you had to act the part.

"I need a favor," Jack said.

"Don't do favors."

"It's for Lockhart. He's good for it."

Snyder considered this. Jack and Ethan weren't the type of prisoners who normally needed favors, or owed them. He could tell the guard was wondering what benefit there might be for having such an owed favor sitting in his pocket.

"What do you need?"

Jack nodded toward the door of the plate factory. "Any other guards inside?"

"One."

"Can you get him to come out here?" Jack said. "Then if you hear some commotion, y'all take your time getting in there to see what the fuss is about."

Guards got this kind of entreaty from time to time—that's how most hits happened—but usually there was a big price tag assigned to it. Not a promise.

And someone like Jack, who kept to himself, wasn't the kind of person who usually made this kind of request.

"This some kind of payback for this morning?" the guard asked.

"Something like that."

The guard shook his head. "You're asking too much. Not offering enough in return."

"I ain't gonna kill him," Jack said. "I need to ask a question is all."

"I don't need any attention on me," Snyder said.

"What do you want?" Jack said.

Jack feared for a moment that the guard would ask for a blowjob.

"Got someone in Block A who owes me money," Snyder explained. "Said his sister was gonna pay me, but she hasn't yet. Next time she comes to visit, I need her to see him not looking so good. Some bruises. Maybe a couple broken fingers."

Jack had heard Ethan talk about his life before prison, the things he'd done. Ethan wouldn't want to go back to that kind of lifestyle. But Jack also knew how badly Ethan needed the information he was asking for. Ethan would consent to Jack making the deal, even though Ethan would probably never follow through on it.

"Lockhart will take care of it," Jack said.

"He better," the guard said. "Or it will come out of *your* ass."

With that, the guard ducked inside the doorway and called out to the other guard.

"Come here for a second," he said. "Got a question for you."

A few seconds later, the guard stepped out. A young guy. Green. He would do whatever Snyder asked him to.

"Make it quick," Snyder said to Jack.

Jack hesitated at the threshold. This was the first time since he was arrested that he was entering a situation with the intention to commit violence. He had defended himself numerous times, but that had been instinct kicking in. Even when he was at his lowest, hating himself for what he'd done, wishing he was dead, he still fought back when someone tried to kill him.

But this time he was starting a fight.

And even though Ethan was the only person in the prison he cared about—and who cared about him—he resented his friend for asking this of him. He wasn't sure things would be able to go back to normal when Ethan returned.

But he stepped through the doorway anyway.

63

Ethan
18 hours, 39 minutes remaining

"I'M GOING TO change my clothes," Ethan told Whitney.

Back in the bathroom, he pulled off his suit jacket and dress shirt. His only T-shirt was damp with sweat. He went downstairs to the garage and rummaged through his box of clothes. He found boxers, socks, and a T-shirt, and he put them all on in the cold garage. He put on a different pair of jeans, found a thick sweatshirt that fit him tightly. He tossed his ruined suit back into the box it had come from. Somehow in his melee with Bruce, the glass display on his watch had been smashed and the numbers were reading nonsense, so he tossed that in with the clothes.

As he was climbing back up the stairs, he heard Whitney call to him. "The phone's buzzing."

"Go ahead and get it," he said, picking up his pace.

"Not yours," she said. "Bruce's."

She held the phone up and pointed the screen at him as he approached. The display said simply "BOSS."

Ethan snatched it and answered.

"Yeah."

There was a pause, then Shark said, "Ethan?"

"You said I'm not a threat to you?" Ethan said. "Once you take a look at the latest lackey I've taken out, you might think differently about that."

Another long pause. "This is a cell phone, Ethan. You might be careful what you say."

Ethan answered, "I'm talking about your fantasy football roster, Shark."

"Fantasy football?"

"Yeah," Ethan said. "You've got another offensive lineman on injured reserve. That's two down. There's not much protection left for your quarterback."

Shark laughed into the receiver, a deep hearty laugh that struck Ethan as a little false. *I am getting to him,* Ethan thought.

"I'm not scared, Ethan. My defensive back is the one you need to worry about. That guy'll cut your offense to pieces."

Shark hung up.

"What did he say?" Whitney asked.

"He said Stuart Kicking Bird is going to cut my fingers off," Ethan said. "Or kill me. He wasn't clear which."

CHAPTER

64

Jack
18 hours, 38 minutes remaining

INSIDE THE PLATE factory, fifteen or so men worked at various stations. A machine that looked like a small newspaper press spooled huge rolls of aluminum through its wheels, printing *NEVADA* over and over atop an illustration of mountains. Another station cut the aluminum sheets. Another embossed the numbers and letters. Finally, the plates rolled down a conveyer belt to a man stacking them onto a cart, where another man took them in pairs and slid them into paper sleeves.

That last person was Miguel, the toothless kid from the yard. The guy in the keno club.

Jack looked around, thinking of what to do. His hands were shaking. He knew he needed to get this over with before his nerves were fried and he couldn't go through with it. And the clock was ticking—the guards wouldn't wait outside forever.

He studied the machine that cut the plates. The operator moved a large sheet of aluminum into place then reached up with both hands to press two buttons. A heavy boom lowered and, with a loud *thwack*, blades the size of two-by-fours came down and snapped through the sheet to make the individual license plates.

The blades could cut through a human hand like a machete through a stick of butter, but the machine was set up so you needed both hands to lower the blades. The operator could never have one hand on the plate when triggering the cut.

Jack wanted to turn around and walk out, tell Snyder to forget it. Yeah, Ethan's investigation would stall without his help, but that might be the best thing for him. If Ethan kept going, he was liable to end up dead. Or screw up so bad that he'd never get parole. Jack might be doing him a favor to walk away.

But he had given Ethan his word. Where he came from, that meant something.

He stepped forward, approaching the Mexican kid from behind. The room was noisy enough that the kid wouldn't hear him approach. Jack reached beside the kid onto the cart of license plates and picked up a stack of them. He was surprised by the weight. He lifted the brick of plates over his head, squeezing to give them the mass of a single object. Only then did Miguel look up. His eyes went wide.

Smash his face, Jack told himself. *Don't hesitate. Don't hesitate!*

But he was hesitating.

The kid jumped to his feet. He held a license plate in his hand and swung it toward Jack like it was a knife. Jack brought the stack of plates down on the slashing hand. All of the plates—the one in the kid's hand and the stack Jack was holding—spilled across the floor, clattering loudly.

The kid backed up, getting into a fighting stance. His posture looked like a knife fighter, but his hands were empty. Jack brought his arms up, trying to remember what he learned from a one-day boxing lesson in basic training. He'd blown his surprise, and now there was no telling what would happen.

The rest of the inmates had stopped what they were doing and turned their attention to Jack. No one attempted to intervene. The guards did not return. But Jack didn't have long.

Miguel smiled, showing the gap in his teeth.

"This is too good, amigo," he said. "You giving me a second chance for my payday."

Jack thought of how close he'd come to being killed yesterday, and anger surged through him. He charged forward, swinging his left fist in a wide arc toward the kid's ribs. The kid was fast and moved his arms to block the incoming blow. But Jack's left had been a feint. The real attack came next, a driving right aimed at the center of the kid's head. The kid saw it coming and froze like a deer in front of a pickup's headlights.

Jack's fist smashed into the kid's face, a solid, electrifying hit that filled Jack with a sickening sense of satisfaction. The kid dropped onto his butt and then rolled backward, blinking back tears. Jack didn't give him time to recover. He grabbed the kid's wrist, twisted it in a way he'd learned in the military, and forced Miguel to crawl toward the big cutting machine. When Miguel resisted, Jack gave the hand a twist. The kid inhaled sharply. Jack slammed him against the cutting machine.

"No," the kid gasped, knowing what Jack was trying to do.

Jack shoved his head into the space where the aluminum sheets rested. If the blade came down now, it would cut the kid's head off at the neck, and transform his skull into the dimensions of a license plate.

"It will take me a fraction of a second to get my hands to the buttons," Jack growled, his voice hoarse. "Faster than you can pull your head out."

This was true. As soon as Jack let go, the kid could start backing out, but with Jack's body leaning against his, he had no leverage. He might get far enough that only the top few inches of his skull would come off. But if Jack wanted to kill him, he could—that was clear to both of them.

Jack had entered the room intending only to bluff the kid. But he was in a rage now. If the kid refused him, Jack would go through with it.

"Please, man, please. I'm sorry."

"Shark's ledger," Jack said, his teeth clenched. "What's the code?"

"What?"

"Don't play stupid," Jack roared. He didn't recognize his own voice. He didn't like the person saying the words. "Tell me the code to Shark's ledger or you die. Simple as that. You're not the first person I've killed. Don't think I won't do it."

Miguel hesitated, and Jack released a little pressure from his wrist. He meant this to give the impression that he was about to reach for the buttons.

It worked.

"Okay, okay," the kid screamed. "I'll tell you."

It took only a few seconds to explain the code. When he was finished, Jack yanked him out and shoved him across the floor. His foot slipped on some of the fallen plates, and he stumbled, tried to stand, slipped again, and crawled away. He looked back at Jack when he thought he was at a safe distance. His cheek was starting to swell where Jack had hit him. But he looked relieved, glad to accept his injury in lieu of what had almost happened.

Jack walked away without a word. As he exited the factory door, the guard, Snyder, looked up and said, "Inmate, is something happening in there?"

He said the words in a rehearsed tone of pretense. He knew damn well something had happened in there. But if there were any questions later, he wouldn't have to lie about what was said, and the younger guard could back him up.

"I think somebody tripped," Jack said, and kept on walking.

When he rounded the corner, out of sight of anyone from the factory, he dropped to his hands and knees and vomited up all the Cracker Barrel he'd eaten for lunch.

CHAPTER

65

Ethan
18 hours, 3 minutes remaining

Ethan checked the time. Daryl had told him an hour, but he expected it to take longer than that. His phone buzzed, but it was Hughes, and Ethan ignored it.

"How are you feeling?" he said to Whitney.

"I'm feeling all right," she said, and she shook a bottle of pills. "These things aren't nearly as fun when you're actually in pain."

"I'm sorry I got you involved in this," Ethan said.

"I'm the one who should be sorry," Whitney said. "When your sister told me she wanted to get a job at Shark's club, I should have done everything in my power to talk her out of it."

"You and I both know that no one could talk Abby out of something when she made up her mind."

They heard a phone buzz. He was relieved to see it was his burner, not Shark calling again.

"Daryl," he said when he answered. "That was fast."

"Not Daryl. Jack." His voice was cold, distant, thicker somehow.

"Hey, man, what happened? You okay?"

"I got the information you needed."

"Fantastic."

Jack explained, in the same distant voice, how each entry contained a date and GPS coordinates. The first two digits of the years were left off entirely, but the rest of the date would either be at the beginning or the end. This made it harder to spot a pattern.

"The rest of the numbers are GPS coordinates," Jack said. "All of the locations should be in either Lake Tahoe or the Black Rock Desert."

Ethan looked through the ledger and immediately saw what Jack was talking about. Reading the numbers required some interpretation, since they were written in increments of one to eighty—all on a keno card—but now that he knew what he was looking for, it was easy to see.

He hoped Jack hadn't had too much trouble getting the information.

"How did you get him to talk?"

"I asked and he told me," Jack said, but his voice was still hollow.

"Are you hurt?" Ethan asked, but the line was silent for a moment, and then Daryl was on the phone.

"Okay," he said. "I'm putting Jack back into general for the night. If the guards are after him, he'll be safer around witnesses. After that, I'm going home. My phone will be off. I'll be there tomorrow morning when you're due back. If you're so much as a second late reporting, I will personally attend every parole hearing from now to eternity and advocate that you stay locked up for the rest of your life. Got it?"

"Got it."

"I've stuck my head out for you, Ethan. Don't screw me over."

With that, Daryl hung up.

He'd betrayed Daryl's trust, and now Jack was mad at him too. And he couldn't blame either of them.

"Well?" Whitney said.

"The good news is I got the code," Ethan said.

"And the bad news?"

"I think I've lost my only friend and the only other person who was ever on my side."

Whitney smiled sympathetically. "I'm still your friend," she said. "I'm still on your side."

*   *   *

Whitney vaguely remembered Abby having a GPS from the time they went camping together at Yosemite. They searched the garage for it. Besides Ethan's boxes, there weren't many storage containers. Whitney opened one with Abby's camping equipment and found what they were looking for.

Ethan was unsure how to use it, but Whitney figured it out quickly. They sat at Abby's table and looked through the ledger. Ethan was thankful for Whitney's help. She was able to figure out how to interpret the numbers much quicker than he could.

She pointed to the most recent entry. In the long stream of numbers, she showed him what she thought was the date, then the GPS coordinates.

"See," she said, "this was yesterday."

"Anton," Ethan said. "Last night."

She plugged the numbers into the GPS.

"Looks like they buried him in the Black Rock Desert," she said.

"Okay, so do any numbers correspond with Abby?"

The second to last number was something from only a week ago—"Jesus," Ethan said, "how many people does Shark kill?"—and the coordinates indicated Lake Tahoe. The third from the last entry was another Black Rock coordinate—and the date was two days after Abby's disappearance. One day before that—the day after Abby was last seen—was another entry, but this one only showed the date. There were no GPS coordinates.

"What do you make of that?" Whitney asked.

The only thing Ethan could think was that they'd planned to get rid of a body that day but were delayed for whatever reason. So they wrote a completely new entry the next day.

Whitney agreed that was the only thing that made sense.

"If Abby's in here," Whitney said, tapping the date with the Black Rock coordinates, "this has got to be it."

"Let's go." Ethan said, and the weight of what they were about to do hit him.

They were going to dig up the dead body of his sister.

66

Jack
17 hours, 46 minutes remaining

DARYL AND JACK were walking back to the solitary wing of the prison. Neither spoke. Jack was in a daze of sorts. He kept thinking about the way he'd shoved the kid's head into the machine, how ready he'd been to press the buttons and turn his head into a rectangle. Today he'd seen a side of himself he'd never wanted to see again.

Ethan was the best part of his life in prison. His only friend. Ethan had saved his life more than the two times today. But Ethan had also called on him to commit violence in service to that friendship, and Jack couldn't let it go. He had always known the friendship would come to an end. Ethan would be paroled in a few years, and Jack would likely grow old in prison. But when he'd said goodbye to Ethan this morning, he hadn't realized that he was most likely saying goodbye to the way things were.

"You know," Daryl said, as they arrived at the gate to general, "I think there are going to be some openings soon at Northern Nevada Correctional Center in the horse program."

Jack arched his eyebrows. They stopped outside the door before going through.

"I hear you're good with horses," Daryl said.

"I grew up with horses," Jack said. "I worked with them all my life. Well, until . . ."

He didn't need to finish—he'd worked with horses his whole life until he shot up a meth house and got his brother brain damaged.

"I'll put your name down," Daryl said. "No guarantees."

"Appreciate that," Jack said.

In the program Daryl was talking about, the Bureau of Land Management rounded up wild horses from throughout Nevada and brought them in for prisoners to work with. Once the inmates tamed the horses, the state put them up for adoption. It was far from going home to Montana, but for someone who had done what Jack had, it was the best life he could hope for.

Daryl extended his hand, and the two shook on it.

It felt as if there was some new, small kinship between them. They had both liked Ethan, and they both now felt betrayed by him, used by him. Jack knew that the main reason Daryl was making this offer was because it would hurt Ethan a little bit. He wasn't going so far as revoking Ethan's furlough or making a negative recommendation for parole. This was a smaller treason, a passive-aggressive jab that could look like a favor.

The thing is, Jack realized, Ethan would be happy for him. He wouldn't be hurt. Ethan's own loneliness in prison was a small inconvenience for knowing that his friend would be doing something that he loved.

With this thought, he was filled again with uneasiness for Ethan. Whether Jack could forgive him or not, the truth was there was a good chance his friend would never come back to prison at all.

By tomorrow morning, he might be as dead as his sister.

67

Ethan
17 hours, 31 minutes remaining

THEY FIGURED SHARK and the police would both be looking for Whitney's car, so they swapped it for the truck. Ethan pulled his old pickup out of the garage, and Abby hid her Prius inside. Careful to minimize the use of his right hand, he grabbed the shovels out of the car and tossed them into the truck bed.

When they got to the interstate, he cranked down the window and tossed Bruce's phone onto the blacktop. He watched it bounce on the pavement in the rearview mirror.

"I'm not sure if they track those things," Ethan said. "But just in case . . ."

"Probably a good idea," Whitney said.

It felt strange to be driving after five years without touching a steering wheel. But the truck was like an old glove that would always fit. Not that a glove would fit on his hand now. It was swollen up like a balloon. He'd left the frozen vegetables behind at Abby's place, and his hand throbbed and pulsed with heat. The soreness wasn't terrible unless he tried to bend his fingers, but when he did, tendrils of pain needled their way up his arm.

Hughes called Ethan's phone again, and they ignored it.

"How was the funeral?" Whitney asked.

"Weird," he said.

"I wish I had been there," she said. "I feel like a shitty friend."

"You know Abby wouldn't think that."

Ethan could sympathize with her. He felt like a shitty brother for talking to Shark there. He hadn't treated the service with the gravity it deserved. It was as if the funeral wasn't real with all the pretense. Not just the pretense between him and Shark. But the whole charade of having a casket to begin with. The farce of burying something when there was nothing to bury.

Whitney leaned against the door, her arms wrapped around her body. The truck's old heater was just now starting to warm the cab.

"You can get some sleep, if you'd like," Ethan said. "We've got a hundred miles till we get there."

"I won't be able to sleep."

"Doesn't that stuff make you drowsy?" he said, referring to the painkillers.

"Not if you're actually in pain," she said. "It goes right to your pain receptors. If there's nothing wrong, that's when it knocks you out. You sure you don't want one?"

Ethan felt sore all over: his fist, his face, his ribs. Mostly, though, he felt exhausted. He'd been awake for something like thirty hours. And despite what Whitney said, he was afraid the drugs would make him groggy. He needed to be alert.

"No," he said. "I'm okay."

He got off the interstate and headed north. Soon they were out of the suburbs and surrounded only by rolling brown hills. The wind buffeted the truck.

They entered the Paiute reservation and came to Pyramid Lake and skirted its southern edge. The water was gray, the desert hills around it were brown and bleak. The pyramid-shaped tufa formations stood in the distance like strange tumors in a desert landscape where they didn't belong.

Lake Tahoe was more beautiful, but Ethan had always liked coming to Pyramid Lake when he was a kid. The lake basin wasn't crowded like Tahoe, the water not as cold.

"When was the last time you saw Abby?" Ethan said.

"At work," Whitney said. "It was nothing out of the ordinary. I don't even remember what we said to each other."

The highway entered Nixon, the Paiute community east of the lake, and the speed limit dropped to twenty-five. Ethan knew the police were serious about catching speeders, so he slowed down and hit the cruise control as they crept through the town.

"I talked to her on the phone the night it happened, maybe only a few hours before," Whitney added.

"You didn't tell me that," Ethan said.

"And I was supposed to see her that morning. We were going to drive down to Mammoth to go snowboarding."

"You were?"

"I drove over to her place and knocked on the door. It was like three o'clock in the morning."

"Three?" Ethan said.

"Yeah," she said. "It takes a long time to get to Mammoth, and we had big plans to do a full day of riding."

Whitney was quiet a minute.

"I pounded on the door," Whitney said, her voice cracking. "I called her phone. I thought, 'That bitch is sleeping through it all.' I didn't bring my key. I hadn't even thought about it." She began to cry. "I yelled up to her room and said, 'I'm going back to get my key, you bitch.' But I drove home and went back to bed. It was three in the morning. I was tired too, you know. I thought, 'If she's going to sleep, I might as well too.'"

"Jesus Christ," Ethan said. "The killer was probably inside."

"I know," Whitney said, wiping her tears with her hands and then wiping her nose with her shirtsleeve. "If I had gone back, maybe I could have saved her. Maybe she'd still be alive."

"Why didn't you tell me this before?" Ethan said.

"Because it's my fault she's dead," Whitney said, beginning to cry. "I was too lazy to go back."

Ethan pulled the truck over onto the shoulder. He put the gearshift in park and reached across to her. She leaned into him and sobbed against his neck.

"Shh," Ethan said. "If you had gone in there, you could be dead too."

"So what?" she said. "At least I could have tried to do something. I was home sleeping while the killer was hauling her body out of the house."

"Shh," he said again because he didn't know what else to say.

As she cried, he tried to remember what Whitney had been like when she was a child. He hadn't known her well but had always thought of her as smart, witty. He remembered a handful of friends coming in and out of Abby's life, but those girls fell away over time. Abby—who had always had a dynamic, infectious personality—had probably grown bored with them. But Whitney had always seemed Abby's equal. He couldn't remember the last time he'd seen her, and tried to think of what Abby might have said about her during her visits to the prison. There might have been a mention of the two of them getting an apartment together a few years ago, but that was all he could think of. If she'd mentioned Whitney was going to be working with her at the club, he had forgotten. He'd been in such a rage about the news that he hadn't paid attention to whatever else she'd said.

He felt a sickening, guilty dread squirming in his stomach.

"You know what happened the last time I saw her?" Ethan said.

"I do."

"You do?"

"She was my best friend, Ethan. She told me." She sat up. Her eyes were red from crying.

"I told her not to bother coming back unless she quit," he said. "And the next time she came, I refused to see her. So she didn't come back. That was two years ago."

"I'm sorry," Whitney said. "In hindsight, you were justified. She and I never should have gone to work at Dark Secrets."

"I still can't believe that FBI asshole convinced her to rat out Shark. Christ, I would have been out in *two* years."

As he said the words, though, Ethan knew he was trying to divert the blame. This was all his fault. He was the one who'd gotten involved with Shark in the first place, the one who didn't rat out Shark when he'd had the chance, the one who'd negotiated for Shark to look after her. He'd not only showed her the door to that world, he'd opened it wide so she could walk through. And then he'd gone to prison, abandoning her to live in that world without him.

68

Shark
17 hours, 5 minutes remaining

Kicking Bird pulled Shark's Escalade into a parking spot in front of Blake's apartment complex. Shark wouldn't normally come along for something like this, but he wanted to see Blake for himself.

He wanted to make sure Blake wasn't lying.

He and Kicking Bird climbed out of the vehicle and stepped briskly up the walk. Blake lived on the second floor, with an apartment overlooking a golf course. Shark tried the door handle and found it locked. He knocked gently on the door, making the sound deliberately meek. Let Blake think it's someone else.

A few seconds later, Blake cracked the door and saw him.

"Just came by to check on you," Shark said, making his voice so thick with concern that Blake would know it was a lie. "Wanted to make sure you weren't too banged up."

Shark offered him his most insincere smile. He wouldn't be here if it wasn't for any reason other than Blake fucking up so badly. And Blake knew it. Shark sometimes liked the way pretense made people squirm more than outright anger.

Blake's eyes drifted over Shark's shoulder to Stu standing behind him, and he had to clear his throat before speaking.

"Sure," Blake said. "Yeah. Come on in."

Blake looked like he was going to piss his pants but played it off like their visit was no big deal. He gestured for them to sit down in his living room. The TV was paused on some kind of zombie show. A bong sat on the coffee table next to a couple of empty beer bottles and an ashtray full of butts. Blake wore sweatpants and a Nike T-shirt that said "JUST DO IT."

More like "JUST FUCK IT UP," Shark thought.

Blake eased down on the couch, and Shark sat next to him. Stu stood leaning against the counter that separated the carpeted room from the kitchen.

"So how's my boy?" Shark said.

"I'm not gonna lie to you," Blake said. "I'm in rough shape."

He winced and held his ribs—he wasn't acting.

"Your old friend's become a pain in my ass," Shark said.

"He really messed me up," Blake said. "Have you seen Wayne?"

Shark nodded. "Ruptured testicle and a broken nose."

"Ouch," Blake said. He told Shark he thought he had some broken ribs. And when he took a piss, there was blood in his urine. He wasn't lying.

Shark affected a look of concern, but he wanted Blake to see through it and could tell that he did.

Kicking Bird said, "Your old friend took Bruce out too."

"Really?"

"He's in the hospital. Now he's blind in both eyes."

"What?"

Blake looked to Shark, who nodded gravely.

Blake flopped back. In his astonishment, he seemed almost proud. Like his old friend was proving to be a decent adversary for Shark. Then he remembered who was watching him, and his expression changed to anger.

"That stupid son of a bitch," Blake said. "I guess prison's made him crazy."

"Stu's going after him," Shark said. "I want you to go along."

"I would love to," Blake said. "Believe me. I'd like to get some payback. But man, I'm messed up. I'm telling you: I've never hurt this much before."

Shark looked around the apartment. What a mess. Blake's clothes from last night were discarded on the carpet. His boots were lying by the door. His two guns—the one he kept in the shoulder holster and the other in his boot—were lying on the floor like toys he hadn't picked up.

Shark turned his gaze back to Blake. He was satisfied that Blake wasn't faking his pain. Ethan really had beaten the shit out of him. But he sensed there was something more in his hesitation to go after Ethan. Some lingering loyalty to his old friend.

"I'd only hold him back," Blake said.

Shark looked at Kicking Bird and gave him a nod. Without a word, Kicking Bird went to the door and left.

"Well, I hope you feel better," Shark said matter-of-factly, but he didn't get up to leave.

They sat in awkward silence for a minute until there was a noise at the door and Kicking Bird was back. He came into the apartment with a roll of Visqueen under his arm.

"What the hell are you doing?" Blake said.

Kicking Bird ignored him and kneeled to unspool the clear plastic.

"I'm coming," Blake said, rising to his feet despite the pain. "I'm okay."

He pointed toward his bedroom.

"I need to change," he said. "Give me a minute. I'll be right there."

Shark nodded.

Blake hurried into his bedroom. He closed his door. He came out fully dressed and exhaled in relief when he saw that Kicking Bird had rolled the plastic back up.

Blake picked his guns up off the floor. He tucked the one into his boot, then wrapped the shoulder holster around his body. Every movement, Shark could tell, was agonizing. Shark grinned, seeing him in pain.

"Ready," Blake said, although he looked like he belonged in a hospital bed.

Shark rose and put a hand on Blake's shoulder. He'd gotten the message loud and clear: he'd screwed up. And now, to make things right, it was either his head or Ethan's.

"Glad to see you're feeling better."

69

Taylor
16 hours, 45 minutes remaining

TAYLOR WAS GETTING ready to leave the office. It was his day off and somehow he had spent the whole day at work. His wife was going to kill him. When he'd left this morning, he'd promised to be back in time to make a trip to Home Depot with her to look at paint samples. But after he'd talked to Ethan Lockhart and that gangster Shark D'Antonio, he'd come back to the office to glance back through the Abby Lockhart file. Hours had drifted by.

It was an unusual case. Blood on the scene, but no body. Sister of a convicted felon. Employee of a crime boss. Girlfriend of an FBI agent.

Taylor had been secretly relieved when feds had taken over jurisdiction. This was the kind of case that wouldn't get solved for years. He'd been glad that it wouldn't have to be his problem anymore. But now he felt guilty for how willingly he'd stepped aside. Abby Lockhart might have been a stripper, but she was still a person—still had a mother who mourned her, a guilt-racked brother desperate for closure.

He hadn't figured out anything new today. But he had decided he would call Brian Hughes on Monday and see about reinserting himself in the case.

He closed the folder and stood up, and that's when Marquez, the lieutenant on duty over the weekend, poked his head into Taylor's office.

"You're not going to believe this," Marquez said.

Marquez was the best source for knowing what was going on throughout the department. He was always gossiping. Most of it was useless information, but if Taylor ever needed to know the status of another detective's case, he always went to Marquez. And it was Marquez who'd known enough to call him in this morning when the report said it was a couple of Shark's guys who were spotted limping and bloody in the Neptune.

"Do I want to know?" Taylor said. "I was just about to go home."

"You know the bouncer that was hospitalized last night?" Marquez said. He was holding some kind of paper in his hand. "The one who works at Dark Secrets."

Taylor nodded.

"His twin brother just joined him at the hospital. This one's hurt even worse."

"No shit," Taylor said, feeling suddenly sick to his stomach.

"Officers responded to some kind of assault at a downtown condo. Condo belongs to a girl who works at Dark Secrets. She left with the suspected assailant. Maybe kidnapped. We're not sure yet."

"You got an ID on the assailant?"

"Surveillance footage inside the elevator."

He held out the piece of paper he'd been holding. It was a grainy black-and-white printout of a photograph showing a man standing in an elevator with a woman whose face was obscured by her hair.

He thought he knew who she was. He definitely knew who the man was.

He saw the time stamp on the image.

"Son of a bitch," he said. "This was right after I talked to him."

He remembered Ethan telling him he was going to visit with his mom.

"Goddamn liar," Taylor said.

"You should have brought him in, amigo."

"I won't make the same mistake twice," Taylor said, pulling out his phone to call his wife.

He wouldn't be home anytime soon.

70

Ethan
16 hours, 11 minutes remaining

A s Ethan and Whitney approached the Black Rock, alkali fields began to appear in the desert, the fine sand drifting onto the road like powdery snow. They drove through Gerlach, the blink-and-you-miss-it town at the southern end of the desert. There was almost nothing to the town, but there was an old diner. They hadn't eaten since breakfast, and Ethan thought about stopping. But he wanted to find the grave before the sun went down. They could dig in the dark, but they might need light to at least find the location.

He asked Whitney if the more recent burial was closer, and she said it was. The entry that corresponded with Abby's disappearance was another twenty miles deeper into the desert.

"Let's stop at that most recent one first," Ethan said. "It will be fresher and easier to find. We can figure out how accurate the numbers are."

He pulled off the highway and into the desert. The pale brown surface stretched in front of them for a hundred miles. Distant mountains proved that the desert was finite, but still it was enormous. There were no obstacles in sight.

This time of year, the playa—that's what people called it—could get muddy, so Ethan put the truck into four-wheel drive. He accelerated. A cloud of dust trailed the truck like the wake of a speedboat on water. They could see nothing behind them, just kicked-up dirt. Ahead of them, more flat hardpan.

Whitney told him to slow down and which direction to angle the truck. When they were close, he saw it, a scar in the desert surface about the size of a twin mattress. Whoever had buried the body had done a good job of packing down the soil, and it looked like they had driven back and forth over the spot for good measure. But the ground definitely looked different from the surrounding desert, which was unblemished except for the spider web of natural cracks in the dried alkali.

"It's strange to think there's a dead body down there," Whitney said.

Ethan pictured Anton, wrapped in bloody plastic.

"It's not hidden very well, actually," Whitney said.

Ethan gestured to the desert around them. "It's hidden in all of this," he said. "A thousand square miles of nothing. And once they get a good rain and the soil dries out again, it will blend right in. The next one might be pretty well hidden."

Ethan drove and Whitney navigated. Forty minutes later, they found the grave. It blended in better than the first one, but its traces hadn't disappeared entirely.

They got out and stood next to the scar on the desert floor. Ethan's blood was rioting inside him. Was Abby down there?

He picked up the shovel and tried to wrap his right fist around the wooden handle. The pain was excruciating, and he let go.

"Okay," he said. "I'll take one of those pain pills now."

Whitney tapped one of the pills out of the bottle into his palm. "That violates another condition of your furlough, doesn't it?"

He popped it in his mouth, and said, "At least I haven't driven out of state."

"Yet." She winked at him.

They began to work. The painkillers took effect almost immediately. The pain in his hand didn't disappear entirely, but it felt distant. The rest of his aches vanished in a glow that emanated through his body like the warmth from a whiskey shot.

It was dusk, and the wind died down to a breeze. The temperature was dropping, and Ethan and Whitney breathed out white frosty clouds. They threw shovelful after shovelful. Ethan didn't have gloves; his hands became ice-cold.

In the distance, they saw the occasional trail of dust from cars speeding across the desert. It was hard to judge how far away they were. Five miles. Ten.

Sporadic clouds appeared and the setting sun bathed them in a mixture of pinks, reds, and purples. The color would fade for a moment, then the clouds would be reinvigorated with brightness, changing hue. Once the sun disappeared, the sky faded from dark blue to black, filling with more stars than either of them had ever seen.

Ethan felt small and insignificant under those stars. The universe was so big. It seemed like one dead girl couldn't really matter. But she mattered to him.

If she mattered to no one else, to nothing else under their star or any other, she mattered to him more than anything else ever had or would.

They dug in the dark without speaking.

The moon came up, big and orange, rising over the mountains and floating, nearly as bright and every bit as amazing as the setting sun had been. As they dug, it seemed to shrink and turn from fire orange to bone white. It rose quickly like a balloon, and before long it was high in the sky, hiding the stars in its glow and casting bright light onto the desert. The moonlight reflected so brightly off the playa that the ground looked like snow. The desert was a moonscape, white and pale.

The temperature kept dropping. Whitney had to take a break and sit in the truck with the heater on. Ethan kept digging. The pile of loose dirt grew and grew. His hands ached. They were callused from weightlifting, but even so, blisters were developing in his palms and on his fingers. His mouth was as dry as the desert dirt.

He worked with a singular focus, a strange tunnel vision. He was exhausted—more tired than he had ever been in his life—but he did not slow down.

Abby, he thought, *I'm going to find you.*

His shovel struck something.

CHAPTER

71

Ethan
12 hours, 2 minutes remaining

WHATEVER HE HIT wasn't hard. It was solid, but it had give. He was certain it was a body.

He knelt and scraped away dirt with his hands. He uncovered a swatch of fabric—a T-shirt or a blouse—and he began digging with his hands. Whitney joined him. They were both in the hole, frantic to uncover the rest of the body. They revealed a shoulder and then worked toward the head. Ethan clawed the cold ground. Dirt filled the spaces under his fingernails.

They uncovered a jawline.

There was stubble on it.

"What the hell?" Ethan said. "It's not Abby."

He grabbed a shovel—no longer careful—and wedged it under where the head would be. He leveraged up the skull.

The dead body belonged to a man.

Ethan grabbed ahold of the man's collar and pulled, working his head and shoulders out of the grave before collapsing back on his haunches and breathing heavily.

The dead man's skin was bluish in the moonlight and pulled taut against his skull, but there was no real rotting yet. The cold had preserved him. Decomposition would begin in the spring when the worms and insects started to eat him. His eyes were sunken into the sockets, and dirt was caked into the holes. There was a faint stench mixed with the smell of the soil, like spoiled meat left in the refrigerator too long.

Whitney took a few steps away and retched.

Ethan went to her and laid a hand on her back.

"I knew him," she said, wiping a hand across her mouth. "He did some work for Shark. He was from Wisconsin or someplace like that. Everyone said he moved back home. He was a nice kid."

"I'm sure he was," Ethan said without much conviction.

He was exhausted and in a daze—unsure how to continue and lacking the strength even if he did know what he should do.

"I was sure it was going to be Abby," he said.

He turned back and looked at the dead body. He noticed something beneath the body. Something was reflecting in the moonlight.

Plastic.

"Wait," he said, and grabbed a shovel.

He sunk it in next to the body and began prying up the man's waist, his legs. When the body was loosened enough, he grabbed it and dragged it out of the grave. Whitney watched, her face pale and horrified.

Deeper in the grave, underneath where the man had been buried, there was another body, this one enclosed in plastic the way Kicking Bird and Bruce had wrapped Anton.

Ethan dug with his hands again. Whitney joined him. They uncovered where the face would be, its features obscured by multiple layers of the plastic wrap. Ethan tore at a layer, tore at the second. He stopped with one layer of plastic to go.

The body inside was a Black man with a goatee.

Two bodies. Neither of them Abby.

*   *   *

Ethan and Whitney were both in the hole, slumped against the slopes of dirt. Ethan's limbs trembled. He was hungry, exhausted, cold.

He was defeated.

"What now?" Whitney said.

"Just because we didn't find her doesn't mean Shark didn't kill her, right?" Ethan said.

"I guess."

"I mean, they don't put all the bodies in that stupid ledger, do they?"

"I don't know," she said.

There had been the blank entry the day before this one. Only a date. No coordinates. What did that mean?

Ethan shivered. Digging had kept him warm, but now he wasn't moving and the sweat against his body was growing cold.

"I'm going to see Shark," Ethan said. "I'm going to trade him his money for information. Even if it kills me."

"That's not a good idea, Eth—"

"Shh," Ethan said. "Quiet."

He'd heard something. He stood up out of the hole. A car was coming toward them. Its lights were off, but it was visible in the moonlight. It was close—only about fifty yards away—and coming fast.

Ethan wondered how he hadn't heard it earlier. Then he realized whose car it was.

CHAPTER

72

Abby
3 weeks ago

ABBY PACED THROUGH her apartment, checking the window, then walking away, only to return a few seconds later. When she finally saw Brian's car pull down the street that ran between the townhomes, she couldn't contain herself, and she ran downstairs to meet him at the door.

He looked tired, the weariness of a long day coming through his eyes. But he brightened when he saw her and flashed his charming, white-teeth smile.

"Hey, good lookin'," he said.

"I've got something," she said.

He didn't seem to hear her. He leaned in to kiss her, but she turned and headed back up the stairs.

"Come on," she said.

He came up and sat down on her couch, leaning back and crossing his legs out in front of him like he was settling in to watch a movie. "Okay, what have you got?"

She told him standing up, pacing back and forth again. She was too nervous to sit down. She explained that she and a couple other girls had come back from a private gig at the Sandstorm, a bachelor party in one of the penthouses. They'd ridden in the limo, like they always did, and the club's newest bouncer, Lee, had driven them and worked as their security. He was a big farm boy from somewhere in the Midwest, strong but a little too earnest and innocent for the line of work he was in. More likeable than most of the other options though:

Bruce, Wayne, Anton. Even Blake, whom she'd known since she was a kid, got on her nerves lately.

Lee had pulled the limo into the warehouse, and the girls had exited reluctantly, not particularly excited to be back. Abby had been back in the dressing room for about ten minutes, getting ready to step back into the stage rotation, when she'd realized that she was missing a stocking. She went back to the limo to look for it.

She was inside, feeling around underneath and behind the cushions, when the door from the club banged open. Shark and Stu and the new guy, Lee, walked in. Without stopping to think about it, Abby reached up and switched off the interior light, then tried to remain still. She could see them through the tinted windows, but she thought with the lights off inside she'd be invisible to them. Shark was pissed, going on and on about how some kind of payment kept coming up short.

Lee was saying that the guy who owed Shark the money wasn't giving him enough.

"Yeah?" Shark said. "Well, he called and said he was giving you the full vig, so *you* must be skimming."

"Oh, that's total bullshit," Lee said.

He was either a good actor or he was genuinely stunned that someone would lie like that. He seemed sickeningly naive for someone who knowingly worked for a gangster.

"Next time I want the full payment," Shark said, "with arrears."

"What if he doesn't—"

"It's your job to make him pay," Shark said. "That's why I pay you. If he says he doesn't have enough, you make him understand that he does."

Lee nodded his head. "Okay. I'll get him to pay."

They were quiet for a few seconds and then Shark said, "What are you waiting on?"

"Oh, sorry," Lee said, and then left.

Shark and Stu lingered in the warehouse. Abby stayed hidden in the car, her body vibrating from the beating of her heart.

"That kid's got turds for brains," Shark said.

"You believe him?" Stu asked.

"I do," Shark said. "But it doesn't matter. If he can't get someone to pay up, he ain't worth a puddle of piss to me."

Abby heard footsteps as they headed back to the club. She shifted so she could see them through the tinted window. Stu turned his head and looked her way. Her breath froze in her throat. For a terrifying split second, it seemed he was staring directly at her, and then he turned away.

Before they walked through the door, Shark said, "If the next payment's short, you're gonna punch his number. Got it?"

"Which one?" Kicking Bird asked.

And then they were through the door, and Abby was alone in the warehouse. Now, after telling the story to Brian, she waited for him to respond.

"What did he mean by 'Which one?'" Brian asked.

"Either Lee or the guy who's been stiffing them on the payments. Stu wasn't sure which one he was supposed to kill."

"And you didn't hear his answer?"

Abby shook her head.

"Or the name of the guy who owes Shark?"

"No."

Brian leaned his head back, closed his eyes, and pinched the bridge of his nose like he had a headache. He didn't seem nearly as excited as Abby had expected him to be.

"They're going to kill somebody," Abby said. "You've got to do something about it."

"Okay," Brian said, his voice sounding almost bored, "if they kill that guy Lee, then this info will be great. You can testify. But we'll need other evidence. Like a body. And we pretty much never find the bodies of people who cross Shark. They disappear. And you don't know the other guy's name, so if he goes missing, we won't even know he's connected to Shark. That won't help much either."

Abby stared at Brian. He seemed to be missing the point entirely.

"Shark is going to kill someone," she said. "Can't you go arrest him?"

"For what?" Brian said. "Conspiracy to commit murder? Shark will say he was using a figure of speech. It would never stick. And then the witness"—he pointed to Abby—"would disappear off the face of the planet."

Abby felt sick to her stomach. She sat on the other side of her L-shaped couch, perpendicular to Brian. She had been so excited—she was going to do something important, save someone's life. Now she felt stupid.

"Look," Brian said, "this is good information. We're making some progress. But we need a lot more."

"They're going to kill him, Brian."

"Nothing I can do about that."

Abby stood up and paced into the middle of the room. She whirled on him. "Are you kidding me?" she said.

"Hey, don't get all bent out of shape."

"Bent out of shape?" she said. "Why would I be bent out of shape? I just told you a criminal is going to murder someone, and you don't give a shit. Why would that bother me?"

Brian sat up. He put his arm out as if that would calm her down.

"You don't know how the law works," he said. "There's nothing we can do here."

"The law?" Abby said. "I don't give a shit about the law. I'm talking about doing what's right. We have to save him."

Brian flopped back against the couch. "You're being naive."

Abby stomped across the room and stopped at the window. She stared out at the darkness. She felt sick. She'd been sleeping with Brian for a couple months now. He was cute. She liked him. And she'd thought they were a team—she was going to help him take down Shark. Now she wondered if she'd been duped all along. Did he really think she could do anything for him? Or was he just using her for easy, no-strings-attached sex?

Brian rose and walked over to her.

"I'll warn him myself," she said.

Brian shook his head vigorously. "No," he said. "If you do that, you'll be dead too."

"I can't just let him die," Abby said.

"He made his bed by working for Shark in the first place."

He wrapped his arms around her waist and bent his face down to kiss her in the crook of the neck. She squirmed away, suddenly repulsed by him.

"Brian," she said, pointing toward the stairs, "I want you to leave."

"Don't overreact."

"I want you to leave now!" she yelled.

Her voice broke on the last syllable.

Brian reached for her. "Don't cry, honey."

She swatted his hands away. She stared at him, her chest rising and falling as if she had been in a physical fight. She knew he was right—this whole thing was bigger than what she'd realized she was signing up for. She'd known crossing Shark was going to be dangerous, but she hadn't realized how morally compromising it was going to be.

"Look," he said, his voice softening, "I didn't—"

"I want to be alone," she said, and she turned and went upstairs to her bedroom. She didn't run, but she walked quickly. She slammed the door and locked it. Brian came and knocked gently, calling to her. She sat on her bed and didn't answer.

"Abby," he said, "please talk to me."

She was silent. He waited on the other side of the door. Finally, after several minutes, he said, "Okay, Abby, I'll go. But I'm going to call you tomorrow. We'll figure this out. Don't do anything rash before then. Please."

She waited until she saw his car drive by before walking down to the bottom level and locking the front door.

Then she sat on the lowest step and put her head in her hands. She felt like a small, silly girl, no closer to freeing her brother than she'd been before she met Brian Hughes. No closer than she'd been before she went to work at Dark Secrets. No closer than that day she'd sat in the courtroom, unable to speak up in his defense.

She was the same scared little girl, and she hated herself for it.

CHAPTER

73

Ethan
10 hours, 9 minutes remaining

THE HEADLIGHTS FLASHED on, blinding Ethan, and the car came skidding to a stop in front of them. A cloud of dust filled the headlight beams.

The BMW's doors flew open, and men stepped out of each side. The headlights made it hard to see, but Ethan could tell who they were by the shapes. Blake stood on the driver's side, pistol in hand. Kicking Bird stood on the passenger side with a shotgun.

Ethan climbed out of the hole. He stepped over the dead body.

"I warned you," Ethan said to Blake.

Kicking Bird raised the shotgun. "Stay right there," he said.

Ethan did as he was told. The shotgun was a side-by-side double-barrel with the stock sawed off to form a pistol grip and the long barrels sawed down as well. It would have terrible range, but it would make a mess of anything close.

The gun had external hammers, like something out of the 1800s, and both were cocked back.

"I want to see Shark," Ethan said. "I'll tell him where the money is, but I'm not telling either of you two morons. Shark, and only Shark."

"That's good," Kicking Bird said, "because he wants to see you too."

He told them to throw their cell phones to him. Ethan tossed his at Kicking Bird's feet. Whitney said hers was in the truck, and Blake opened the door and verified that it was there.

Kicking Bird held the shotgun at his side. He reached into a pocket and tossed something toward them. Handcuffs landed in the dirt.

"Put those on her," Kicking Bird said to Ethan, gesturing with a head nod toward Whitney.

"Go to hell."

Kicking Bird exhaled impatiently. "We're not driving you two out of here without cuffs on you. Shark wants *you* alive, but there's nothing stopping us from leaving the girl out here."

Ethan reached down and picked up the handcuffs.

"I'm sorry," he said to Whitney.

The light from the headlights blasted one side of her face and left the other side completely in shadow. Her pasty half face looked terrified. He wanted to tell her he would get them out of this, but he didn't want Blake and Kicking Bird to hear him. And he wouldn't believe his own words anyway—so why should she?

He put the handcuffs on her, only latching the first teeth, so the silver rings dangled with slack around her thin wrists.

"Come here, Whitney," Kicking Bird said.

She approached him, and he reached down and squeezed both rings tight against her wrist.

"Ow," she said.

"Okay," Kicking Bird said to Ethan, "you're going to fill that hole back in."

"Like hell," Ethan said.

In a flash, Kicking Bird rapped the barrels of the shotgun against Whitney's head—not hard enough to knock her out, but plenty hard enough to hurt. She doubled over and fell onto her knees. Kicking Bird pointed the shotgun at the back of her head.

Ethan took a step forward, and Blake raised his gun.

"I'll do it this time," Blake said. "Don't think I won't."

Ethan believed him.

"It's simple," Kicking Bird said. "We can't leave here with that hole uncovered. You've got to fill it back in. Blake'll help you."

"Fuck that," Blake said. "My ribs are broken. I can barely walk."

"Either you help cover the hole, or I put you in it."

Blake glared at him. "Fine," he said, jamming his pistol into the shoulder holster. He pointed at Ethan. "You're an asshole."

Kicking Bird continued, "Whitney and I are going to be inside the car. If you try to do anything, I'll kill her without a second's hesitation."

"Come on," Ethan said to Blake. "Let's get this over with."

He and Blake each took a side of the body lying on the ground. Ethan grabbed him under the armpits, and Blake grabbed his legs, groaning in pain.

They dropped the body into the hole and began shoveling.

* * *

Blake was nearly useless. He winced and moaned with every shovelful. After five minutes, his breathing was heavy but shallow. He stopped to smoke a cigarette, but it clearly hurt for him to inhale the smoke. He leaned against the grill of the truck and rubbed his lower back as if that would make his kidneys stop hurting.

"You sure are stupid," he said to Ethan. "You didn't think we'd come looking for you?"

"How'd you know where we were?" Ethan said.

He didn't stop shoveling. Putting the dirt back in the ground was much easier than taking it out, but he was sore and tired and cold. He was ready to sit in a warm car and rest, even if he was a prisoner.

"We're not stupid, Ethan," Blake said, tossing his cigarette away and lighting another instead of helping. "Stu knew you took the journal. And he knew this was the only entry even close to Abby's disappearance."

"So you've got the codes written down somewhere else?"

"No, dumbass," Blake said, hooking his thumb toward the car. "Who do you think dug this grave?"

Ethan stopped, leaned on the shovel and looked at Blake. The headlights from the BMW were still blasting them, so Blake was mostly in silhouette.

"What's with the two bodies?" Ethan said.

"The kid helped Stu dig the hole. He didn't know Stu was going to leave him in it too." Blake sauntered over to pick up his shovel.

"Who's the guy in the plastic?" Ethan said.

"Guy who owed money," Blake said. "The kid was his collector. Payments started coming up short. Guy blamed the kid. Kid blamed the guy. Shark said to get rid of them both."

"How much did he owe?"

"A hell of a lot less than you do," Blake said.

He leaned over and started shoveling again, the last inch of his cigarette still in his lips. He grunted with every movement. Ethan considered telling him that Whitney had a sack full of painkillers in the truck, but he preferred his friend continue to suffer.

"What's with the blank entry in the journal?" Ethan said. "It matches Abby's disappearance."

"Hell if I know," Blake huffed while scooping a shovelful into the hole. His cigarette was pinched between his lips. "It's not like Shark holds a weekly staff meeting to keep us all up to date on the details."

"Why didn't you do what I said?" Ethan said. "Why didn't you stay away?"

"Fuck you," Blake said, throwing down the shovel. He tossed his cigarette in the hole and got in Ethan's face. "You really blew things up for me."

Ethan stood face to face with him, but he was careful to make no aggressive moves. He knew Kicking Bird was watching, with his shotgun pointed at Whitney.

"I gotta do what I can to make sure I don't end up like that kid down there." Blake pointed to the grave, where one shoe was still visible, sticking up out of the dirt.

"You know if it comes down to it," Ethan said, "I'm going to kill you. I warned you."

Blake started laughing as he picked up his shovel again.

"Don't make jokes," he said. "It hurts too much to laugh."

"You think I'm joking?"

"It ain't gonna come down to it," Blake said. "You ain't gonna get the chance. You'll be dead before the sun comes up. I'm sorry, old friend, but them's the facts."

"If I die," Ethan said, "then Shark doesn't get his money."

"Oh, you'll tell him where the money is," Blake said. "You will. *Then* he'll kill you."

74

Ethan
8 hours, 30 minutes remaining

WHEN THEY FINISHED filling in the grave, Ethan and Blake smacked the mound of dirt with their shovels to pack the dirt down. Ethan's muscles ached, and he didn't have much strength to put behind his swings. The moon had moved far across the sky.

Kicking Bird started the engine of the BMW and eased forward. They stepped out of the way, and the car drove over the mound, backed up, did it again a few times to flatten the layer even more.

When Kicking Bird was done, he pulled the car back to where it had been and stepped out.

He tossed another set of handcuffs to Ethan.

"Listen, Stu," Ethan said. "I know why you guys put a hit out on my cellmate. He and his brother were the ones who shot up the meth lab where your sister was killed."

Kicking Bird seemed to have no reaction.

"The hit failed," Ethan said. "I talked to my caseworker. Jack's fine."

Still no reaction.

"Let us go, and I'll do him for you," Ethan said. "I'll give you the money. Whitney will go live in some other part of the country, and you won't ever hear from her again. I'll go back to prison. Tell Shark we weren't here. The grave was untouched."

Blake laughed.

"What?" Ethan said.

"You're a shitty liar," he said. "That was pathetic."

Ethan turned back to Kicking Bird. "I would do anything to avenge my sister." He held his arms up as if to gesture to the widespread evidence of this. "I think I've proven that. You wouldn't do anything for your sister?"

Kicking Bird was a black silhouette behind the headlights, and Ethan wished he could see his face.

"You wouldn't tell Shark a little lie to avenge her?" Ethan said. "You're that afraid of him?"

"I'm not afraid of Shark," Kicking Bird said finally. "I work for Shark for one reason."

"What's that?"

"He asks me to kill people," Kicking Bird said matter-of-factly.

Ethan felt a lump in his throat. He knew people like that in prison. There weren't many of them—more than just sociopaths willing to kill to get what they wanted. These were the ones who *liked* to kill.

"I'll kill my sister's murderer someday," Kicking Bird said. "Even if I have to wait until I'm eighty years old and your friend finally gets paroled. In fact, I think I prefer that to a stranger doing the job for me."

"At least you know what happened to your sister," Ethan said, trying—fruitlessly, he knew—to appeal to Kicking Bird's sense of compassion. If they had anything in common—anything besides one night on a football field more than a decade ago—it was that both of their sisters had been murdered.

But Kicking Bird didn't take the bait. He pointed the shotgun inside the BMW, presumably where Whitney was sitting.

"Put the handcuffs on," he said to Ethan.

Ethan lifted them out of the dirt. He fastened the first ring around his right wrist. The swelling had spread down his forearm, and even clipping the cuffs to the first tooth made the metal tight. He clipped the other ring around his left hand, in front of his body, being careful to only catch one tooth so that the ring was as loose as possible.

"Tighter," Kicking Bird said.

Ethan held up his wrists. "Come do it yourself," he said.

Kicking Bird said to Blake, "Tighten his cuffs."

Blake took a step forward, and Ethan said, "You touch me and I'll put you down. I don't care if my hands are cuffed. I'll break your fucking neck."

"And then I shoot Whitney," Kicking Bird said.

"And then I come after you," Ethan said.

"And I shoot you before you get within five feet of me."

"And," Ethan said, "Shark's money is gone forever."

Silence.

Stalemate.

Finally, Kicking Bird said, "Put your gun on him, Blake."

Blake obliged, pulling out his pistol and leveling it on Ethan. He backed away several steps so that Ethan couldn't disarm him the way he had last night. Kicking Bird reached into the car, and Ethan heard the thump of the trunk opening. He gestured for Ethan to walk around the car, and Ethan did as he was instructed.

The trunk, lit by a single bulb, was large and empty. No motor oil or jumper cables.

"What are you waiting for?" Kicking Bird said.

Ethan climbed in and lay on his side. The trunk smelled new, with a trace of a plastic odor and something else. Maybe blood. How many bodies had been stored back here?

Kicking Bird and Blake looked down at Ethan, their guns still pointed toward him.

Kicking Bird said to Blake, "You follow in the truck."

"I don't even get to drive my own car?" Blake said, his voice like a whiny teenager's.

"No discussion," Kicking Bird said.

And there wasn't.

Kicking Bird slammed the lid shut without another word.

75

Ethan
7 hours, 53 minutes remaining

THE TRUNK WAS cold inside, but at least he was out of the wind. Just like he had in the prison transport a day and a half earlier, Ethan tried to squeeze his hand out of the cuffs. He'd put them on as loosely as he could, but even so, he couldn't get his hand out of the metal ring. With some lotion or lubricant, he might be able to do it, but there was nothing like that in the trunk. He spent some time trying to wedge up the carpet to get to the jack and—more importantly—the tire iron. But he didn't have enough room to maneuver, and he quickly settled into place, lying on his side.

The car slowed down, stopped briefly, then drove on. They were on the highway now. The suspension vibrated differently over the blacktop than the desert. He heard Kicking Bird's voice, and while he couldn't make out all the words, he could tell he wasn't talking to Whitney. He was making a phone call, now that they were out of the desert and in a service area, and Ethan figured he was reporting to Shark, telling him what had happened.

After that, there was only silence from inside the car. Kicking Bird did not speak to Whitney. He did not turn on the radio. Ethan thought maybe he could hear Whitney crying softly to herself, but it could have been his imagination.

He thought of the second time he and Whitney made love. The first had been passionate, but the second had been slower, more intimate. They'd had time to kiss and touch and—afterward—talk. It was unlike any sex he'd ever had. The reason might have been that he hadn't been near—let alone touched— a woman in five years. But he didn't think that was all there was to it. What was happening between them might be the real thing, and it had seemed unfair that they couldn't explore it further. Now, he felt a growing panic that something far more unfair would occur—that she wouldn't survive the night.

He told himself he should sleep. He was going to need all his physical and mental strength. But he couldn't. The ride was bumpy and uncomfortable. The trunk was spacious, but it wasn't meant for a human to lie curled up in for a hundred miles. More than any of those things, though, he couldn't sleep because he couldn't turn his brain off. He kept running through scenarios, and all of them looked bad.

He knew—logically, if not yet emotionally—that he was probably going to die. They would take him to the warehouse, spread Visqueen out on the floor, and they would kill him. There was no way he could negotiate for his own life. They planned to kill Whitney too, no doubt. But perhaps—if he played his cards right—he could save her. Only he knew where the briefcase was, and however much was in there—somewhere between five hundred grand and a million—was enough that Shark would not let Ethan die without telling him where it was. Ethan would tell him if he let Whitney go.

That was the deal he had to propose.

* * *

He knew when they were getting closer to the city. He could hear other traffic around them. The car began stopping at stoplights. It wouldn't be long. He could tell when they pulled on the interstate because the car was going fast again. He anticipated the exit for downtown, but, instead, he felt the car circle around a ramp and speed up again. Kicking Bird had driven onto 395. Ethan was sure of it. The car was speeding. No stoplights. He thought they were heading south, but couldn't be certain. Then he started to suspect where they were going.

He knew for sure when the car exited the highway and began to climb in elevation. Ethan had to shift his position because the car was now going uphill, speeding and slowing along the curvy Mount Rose Highway.

Kicking Bird was taking them to Lake Tahoe.

Which changed everything.

Once they were out on Shark's boat, Ethan knew, there was no getting out alive for either of them. If he had any chance of saving Whitney, he had to get them to let her go before the boat left the dock.

If he could do that, when they were out on the boat—him, Shark, Kicking Bird, and Blake—he would try to get them to tell him what happened to Abby. He would die. He was sure of that. But he would rather die knowing than not knowing.

This is what he told himself as the car crested the peak and began descending into the Lake Tahoe Basin. He wanted to save Whitney, and he wanted the truth about Abby.

But another idea started to form in his brain. A long shot. A hail Mary. He would almost certainly still die. But there might be a way to avenge Abby too. He might be able to take her killers out with him.

CHAPTER

76

Ethan
4 hours, 19 minutes remaining

W HEN THE CAR finally stopped, they left him inside for a few minutes. He heard Kicking Bird and Whitney's doors open. He heard Blake approach. He heard Shark.

When the trunk popped open, Kicking Bird's shotgun was pointed at Ethan's face. The barrel holes looked at him like big black eyes.

Kicking Bird had ahold of Whitney, and he turned the gun on her, pressing it against her side. She squirmed at the touch of the barrel.

"Try anything," Kicking Bird said, "and I'll put nine steel balls into your girlfriend's guts. Which will leave nine for you."

Ethan crawled out of the trunk and stretched. He rolled his head from side to side. The air up here was even colder than in the valley, but, mercifully, there was no wind. Hills of black pine trees rose in the darkness, the snow on the tops visible in the moonlight.

Blake grabbed Ethan by the arm and guided him. They were at a dock on the edge of the lake. Shark stood waiting on one of the boats, wearing the same suit he'd had on that morning at Abby's funeral and leaning against the stainless-steel handrails that bounded the deck. He was smiling, his mouth full of his familiar stubby teeth.

Blake shoved Ethan along the pier. Kicking Bird and Whitney followed. No one else was around. Ethan's breath was like smoke in the darkness.

"Shark," he said, stopping in front of the boat. "I'll tell you where the money is if you let Whitney go. No bullshit."

Shark stood and crossed his arms. "Okay," he said. "Where is it?"

"I want your word, Shark. Your word used to mean something."

Shark was silent for a moment and then said, "You have my word, Ethan."

Ethan didn't believe him. "Okay," he said. "Uncuff her. Put her in my truck."

Shark shook his head. "You go first."

"I don't believe you're going to let her go."

"I don't believe you're going to tell me where my money is."

They were quiet. Then Shark waved for Blake to bring him onto the boat.

"Wait," Ethan said. "Listen. I know you're going to kill me."

Shark breathed through is nose, and it looked like steam coming out of his nostrils.

"I'm dead," Ethan said. "I'm not stupid. But you're not so rich that what's in that briefcase is disposable. I know you want that money. The only way you're getting it is if you let Whitney live."

"We'll see about that," Shark said.

Blake pressed his pistol against Ethan's back and told him to climb aboard.

* * *

Shark's boat was a mid-sized yacht, small for the ocean but big for Lake Tahoe. It had a spacious, glass-encased cockpit, so Shark and Blake and Kicking Bird were shielded from the wind. There was a couch in the cockpit and several chairs—perfect for entertaining, although Ethan suspected Shark did very little of that. Despite the photo on Shark's desk of him on the boat with the two girls, Ethan supposed the boat was used mostly for what it was doing now: dumping bodies. There was a tray near the steering wheel where boaters could put items they didn't want to lose: sunglasses, car keys, wallets. Now it contained Shark's hammer and the cutters they'd used to sever Anton's finger, as well as Kicking Bird's pistol-grip, double-barrel shotgun.

They'd sat Ethan and Whitney in the aft deck, which was spacious, in two cushioned swivel chairs fastened to the deck. The wind pummeled them, and spray from the twin motors coated them in an icy mist. They were both still handcuffed, but they weren't tied in place. There was no need—if they jumped into the frigid lake, they would be dead in minutes, if not seconds.

The surface was black with light reflecting from the moon, like glittering scales on a serpent whose skin stretched in every direction. The water below them was a thousand feet deep, clear as glass in the daytime but opaque now. It was like a void in the universe, an abyss with no bottom. Liquid death. When people drowned in Lake Tahoe, their corpses didn't float to the surface. The water was too cold for bodies to bloat with gas. Ethan imagined his and

Whitney's bodies suspended somewhere in the middle of the icy purgatory, pre-served by the cold water, their hair floating like seaweed, their glassy eyes open, their arms spread as if they'd been crucified.

"I'm sorry," Ethan said to Whitney.

She was shivering violently, and Ethan wasn't sure if it was the cold or the fear. He felt numb. The exhaustion, the cold, the hurt—all of it seemed to add up to numbness. He was aware of what was going on, but he felt strangely removed from it. He didn't feel scared. Fear wouldn't help him, so he wasn't allowing himself to experience it.

"They're going to kill us, aren't they?" Whitney said.

"Yes," Ethan said.

The boat bounced as it skimmed across the water, jostling them. Shark, Blake, and Kicking Bird were a good ten feet from them, and with the sound of the motors and splashing water, Ethan couldn't hear what they were talking about. He assumed they couldn't hear him and Whitney either.

"They're going to torture us first," Ethan said. "I'm going to try to get them to focus on me. I'll goad them into it."

Whitney's skin was as white as paper. Her lips, so naturally red before, were purplish and pale. Her hair whipped around her. He wished there was some way, some universe where he hadn't gone to prison and Abby had never died and he and Whitney had somehow gotten together under other circumstances.

"I'll tell them what they want to know," Ethan said. "I won't let them hurt you."

"You mean before they kill me?"

Ethan glanced toward Shark and the others.

"There's still a chance you'll make it," Ethan said. "I'm going to try something."

"What?"

The boat was slowing down.

"You think you can figure out how to drive this boat back to shore?" Ethan said.

Whitney stared at him.

"What do you mean there's a possibility *I'll* make it?" she said.

Ethan

3 hours, 36 minutes remaining

THE BOAT STOPPED. It rose and fell on the waves created from its own wake. Cold emanated from below like the icy breath of some great primeval creature.

Shark and the others walked from the cockpit.

"Are we still in Nevada?" Ethan asked. "Or did we cross into California?"

"Nevada," Shark said.

He was holding the hammer. Blake had the bone shears. Kicking Bird had left the shotgun in the tray by the steering wheel.

"Good," Ethan said, grinning. "One of the conditions of my release is I'm not allowed to leave the state."

Shark looked at him, surprised. Then he started laughing. Blake did too. Kicking Bird even cracked a smirk.

Shark put a hand on Ethan's shoulder.

"I've missed you."

Ethan stopped smiling. "Then why'd you kill my sister?"

"This again."

"I know you killed her, Shark," Ethan said. "Stop lying about it."

Shark stepped away, acting exasperated, and Blake stepped in to do the talking. He was probably trying to save face for having let Ethan break up the poker game and walk away with the money. He wanted to make sure that he didn't get dumped out here in the lake with Ethan and Whitney.

"Ethan," Blake said, practically yelling, "for the last goddamn time, we did not kill your sister."

"Bullshit. She was talking to the feds, so you killed her like you killed that guy Anton."

Blake stared at him, his mouth hanging open. "Abby was talking to the feds?"

"Go to hell. Don't act like you didn't know?"

Shark stepped away and leaned against the railing, strangely quiet. Ethan felt certain Shark knew something Blake didn't.

Ethan let out a frustrated groan. "Look around, Shark. We're in the middle of Lake fucking Tahoe. Stop fucking pretending."

Blake looked back and forth between Ethan and Shark.

"Shark," Ethan said, standing up. Blake grabbed him by the shoulder and forced him back into his seat, but Ethan kept talking. "I know you know she was talking. To that Brian Hughes douchebag, the same guy Anton was talking to."

"You're only repeating the name you heard Anton say," Blake said.

It was telling that Blake was the one showing surprise, not Shark.

"Do you know what Hughes looks like?" Ethan asked Blake.

"Yes."

"There's an envelope in my jacket pocket," Ethan said. "Take a look."

He hated to show them the pictures, but once they killed him, they'd find them anyway.

Shark gestured to Blake, and like a good dog, he obeyed. He handed the envelope to Shark. Shark fumbled with opening the envelope because he was still holding the hammer. He tucked it under his arm and started pulling out photographs.

Shark raised his eyebrows. "It's a pity I never got your sister to fuck me," he said, cocking his eyes to Ethan. "I would have if it wasn't for you. You think I'm such a bad guy, but I was always respectful to her." He shifted his eyes to Whitney. "This one too. I would have made her mine, but I figured she was part of the deal with Abby. So I kept my hands off."

"Go fuck yourself," Whitney spat.

Ethan leaned back in his chair, a wave of sickness flooding through him. He wasn't getting anywhere. They were still going to die. And he was going to die not knowing what happened to Abby.

"Shark," Ethan said softly, deferentially, "do you know what happened to my sister?"

Shark looked at Ethan, at first with pity, but then his expression changed to anger—like he'd put up with Ethan's games long enough.

"You don't get to ask the fucking questions," he said, and then he squatted and got close to Ethan's face. His teeth were gritted, and he almost growled the words. "I do."

78

Ethan
3 hours, 24 minutes remaining

Shark stared at him, close enough that Ethan could smell his body odor, a pungent, acidic smell.

"I only have one question," Shark said, "Where's my fucking money?"

Ethan could see there would be no reasoning with him. Time for plan B— if there was any chance of saving Whitney, he needed to act now.

"Answer me, Ethan!"

Ethan spat in his face.

Shark raised the hammer.

"Go ahead," Ethan said, holding his head up defiantly. "Kill me. Drop my body in the lake. Your money might as well be down there with me."

Shark breathed heavily through his nose, his lips closed tight. He wiped the spit off his face with his coat sleeve. He took a step back and gestured toward Blake.

"Take one of his girlfriend's fingers," he said. "Then we'll see how fucking insolent he is."

Blake started toward Whitney. He still looked a little shaken that Abby had talked to the FBI. He, at least, hadn't been a part of her murder. But he wasn't going to turn against Shark. Ethan knew that.

"You're a fucking pussy, Blake," Ethan said, rising to his feet.

Kicking Bird stepped away from the railing, snapping out the blade of his knife.

"I beat the shit out of you," Ethan said. "I put your head in the toilet. Now you're going to hurt *her*? You always were a fucking coward."

"Ethan," Blake said, "don't make this—"

"You're fucking pathetic," Ethan said. "I know it. Shark knows it. Stu knows it. You were my best friend, but now you're a fucking chickenshit little pussy."

Blake put his hand against Ethan's chest to shove him back into the seat, but Ethan pushed his arm out of the way with his cuffed hands. He got in Blake's face.

"You're going to cut off a little girl's finger? If you had any balls you'd cut off mine." He held up his cuffed hands.

Blake took a step back and looked to Shark, who had an amused expression on his face.

"Fuck it," Shark said. "Do as the man asks."

Blake pushed Ethan, and Ethan let himself go down in the chair this time.

Kicking Bird started over toward them, folding his knife and pocketing it. He'd be the one holding Ethan down.

Ethan said, "Don't bother, Stu. I won't move. I won't fucking flinch."

Kicking Bird stopped but stayed close.

Ethan held his hands up. He kept the swollen one underneath, opening the fingers of his left wide for Blake to take his pick. Blake put the blade of the cutter around the littlest finger on his left hand.

"What a fucking pussy," Ethan said. "Going for the smallest finger. How hard is it to cut off a pinky? Why don't you do some real damage and cut off my fucking thumb, Blake?"

Blake removed the cutters and got into Ethan's face.

"You want me to cut off your thumb?"

"As if you could. These guys were making fun of you when they killed Anton. Said you bitched out and made a mess of things. Couldn't get through the bone."

Blake grabbed Ethan's wrist and shoved the clipper blade around the second knuckle of his thumb.

"Hell, they can sew it back on if you cut it there," Ethan said.

Blake lowered the blade down close to the third knuckle, where the bones met the wrist, deep in the web of flesh between the thumb and forefingers.

"How's that, you son of a bitch?" Blake yelled, his eyes watering. Ethan could see the reluctance in them and hated that their friendship had come to this.

But he couldn't stop now.

"Yeah, there," Ethan yelled. He was crying too.

Blake squeezed. The pain was excruciating, but Ethan held his hands up. He roared through gritted teeth, and, as if not to be outdone, Blake did too.

Shark looked thoroughly entertained, smiling like he was enjoying a surprisingly pleasurable Broadway show.

Blood was pouring out of the cut, but Blake was hung up on the bone. He was squeezing the grips with both hands, but still the blade wouldn't cut through. Blake's face was red. Veins bulged in his forehead.

Ethan yelled, "Come on, you fucking pu—"

The blade broke through the bone with an audible *snap!*

Ethan gasped, a noise that sounded almost orgasmic. Blake exhaled as if he'd been holding his breath the entire time. He withdrew the cutters.

The blades had cut deep into the fleshy web of Ethan's hand, but not quite through all of it. Ethan's thumb dangled from a filament of skin. The blood steamed in the cold.

Shark let out a chuckle. "Well," he said, "I can't say I've ever seen anything like that before."

Ethan fell onto the deck, curling into a fetal position with his head on the wood and his arms underneath his body.

"Who's the pussy now?" Blake said, standing over Ethan.

Ethan groaned and tried to work the cuffs off his left hand. He tried not to move his arms too much so what he was doing wouldn't be obvious. The blood made his arm slick, and the ring slid easily, but it caught the exposed gorge of the cut. Ethan felt tsunamis of dizziness, each one exponentially stronger than the one before.

Don't pass out, he told himself. *You can't die yet.*

He worked the cuff around his dangling thumb and suddenly his hands were free. He held them beneath him, trying to breathe in slow, deep breaths. If he passed out, it was over.

"Blake," he groaned, "I loved you like a brother." He tried to blink away the tears. He would need to see.

He shifted toward Blake's feet and clutched his friend's pant leg. He kept his hands together, mostly concealed by his body.

"I would have done anything for you," he moaned, as he eased Blake's pant leg up.

"Ethan," Blake said, breathless. "I . . ."

He seemed lost for words.

Ethan put his fingers on the derringer hidden in Blake's boot. He might have had difficulty bending the fingers on his swollen hand to grip the gun, but all his pain receptors were preoccupied elsewhere. He took one final deep breath.

Then he yanked the pistol free and stood.

He shot the biggest threat first. The bullet hit Kicking Bird in the chest and he staggered back, more from surprise than the force of the bullet.

Ethan swung the gun on Shark, but Blake pushed his arm down. "What are you doing, man?" Blake said. He seemed genuinely surprised.

Ethan spun around, bringing up his left arm, and drove his elbow into Blake's face. Ethan's dangling thumb flopped around, and the pain threatened to buckle his knees.

Blake fell on his butt at the side of the boat. He reached in his jacket and brought out his pistol. He squeezed the trigger, and amid the bark of the gun, Ethan heard the whine of a bullet zip past his ear.

Ethan fired back—his last shot with the little Derringer—and a third nostril opened on the bridge of Blake's nose. His body collapsed into a flaccid pile.

Out of the corner of his eye, Ethan saw Shark coming at him. He threw up his left arm in defense, and Shark smashed his hammer into Ethan's wrist. The bone crunched, and fresh waves of pain sluiced through Ethan's arm. He dropped to his knees, scrambling toward Blake's body. He kept his left arm raised in defense and reached blindly for the gun in Blake's hand.

Shark lifted the hammer again. Ethan found the pistol and pressed it against the meat of Shark's leg. He squeezed the trigger and shot him through the thigh.

Shark erupted with a cry and hopped away on one leg, a dance that might have looked comical given different circumstances.

Ethan stood again. Whitney had retreated to the edge of the boat and was curled up. Kicking Bird was getting to his feet, knife in hand.

Ethan shot him again. Another body shot, but this time with a bigger caliber. Ethan turned the gun on Shark even before Kicking Bird fell. Shark saw the gun and stumbled backward. His legs crashed into the sidewall and he tumbled overboard. There was a splash and then howling.

Ethan hadn't planned on shooting him. He still wanted answers.

"Oh God," Shark yelled from the water. "Oh God."

Ethan walked over to the side of the boat. The water wasn't choppy, but the boat bobbed slightly. Ethan's vertigo made every step on the deck precarious.

Shark was splashing in the black water. He clawed at the side of the boat. "Help me," he said. "I can't swim."

Ethan held the gun on him. "Do you know what happened to my sister?"

"I'll tell you what I know," Shark said, the words coming out in gasps.

Ethan turned to look for a life preserver and saw Kicking Bird coming at him. He threw his left arm up and Kicking Bird slashed it with his knife. The pain was distant, as if his arm's nerves had shut down from overload. Kicking Bird slashed again, and Ethan accepted another wound on his arm. He swung Blake's pistol, but Kicking Bird caught it with his free hand.

Ethan tried to backpedal but lost his footing and fell, Kicking Bird coming down with him. Ethan's back was against the sideboard. He tried to jerk his gun hand free of Kicking Bird's grip, but he had no strength. Kicking Bird spun the knife in his hand—positioned to stab instead of slash—and brought it down hard. Ethan caught it again with his left forearm. The blade sunk an inch or two, and those nerves came back to life. Ethan roared.

He caught a glimpse of movement through his tunnel vision, and Kicking Bird froze. The barrels of the shotgun were pressed against Kicking Bird's temple. Whitney held the gun with her cuffed hands. She cocked both hammers with her thumbs. Kicking Bird turned his head slowly and faced the double barrels.

Ethan opened his mouth to tell Whitney to shoot, but she was ahead of him.

She squeezed both triggers.

Hot blood and bone chips splattered against Ethan's face.

79

Ethan
2 hours, 59 minutes remaining

WHITNEY DROPPED THE shotgun and reached for Ethan, throwing her cuffed arms over his head. He hugged her with his good arm but didn't let go of the pistol. She held onto him with a vise's strength. She was sobbing. Gun smoke hung in the air.

"Whitney," he said. He could hardly hear his own voice through the ringing in his ears. "I've got to get up. Shark."

She eased up, and he ducked out of her arms. He stepped away from Kicking Bird's faceless body and looked over the edge of the boat. The moonlight glistened on the black water. Shark was nowhere. Ethan hobbled around the perimeter.

"Shark!" he shouted.

On all sides of the boat, the water was empty.

Ethan staggered over toward Blake, hoping that perhaps he was still alive. But his friend's body was limp against the sidewall, his legs stretched out like he was relaxing, his chin resting on his chest. Ropes of black, moonlit blood stretched from his open mouth.

They were all dead—everyone who might know anything.

Ethan raised his head to the sky and screamed, *"Abby! Where are you?"*

Then he collapsed onto the deck.

CHAPTER

80

Whitney
2 hours, 54 minutes remaining

WHITNEY CROUCHED OVER Ethan. He was conscious, but she didn't know for how long.

"Stay awake," she said.

He stared at the sky, and Whitney knew that was all the response she was going to get out of him. She crawled to Kicking Bird's body. He lay on his side, the back of his skull opened up, with chunks of bone exposed like wedges from a broken watermelon. Whitney searched through his pockets to find the keys to her handcuffs.

She fumbled with the keys for a few seconds and finally got the cuffs undone. She searched for a first-aid kit and discovered a briefcase-sized canvas kit fastened with Velcro to a spot under the steering console.

There was a pill-bottle container of something called Wound Sealant, and she poured all of it on the wound on Ethan's thumb. He squirmed on the deck but held his hand steady for her. She pulled open a plastic vacuum-sealed pouch labeled trauma dressing. She tried to wrap it around his thumb, but there was no good way to cover the entire wound. Ethan screamed and pounded on the deck with his usable hand. Blood soaked through the bandage immediately. She found towels—beach towels and hand towels—and wrapped his hand in one of the smaller ones.

But the blood was still coming. And there were all kinds of knife wounds on his forearm.

He saved my life, she thought. *I can't let him die.*

"We've got to get your jacket off, Ethan. I can't work around it."

She released the pressure on his bandages and unzipped his jacket. She pulled his other arm, the one with the swollen hand, out first. Then, as gently as she could, she worked his mangled arm out of its sleeve. It was hard—the arm was swollen and his dangling thumb dragged against the leather. Ethan was gritting his teeth and taking shallow breaths.

She pulled off her belt, a thin strip of leather, and looped it under his armpit. She yanked it as tight as she could and looked around. Kicking Bird's knife was within reach, lying on the deck. She grabbed it and jammed a new hole into the belt. She fastened the belt strap tight against his artery. Then she wrapped his hand up in a towel again and secured it with medical tape. He'd been close to hyperventilating, but once she finished wrapping his hand, his breathing leveled off.

She dug around in the first-aid kit.

"It's your lucky day," Whitney said.

"I don't feel lucky."

"There's an IV."

She tried to remember what to do from a nursing class she'd had before dropping out of school. She used Kicking Bird's knife to cut along the seam of his shirtsleeve. Now she could see his arm was definitely broken. She could tell by the swelling and the bruising and the way the ulna—the smaller of the two bones—seemed to be bent inward. At least the bone wasn't sticking out through the skin.

She jammed the needle into the big vein in the crook of his right arm. She left the catheter sticking out of his skin, unrolled the IV tubing and plugged it, then stretched a stick of medical tape and fastened the catheter in place. She tucked the bag into the collar of his shirt.

"Sit up," she said.

"Are you kidding?"

She grabbed him around the neck and pulled him into a sitting position. He groaned but stayed upright.

"Keep your arm down," she said. "The stuff will drain into your body."

Whitney dressed the other wounds quickly, using the large trauma bandages. His leather jacket had probably lessened the damage, but there was still plenty of it.

Whitney didn't know what to do with the broken bone, but she was satisfied she'd at least triaged all the bleeding wounds.

Whitney kissed Ethan's cheek. "All better?"

He grinned slightly. "Good as new."

Whitney let out an uncomfortable laugh. "It's nice to see you haven't lost your sense of humor," she said.

He looked like he was about to pass out

81

Ethan
2 hours, 31 minutes remaining

Ethan felt unconsciousness threatening. He was tempted to let himself go under. What a relief it would be to sleep. And if he died, so what?

He fought only because he didn't want to put Whitney through that. She was trying hard to keep him alive. He couldn't disappoint her.

She found Blake's cell phone, but there was no service this far out on the lake. "Is there a radio on this thing?" she said.

She looked and found something that looked like one, but she didn't know how to work it.

"I told you you were going to have to figure out how to drive this boat," Ethan said from the deck floor.

She made him get up. He moaned as she pulled him off the deck. She supported most of his weight, and they staggered to the cockpit. She helped him lie down on the cushioned couch. She took the IV bag and wedged it into a handgrip above the couch.

The key was in the ignition, and she turned it. The motors fired but then quickly died.

"That's the gas," Ethan said, pointing from where he lay to a lever on the console.

Whitney tried again, this time easing the lever up as the motors started to spin. The engines caught and the boat started idling forward. She eased the gas up, and the boat accelerated across the water, bobbing up and down in great splashes. She gave it more gas, and soon they were skimming across the surface.

She pointed the boat toward the lights on the shore. The sky had started to lighten. Instead of blackness full of stars, the atmosphere was now dark blue with only a handful of lights still shining through. The moon had traveled the length of the sky since they first saw it rise over the Black Rock Desert. It hovered above the mountains.

"Whitney?" Ethan called.

"Yeah," she said.

"I want you to take me back to prison."

"No way. As soon as we get to shore, I'm calling you an ambulance."

"I'm in a shitload of trouble," Ethan said. "There's a guy there. My caseworker. He's always had my back. He can run interference with the cops and the feds. If I report back to prison on time, that will go a long way toward showing them I'll cooperate. I don't need 'fugitive from justice' on the list of things they can throw at me."

"There's still a chance they could save your thumb, Ethan."

"I don't care."

"You're crazy," she said.

"I know," he said. "We'd be dead if I wasn't."

What he'd told her was only partly true. He really wanted to go back to prison because that was his home now. It was where he felt safe. He'd gone out into the world and this is what had happened. He knew, logically, that he wouldn't be in prison right away. They would rush him to the hospital after they got one look at him. But the *idea* of prison was welcoming. To be incarcerated, whether in his jail cell or in a hospital room. There would be guards to protect him. From the world but also from himself. He would be safe again.

He might never get out again, but he didn't care.

"I'm going to tell them that you were my hostage," he went on.

"No."

"I don't think there's any other way."

"Stop it, Ethan."

Behind them, the motors threw up white plumes. The sky was turning a lighter and lighter blue each second.

"You were my hostage," Ethan said. "We have to have our stories straight."

Whitney said nothing.

Ethan closed his eyes.

He stood over the abyss. He thought about diving in. Why not? Abby was down there waiting for him.

"Not yet," he muttered.

He opened his eyes. The sky seemed much lighter than it had a second ago.

82

Ethan
1 hour and 56 minutes remaining

SHE FOUND THE marina easily enough, and instead of searching for Shark's slip or an open place on any pier, she aimed the boat at the loading ramp and revved the engine. The boat ran aground with a terrible screeching sound as the fiberglass slid across the pavement. The propellers screamed as they dug into concrete. Ethan almost tumbled off the couch but was able to hold on with one hand. The engine stalled, and black clouds of smoke poured out of the motors. Now that it was no longer floating, the boat listed to one side.

The dead bodies were stiff. The blood splattered and pooling about the deck had turned to ice. The strawberry preserves oozing out of the cavern in Kicking Bird's face had frozen his head to the deck. Icicles of blood hung from Blake's mouth. Whitney dug through Blake's pockets. She found Ethan's cell phone and truck keys. Ethan was impressed with her strength under the circumstances, proud of how in control she was.

"Grab those," Ethan said and pointed to the envelope of photos stuck in an icy puddle of blood.

She pried them loose and then lowered a ladder attached to the side closest to the ground. She climbed down first and helped him descend, then she supported his weight as they walked the ramp to the parking lot. She kept the first-aid kit in one hand.

She opened the passenger door to his truck. He fell on his side on the bench seat, but once he was there, he was able to sit upright. She took the IV bag and wedged it into a hand strap on the ceiling next to the door.

She ran around to the other side and started the engine. Her cell phone was where she'd left it on the seat. Ethan read her mind and asked her again not to call 911. She turned the heater up all the way and looked around for her bag of pharmaceuticals. It was on the floor by Ethan's feet. She tapped two oxycodone onto Ethan's swollen palm, paused for a second, and then added a third. He popped them into his mouth but had to work hard to swallow them.

"What I wouldn't do for a fucking glass of water," Ethan said after he got the pills down.

"We can stop at a drive-thru," Whitney quipped.

He chuckled. She gunned the engine and took off.

83

Ethan
1 hour, 12 minutes remaining

ETHAN'S LEFT ARM had tingled for a while, but now he had no sensation in it at all.

"I've got to undo this tourniquet," he said. "I don't want to lose my arm entirely."

He had trouble working the strap, and Whitney reached over to help. A warmth rush into his arm, and he hoped that the wounds had congealed enough to stop a fresh stream of blood.

Ethan leaned against the glass. The cab of the truck smelled like Blake's cigarette smoke. The truck sped over the highway running alongside the lake, and Ethan looked out over the surface. The water was a deep cobalt, glimmering in the morning sunlight. Smooth, like blue glass. Shark was down there somewhere, floating a hundred or two hundred or five hundred feet below the surface.

The highway veered away from the lake, and now his view of the water was obscured by a forest of pine trees. His eyesight seemed to focus incredibly, like he could see the detail in everything he looked at: the trees, the glinting water beyond, a hawk hanging in the breeze.

Ethan couldn't believe what had transpired. Everything had happened so fast that he could hardly remember the order of events. And all of it was for nothing. He'd killed the people he had gone to prison to protect, and he hadn't found out what happened to Abby.

He let his body fall over on the bench seat. He cradled his left arm and started to cry. He buried his head into the truck seat and sobbed the way he'd been unable to at Abby's funeral.

"I'm sorry, Abby," he said. "I'm sorry."

Whitney put her hand on his shoulder and rubbed his arm gently.

"Shh," she said, as if he were a baby crying before bedtime. "Shh."

When some time had passed, Whitney said, "We don't have to go to the prison. You could run. I could go with you. Maybe we didn't find Abby's killer, but something good could come from this. You and me—Abby would be okay with that."

Ethan sat up.

"I need medical attention," he said, his voice low and matter-of-fact. "You saved me, Whitney, but I'm going to need real help."

She was crying as she steered.

"And living on the run is no way to live," he said. "You deserve better."

"I would do it for you," she said.

"But I wouldn't do it *to* you," he said.

CHAPTER

84

Ethan
32 minutes remaining

WHEN THEY LEFT the curvy highway and descended into Carson City, Ethan pulled down the sun visor and looked at himself in the mirror. He tried to wipe away the blood, but it was caked on.

He dug into his pockets with his swollen hand, first the right and then, across his body, the left. He dumped the business cards and the envelope of pictures out onto the bench seat. Shark's ledger was lying on the floorboards, and Ethan bent over to pick it up. He tossed it on the pile of paperwork—everything he'd acquired during his investigation. None of it had amounted to anything.

They were close to the prison now. The traffic was sparse on the cold Sunday morning. Fast-food restaurants and slot casinos lined the roadway, but the parking lots were nearly empty.

Ethan grabbed his phone off the seat and saw that he had five missed calls, all from Hughes. He thought about calling him and telling him to go to the marina where Shark kept his boat.

Fuck that guy, Ethan thought.

Instead, he called his mom. She didn't pick up.

"Mom," he said to her voicemail. His breathing became heavy and his voice quivered. "I tried," he said. "I tried but I failed. I'm sorry." His voice cracked and he took a deep breath. "I would love it if you would come visit me. If you could find it in your heart to do that."

He couldn't say anymore, so he ended the call. He dropped the phone on the seat and slouched back, blinking away tears.

The prison was up ahead, its stone walls encircled by tall hurricane fencing topped with razor wire.

Home.

85

Ethan
7 minutes remaining

THE IV WAS empty and Ethan tossed the bag on the floor. He put the tube in his teeth and pulled the needle out. A trickle of blood ran down his arm.

Whitney crept the truck toward the vehicle entrance of the prison's gravel lot.

"Ethan," she said, "I was wondering something."

"Yeah?"

"Shark's money," she said. "What *did* you do with it?"

Ethan snickered. "I put it in Abby's casket."

"What?"

"I wanted to put it somewhere out of Shark's reach."

Her mouth was open in shock. Even after all that had happened, she was still capable of being surprised. That was probably a good thing.

"I would have given it to you," he said, "but I thought it would be too dangerous if Shark found out you had it."

"Are you going to tell the cops where you put it?"

"No," he said. "I don't want them messing up her grave to get it. I'll say I threw the briefcase in the river. That's not a lie actually. Maybe they'll find the case and think the money fell out."

Whitney stopped the truck. She left the engine running, and they looked at what was ahead.

A twenty-foot-tall gate stood before them, already opened. Daryl was behind the fence as expected. There were three guards on the ground and another with a rifle in the tower gatehouse—also expected. What wasn't expected was Calvin Taylor, there along with two police cars and four uniformed officers.

Taylor was talking to Daryl, probably sorting out what to do. Book him back into the prison then question him? Or arrest him on the spot?

Neither of them was expecting him to show up with a missing thumb and a slew of knife wounds—he was almost amused thinking about how they would sort out all the paperwork he was about to give them.

"What's going to happen now?" Whitney said.

"I don't know," he said, "but I'm probably going to be in there"—he gestured toward the prison—"or another place like it for the rest of my life."

"I don't want you to go," Whitney said quietly. She put the truck in park and scooted over on the seat—squishing the ledger and envelope and cards between them—and hugged him around the neck.

"You go and live a good life, Whitney," he said. "Do it for me and for Abby."

She wept into the crook of his neck.

"We don't have much time," he said. "Here, take these."

She let go of his neck and scooted a few inches away. He handed her the photo envelope. There were droplets of dried blood on the outside, and the ink of the handwritten *ABBY* was now smeared slightly from getting wet on the boat.

"As much as I'd love to get that prick Hughes fired," he said, "I don't want anyone to see those pictures."

She wiped her eyes.

Through the windshield, they could see Daryl and Taylor walk through the open gate and approach the truck. The clock on the dashboard read 8:57.

"This too," Ethan said, reaching for the ledger.

He grabbed it with his swollen hand, but his fingers were numb, and he fumbled trying to pass it to her. The ledger dropped to the floor of the truck, spilling all of the keno receipts onto the mat.

"Shit," he muttered.

"I'll get it," Whitney said, leaning over.

But Ethan was staring at the pile of rectangular papers. Among the receipts were a few envelopes—which they'd checked earlier to find the contents were simply more receipts. However, one of the envelopes caught his eye now. It had *SHARK* written in block handwriting across it. He hadn't paid attention to the writing before. He opened the envelope. The time stamp on the receipt inside showed it was purchased early the morning after Abby's disappearance at the Carson Nugget, which was way down south in Carson City—nowhere near Lake Tahoe or the Black Rock Desert.

The numbers that were played that day were simply 1 and 2, which Ethan knew corresponded to nowhere in Nevada. It was probably in the middle of the goddamn ocean. You have to choose a minimum of two numbers when you play keno, but it looked like whoever bought this card simply did it so Shark could have the receipt. They would have bought 0 and 0 if that had been an option. No, these weren't coordinates. If someone had been killed, that person had not been buried in the desert or dropped into the lake.

She had simply vanished from the face of the earth.

Whitney finished collecting the other receipts and reached to grab the papers in Ethan's hand, but he held onto them. He was staring at the *SHARK* envelope. He recognized the handwriting now.

Someone knocked on the truck window—Taylor or Daryl or one of their men—but Ethan didn't lift his eyes.

"Ethan?" Whitney said. "You okay?"

"I know what happened to Abby," Ethan said, raising his head to stare into Whitney's eyes. "I know where she is."

CHAPTER

86

Abby
3 weeks ago

Abby woke up with a desert in her mouth. Her head was pounding. She wasn't sure where she was. She must have done something stupid—drunk too much or, worse, gone home with a customer.

She looked around and quickly figured out neither of those things had happened. She was in a bare room with cinderblock walls peppered with tiny drill holes. It reminded her of the soundproofing in her high school band room. The space was lit brightly by a single bulb in the ceiling, and the air was warm from an electric space heater plugged into the room's only socket. Abby took all this in from where she was lying, on a twin-sized mattress on the floor.

The room had one door, a big metal thing with no handle on this side. In front of the door sat a plastic tray with food on it, like you might get from room service. A tin lid covered the meal, and a plastic cup of liquid stood next to it. She crawled over and grabbed the cup, which held water. Her mouth was unbearably dry, and all she wanted was a drink. Then she'd figure out what the hell was going on.

She swished the water around in her mouth. It tasted funny, and she wasn't sure if it was the water or her taste buds.

A memory from last night flooded into her mind, and she spit the water out.

Brian had been over. They'd had a fight, and he'd left. It was late and she'd wanted to go to bed. Whitney was going to be over early so they could drive to Mammoth to snowboard. She'd thought about texting Whitney to cancel, but decided that maybe a day away was what she needed. Maybe it was time to finally tell Whitney the real reason she'd wanted to go to work at the club.

She walked over to her window to close the blinds, and she saw Robert on his balcony waving to her.

"Hey," he said when she stepped outside. "I noticed you were still up."

"About to go to bed," she said.

"Can I come over?"

"I'm tired."

"My sister died," he said. "I don't want to be alone."

Abby wanted to tell him no—she didn't really like to have much to do with him except buy drugs every now and then—but she couldn't bring herself to do it. She couldn't imagine losing a sibling. She'd been devastated when Ethan had gone to prison. What if he'd *died*?

Besides, she wasn't sure she'd be able to sleep anyway with everything that was on her mind: what to do about Lee, what was going to happen with Brian, what she could do—if anything—for Ethan.

Screw it, she thought. *Maybe I can stay up until Whitney gets here. I'll sleep while she drives.*

He took his sweet time coming over, and every second she waited, she regretted agreeing to this. But he showed up with two cups of coffee, which explained the delay.

They sat in her living room and she asked him what had happened.

"Car accident," he said, but he didn't seem sad. He seemed jittery. Almost upbeat. Nervous.

Waves of sleepiness started to wash over her immediately. She thought, for a moment, that she was just exhausted after a long day. But then she realized something was wrong.

"Did you fucking roofie me?" she said.

He started laughing. "It's something a little more powerful than Rohypnol."

She wanted to stand and tell him to get the hell out. But she couldn't find the strength to get off the couch. That was the last thing she remembered.

Now she stood up and started pounding on the metal door.

"Hey, you motherfucker! Open this goddamn door!"

There was a twinge of pain in one arm, and she noticed that there was a small Band-Aid taped in the crook of her elbow.

"What the hell?"

She pulled the bandage and saw a small red dot, a needle hole like she was injected with heroin or had her blood drawn. She looked at her other arm and found another Band-Aid and another needle mark. A chill ran down her back.

She noticed for the first time—she was still groggy despite the adrenaline cours-
ing through her veins—that there were maroon stains on her clothes.

Blood.

She examined herself for other wounds but found nothing besides the pin-
pricks in her arms.

She smacked her palm against the door. She yelled and yelled. Finally, she
heard a door open from above—she must have been in a basement—and footsteps on the concrete floor.

"Abby," Robert said from the other side of the door. "How are you?"

"How the fuck do you think I am? Let me out of here or so help me."

"Why don't you calm down?" he said. "I made some food for you."

She lifted the lid of the metal dish sitting on the floor by the door. There
was a chicken breast inside, with asparagus spears and mashed sweet potatoes.

"What, so I can pass out and you can rape me? Fuck you."

She had the horrific thought that maybe she'd already been raped. She felt
around on her body. Her breasts. Between her legs. She was wearing the sweatpants and sweatshirt she'd had on last night. They were stained with dried
blood but they didn't look like they'd been removed. Her bra was clasped, her
panties weren't askew. She wasn't sore anywhere. Except her arm and her head.

"You're going to have to eat, Abby."

"If you try to touch me," Abby said, "I'll gouge your eyes out with my fingernails. I'll tear your balls off with my bare hands. Don't think I won't."

"I can't talk to you when you're like this." He walked away.

She yelled for him to come back, but his footsteps went up the stairs and the
door closed.

She turned around, her back to the door, and surveyed the room. She felt
the strong urge to cry, to slump to the floor and curl into a ball and sob.

She wouldn't let herself.

I've got to figure this out, she thought.

Abby sat with her back to the wall and put her hands in her hair. She stood
up and paced around her cell. Besides the mattress and the food tray, there was
only a porcelain toilet. There was no sink, and she had the strange thought that
Ethan's cell was probably nicer than this one. This brought home the horror of
the situation she was in, and she felt a wave of terror sluice through her
bloodstream.

She took the metal lid and started banging on the door with it—a loud
metallic clanging. Robert came down the stairs.

"Here's what's going to happen," Abby said. "You're going to bring me my
food in cans. Packaged foods that haven't been opened. And bottled water—
seals intact. I'm not eating anything you could dissolve drugs into. Got it?"

"You don't make the rules, Abby."

"The hell I don't," she said. "You might as well open your little hatch and take this food away."

He didn't.

For what must have been at least twenty-four hours, he left the food in her cell, and Abby willed herself not to take a bite, not a single swig of water. She lifted the lid off the back of the toilet and cupped the water inside, slurping it down.

Her stomach cramped. Her body trembled with weakness.

Finally, he came and told her to stand in the corner, away from the door.

"Go to hell," she said.

"I've got some food for you," he said. "Packaged food. You lost a lot of blood, Abby. You need to eat."

She did as he told her and stood on the other side of the cell. He opened the hatch, and she saw about half of his face, staring in at her. His expression seemed normal, like he was feeding a pet. He pulled the tray out of the room and slid a new one in. There was a can of soup with a pull-tab to tear the lid off, along with two pudding packets. A single bottle of Gatorade.

When he pulled the hatch closed, she examined each item as carefully as possible, trying to find places where the packages had been subtly opened or needle holes where something could have been injected inside. When she was satisfied, she popped the lid off the Gatorade. She drank half the bottle and made herself stop. Then she pulled the lid off the can of soup and poured a glob into her mouth. He hadn't given her any utensils.

She ate all the food but made herself leave a couple swallows of sports drink. She was still hungry, and there was no telling when he would bring her more.

I have to survive, she thought. *I have to stay alive until someone saves me.*

Her boyfriend worked for the FBI. He would be looking for her. But as she thought about it, she had an awful realization: Brian would think Shark had killed her. He'd warned her over and over about the dangers of double-crossing Shark. No doubt he was sitting somewhere thinking his fears had come to fruition.

She was sure he was out there investigating the wrong clues.

She thought of Ethan.

She remembered when she was a teenager and she'd almost drowned. She'd been underwater, unable to breathe, the dark blue around her turning darker every second. She had pleaded for him in her mind—*Ethan, help!*—and, as if through telepathy, he had jumped in to save her.

Ethan, she thought again, as she had nine years ago when she was drowning. *Help me!*

But Ethan was in prison.

This was what made Abby finally break down and cry.

87

Ethan
1 minute remaining

ETHAN STEPPED OUT of his truck. Daryl and Taylor were flanked by the four officers and two prison guards. Ethan held his hands up, not in a surrender position, but in a gesture that meant they should keep their distance.

"I need to talk to Taylor," he said.

"I'm here to arrest you, Ethan. We'll have plenty of time to talk after . . ." He trailed off, seeing that Ethan had blood all over him.

"Holy Jesus," Daryl said. His jaw dropped open. One hand went involuntarily to his mouth. "What happened?"

"I need a minute, Daryl," Ethan said, holding up his index finger on his swollen hand. "Taylor, please."

Daryl started yelling toward the gate. "Call 911. And get whoever is in the infirmary to come down here ASAP."

One of the guards took off to make sure this message was delivered, but everyone else stayed put, unsure what to do. Whitney hopped out of the truck and circled around to join them.

Ethan ignored all of this and focused on Taylor's face. The man looked angry. This wasn't how he'd planned to spend his Sunday morning, and he undoubtedly regretted not taking Ethan into custody yesterday. He looked like he'd been up all night.

"Look at these," Ethan said, holding with one hand the envelope with Abby's photographs and the envelope that held the keno receipt. "Would you say these are in the same handwriting?"

Taylor looked at both. The words *ABBY* and *SHARK* were both written in block letters, which, to Ethan's eyes, looked like they'd been written by the exact same hand. *ABBY* was smeared slightly, and there was blood on the envelope, but still the word was easily legible.

"I'm no handwriting expert," Taylor said.

"Come on!" Ethan said in frustration.

"But," Taylor added, "they look the same as far as I can tell. Where did you get them?"

Ethan explained that *SHARK* came from Shark's ledger, which showed, in code, the locations of the people he'd killed. The large envelope was from Abby's neighbor, who had been illegally photographing her.

"And look," Ethan said, wedging the large envelope under his armpit so he could open the smaller one and show Taylor the keno receipt. "The date. It corresponds exactly with Abby's disappearance."

"I'm not following," Taylor said.

"Shit," Ethan spat in frustration.

He didn't know how to explain what he was thinking in a clear and succinct way, how he could catch Taylor up in only a minute or two on all he'd learned in the last forty-eight hours.

"When Shark gets rid of bodies," he said, "he keeps track of them in a ledger. He uses a code that makes it look like it's a record of keno numbers he's played. That way, if you or the feds ever get ahold of it, you won't know what you've got."

"And Abby's in there?"

"Not exactly," Ethan said. Whitney helped him by holding the book open and pointing to the entry. "Whitney and I thought they just didn't go through with hiding her body that night and did it the next day. But look . . ." Whitney showed the keno receipt with the *1* and *2*. "Shark always got his normal guys—Kicking Bird or Blake or whoever—to get rid of the bodies and write them in the ledger. But for whatever reason, he used someone else this time. Shark didn't record any coordinates in the book because the 1 and 2 on the receipt are meaningless. I don't think Shark knew where Abby was taken."

Taylor looked skeptical.

"That's a lot of conjecture based on two words written in block letters," Taylor said.

"There's more," Ethan said.

He held up the envelope with *SHARK* written on it. The envelope itself was blank except for a preprinted return address. There was no name, just a two-line street and town in Alpine County, California, about fifty or sixty miles from where they were standing.

Ethan reached back into the truck and snatched the other envelope—the one he'd taken from Robert Winther's townhome to put all the cards and paperwork in—and held it up to Taylor next to the other one.

The addresses were the same.

"One of these is from Shark's murder ledger, containing the receipt I'm talking about," Ethan said. "The other is from Robert's townhome across the street from Abby."

Taylor looked back and forth, thinking.

"It's her *neighbor*," Ethan yelled. *"He has a cabin in Alpine County!"*

"Jesus," Taylor said. His expression of anger had dissolved.

"I'm telling you: it's him. All the other receipts are from Reno casinos. Or Tahoe. But this one was purchased at the Carson Nugget." Ethan pointed in the direction of where the casino would be, probably only two or three miles from here. "It's on his way to the cabin. When he delivered the receipt, he stuck it in one of his own envelopes and wrote *SHARK* on it. He probably left it at the bar while Shark was out, thinking Shark would throw the envelope away and only keep the receipt."

"But Robert Winther came to us with a photograph," Taylor said. "Why would he do that if he wasn't trying to help?"

"He showed you the picture of Hughes, didn't he?"

"Yeah."

"And what did you do?"

"I gave it to Hughes."

"And what did he do?"

"Buried it, I assume," Taylor said, keeping his voice low. "He'd lose his job if it came out he was sleeping with an informant."

"Exactly," Ethan said. "Robert made it sound like he didn't know who Hughes was, but that was bullshit. He'd been spying on them for god knows how long. He probably spotted his gun or his badge. Robert knew that photograph would keep eyes off him. Or, if Hughes didn't bury it and he got into trouble, it would derail the whole investigation. Either way, it's a distraction. As soon as he brought you that photo, no one so much as looked his way. You never thought of him as a serious suspect."

Ethan took a breath, then added regretfully, "And neither did I."

CHAPTER

88

Abby
2 weeks ago

ROBERT BROUGHT ABBY food almost every day, but it was only a can and a bottle of water. Twice, he brought bottles that had already been opened, and she made herself not drink them. He also included unpackaged food. An apple one day. A muffin the next. A smelly burrito from Taco Bell. She didn't allow herself to eat anything suspicious.

Her stomach always ached. Her head throbbed. Her ears started ringing.

She remembered almost drowning. It was horrifying, but at least it would have been fast. A few quick seconds of panic. But this was agonizingly slow.

"Hey, Abby," Robert said from the hallway as he knelt to unlatch the panel at the bottom of the door. "Dinnertime."

She despised Robert's visits. He was often gone for days at a time, and during those periods, she felt an overwhelming sense of relief. When he was here, and she could hear his footsteps overhead or he came down into the basement to talk to her, her stomach knotted with fear. She was so weak she knew she couldn't fight him off if he opened the door. She always acted tough, to keep him at bay, and when he was home, she worried every minute that he would call her bluff.

She'd always thought of him as a harmless weirdo, but she understood now that she'd never seen him at all. When his eyes—beady black marbles buried in the pudgy dough of his face—had lingered on her in the past, she'd just thought he was a horny, socially awkward single guy, just like a lot of the customers at the club. But now when she looked back and thought about it, she could see there'd always been something more threatening about him. Something in his eyes and in his manners had been there all along, suggesting that if he could slip free from the bonds of normal society, there was no telling what he would be willing to do to her.

She'd spent the last two years around dangerous men. It turned out she'd been blind to the most dangerous one in her life.

"What the fuck is this?" Abby said, after Robert slid a new tray into her cell: a warm hamburger, French fries, and a cookie.

"Sorry, Abby," he said, sounding almost jolly. "No more packaged foods. And I've shut off the water to your toilet."

The aroma was torture. She was salivating so badly she had to wipe her mouth with her shirtsleeve.

"Why are you doing this?" she croaked.

"Oh, Abby," he said jovially. "I wanted you for a long time. I just couldn't figure out how to make it happen. You're not the first girl to stay with me in this room. It's easier when they're transient. Homeless or something. But I knew people would look for you. I wasn't afraid of the cops figuring it out, but I knew you were special to Shark and he'd send his people to find you. You were off-limits. And then," he added, "you went and screwed that FBI agent."

Once Robert had realized who she was sleeping with, he'd hatched a plan. He showed the pictures to Shark—just of her talking to the agent, not them together in bed.

"You really should be thanking me," Robert said. "When I showed him the pictures, Shark badly wanted to kill you himself—said he had a perfect spot in the desert with your name written on it—but I convinced him to let me have you."

Because she was talking to the feds and because she was Ethan Lockhart's sister, Robert sold Shark on the idea that there would be extra heat when she went missing—and Shark would do well to be more removed from the crime. He told Shark what day he planned to do it, which would allow Shark and his men to secure airtight alibis.

Robert had drawn Abby's blood and spread it on the floor to make it look like she'd been murdered. He wanted to fool Shark as much as he did the police—everyone needed to believe she was dead.

"I poured it all over the floor and rolled you around in it," he said. "I was going to use it to write some Satanic bullshit on the walls to throw people off even more, but your pal Whitney interrupted me before I could put the finishing touches on the scene."

As soon as he'd gotten Abby in the car, he'd hooked an IV to her—hence the needle hole in the other arm—to make sure she didn't die.

As Robert spoke, Abby curled into a tight ball, holding herself and rocking back and forth. She wasn't crying. Those days had passed.

"How much did you pay him?" Abby said, wondering how much her life had been worth.

"Nothing." Robert laughed. "I offered. Money, drugs, favors. But it turns out he only wanted one thing. He wanted me to play a game of keno at one of the casinos that same night and give him the receipt."

Shark told him what numbers to play, and when Robert asked why, he explained that he wouldn't tell any of his crew of the deal they'd struck, but he did want some kind of trophy to remember her by.

"That's how he put it," Robert said. "I don't understand how a keno receipt could be a trophy, but what do I care. I got what I wanted. I have my own trophy."

89

Ethan
12 minutes past

DARYL HAD BEEN listening to Ethan talk to Taylor, but at the first chance to interrupt, he said, "Ethan, it's past nine o'clock." He gestured to a medic hurrying toward them. "We've got a doc here."

"Give me a fucking minute!"

Daryl recoiled.

"Just one moment," Taylor said to Daryl, keeping his voice calm to quell all the confusion around them. None of the guards or cops he had brought with him seemed to know what to do.

To Ethan, Taylor said, "I'll look into it. I promise."

"Can you get a search warrant for his cabin? How long will it take?"

"Uh," Taylor said, "there are jurisdictional issues."

"How fucking long?"

"Well, it's a Sunday. I'll make some calls tomorrow. If there's enough circumstantial evidence, maybe next week, if we're lucky."

"But what if she's still alive?" Ethan pleaded. "You said yourself that she shouldn't have been declared dead without a body."

"She lost a lot of blood, Ethan. I don't want you getting your hopes up."

Ethan thought about how much blood he'd lost. At least a liter, probably more. He still had fight left in him.

Abby was a fighter too.

Ethan pictured the police bringing the guy in for questioning, asking his whereabouts on the dates of the crime, letting him go while they tried for a warrant. He'd clean up whatever evidence there was. And if Abby was still alive, he'd kill her and get rid of her body.

"What if she's still alive now but she's dead by the time you get to her?" Ethan said.

Taylor went silent. Everyone was staring at him: Whitney, Daryl, a doctor, the guards and deputies.

"We need to go to his cabin right now," Ethan pleaded, holding up the envelope. "I have the address. Let's beat down the goddamn door. Find her!"

Taylor shook his head. "I can't even cross the state line without making a half-dozen phone calls."

"Ethan," Daryl said softly, his friendly tone back. "It's time to come with us, buddy. We'll take care of everything. You need a doctor, my friend."

Ethan looked at Whitney. Tears were brimming in her eyes. Her face looked scared and horrified and—underneath all that—yearning. *Could there be a chance to save Abby?*

Some of the men already had their hands on their holstered pistols, ready to draw if Ethan didn't come willingly.

"Ethan," Taylor said in a relaxed tone, probably trying to calm the police and prison officers as much as him, "you have to come in now. Time's up."

Ethan thought about trying to jump into the truck and take off. But police didn't mess around when it came to escaping convicts. He could go for one of their guns, but that would get him killed even quicker. He could grab Whitney, pretend she was a hostage. They might not fire if he used her as a shield. But as much as Ethan loved Abby—as much as he wanted to save her—he could not put Whitney in harm's way anymore. He could not sacrifice Whitney to save Abby.

"Please," Ethan said to Taylor, but the detective's expression told him that there were no options.

Ethan was out of time. It was as simple as that.

It was over.

Then he saw movement out of the corner of his eye and looked up. A familiar sedan was pulling up next to his truck. Brian Hughes sat behind the wheel.

"Wait," Ethan said, almost shouting. He held his hand up to keep the officers at bay. He stared at Taylor. "You said you can't cross the border without making a half-dozen phone calls." He pointed to Hughes as the FBI agent got out of the car. "But *he* can."

CHAPTER

90

Abby
3 days ago

A BBY WAS STARVING.
After not eating for what seemed like days—subsisting on the last of
the water in the toilet tank—she felt overpowering hope when Robert opened
the door to the cellar. Would he bring something she could eat this time? But
when he slid a new tray under her door, she wanted to scream when she saw the
pork chop, applesauce, green beans. A cup of milk.

Robert had made good on his promise of no more packaged foods.

"Abby," Robert called to her from the hallway. "Guess what."

He slid a newspaper under the door.

"You're dead."

Funeral planned for missing dancer. Abby read the headline with trembling
hands. The article said she'd been declared dead "in absentia" and her funeral
was planned for the weekend. The reporter gave the background of her case, but
there wasn't much detail. A quote from a cop saying they were pursuing all possible leads, which sounded to her like they didn't have any.

Abby flipped through the rest of the paper, looking for any information
about what was going on out there. She scanned for an article about Lee—had
Shark killed him?—but the newspaper told her nothing either way. It was life as
usual for the rest of the world. No one knew she was here.

Her body odor disgusted her. The toilet reeked of shit and piss since it
could no longer be flushed.

Later, Robert came back and slid a few cans of food into her cell.

"Make this last," he told her. "I'm going to be gone for a few days and don't want to come back to find you dead."

She was so hungry she knew she would devour it within minutes, no matter how much she told herself to ration it.

"I'm heading to the city," he announced. "I'm going to your funeral."

91

Ethan
23 minutes past

B RIAN HUGHES CHARGED into the crowd of prison officials and cops with an arrogance that parted them out of his way.

"I got word that there's a goddamn bloodbath at the marina where Shark keeps his boat," he said. "I was on my way to the lake but I made a U-turn. If anyone is going to tell me what the hell's going on, it's you." He looked Ethan up and down, taking in the blood and the bandages. "I think I made the right call. What the hell happened up there, Ethan?"

"I'll tell you on the drive to California," Ethan said.

"What?" Hughes smirked.

"No," Daryl said. "You're not going anywhere. You are officially in the custody of the Nevada State Prison system now."

"Not yet," Ethan said, pointing to the gate, only a few feet away. He hadn't crossed over the threshold to the prison.

"Well, then you're late," Daryl said. "Which makes you a fugitive."

The guards moved to take Ethan into custody, but the officers Taylor brought with him bristled and moved to arrest him instead. Hughes lifted his arms to halt them. "Wait. I want to hear this."

"Just you and you," Ethan said, gesturing to Taylor and Hughes. "Tell all these other assholes to give us some goddamn space."

Daryl wouldn't have it. "You are in *my* custody."

"Fine," Ethan said, "but get everyone else back."

Daryl and Taylor told their associates to stand back about fifteen feet. Ethan asked Whitney to stay too, and the five of them—Ethan, Whitney, Taylor, Hughes, and Daryl—stood in a tense huddle. Then Ethan repeated everything he'd told Taylor—the similar handwriting, the address.

"You're grasping at straws," Daryl said.

"No one fucking asked you," Ethan growled.

But Brian looked intrigued. "Damned if the handwriting on those envelopes doesn't look identical. Are you lying to us? Did you take all of this from Winther's apartment?"

Whitney came to Ethan's defense, adamant that one came from Shark's office, the other from Robert's.

"Does Robert Winther even know Shark?"

"He was a customer at Dark Secrets," Whitney said. "I think he used to sell Shark prescription meds."

The guards and police who'd stepped back were slowly encroaching back toward Ethan.

"The problem," Hughes said, looking at Taylor for confirmation, "is that none of this is going to be admissible in court. We've got a felon who stole all the evidence and whose testimony isn't going to be worth jack shit."

"I'm not talking about taking this to court," Ethan snapped. "We need to go to his house in Alpine County. Right now."

"We?" Hughes said. "Maybe Taylor and I can go check it out together, but you're going back behind bars, my friend. Or to a hospital. There's nothing I can do about that."

Ethan felt himself on the verge of exploding.

"Listen, Brian," he said, his voice hoarse and unrecognizable. "You got me out. You took the leash off and said, 'Go wreak havoc.' Well, I did. And I did all the messy work you couldn't do yourself. You can't put me back in the cage. Not now."

Neither Hughes nor Taylor said anything. From the moment he met Hughes, Ethan knew the agent played fast and loose with the rules, and he hoped a guy willing to sleep with an informant and pull strings to get a prisoner released wouldn't mind rewriting the rules now too.

Ethan was unsure how much to reveal but decided not to hold back. Hughes needed more incentive.

"Shark is dead. You'll never get the big arrest you've been working for. If you want to be on the news and get that promotion, you'll have to do it by bringing home all the skeletons he buried in his closet. I spent last night digging up a grave in the Black Rock Desert. I saw the bodies of two of Shark's victims myself. I know where dozens of others are located, including your informant, Anton. But I won't cooperate unless you take me to that cabin right now."

"And if you find Abby, that's another feather in your cap," Whitney added. "And if she's still alive, you'll be a hero."

There was also the matter of saving a person Hughes claimed to care about. If Abby had been special to him, if she had been more than a hot piece of ass and a means to an end, maybe he would take the risk. Ethan hoped there was a decent human being underneath that suit and behind that badge.

But Hughes still seemed undecided.

"Listen," Whitney interjected, reaching over and plucking the envelope of photographs out of Ethan's swollen hand. "How about we just make this simple for you. Either you take Ethan with you, or I take this envelope to the *Reno Gazette-Journal* and show them what's inside."

She pulled out a photo of Abby straddling the FBI agent, both of them naked. Whitney held it out to Hughes, using the envelope as a shield so only he—and not Daryl or Taylor—could see the image.

"This one has a particularly good view of your face, I think."

"Fine," Hughes said, exhaling loudly. "It's my ass either way, I guess."

92

Abby
Yesterday

THE HOUSE HAD been silent for a long time. A day? Two? It was hard to judge time when all you did was slip in and out of consciousness, thinking only of food when you were awake, seeing nothing but nightmares when you slept.

When the cellar door finally banged open, it startled Abby out of a nearly catatonic state. Robert stormed down the stairs. He strode directly to Abby's door and threw open the food hatch at the bottom. From across her cell, she could see his face appear.

"You goddamn bitch!" he shouted.

She was lying down and didn't raise her head. She stared at him, saying nothing. There was a bruise on his cheekbone.

"You see this?" he said, pointing to the patch of swollen, purple flesh. "This is your fault. You're going to pay, you whore."

She had no idea what he was talking about.

"No more food," he roared, slamming the hatch closed.

She sat up. "That little bruise is nothing compared to what I'll do to you," she yelled. "You come in here, I'll stick my finger in your eye all the way to the last goddamn knuckle."

"I'm coming in there!" he yelled as he went back down the hall. "I'll wait until you're so weak you can't move."

The truth was Abby was already there. Yelling the threat had taken all of her strength. One last bluff. If he came in, she wouldn't be able to fight. She had nothing left, and if he kept his word and didn't bring food, in another day she wouldn't care what he did to her.

She'd be dead.

93

Ethan
31 minutes past

"I'M GOING TO get into a whole heap of trouble over this," Daryl said.

"Tell anyone who asks that we need Ethan to aid in a federal investigation," Hughes told him.

"We can take my car," said Taylor, who seemed game for this little adventure now that Hughes could take the blame if anything went wrong. "We'll lock Ethan in the back. He'll still be in custody."

"What if he dies?" Daryl said. "He looks like he's on death's door."

"I won't die," Ethan said, sounding like his vocal cords had been run over with a belt sander.

None of them knew what was underneath the bandages. The towel was soaked with blood, but at least they didn't know that his thumb was dangling by a thin piece of skin.

Taylor opened the rear door for Ethan. He turned to say goodbye to Whitney. She wrapped her arms around him in a tight hug, which he returned the best he could with his swollen right and ruined left arm.

"Hang on to the ledger," he whispered. "And the photos. Hide them somewhere. I'll let you know if it's okay to share them with the FBI or the police."

She kissed his cheek.

"Go find our girl," she said. "Dead or alive—bring her home."

He kissed her forehead, letting his lips linger on her skin, knowing he would probably never touch her again.

* * *

Taylor drove with Hughes riding shotgun. Ethan slumped in the back. His heart was pumping rapidly and erratically, yet at the same time he felt like he could drift off to sleep. He remembered looking out the window of the transport van as it drove away from the prison—the memory seemed a lifetime ago.

Taylor took East Fifth Street to Carson Street, where they passed small casinos, auto dealers, and fast-food restaurants. Instead of turning off to go to Lake Tahoe, where Ethan and Whitney had come from, he headed south on US 395 and into Douglas County. City streets turned to ranch land. Taylor turned on his lights but kept the siren silent, driving fast but not recklessly.

It was beautiful country with majestic mountains off to the right, rising steeply out of the foothills. The fields they drove through were brown. Ethan spotted two bald eagles perched on fence posts. They migrated here each year to feast on the afterbirth left in the fields during calving season.

As Taylor drove, Hughes was on the phone, listening more than talking. Finally, he hung up.

"Two dead bodies at the Lake Tahoe marina," he said, craning his neck to look back at Ethan. The metal netting separated them. "The bodies haven't been identified, but the boat was registered to Stanley D'Antonio. Spill, Ethan."

"They took Whitney and me out there to kill us," Ethan said. "I killed them instead."

"Jesus," Hughes said, laughing a little. "You are one crazy son of a bitch."

Hughes wanted more, and Ethan explained what had happened during the course of the furlough in a tired, emotionless monotone. It was most of the truth. He left out that he'd taken Shark's money. He left out that Whitney had fired the shot that killed Kicking Bird.

At the north end of the town of Minden, the road forked from Highway 395 to 88, and soon after that the car approached the state line. A small sign read "Welcome to California."

Ethan began to laugh.

"What's so funny?" Taylor asked.

"Just thinking of the conditions of my release. I'm not supposed to cross the state line."

"How many of your conditions didn't you break?" Hughes asked.

"Not one."

Outside, the land became wooded and hilly. They were rising in elevation as they curved around south of the Lake Tahoe Basin. Patches of snow spotted the ground at first, and soon all of the landscape was covered in an icy white blanket.

"How are we going to do this?" Taylor asked. "We don't have a warrant."

Before leaving, Taylor had plugged the address into his GPS. They were fifteen minutes away.

"If he's not there," Hughes said, "I'll swear I heard a woman screaming, and we'll kick the door down and search."

"And if he is there?"

"I don't know," Hughes said. "Maybe he'll let us in."

Ethan didn't think that was likely, but he knew Hughes would break the rules to get himself into that house

"Why are you going along with this, Taylor?" Hughes said conversationally. "You seem like a by-the-book kind of guy."

Taylor frowned. He glanced at Hughes next to him. "I guess I'm feeling a little guilty for being so quick to hand this case off to the feds. I should have looked deeper."

Hughes didn't say anything.

"And," Taylor added, "I'm a homicide detective. It's rare that I get the chance—even a slim one—to save a person before they're murdered."

Taylor turned off his flashers. He drove slowly, the tires crunching over the icy roads. They were on winding dirt roads now, where no snow plow traveled. But Taylor knew what he was doing, navigating the conditions fine in the sedan, and soon the voice on the GPS told them they'd arrived at their destination.

94

Ethan
1 hour, 17 minutes past

HUGHES CHECKED HIS phone. "No cell service."

Taylor turned up the police radio, where they could hear the local dispatcher talking between bursts of static.

"If we need to call it in, we can use the radio," Taylor said.

The cabin was nice, but not fancy. Hewed fir logs made up the outer walls. A wooden porch wrapped around half of the building. Taylor pulled into the driveway, squeezing his car between a scattering of tall trees, and drove straight to the front porch.

"Ethan," Taylor said, "why don't you duck down for a minute. Maybe it's better he doesn't see you."

Ethan did as he was asked, but said, "You should leave my door cracked. In case you need me."

Hughes laughed. "We're not stupid, Ethan. I'm already going to have a hard time explaining this. If I don't bring you back, there will be no bottom to the deep shit I'll be in."

Ethan wanted to argue, but Taylor and Hughes were already stepping out of the car, and the front door of the cabin was swinging open. Ethan kept his head down but peeked just enough so he could see. Robert Winther stood at the threshold, smiling politely.

"Hello there," Robert called.

"Mr. Winther," Taylor said, crunching through the snow on his way to the porch. "We met before. Detective Calvin Taylor. I was wondering if we could have a moment of your time."

Robert did a double take when he saw who Taylor was with.

"Sure," he said. "Come on in. I was just making some tea."

Taylor and Hughes climbed the stairs and stepped into the house. Robert closed the door behind them. Ethan didn't think he'd been spotted. He wanted so badly to be in there, to know what was going on. His heart jackhammered. If they walked out as nonchalantly as they walked in and told Ethan he was mistaken, Ethan didn't know what he would do. He'd probably thrash around in the back seat like a caged animal.

Minutes ticked by. Taylor had turned the engine off and the vehicle was getting cold, but Ethan was sweating underneath his shirt.

"Come on," he muttered. "What's taking so goddamn—"

Gunfire erupted from within the house. The shots weren't loud, but it was clear what they were. There were several muffled pop pop pops, followed by a barrage of louder blasts.

Then there was silence.

"Fuck," Ethan said.

He assumed the first shots came from Winther, the return fire from Taylor and Hughes. But no one came outside, and Ethan couldn't hear anyone inside.

He tried the car door.

It wouldn't open.

He lay down on this back and began kicking the side window. He didn't know if it was even possible to break it. He couldn't seem to get the right leverage to put any weight behind his kicks. But with each kick, his body jolted, sending waves of pain through his left arm.

He gritted his teeth and positioned his right arm over his head, pushing against the opposite door. He growled as he slammed both feet against the window, and the glass turned into a spiderweb of shards. He kicked at it a few more times to knock it all the way out, then he crawled head first through the opening. He tried to cradle his bad arm the best he could, but every movement hurt. As he collapsed into the snow, the pain was explosive and took his breath away.

He struggled to his feet and staggered up the snow-covered walkway like a drunk. All his muscles seemed to have a mind of their own, refusing to move with the quickness he wanted.

The front door burst open, and Ethan flinched, expecting to see an armed Robert Winther come out shooting. Instead it was Taylor, crawling forward on his knees. His pistol was in one hand while the other held his abdomen, which was leaking blood so dark it looked like motor oil.

Taylor looked surprised to see Ethan coming up the stairs.

"Got to call for help," the detective gasped, unable to stand.

"Is Abby in there?"

"Don't know," Taylor gasped.

Ethan wanted to go into the house, but he knew Taylor might not make it to the car without him. He grabbed Taylor and dragged him to his feet. He supported most of the big man's weight and hauled him down the stairs and through the snow. He threw open the front car door and thrust Taylor inside.

"I think I got him," Taylor panted to Ethan as he reached for his radio. "Wounded him anyway."

"Hughes?"

"Dead."

Taylor started barking into the police radio, telling whoever was listening that an FBI agent was down and that he needed backup immediately.

Ethan turned back to the cabin and followed the trail of Taylor's blood back up the stairs.

"Ethan, don't go in there!" Taylor called.

Ethan ignored him.

CHAPTER

95

Ethan
1 hour 44 minutes past

THE FIRST THING he saw when he stepped over the threshold was Brian Hughes, sitting in a chair with his head back like he was taking a nap. Blackish brain-thick blood was oozing down his face from a hole where one of his eyes had been.

It took Ethan only a second to see where Taylor had been sitting because of the bloody trail leading from a cushioned chair to the front door. At the opposite side of the room, several bullets had punched holes in the sheetrock at the hallway entrance, where Winther probably came into the room with a gun instead of the tea he'd promised. One of the holes was surrounded by a small crimson spray pattern, only about a foot and a half from the floor.

Ethan surveyed the blood trail Robert left behind. There were only a few drops—he wasn't badly injured. Ethan walked over to Brian Hughes's body and took the FBI agent's Glock out of his shoulder holster. He examined the gun and made sure there was a round in the chamber.

Ethan pushed further into the cabin. The corridor he followed led into the kitchen. A carton of eggs sat on the counter next to a cutting board with diced mushrooms and peppers piled next to a long kitchen knife. It looked like Robert had been in the middle of making an omelet when Hughes and Taylor interrupted his morning.

"Abby!" he yelled. "Abby."

He felt like he was underwater—everything was undulating. His breathing filled his hearing, as if his ears were plugged. He thought he could make out a woman's voice calling for help but couldn't be sure if it was his imagination. He followed the blood droplets to the back door and stepped onto the porch. A vast expanse of forest lay before him. Trees bare from winter cast long shadows across the snow.

He spotted Winther, gun raised, hiding partially behind a tree. A flash of light came from the barrel, and Ethan felt a sharp sting low in his chest.

Ethan raised his own gun and fired a volley. Chunks of bark exploded from the tree. Winther took cover behind the trunk, mostly out of sight. One shoulder was visible around the edge of the bark, and Ethan tried to hit it. The shot sailed into the woods, sending up a puff of snow twenty feet away. Winther repositioned himself so he was better hidden.

The hole in Ethan's ribcage burned like he'd been stabbed with a red-hot poker. Blood trickled down his stomach, but he willed himself not to look down. He kept his arm raised, gun ready for any movement from Winther. He felt lightheaded, on the verge of passing out.

Stay alive, he told himself. *Just a little longer.*

He started down the stairs along the path of Winther's blood. He staggered forward, trying to maintain his footing in the snow. He'd never felt so tired, like he could just close his eyes and fall asleep standing up.

The tree was fifteen yards away.

Twelve yards.

Ten.

Winther lunged out, gun raised.

Ethan fired.

Winther's head whipped backward, and he fell into the snow, his arms stretched wide like he was making a snow angel. The gun, a little six-shot .38, was still in his hand, pointed out into the trees. He squeezed the trigger. The shot rang into the woods. He pulled the trigger again, unable to lift his arm, and the gun clicked empty.

Ethan approached, dragging his feet through the snow. He stood over Robert, keeping his gun pointed at the man's face.

Winther blinked, trying to orient himself. He had a bruise on his cheek from where Ethan had punched him two days ago, but that was the least of his worries. Taylor had gotten him high in the thigh, not much more than a nick actually, judging by the slow blood flow. But Ethan's shot had hit him in the face on the right side of his jaw. It looked like it hadn't hit brain or skull, but Winther's cheek was swelling like it was full of cotton, and blood filled his mouth like a pond. He coughed it out and moved his lips like he was trying to speak, but only grunts and gurgles came out.

Ethan raised the gun to shoot him through the brain. He hesitated. He wasn't sure if finishing off Winther would be monstrous or merciful.

As he thought about it, he noticed sirens wailing in the distance. Ethan felt himself teetering. His arm dropped to his side. His vision was growing dark despite the bright sunlight glaring off the snow. He looked down at his chest. A chunk of what looked like marshmallow was hanging out of his wound.

A piece of lung.

Winther might survive, he thought. *But I won't.*

The wound seemed to be located toward the bottom of the lung, and he hoped this meant the blood would flow out of his body, rather than filling up the air sack and drowning him from inside. He felt a tightness in his chest, and the injury made a sucking sound when he breathed. He spit a red glob into the snow.

He raised the gun again and aimed at Winther's face. He put his finger inside the trigger guard. He hesitated again. The screaming he'd heard earlier was back. The woman's voice. Coming from inside the house.

Winther's eyes stared vacantly at the tree canopy above them. Steam rose from his blood, but no clouds of breath escaped his mouth or nose.

I guess I was wrong, Ethan thought. *Neither of us is going to make it.*

He jammed the gun into the belt of his jeans and turned back toward the cabin, wading through tendrils of darkness that seemed to slither from the shadows of the trees.

CHAPTER

96

Ethan
2 hours past

E THAN STUMBLED AROUND inside the cabin, searching. He found a door and yanked it open to reveal a small office. The lights were on, and the walls were papered with photographs of women. Some were like the shots of Abby, voyeuristic pictures taken from afar, but most of them were of women who were asleep or unconscious. All lying in a cinderblock room, their mouths spilling drool, their eyes—the ones that were open—as vacant as glass. He wasn't sure if some of them were drugged or dead.

He didn't see any pictures of his sister.

"Abby!" he yelled, returning to the front room where Hughes had been killed. The door stood open, and Ethan spotted Taylor out by the car. The detective had fallen and lay unmoving in the snow.

The sirens were loud now, but he still couldn't see any flashing lights coming down the road through the trees. He circled back inside the cabin. He saw a door that he'd passed before because it looked like it might be a pantry. It was locked. He took a few steps back. He put everything he had into ramming the door with his shoulder. The wood split apart and he fell forward, rolling down a staircase onto the concrete floor of a basement. His left hand was howling at him.

He sat up. He coughed and large flecks of blood splattered the cinderblock wall. He examined the blood, saw the tiny slivers of lung.

The corridor was probably fifteen feet long, lit by a bulb in the ceiling. Despite the light, blackness crowded Ethan's vision, like he was diving deeper and deeper into water where the sun could no longer reach.

"Not yet," he said aloud.

He heard a female voice. "Hello?"

He wasn't sure where the voice was coming from. Everything sounded muffled, like his head was underwater. He looked up the stairs, but no one was there.

"Abby," he said.

He heard the voice yell, *"Help! Help me!"*

Ethan staggered to his feet and started down the hall to the only door, the source of the voice.

"Abby!" he yelled.

Buried beneath the ringing in his ears, he heard a voice softly say, "Ethan?"

"Abby?"

"Ethan!"

They began yelling to each other. Ethan shook the knob, which was locked. The deadbolt on the door required a key. He slapped the metal with his hand. Even healthy, he wouldn't be able to knock it down.

He sobbed as he collapsed onto his knees and then slid down onto the floor. Inside, he could hear her crying. The door had some kind of extra hinge so Winther could open the bottom, but even that was secured with a small padlock.

Ethan put his face to the floor and looked under the crack. He could only see one of Abby's eyes—recognizable and beautiful and scared—looking back at him. He jammed his swollen fingers under the door and she touched them with hers. Darkness swirled around him again, and he thought about giving up. She would be okay. But he couldn't rest until she was free from this prison. Until he saw her face one last time, held her in his arms.

He remembered the gun in his waistband.

"Get down," he shouted. "I'm going to shoot the lock."

He could see enough of her from under the door to know she'd closed her eyes and put her hands over her head. He aimed upward, so the bullets would sail over her. He yanked the trigger and shot the doorknob and deadbolt over and over again, filling the air with the smell of gunpowder. When the gun clicked empty, Ethan couldn't hear it through the ringing in his ears.

Abby threw open the door. She fell onto Ethan, hugging him and crying. Her face was thin, the skin pulled close to the bone, and her hair hung greasy and listless. But her eyes were the familiar electric eyes of his sister, and relief washed through him like an injection of morphine.

Okay, Ethan thought, *I can die now.*

"Oh God," Abby said, seeing the bullet wound in his chest and taking in the sight of all the blood and bandages. "Help!" she yelled, turning toward the stairway. "Someone he—"

Her voice morphed into a scream.

Robert stood at the top of the stairway. He looked like a zombie, with red ropes dangling from his mouth. The .38 was gone, but he'd replaced it with the knife from the kitchen counter.

He began to descend. Abby ran back into her cell. Ethan wanted to rise—he knew he *had* to rise—but he had no strength left. He lay in a heap, unable to move. Robert came to the foot of the stairs and continued forward. When he was close to Ethan, he began to kneel, drawing the knife back. Ethan had come this far and could go no further. He was going to die and his sister still wasn't safe.

Abby jumped from behind her doorway and swung the heavy rectangular lid of a toilet tank. It connected with Robert's forehead—making a sound like a rubber mallet striking a bell—and Robert flew backward, the back of his head cracking against the bottom step. The knife clattered to the concrete. Robert lay unmoving, his forehead dented in and already turning blue.

Abby looked emaciated—like a cancer victim—but she still had fight left in her. With twig arms, she hefted the porcelain block over her head, ready to slam it down on her abductor's head again.

"I told you I would kill you, you motherfucker!"

She noticed movement by the stairs and hesitated, keeping the slab aloft.

"Freeze!" a voice shouted.

A uniformed deputy aimed his gun at her from the top of the stairs. Abby stared up at him, arms trembling. She let the toilet lid drop to her waist. She tossed it aside and it crashed loudly against the floor, splitting in two.

"My name is Abby Lockhart," she called up, out of breath. "I've been abducted and held prisoner. My brother saved me. Get paramedics. He's been shot."

She turned from the cop and knelt and held Ethan's head in her hands. Above her, the deputy shouted something into his radio.

"You came for me," Abby said, crying and smiling.

Ethan's mouth curved into the hint of a grin.

"Of course I did," he said, his voice no more than a whisper.

Then the darkness started to swirl around him again. This time there was no stopping it.

He closed his eyes and pictured her face as he saw her at the end—smiling and safe. He held the image in his thoughts. Then the blackness wrapped itself around him like a funeral shroud.

He did not dive into the abyss.

The abyss rose up and swallowed him.

EPILOGUE

Four months later

THE BLACKNESS BEGAN to soften, changing at first to a dark blue, then transforming to an icy hue, like looking into the watery crevasse of a glacier. The shifting colors of the prison window—the rectangular block of glass crosshatched with iron rods—signaled the coming of morning. The obscured view of the outside world took on a pinkish hue, like blood in water, and then changed to a murky yellow.

Ethan stared from his bunk, his mind lost in thought.

He hadn't slept much. He never did these days. He often awoke from nightmares, usually reenactments from his furlough that didn't go the way they had in real life. He had to relive having his thumb cut off, only he couldn't get the handcuffs off afterward. Or he was digging up the grave in the Black Rock, but Abby's face was behind the plastic.

Ethan made sleep come and take him by force. At lights out, he would lie in the gray-dark, his eyes open, never submitting to sleep without a fight. Some nights, he stayed this way until dawn, eyes wide, afraid of what lay lurking in his darkness.

The morning was a relief. But he still wasn't used to not having Jack in the cell with him. Jack had never been a noisy cellmate, but without him, the absence of any sound at all bothered Ethan. No matter how noisy the rest of the prison became—and it was truly raucous for most hours of the day—Ethan found the quiet of his own cell unnerving.

He hopped down off the bunk, cast a glance at the empty mattress where Jack used to lie, and walked to the toilet to relieve his bladder.

Jack had received his transfer orders for the conservation camp and was gone before Ethan ever got out of the hospital. Daryl, his other ally, had been transferred to the Warm Springs Correctional Center, the nearby women's prison. Ethan didn't know if this was his choice or a punishment, but Ethan figured Daryl might do some good there, with inmates who actually wanted reform. As for Jack, he was working with horses every day. For a criminal like him—serving consecutive life sentences and unlikely to be paroled until he was old—it was the closest thing to salvation he could possibly expect.

Ethan didn't know what kind of salvation he could expect for himself. When he got out, who would he be? Could he still be the man he'd hoped to become?

He didn't know.

As he urinated, he lifted his left hand, moving it this way and that. Without the thumb, it looked almost like a flipper. The nub where his thumb used to be was red, like a burn, but the pain had mostly gone away. The worst was that the ghost of his thumb itched, and he caught himself several times a day reaching to scratch it.

He'd been in a lot of pain for the first couple of months—the broken arm, the knife wounds, the bullet in his lung, not to mention the surgery to repair the mess inside his chest cavity—but he'd mostly healed at this point.

At least physically.

He wasn't sure the other wounds would ever go away.

He'd sacrificed himself in every way to save Abby. His physical body. His mental state. Who he was, who he wanted to be.

In the end, he'd even sacrificed his life.

For two minutes.

Then the paramedics had zapped him with their paddles and brought him back. Abby told him later that they would have let him stay dead if it hadn't been for her. Two ambulances had arrived simultaneously, with one set of paramedics helping Taylor in the snow. The other pair didn't seem to know who to try to save first. Robert Winther, with the dent in his forehead and bullet hole in his face? Or Ethan?

No, she'd screamed, when they'd knelt next to Winther. *My brother first!*

And they listened.

Now here he was, staring at his blurry reflection in the metal mirror over his toilet. Pale. Hollow-eyed. Nine fingers instead of ten. But alive.

In fact, the paramedics had managed to save all three of the wounded men. Robert Winther spent a month in a coma, and by all accounts remained a vegetable, drooling on himself and barely able to chew his own food.

Which was fine with Ethan.

Taylor, last he heard, was still off duty, but he was out of the hospital and expected to recover. Brian Hughes hadn't made it, of course. If things had gone differently, he might have been fired from the FBI in disgrace. Instead, he died a hero. His death had only added to Abby's trauma. Ethan maintained he wasn't good for her, but she'd felt something for him and, she insisted, he'd felt something for her— they weren't just using each other. Besides, he'd died trying to save her. She might carry a torch for him forever.

Ethan could live with it. Hughes had gotten him out of prison, after all. The least he could do was not try to taint Abby's memory of him.

Ethan dressed for the day, putting on the identical denim he'd worn the day before and the day before that, and waited for the guards to open the cells for breakfast. Fifteen minutes later, as he walked to the cafeteria, the cons he passed spoke to him briefly or at least gave him a respectful nod. He'd been a celebrity since he returned. Most of the cons in the joint had, at some point, approached him to shake his hand or clap him on the back or tell him he'd done a good job. The guards too. They were all proud of him—one of their own had gone out and done something good, something amazing.

"Yo, Lockhart," one of them said to him now. He was a longtime con, *in for all day and night.* "Any word on extradition?"

Ethan shook his head. "No," he said. "I bet they'll keep him in California for a while."

Police had found the bones of four other women buried on Robert Winther's property. Since two of the victims had disappeared from Nevada and two from California, the states were in a pissing match over who got to prosecute first. Ethan didn't care either way. He was brain-damaged—Abby had seen to that—and would probably spend the rest of his life in a mental hospital regardless of how many guilty verdicts came down on him.

"Well," said the con, someone Ethan had never spoken to in the first five years of his prison sentence, "don't you worry: if that son of a bitch ever shows up in this prison, he won't live through the first day."

During the past few months, a half-dozen men had told him something similar. He was surrounded by robbers and burglars and murderers, but they all understood a brother's love for his sister. And what Robert Winther did was beyond the pale, even for these men. There were unwritten laws that even criminals weren't allowed to break.

Sometimes Ethan wished he'd fired that bullet through Robert Winther's brain to save everyone the trouble of dealing with him now.

Sometimes he was glad he hadn't.

After breakfast, he walked over to the weight area and picked up a dumb-bell with his left hand. It felt weird to hold it without any thumb, but he did his best to wrap his fingers around the handle and grip it in place. He tried some arm curls. The strength of his arm was more of an issue than the missing digit. The limb had been slashed and stabbed and broken, and had atrophied while inside its casts and bandages.

A few days ago, he'd also started running around the yard. He hadn't made it far. It was obvious his lung strength would be slower to come back than his arm strength. Today, he didn't want to get all sweaty and out of breath anyway, so he only lifted for a little while, then stood up against a wall, trying to enjoy the sun-shine while he waited for the moment he'd been looking forward to all morning.

Visiting hours.

* * *

He sat on the stool in front of the foot-thick glass, waiting. He knew they were coming long before he saw them because the men in the queue all started whis-tling and catcalling.

"Show some respect," someone shouted. "That's Lockhart's sister."

With this, the uproar died down to a murmur, but the men still whispered "Damn" and "Look at that," even though many of them were probably waiting for their own wives or girlfriends.

Finally, Abby and Whitney popped into view, smiling and beautiful. They wore shorts and T-shirts cut into baggy tank tops, which only partly covered bikinis underneath. They had sunglasses tucked into their hair and flip-flops on their feet. Abby carried a newspaper that she laid face down on the desk. Ethan wasn't sure why she'd brought it, but figured they'd tell him in time.

For now, he focused on them. Abby had put back on the weight she lost and was looking fit and strong. Whitney hadn't changed at all—her smile was as heart-melting as ever—but he knew she was dealing with a lot of trauma. He was sure she was having nightmares too.

Abby and Whitney huddled together to talk to him since there was only one telephone on their side. He picked up his own, using his right hand even though the receiver was on the left side.

"Well, don't you two look like a summer day," Ethan said. "You look like you're going to the beach."

"Maybe we are," Whitney said with smile.

"Isn't the water still a bit cold?"

"We brought wetsuits," Abby said.

Abby and Whitney had been in to visit him often, usually together, sometimes separately. Sometimes with Ethan's mom. The times alone with

Whitney could be awkward, as they didn't openly discuss what had happened between them and what might become of them now. Ethan considered asking her not to return—to tell her she needed to find some normal guy outside. But he wanted to see her. Maybe that was selfish, but after everything he'd been through, he wasn't ready to cut loose one of the only good things left in his life.

Besides, there was a chance he might not be in prison for much longer.

Abby had been fighting tirelessly for his release—talking to lawyers, calling every government official she could find. Ethan rescued her from her prison cell. Now she was determined to do the same for him. He might have broken an extensive list of laws during his forty-eight-hour furlough—not to mention all six conditions of his release—but he'd saved a missing woman and caught a murderer who had already killed at least four others. And he'd helped police solve numerous murder and missing-persons investigations by turning over Shark's ledger. The news channels were ripping the police and the FBI to pieces and lauding Ethan Lockhart as some new brand of American hero. He had so far been unwilling to tell his legal team—and he had a whole team; they'd lined up to work with him—to get him network TV time and interviews with *The New York Times* or *USA Today*. But he could if he needed to, and the politicians and bureaucrats all knew it. What they feared even more was Abby going on TV. The media loves nothing more than a pretty girl in peril, and if she sat down with Savannah Guthrie on the *Today Show*, advocating for Ethan's release, it would only make the state look worse.

Ethan might have to quietly finish the two years before he was eligible for parole on his original sentence—to allow the whole law enforcement system to save face—but if Abby got her way, he wouldn't even need to do that.

"The governor's office is involved," she said. "I think a pardon is a real possibility. They're trying to figure out a way to spin things. They want this to be a feel-good story, not a PR nightmare."

Ethan shrugged, as if to say, *Maybe, maybe not.*

"They don't want to come across like they're encouraging vigilantes, but they've got the pictures of the pretty victims plastered all over the media, and one of those girls is alive today because of you."

"If I have to stay in here until I die of old age," Ethan said, "it was worth it."

"But I want *you*, big brother. I want you out in the world, having a good life." Tears filled her eyes. "I want you to live for me."

Ethan frowned, as if to say, *I haven't given you enough?*

"You can't save me and then make me feel guilty the rest of my life because you're not living yours."

This struck home with him.

"If I get out," he said, "I promise I'll try to live as happy and normal a life as possible."

"Good," she said, "because that's what I'm trying to do."

Their moods shifted, and he could tell there was something they wanted to talk to him about.

"We signed up for college classes," Abby told him.

"That's great," Ethan said, thrilled that they were putting stripping in their rearview mirrors for good.

"In Arizona," Whitney added, wincing as she delivered the unexpected news.

"Oh," Ethan said, then recovered and told them that this was fantastic.

They explained that they wanted to get out of Reno and get away from all the media coverage and bad memories. A new place might be what they needed to heal from the traumas they'd endured. They'd registered for classes at Arizona State and planned to drive down to Phoenix in the next few weeks to find an apartment.

"When you get out," Abby said, "you can come live there too."

Whitney nodded her head in agreement, but Ethan wasn't so sure. It was doubtful that he'd be released without any conditions. Like before, leaving the state might be on the list of prohibited activities. He didn't mention this to them, though. He wanted them both to be happy. Wanted that more than his own happiness.

The clock on the wall behind them was ticking, and their time was running out. It seemed like time was always running out.

Whitney said to Abby, "Should we tell him now?"

"Guess what happened?" Abby said, unable to control her spreading smile.

"What?"

"It's really weird," she said, "but . . ."

She lifted the newspaper and put the cover against the glass for him to read. He leaned in close to study it. His eyes widened.

There was a front-page article about how someone had broken into the cemetery where Abby's casket had been buried and dug up her grave. They'd stolen the keepsakes and mementos that people had put inside.

"Isn't it weird that someone would dig up *my* grave?" she said. "Why would someone do that?"

Ethan leaned back in his chair and let out a hearty laugh. He was glad Abby and Whitney would have the money. They deserved it.

Call it severance pay from Dark Secrets.

Since being locked back behind bars again, he'd worried about Abby—and Whitney too—but as they all laughed together, he felt a sense of calm. They had money for a brand-new start and plans to rebuild their lives in a new place, far from ghosts that would haunt them here.

They were going to be okay.

And as he laughed, Ethan felt reassured that he would be too—whether he was released from prison or had to spend another decade in here. If Abby and Whitney were okay, wherever they were, he would be okay, wherever he was.

LATER

WHITNEY DROVE THE truck, and Abby held her arm out the window, letting it dance in the wind. Her hair whipped around her neck and shoulders. The air was chilly in the mountains, not hot as it had been in the valley, but she didn't mind. This was one of the first days since the abduction that she felt good. Really happy.

They drove along the northeast shore of the lake, the same route—only in reverse—that Whitney had taken Ethan after they'd escaped Shark's boat. When they came to the stretch of highway near the East Shore beaches, Whitney parked on the shoulder, which would be packed in another month but was empty today.

They jumped out of the truck, grabbed two duffel bags out of the bed, and headed down the dirt path that wound through the pine forest. Abby hadn't been back here since she almost drowned, and she felt a strange sort of excitement about returning—like she was coming back to conquer her fear. The clandestine nature of what they were doing also felt exciting, like they were George Clooney and Brad Pitt in *Ocean's 11*—only instead of stealing money they were hiding it.

Since Abby's rescue, she and Whitney had both moved out of their apartments and into a new one together, roommates like before. Most of the past few months had been spent healing: holding each other after one or the other woke up screaming; checking and double-checking that their doors were locked, windows bolted, alarm set; encouraging each other to eat when they had no appetite; and taking turns crying, one listening while the other recounted a portion of what had happened.

It had been Whitney's idea to dig up the grave. And Abby's idea to leave Ethan's share beneath Coffin Rock, where he could pick it up when he got out.

It would be easier to get a safety deposit box—or to just hang onto it and hand it to him—but where was the fun in that?

Abby stepped off the trail and out onto the sand and took in the sight of Lake Tahoe, the afternoon sun reflecting on the blue surface like glittering golden scales. Whitney came up behind her, and the two stared together at the expanse of cobalt blue and the mountains that rimmed it, their peaks still topped with snow. In another month—when the water was warm enough that people actually dared to swim—the beach would be crowded, but today they had it to themselves.

They laid their towels out and stripped down to their swimming suits like this was an ordinary day at the beach. But then they reached into the duffel bags and pulled out full-body wetsuits and squeezed their limbs into the tight fabric.

They'd planned to swim from shore, but Abby looked up at the cliff and said, "Should we?"

Whitney followed her gaze. The sheer rock face towered above them. "I'm game."

Abby grabbed the black plastic bag with the money, which was about the size of two or three hardback books stacked on top of each other. They'd used the reverse setting on an air mattress pump to pull all the excess air out of the garbage bag, then secured it with duct tape.

They scrambled up the rocks in their bare feet and made it to the top, breathless. The view from up here was spectacular, and they took in the vastness of the lake—its depth and its beauty. Lake Tahoe was a natural wonder. It was a thousand feet deep and two million years old. The water so clear you could see sixty feet into its depths. So cold that corpses didn't bloat and float to the surface.

"You know," Whitney said, "somewhere out there is Shark's body."

"I hadn't thought about that," Abby said. "You still want to go through with this?"

Whitney nodded. "Yeah. Screw him. His ghost can watch over Ethan's money."

Abby giggled, and the two girls laughed together.

"You ready?" Whitney asked.

"No," Abby quipped, but really she was.

The view from Coffin Rock wasn't as scary as it used to be. It didn't seem quite so high.

"You?"

"I guess," Whitney said. "On the count of three?"

"Sure."

Abby looked down where the wavelets met the cliff face. She could see through the aqua water to the rocks underneath. She'd been down there before, full of pain and panic, and it hadn't been long before she'd blacked out.

She wondered how well they'd be able to navigate the watery underworld now, exploring down there for the first time. Would they even be able to find Ethan's cave?

She wished her brother was here. The frightening parts of life always felt safer when he was around. But at least she and Whitney were here for each other. If one got into trouble, the other could help. Besides, they were doing this *for* Ethan.

Abby had been through a lot. She could face this challenge without him.

"One," they said together.

Abby held tight to the money with her left hand and reached out to take Whitney's with her right.

"Two."

You can do this, Abby told herself and realized she didn't really need the pep talk. She *could* do this. She knew it.

"Three!" they shouted, and together they leapt.

They sailed off the cliff, letting out joyful shrieks—more thrilled than scared—as they plunged toward the surface below and the unknown world that lay on the other side.

ACKNOWLEDGMENTS

S PECIAL THANKS TO my amazing agent, Amy Tannenbaum, and the whole team at the Jane Rotrosen Agency. The book is better because of Amy's help, and it wouldn't be in print without her.

Special thanks also to Jessica Renheim of Crooked Lane Books, along with Melissa Rechter, Madeline Rathle, Rebecca Nelson, and everyone at Crooked Lane who had a hand in developing the book for publication. Thank you to editor James Bock for his careful and thoughtful work on the manuscript, which was invaluable in shaping and polishing the final draft.

Some family and friends read early drafts, and I'm grateful for their feedback: Tiffany Bourelle, Ed Bourelle, Samantha Tetangco, Evan Morgan Williams, Aeryn Rudel, and Shane Higbee.

I'm especially grateful to my wife, Tiffany, and my extraordinary children, Ben and Aubrey, who all patiently accept that if they hear some noise at three o'clock in the morning, it's just Daddy, who can't sleep and is getting up to write.